THE
WOMAN
WITH THE
BLUE STAR

Also by Pam Jenoff

THE
WOMAN
WITH THE
BLUE STAR

PAM JENOFF

PARK
ROW
BOOKS

PARK
ROW
BOOKS™

ISBN-13: 978-0-7783-1154-6

The Woman with the Blue Star

This edition published by arrangement with Harlequin Books S.A.

Park Row Books
22 Adelaide St. West, 40th Floor
Toronto, Ontario M5H 4E3, Canada
ParkRowBooks.com
BookClubbish.com

Printed in U.S.A.

To my shtetl…I'll be seeing you.

THE
WOMAN
WITH THE
BLUE STAR

Prologue

Kraków, Poland
June 2016

The woman I see before me is not the one I expected at all.

Ten minutes earlier, I stood before the mirror in my hotel room, brushing some lint from the cuff of my pale blue blouse, adjusting a pearl earring. Distaste rose inside me. I had become the poster child for a woman in her early seventies—graying hair cut short and practical, pantsuit hugging my sturdy frame more snugly than it would have a year ago.

I patted the bouquet of fresh flowers on the nightstand, bright red blooms wrapped in crisp brown paper. Then I walked to the window. Hotel Wentzl, a converted sixteenth-century mansion, sat on the southwest corner of the Rynek, Kraków's immense town square. I chose the location deliberately, made sure my room had just the right view. The square, with its concave southern corner giving it rather the appearance of a sieve, bustled with activity. Tourists thronged between the churches and the souvenir stalls of the Sukiennice, the massive, oblong cloth hall that bisected the square. Friends gathered at the outdoor cafés for an after-work drink on a warm June evening, while commuters hurried home with their parcels, eyes cast toward the clouds darkening over Wawel Castle to the south.

I had been to Kraków twice before, once right after communism fell and then again ten years later when I started my search in earnest. I was immediately won over by the hidden gem of a city. Though eclipsed by the tourist magnets of Prague and Berlin, Kraków's Old Town, with its unscarred cathedrals and stone-carved houses restored to the original, was one of the most elegant in all of Europe.

The city changed so much each time I came, everything brighter and newer—"better" in the eyes of the locals, who had gone through many years of hardship and stalled progress. The once-gray houses had been painted vibrant yellows and blues, turning the ancient streets into a movie-set version of themselves. The locals were a study in contradictions, too: fashionably dressed young people talked on their cell phones as they walked, heedless of the mountain villagers selling wool sweaters and sheep's cheese from tarps laid on the ground, and a scarf-clad *babcia* who sat on the pavement, begging for coins. Under a store window touting Wi-Fi and internet plans, pigeons pecked at the hard cobblestones of the market square as they had for centuries. Beneath all of the modernity and polish, the baroque architecture of the Old Town shone defiantly through, a history that would not be denied.

But it was not history that brought me here—or at least not that history.

As the trumpeter in the Mariacki church tower began to play the Hejnał, signaling the top of the hour, I studied the northwest corner of the square, waiting for the woman to appear at five as she had every day. I did not see her and I wondered if she might not come today, in which case my trip halfway around the world would have been in vain. The first day, I wanted to make sure she was the right person. The second, I meant to speak with her but lost my nerve. Tomorrow I would fly home to America. This was my last chance.

Finally, she appeared from around the corner of a pharmacy, umbrella tucked smartly under one arm. She made her way across the square with surprising speed for a woman who was about ninety. She was not stooped; her back was straight and tall. Her white hair was pulled into a loose knot atop her head, but pieces had broken free and fanned out wildly, framing her face. In contrast to my own staid clothing, she wore a brightly colored skirt, its pattern vibrant. The shiny fabric seemed to dance around her ankles by its own accord as she walked and I could almost hear its rustling sound.

Her routine was familiar, the same as the previous two days when I watched her walk to the Café Noworolski and request the table farthest from the square, sheltered from the activity and noise by the deep arched entranceway of the building. Last time I had come to Kraków, I was still searching. Now I knew who she was and where to find her. The only thing to do was to summon my courage and go down.

The woman took a seat at her usual table in the corner, opened a newspaper. She had no idea that we were about to meet—or even that I was alive.

From the distance came a rumble of thunder. Drops began to fall then, splattering the cobblestones like dark tears. I had to hurry. If the outdoor café closed and the woman left, everything I came for would be gone.

I heard the voices of my children, telling me that it was too dangerous to travel so far alone at my age, that there was no reason, nothing more to be learned here. I should just leave and go home. It would matter to no one.

Except to me—and to *her*. I heard her voice in my mind as I imagined it to be, reminding me what it was that I had come for.

Steeling myself, I picked up the flowers and walked from the room.

Outside, I started across the square. Then I stopped again. Doubts reverberated through my brain. Why had I come all of this way? What was I looking for? Doggedly, I pressed onward, not feeling the large drops that splattered my clothes and hair. I reached the café, wound through the tables of patrons who were paying their checks and preparing to leave as the rain fell heavier. As I neared the table, the woman with the white hair lifted her gaze from the newspaper. Her eyes widened.

Up close now, I can see her face. I can see everything. I stand motionless, struck frozen.

The woman I see before me is not the one I expected at all.

1

Sadie

Kraków, Poland
March 1942

Everything changed the day they came for the children.

I was supposed to have been in the attic crawl space of the three-story building we shared with a dozen other families in the ghetto. Mama helped me hide there each morning before she set out to join the factory work detail, leaving me with a fresh bucket as a toilet and a stern admonishment not to leave. But I grew cold and restless alone in the tiny, frigid space where I couldn't run or move or even stand straight. The minutes stretched silently, broken only by a scratching—unseen children, years younger than me, stowed on the other side of the wall. They were kept separate from one another without space to run and play. They sent each other messages by tapping and scratching, though, like a kind of improvised Morse code. Sometimes, in my boredom, I joined in, too.

"Freedom is where you find it," my father often said when I complained. Papa had a way of seeing the world exactly as he wanted. "The greatest prison is in our mind." It was easy for him to say. Though the manual ghetto labor was a far cry from his professional work as an accountant before the war, at least he was out and about each day, seeing other people. Not cooped up like me. I had scarcely left our apartment building since we were forced to move six months earlier from our apartment in the Jewish Quarter near the city center to the Podgórze neighborhood where the ghetto had been established on the southern bank of the river. I wanted a normal life, my life, free to run beyond the walls of the ghetto to all of the places I had once known and taken for granted. I imagined taking the tram to the shops on the Rynek or to the *kino* to see a film, exploring the ancient grassy mounds on the outskirts of the city. I wished that at least my best friend, Stefania, was one of the others hidden nearby. Instead, she lived in a separate apartment on the other side of the ghetto designated for the families of the Jewish police.

It wasn't boredom or loneliness that had driven me from my hiding place this time, though, but hunger. I had always had a big appetite and this morning's breakfast ration had been a half slice of bread, even less than usual. Mama had offered me her portion, but I knew she needed her strength for the long day ahead on the labor detail.

As the morning wore on in my hiding place, my empty belly had begun to ache. Visions pushed into my mind uninvited of the foods we ate before the war: rich mushroom soup and savory borscht, and pierogi, the plump, rich dumplings my grandmother used to make. By midmorning, I felt so weak from hunger that I had ventured out of my hiding place and down to the shared kitchen on the ground floor, which was really nothing more than a lone working stove burner and a sink that dripped tepid brown water. I didn't go to take food—even if there had been any, I would never steal. Rather, I wanted to see if there were any crumbs left in the cupboard and to fill my stomach with a glass of water.

I stayed in the kitchen longer than I should, reading the dog-

eared copy of the book I'd brought with me. The thing I de-
tested most about my hiding place in the attic was the fact that
it was too dark for reading. I had always loved to read and Papa
had carried as many books as he could from our apartment to
the ghetto, over the protests of my mother, who said we needed
the space in our bags for clothes and food. It was my father who
had nurtured my love of learning and encouraged my dream of
studying medicine at Jagiellonian University before the German laws made that impossible, first by banning Jews and later
by closing the university altogether. Even in the ghetto at the
end of his long, hard days of labor, Papa loved to teach and discuss ideas with me. He had somehow found me a new book a
few days earlier, too, *The Count of Monte Cristo*. But the hiding place in the attic was too dark for me to read and there was
scarcely any time in the evening before curfew and lights-out.
Just a bit longer, I told myself, turning the page in the kitchen. A
few minutes wouldn't matter at all.

I had just finished licking the dirty bread knife when I heard
heavy tires screeching, followed by barking voices. I froze, nearly
dropping my book. The SS and Gestapo were outside, flanked
by the vile Jüdischer Ordnungsdienst, Jewish Ghetto Police, who
did their bidding. It was an *aktion*, the sudden unannounced arrest of large groups of Jews to be taken from the ghetto to camps.
The very reason I was meant to be hiding in the first place. I
raced from the kitchen, across the hall and up the stairs. From
below came a great crash as the front door to the apartment
building splintered and the police burst through. There was no
way I could make it back to the attic in time.

Instead, I raced to our third-floor apartment. My heart
pounded as I looked around desperately, wishing for an armoire or other cabinet suitable for hiding in the tiny room,
which was nearly bare except for a dresser and bed. There were
other places, I knew, like the fake plaster wall one of the other
families had constructed in the adjacent building not a week

earlier. That was too far away now, impossible to reach. My eyes focused on the large steamer trunk stowed at the foot of my parents' bed. Mama had shown me how to hide there once shortly after we first moved to the ghetto. We practiced it like a game, Mama opening the trunk so that I could climb in before she closed the lid.

The trunk was a terrible hiding place, exposed and in the middle of the room. But there was simply nowhere else. I had to try. I raced over to the bed and climbed into the trunk, then closed the lid with effort. I thanked heavens that I was tiny like Mama. I had always hated being so petite, which made me look a solid two years younger than I actually was. Now it seemed a blessing, as did the sad fact that the months of meager ghetto rations had made me thinner. I still fit in the trunk.

When we had rehearsed, we had envisioned Mama putting a blanket or some clothes over the top of the trunk. Of course, I couldn't do that myself. So the trunk sat unmasked for anyone who walked into the room to see and open. I curled into a tiny ball and wrapped my arms around myself, feeling the white armband with the blue star on my sleeve that all Jews were required to wear.

There came a great crashing from the next building, the sound of plaster being hewn by a hammer or ax. The police had found the hiding place behind the wall, given away by the too-fresh paint. An unfamiliar cry rang out as a child was found and dragged from his hiding place. If I had gone there, I would have been caught as well.

Someone neared the door to the apartment and flung it open. My heart seized. I could hear breathing, feel eyes searching the room. *I'm sorry, Mama*, I thought, feeling her reproach for having left the attic. I braced myself for discovery. Would they go easier on me if I came out and gave myself up? The footsteps grew fainter as the German continued down the hall, stopping before each door, searching.

The war had come to Kraków one warm fall day two and a half years earlier when the air-raid sirens rang out for the first time and sent the playing children scurrying from the street. Life got hard before it got bad. Food disappeared and we waited in long lines for the most basic supplies. Once there was no bread for a whole week.

Then about a year ago, upon orders from the General Government, Jews teemed into Kraków by the thousands from the small towns and villages, dazed and carrying their belongings on their backs. At first I wondered how they would all find places to stay in Kazimierz, the already cramped Jewish Quarter of the city. But the new arrivals were forced to live by decree in a crowded section of the industrial Podgórze district on the far side of the river that had been cordoned off with a high wall. Mama worked with the *Gmina*, the local Jewish community organization, to help them resettle, and we often had friends of friends over for a meal when they first arrived, before they went to the ghetto for good. They told stories from their hometowns too awful to believe and Mama shooed me from the room so I would not hear.

Several months after the ghetto was created, we were ordered to move there as well. When Papa told me, I couldn't believe it. We were not refugees, but residents of Kraków; we had lived in our apartment on Meiselsa Street my entire life. It was the perfect location: on the edge of the Jewish Quarter but easy walking distance to the sights and sounds of the city center and close enough to Papa's office on Stradomska Street that he could come home for lunch. Our apartment was above an adjacent café where a pianist played every evening. Sometimes the music spilled over and Papa would whirl Mama around the kitchen to the faint strains. But according to the orders, Jews were Jews. One day. One suitcase each. And the world I had known my entire life disappeared forever.

I peered out of the thin slit opening of the trunk, trying to see across the tiny room I shared with my parents. We were lucky, I knew, to have a whole room to ourselves, a privilege we had been given because my father was a labor foreman. Others were forced to share an apartment, often two or three families together. Still, the space felt cramped compared to our real home. We were ever on top of one another, the sights and sounds and smells of daily living magnified.

"Kinder, raus!" the police called over and over again now as they patrolled the halls. *Children, out.* It was not the first time the Germans had come for children during the day, knowing that their parents would be at work.

But I was no longer a child. I was eighteen and might have joined the work details like others my age and some several years younger. I could see them lining up for roll call each morning before trudging to one of the factories. And I *wanted* to work, even though I could tell from the slow, painful way my father now walked, stooped like an old man, and how Mama's hands were split and bleeding that it was hard and awful. Work meant a chance to get out and see and talk to people. My hiding was a subject of much debate between my parents. Papa thought I should work. Labor cards were highly prized in the ghetto. Workers were valued and less likely to be deported to one of the camps. But Mama, who seldom fought my father on anything, had forbidden it. "She doesn't look her age. The work is too hard. She is safest out of sight." I wondered as I hid now, about to be discovered at any second, if she would still think she was right.

The building finally went silent, the last of the awful footsteps receding. Still I didn't move. That was one of the ways they trapped people who were hiding, by pretending to go away and lying in wait when they came out. I remained motionless, not daring to leave my hiding place. My limbs ached, then went numb. I had no idea how much time had passed. Through the slit, I could see that the room had grown dimmer, as if the sun had lowered a bit.

Sometime later, there were footsteps again, this time a shuffling sound as the laborers trudged back silent and exhausted from their day. I tried to uncurl myself from the trunk. But my muscles were stiff and sore and my movements slow. Before I could get out, the door to our apartment flung open and someone ran into the room with steps light and fluttering. "Sadie!" It was Mama, sounding hysterical.

"Jestem tutaj," I called. *I am here.* Now that she was home, she could help me untangle myself and get out. But my voice was muffled by the trunk. When I tried to undo the latch, it stuck.

Mama raced from the room back into the corridor. I could hear her open the door to the attic, then run up the stairs, still searching for me. "Sadie!" she called. Then, "My child, my child," over and over again as she searched but did not find me, her voice rising to a shriek. She thought I was gone.

"Mama!" I yelled. She was too far away to hear me, though, and her own cries were too loud. Desperately, I struggled once more to free myself from the trunk without success. Mama raced back into the room, still wailing. I heard the scraping sound of a window opening. At last I threw myself against the lid of the trunk, slamming my shoulder so hard it throbbed. The latch sprang open.

I broke free and stood up quickly. "Mama?" She was standing in the oddest position, with one foot on the window ledge, her willowy frame silhouetted against the frigid twilight sky. "What are you doing?" For a second, I thought she was looking for me outside. But her face was twisted with grief and pain. I knew then why Mama was on the window ledge. She assumed I had been taken along with the other children. And she didn't want to live. If I hadn't freed myself from the trunk in time, Mama would have jumped. I was her only child, her whole world. She was prepared to kill herself before she would go on without me.

A chill ran through me as I sprinted toward her. "I'm here, I'm here." She wobbled unsteadily on the window ledge and I grabbed her arm to stop her from falling. Remorse ripped through me. I always wanted to please her, to bring that hard-won smile to her beautiful face. Now I had caused her so much pain she'd almost done the unthinkable.

"I was so worried," she said after I'd helped her down and closed the window. As if that explained everything. "You weren't in the attic."

"But, Mama, I hid where you told me to." I gestured to the trunk. "The other place, remember? Why didn't you look for me there?"

Mama looked puzzled. "I didn't think you would fit anymore." There was a pause and then we both began laughing, the sound scratchy and out of place in the pitiful room. For a few seconds, it was like we were back in our old apartment on Meiselsa Street and none of this had happened at all. If we could still laugh, surely things would be all right. I clung to this last improbable thought like a life preserver at sea.

But a cry echoed through the building, then another, silencing our laughter. It was the mothers of the other children who had been taken by the police. There came a thud outside. I started for the window, but my mother blocked me. "Look away," she ordered. It was too late. I glimpsed Helga Kolberg, who lived down the hall, lying motionless in the coal-tinged snow on the pavement below, her limbs cast at odd angles and skirt splayed around her like a fan. She had realized her children were gone and, like Mama, she didn't want to live without them. I wondered whether jumping was a shared instinct, or if they had discussed it, a kind of suicide pact in case their worst nightmares came true.

My father raced into the room then. Neither Mama nor I said a word, but I could tell from his unusually grim expression that he already knew about the *aktion* and what had happened to the other families. He simply walked over and wrapped his enormous arms around both of us, hugging us tighter than usual.

As we sat, silent and still, I looked up at my parents. Mama was a striking beauty—thin and graceful, with white-blond hair the color of a Nordic princess'. She looked nothing like the other Jewish women and I had heard whispers more than once that she didn't come from here. She might have walked away from the ghetto and lived as a non-Jew if it wasn't for us. But I was built like Papa, with the dark, curly hair and olive skin that made the fact that we were Jews undeniable. My father looked like the laborer the Germans had made him in the ghetto, broad-shouldered and ready to lift great pipes or slabs of concrete. In fact, he was an accountant—or had been until it became illegal for his firm to employ him anymore. I always wanted to please Mama, but it was Papa who was my ally, keeper of secrets and weaver of dreams, who stayed up too late whispering secrets in the dark and had roamed the city with me, hunting for treasure. I moved closer now, trying to lose myself in the safety of his embrace.

Still, Papa's arms could offer little shelter from the fact that everything was changing. The ghetto, despite its awful conditions, had once seemed relatively safe. We were living among Jews and the Germans had even appointed a Jewish council, the Judenrat, to run our daily affairs. Perhaps if we laid low and did as we were told, Papa said more than once, the Germans would leave us alone inside these walls until the war was over. That had been the hope. But after today, I wasn't so sure. I looked around the apartment, seized with equal parts disgust and fear. In the beginning, I had not wanted to be here; now I was terrified we would be forced to leave.

"We have to do something," Mama burst out, her voice a pitch higher than usual as it echoed my unspoken thoughts.

"I'll take her tomorrow and register her for a work permit," Papa said. This time Mama did not argue. Before the war, being a child had been a good thing. But now being useful and able to work was the only thing that might save us.

Mama was talking about more than a work visa, though. "They are going to come again and next time we won't be so lucky." She did not bother to hold back her words for my benefit now. I nodded in silent agreement. Things were changing, a voice inside me said. We could not stay here forever.

"It will be okay, *kochana*," Papa soothed. How could he possibly say that? But Mama laid her head on his shoulder, seeming to trust him as she always had. I wanted to believe it, too. "I will think of something. At least," Papa added as we huddled close, "we are all still together." The words echoed through the room, equal parts promise and prayer.

2

Ella

Kraków, Poland
June 1942

The early-summer evening was warm as I crossed the market square, weaving my way around the fragrant flower stalls that stood in the shadow of the Cloth Hall, displaying bright, fresh blooms that few had the money or inclination to buy. The outdoor cafés, not bustling as they once would have been on such a pleasant evening, were still open and doing a brisk business serving beer to German soldiers and the few foolhardy others who dared join them. If one didn't look too closely, it might seem that nothing had changed at all.

Of course, everything had changed. Kraków had been a city under occupation for nearly three years. Red flags with black swastikas at the center hung from the Sukiennice, the long yellow cloth hall that ran down the middle of the square, as well as the brick tower of the Ratusz, or town hall. The Rynek had been renamed Adolf-Hitler-Platz and the centuries-old Polish street names changed to Reichsstrasse and Wehrmachtstrasse, and so on. Hitler had designated Kraków as the seat of the Gen-

eral Government and the city was choked thick with SS and
other German soldiers, jackbooted thugs who walked down the
sidewalk three and four wide, forcing all other pedestrians off
their path and harassing ordinary Poles at will. At the corner a
boy in short pants sold the *Krakauer Zeitung*, the German pro-
paganda paper that had replaced our own newspaper. "Under
the Tail," people called it in irreverent whispers, implying that
it was only useful for wiping one's backside.

Despite the awfulness of the changes, it still felt good to be
out and have the sunshine warm my face and to stretch my legs
on such a beautiful evening. I had walked the streets of the Old
Town every day I could remember of my nineteen years, first
with my father as a child and later on my own. Its features were
the topography of my life, from the medieval Barbican for-
tress and gate at the end of Floriańska Street to Wawel Castle
seated high atop a hill overlooking the Wisła River. Walking,
it seemed, was the one thing that neither time nor war could
take from me.

I did not stop at the cafés, though. Once I might have sat
with my friends, laughing and talking as the sun set and the
lights went on for evening, sending pools of yellow cascad-
ing against the pavement. But there were no nighttime lights
now—everything was dimmed per German decree to disguise
the city against a possible air raid. And no one I knew made
plans to meet anymore either. People were going out less, I reminded myself often as the invitations that had once been plen-
tiful dwindled to nothing. Few could purchase enough food
with ration cards to entertain at home either. Everyone was too
caught up in their own survival, and company was a luxury we
could ill afford.

Still, I felt a pang of loneliness. My life was so quiet with Krys
away and I would have liked to sit and talk with friends my own
age. Brushing the feeling aside, I circled the square once more

studying the shop windows, which displayed fashions and other wares almost no one could afford anymore. Anything to delay going back to the house where I lived with my stepmother.

But it was foolish to stay on the street much longer. The Germans were known to stop people for questioning and inspection with increasing frequency as night fell and the curfew drew closer. I left the square and started down the grand thoroughfare of Grodzka Street toward the house just steps from the city center where I had lived my entire life. Then I turned onto Kanonicza Street, an ancient and winding way paved with cobblestones that had been smoothed by time. Despite the fact that I dreaded encountering my stepmother, Ana Lucia, the wide town house we shared was still a welcome sight. With its bright yellow facade and well-tended flower boxes in the windows, it was nicer than anything the Germans thought a Pole deserved. Under other circumstances it surely would have been confiscated for a Nazi officer.

As I stood in front of the house, memories of my family danced before my eyes. The visions of my mother, who had died of influenza when I was a toddler, were the least clear. I was the youngest of four children and had been jealous of my siblings, who had so many years with our mother, whom I had scarcely known at all. My sisters were both married, one to an attorney in Warsaw and the other to a boat captain in Gdańsk.

It was my brother, Maciej, closest to me in age, whom I missed the most. Though he was eight years older, he had always taken time to play and talk with me. He was different than the others. He had no interest in marriage, nor the career choices my father had wanted for him. So at seventeen, he fled to Paris, where he lived with a man named Phillipe. Of course, Maciej had not escaped the long arm of the Nazis. They controlled Paris now, too, darkening what he had once called the City of Light. But his letters remained upbeat and I hoped that things were at least a bit better there.

For years after my siblings left, it was just me and my father, whom I had always called Tata. Then he began making trips to Vienna for his printing business more often than he had. One day, he returned with Ana Lucia, whom he had married without telling me. I knew the first time I met Ana Lucia that I would hate her. She was wearing a thick fur coat with the head of the animal still attached around the collar. The poor thing's eyes stared at me piteously, filled with recrimination. A whiff of her too-heavy jasmine scent filled my nose as she air-kissed my cheek, her breath an almost hiss. I could tell from the cold way she appraised me upon our first meeting that I was not wanted, like furniture that someone else had picked out, which she was stuck with because it came with the house.

When the war broke out, Tata decided to renew his army commission. At his age, he certainly did not have to go. But he served out of a sense of duty, not just to country but to the young soldiers, barely more than boys, some of whom had not been born the last time Poland went to war.

The telegram had come swiftly: missing, presumed dead on the Eastern Front. My eyes stung now as I thought of Tata, the pain as fresh as the day we had learned the news. Sometimes I dreamed that he had been captured and would return to us after the war. Other times, I was angry: how could he have gone and left me alone with Ana Lucia? She was like the evil stepmother in some childhood story, only worse because she was real.

I reached the arched oak doorway of our house, started to turn the brass knob. Then hearing boisterous voices inside, I stopped. Ana Lucia was entertaining again.

My stepmother's parties were always loud. "Soirees," she called them, making them sound grander than they were. They seemed to consist of whatever decent food could be found these days, paired with several bottles of wine from my father's dwindling cellar and some vodka from the freezer, watered down liberally to make it stretch. Before the war, I might have joined her parties, which were filled with artists and musicians and intellectuals. I loved to listen to their spirited debates, arguing ideas long into the night. But those people were all gone now, having fled to Switzerland or England if they were able, the less lucky ones arrested and sent away. They had been replaced by guests of the worst sort—Germans, the higher ranking, the better. Ana Lucia was nothing if not a pragmatist. She had recognized early on in the war the need to make our captors into friends. The table was filled every weekend now with thick-necked brutes who fouled our house with cigar smoke and soiled our carpets with mud-stained boots they did not bother to wipe at the door.

At first, Ana Lucia claimed that she was fraternizing with the Germans to get information about my father. That was in the early days, when we still hoped he might be imprisoned or missing in action. But then we received word he had been killed and she continued to socialize with the Germans more than ever before. It was as if, freed from the pretense of marriage, she could be exactly as awful as she wanted to be.

Of course, I did not dare to confront my stepmother about her shameful actions. Since my father was declared dead and had not prepared a will, the house and all of his money would legally go into her name. She would happily cast me out if I made trouble, replace the furniture she had never wanted in the first place. I would have nothing. So I treaded lightly. Ana Lucia liked to remind me often that it was thanks to her good graces with the Germans that we remained in our fine house with enough food to eat and the proper stamps on our *Kennkarten* to enable us to move freely about the city.

I stepped away from the front door. From the pavement, I looked sadly through the front window of our house at the familiar crystal glasses and china. But I did not see the horrid strangers who now enjoyed our things. Instead, the visions in my mind were of my family: me wanting to play dolls with my much older sisters, my mother scolding Maciej that he would break things as he chased me around the table. When you are young, you expect the family you were born into to be yours forever. Time and war had made that not the case.

Dreading Ana Lucia's company more than the curfew, I turned away from the house and started walking again. I was not sure where I was headed. It was almost dark and the parks were off-limits to ordinary Poles, as were most of the better cafés, the restaurants and movie theaters, too. My indecision in the moment seemed to reflect my larger life, caught in a kind of no-man's-land. I had nowhere to go, and no one to go with. Living in occupied Kraków, I felt like a pet bird, able to fly just the tiniest bit, but always mindful of being trapped in a cage.

It might not have been like this if Krys was still here, I reflected as I started back in the direction of the Rynek. I imagined a different world where the war had not forced him to leave. We would be planning a wedding, maybe even married by now.

Krys and I had met by happenstance nearly two years before the war broke out when my friends and I had stopped off for a coffee at a courtyard café where he was making a delivery. Tall and broad-shouldered, he cut a dashing figure as he strode through the passageway carrying a large crate. He had rugged features, which appeared to be cut from stone, and a leonine gaze that seemed to hold the entire room. When he passed our table, an onion fell from the crate he was carrying and rolled close to me. He knelt to retrieve it, and looked up at me and smiled. "I'm at your feet." I sometimes wondered if he had dropped the vegetable deliberately or if it was fate that sent it spinning in my direction.

He invited me out for that very night. I should have said no; it was not proper to accept a date on such short notice. But I was intrigued and, after a few hours at dinner, smitten. It was not just looks that drew me to him. Krys was different from anyone I had ever met. He had an energy that seemed to fill the room and make anyone else present fade away. Though he came from a working-class family and had not finished high school, much less gone to college, he was self-taught. He had bold ideas about the future and how the world should be that made him seem so much bigger than everything else around us. He was the smartest person I had ever known. And he listened to my opinions in a way that nobody had.

We began spending all of our free time together. We were an unlikely couple—I was sociable and liked parties and friends. He was a loner who shunned crowds and preferred deep conversations while taking long walks. Krys loved nature and showed me places of rare beauty outside the city, ancient forests and castle ruins buried deep in the woods that I had not known existed.

One evening, a few weeks after we had met, we were walking along the high ridge of St. Bronisława Hill, a hill just outside the city, heatedly debating a point about French philosophers, when I noticed him watching me intensely. "What is it?"

"When we met, I expected you to be like the other girls," he said. "Interested in superficial things." Though I might have been offended, I knew what he meant. My friends seemed largely interested in parties and plays and the latest fashions. "Instead, I found you another way entirely." We were soon spending all of our free time together, making plans to marry and travel and see the world.

Of course, the war changed all of that. Krys was not conscripted, but like my father, signed up to go and fight from the start. He had always cared too much about everything and the war was no exception. I pointed out that if he just waited it might be all over before he had to go, but Krys would not be swayed. Worse yet, he had ended things with me before leaving. "We don't know how long I will be gone." *Or if you will return*, I thought, the notion so awful that neither of us could bear to voice it. "You should be free to meet someone else." That was a joke. Even if there had been young men left in Kraków, I would have had no interest. I argued with more force than

my pride now liked to admit that we should not break up, but
rather get engaged or even married before he left as so many
others had done. I wanted at least that piece of him, to have
shared that bond, if something happened. But Krys wanted to
wait, and when he saw things a certain way, there was nothing
in the world that could convince him. We spent the last night
together, becoming more intimate than we should have because
there might not be another chance for a long time, or maybe
ever. I left tearfully in the predawn hours, sneaking into the
house before my stepmother could notice I was missing.

Even though Krys and I were no longer really together, I still
loved him. He had broken up with me only because he thought
it was in my best interests. I felt certain that when the war was
over and he returned safely, we would reunite and things would
be as they were. Then the Polish Army was quickly defeated,
overrun by the German tanks and artillery. Many of the men
who had gone off to fight returned, wounded and downtrod-
den. I assumed that Krys would do the same. But he did not
come back. His letters, which had already grown less frequent
and more distant in tone, stopped coming altogether. Where
was he? I wondered constantly. Surely I would have heard from
his parents if he had been arrested or worse. No, Krys was still
out there, I told myself doggedly. The war had simply disrupted
the mail. And as soon as he could, Krys would return to me.

In the distance, the bells of the Mariacki church rang out,
signaling seven o'clock. Instinctively, I waited for the trumpeter
to play the Hejnał as he had every hour for most of my life. But
the trumpeter's song, a medieval rallying cry that recalled how
Poland had once repelled invading hordes, had been largely si-
lenced by the Germans, who now allowed it to play only twice
per day. I recrossed the market square, considering whether
it was worth stopping for a coffee to pass the time. As I drew
close to one of the cafés, a German soldier seated with two oth-

ers looked up at me with interest, his intent unmistakable. No good would come from sitting down there. I moved on quickly.

As I neared the Sukiennice, I spotted two familiar figures, walking arm in arm and peering into a shop window. I started toward them. "Good evening."

"Oh, hello." Magda, the brunette, peered out from beneath a straw hat that was two years out of fashion. Magda had been one of my closest friends before the war. But I had not seen her or heard from her in months. She did not meet my eyes.

At her side was Klara, a shallow girl for whom I had never much cared. She sported a blond pageboy haircut and eyebrows that were tweezed too high, giving her a look of perpetual surprise. "We were just doing some shopping and are going to stop for a bite to eat," she informed me smugly.

And they had not invited me. "I would have enjoyed that," I ventured carefully in Magda's direction. Despite the fact that we had not spoken recently, some part of me still hoped that my old friend would have thought of me—and invited me to join her.

Magda did not answer. But Klara, who had always been jealous of my closeness to Magda, did not mince words. "We didn't call. We thought you would be busy with your stepmother's new friends." My cheeks stung as though I had been slapped. For months, I had told myself that my friends were no longer getting together. The truth was that they were no longer getting together with *me*. I knew then that the disappearance of my friends had nothing to do with the hardships of the war. They had shunned me because Ana Lucia was a collaborator—and perhaps they even believed that I was, too.

I cleared my throat. "I don't associate with the same people as my stepmother," I replied slowly, struggling to keep my voice even. Neither Klara nor Magda said anything further and there was an awkward moment of silence among us.

I lifted my chin. "It's no matter," I said, attempting to brush off the rejection. "I've been busy. There's just so much I need to get done before Krys gets back." I had not told my friends that Krys and I had ended our relationship. It was not just the fact that we seldom saw each other or that I was embarrassed. Rather, saying it aloud would force me to admit it to myself, make it real. "He'll be back soon and then we can plan our wedding."

"Yes, of course he will," Magda offered, and I felt a twinge of guilt as I remembered her own fiancé, Albert, who had been taken by the Germans when they raided the university and arrested all of the professors. He had never returned.

"Well, we must be going," Klara said. "We have a reservation at seven thirty." For a split second I wished that for all of their rudeness, they might still invite me to join them. Some pathetic part of me would have swallowed my pride and said yes for a few hours of company.

But they did not. "Goodbye, then," Klara said coldly. She took Magda's arm and led her away, their laughter carrying back across the square with the wind. Their heads were tilted conspiratorially toward one another and I felt certain they were talking about me.

Never mind, I told myself, pushing the rejection away. I drew my sweater closer against the summer breeze, which now carried an ominous chill. Krys would be back soon and we would get engaged. We would pick up right where we had left off and it would be as if this terrible intermission never happened at all.

3

Sadie

March 1943

A loud scraping sound below awakened me from sleep.

It wasn't the first time I'd been disturbed by noise in the ghetto at night. The walls of our apartment building, which had been hastily constructed to divide the original dwellings into smaller units, were paper-thin and the ordinarily muffled sounds of daily life passed readily through them. Within our apartment, the night sounds were constant, too, my father's heavy breathing and snores, my mother's quiet grunts as she tried to find a comfortable position to rest her newly swollen belly. I often heard my parents whispering to one another in our tiny shared space after they thought I was asleep.

Not that they tried to hide so many things from me anymore. It had become impossible in the year since I was nearly caught and taken in the *aktion* to ignore the awfulness of our worsening situation. After a grueling winter with no heat and little food, sickness and death were everywhere. People young and old died of starvation and disease or were shot for not obeying the ghetto police orders quickly enough or for some other perceived infraction while lined up for the work details each morning.

We never spoke of the day I was almost taken. But things had changed after that. For one thing, I had a job now, working alongside Mama in a factory making shoes. Papa had used his every influence to keep us together and make sure that we were not assigned to heavy labor. Still, my hands grew calloused and bled from handling the coarse leather twelve hours a day and my bones ached like an old woman's from being endlessly hunched over the repetitive work.

There was something different about Mama, too—at nearly forty, she was pregnant. My whole life, I had known that my parents desperately wanted another child. Improbably now, at the very worst of times, their prayers had been answered. "Late summer," Papa said, telling me when the baby would come. Mama had already begun to show, her rounded belly protruding from her thin frame.

I wanted to be as happy as my parents were about the baby. Once I had dreamed of a younger sibling, someone closer to my own age. But I was nineteen, and might have been starting a family of my own. A baby just seemed so useless, another mouth to feed at the worst of times. It had been just the three of us for so long now. Yet a baby was coming, whether I liked it or not. I wasn't at all sure that I did.

The scraping noise came again louder, someone digging at the concrete. The ancient plumbing must be backed up again, I thought. Perhaps someone was finally fixing the lone, ground-floor toilet, which overflowed constantly. Still, it seemed odd that they were working on it in the middle of the night.

I sat up, annoyed by the intrusion. I had slept restlessly. We weren't permitted to keep the windows open, and even in March, the room was stuffy, the air thick and foul smelling. I looked around for my parents and was surprised to find them gone. Sometimes after I went to bed, Papa would defy ghetto rules and go sit on the front step and smoke with a few of the other men who lived below in order to escape the confines of our room. But he should have been back by now, and Mama seldom left except for work. Something was not right.

Shouting erupted below on the street, Germans barking orders. I tensed. It had been a year since the day I had hidden in the trunk, and though we had heard of large-scale *aktions* in other parts of the ghetto ("liquidations," I'd heard Papa call them once), the Germans had not entered our building since. But the terror had never left me and some instinct told me with absolute certainty that they were now coming again.

I stood and put on my dressing gown and slippers and hurried from the apartment to find my parents. Unsure where to go, I started downstairs. The corridor was dark, except for the faint light that came from the bathroom, so I started toward it. When I stepped into the doorway, I blinked, not only from the unexpected brightness, but also with surprise. The toilet had been lifted completely from its moorings and shoved aside, revealing a jagged hole in the ground. I hadn't known that it moved at all. My father was on his knees on the ground, clawing at the hole, literally chipping away at the concrete edges and making it bigger with his hands.

"Papa?"

He did not look up. "Get dressed quickly!" he ordered more sharply than I had ever heard him speak.

I considered asking another of the dozen questions swirling through my brain. But I had been raised an only child among adults and I was wise enough to know when to just go along. I went back upstairs to our room and opened the rotting wood armoire that held our clothes. Then I hesitated. I had no idea what to wear, but I didn't know where Mama was and I didn't dare bother my father again to ask. Anyway, we had come to the ghetto with just a few suitcases between the three of us; it was not as if I had so much to choose from. I pulled a skirt and blouse from a hanger and started to dress.

My mother appeared in the door and shook her head. "Something warmer," she instructed.

"But, Mama, it's not that cold." She did not answer. Instead, she pulled out the thick blue sweater my grandmother had knit for me last winter and my lone pair of woolen trousers. I was surprised; I preferred pants to skirts, but Mama thought them unladylike and before the war she used to let me wear them only on the weekend when we weren't going out anywhere. When I had finished changing, she pointed to my feet. "Boots," she said firmly.

My boots were from two winters earlier and too snug. "They're too small." We had planned to buy a new pair last fall, but the restrictions on Jews going into the shops had come.

Mama started to say something and I was sure she was going to tell me to wear them anyway. Then she rummaged in the bottom drawer of the armoire with effort and pulled out her own boots. "But what are you going to wear?"

"Just put them on." Hearing her firm tone, I obeyed without asking further. Mama's feet were birdlike, narrow and small, and the boots only a size larger than my own. I noticed then that despite dressing me for colder weather, my mother still wore a skirt—she didn't own pants, and even if she had, they would not have fit over her belly, which seemed to grow rounder by the day.

As Mama finished shoving some belongings in a bag, I looked out the window to the street below. In the faint predawn light, I could see men in uniforms, not just the police but SS as well, setting up tables. Both ends of the street were blocked. The Jews were being forced to gather on Plac Zgody as they did each morning. Only there was none of the order of roll call from when we lined up to go work in the factories. The police were pulling people from buildings and trying to corral the crowds

into lines with truncheons and whips, herding them in the direction of a dozen trucks waiting at the corner. It looked as
though they were taking everyone in the ghetto. I let the curtains drop uneasily.

A spray of gunfire rattled closer to our building than I had
ever heard it. Mama pulled me away from the window and onto
the floor, whether to shield me from seeing or being hit, I did
not know.

When the gunfire had ceased for several seconds, she stood
and pulled me to my feet, then led me away from the window
and ushered me into my coat. "Come, now!" She started for the
door, carrying a small satchel.

I looked over my shoulder. For so long, I had hated living in
the filthy, cramped space. But the apartment that had seemed so
grim was now a sanctuary, the only safe place I knew. I would
have given anything to stay.

I considered refusing. Leaving our apartment now with so
many police on the street seemed foolish and unsafe. Then I saw
the look on my mother's face, not just angry but afraid. This was
not some outing to be taken or skipped. There was no choice.

I followed Mama down the stairs, still not quite understanding. I guessed that we were going outside and joining the others to avoid risking attention or having the Germans come and
order us out. When we reached the ground floor, I started for
the front door. But Mama turned me squarely by the shoulders,
nudging me farther down the hall. "Come," Mama said.

"Where?" I asked. She did not reply but led me back to the
bathroom, as if asking me to go use it one last time before a
long journey.

As we neared the bathroom once more, I heard my father
arguing with a man whose voice I didn't recognize. "Things
aren't ready," Papa said.

"We have to go now," the strange man insisted.

Going anywhere would be quite impossible, I thought, remembering the blockade on the street. I stepped into the bathroom. The toilet was still shoved to one side, revealing a hole in the floor. I was stunned to see a man's head stuck up through it. It looked dismembered, like some oddity at a freak show or carnival. He had a wide face, cherubic cheeks rough and raw from working outdoors in the cold Polish winter. Seeing me, he smiled. *"Dzień dobry,"* he said politely, greeting me as if all of this was perfectly normal. Then he looked at Papa and his expression turned somber once more. "You must come now."

"Come where?" I blurted. The streets were teeming with SS and Gestapo and the Jewish Ghetto Police, who, God help us, were nearly as bad. I looked down at the hole in the floor, understanding. "Surely you don't mean..."

I turned back to Mama, waiting for her to protest. My elegant, refined mother was not about to lower herself through a hole beneath the toilet. But her face was stony and resolved, ready to do what Papa asked.

I, however, was not ready. I took a step back. "What about Babcia?" I asked. My grandmother, who was in a nursing home on the other side of the city, having somehow escaped deportation to the ghetto.

Mama faltered, then shook her head. "There's no time. Her nursing home is not Jewish," she added. "She'll be fine."

Through the window over the sink, I glimpsed crowds of people being herded from the buildings onto trucks. I spotted my friend Stefania in the crowd. I was surprised to see her so far from her own apartment on the other side of the ghetto. I had imagined, too, that because her father was one of the Jewish Ghetto Police, she might somehow be spared, safe. Now she was being taken, just like everyone else. I almost wished I could go with her. But her face was white with fear. *Come with us*, I wanted to shout. I watched helplessly as she was pushed forward and disappeared into the crowd.

Mama stepped around me. "I'll go first."

Seeing her belly, the man in the hole looked surprised. "I didn't know..." he murmured. The man's face wrinkled with consternation. I could see him calculating the extra difficulties childbirth and a newborn would bring. For a second, I wondered if he might refuse to take my mother. I held my breath, waiting for him to say that it wouldn't work and we would have to find another way.

But the man disappeared back into the hole to make way and my mother stepped forward. She handed Papa her satchel, then sat on the ground with effort, putting her legs through the hole. Under other circumstances she would have slipped through easily. "Little bird," our father called her, and the name suited, for she was thin and girl-like even as she approached forty. However, she was bulky now, bearing the rounded stomach on her lithe frame as though holding a melon. Her skirt pulled down embarrassingly, revealing a patch of white belly. I thought, as I often had, that she was too old to be having another child. Mama let out a small yelp as Papa pushed her through the hole, then disappeared into the darkness.

"Your turn," Papa said to me. I looked around, stalling for time. Anything to avoid going into the sewer. But the Germans were at the door of the building now, knocking hard. Soon they would break down the door and it would all be too late. "Sadie, hurry!" he said, and I could hear the pleading in his voice. Whatever he was asking me to do, he was doing to save our lives.

I sat on the ground as Mama had done and stared down into the hole, dark and ominous. A stench filled my nostrils and I gagged. Something rebellious and stubborn arose in me, eclipsing my normal obedience. "I can't." The hole was dark and terrifying, nothing visible on the other side. It was like the time I had tried to jump from a high tree branch into a lake, only a thousand times worse. I could not bring myself to go through with it.

"You must." My father didn't wait for further argument but

shoved me roughly. The bulk of my clothes caused me to stick halfway down and he pushed me again, harder. The filthy edges of the concrete tore at my cheeks, cutting them, and then I was falling into the darkness.

I landed hard on my knees. Cold, foul water splashed up around me from the ground, soaking my stockings. I caught myself to avoid tumbling farther by grasping at a slimy wall. As I stood, I tried hard not to think about what I might be touching.

Papa lowered himself through the hole and landed beside me. From above, someone re-covered the floor. I had not seen anyone behind us and I wondered who, a neighbor Papa had paid perhaps or someone doing a good deed or too scared to drop into the sewer himself. Our last bit of light was eclipsed. We were trapped in the pitch-blackness of the sewer.

And we were not alone. In the darkness, I could hear people moving around us, though I could not tell who they were or how many. I was surprised that there were others. Had they come through a toilet hole to get here as well? I blinked, trying unsuccessfully to adjust my eyes. "What is happening?" a woman's voice asked in Yiddish. No one answered.

I took a breath and started to gag. The smell was everywhere. It was the stench of water filled with feces and urine, as well as garbage and decay that thickened the air. "Breathe through your mouth," Mama instructed quietly. But that was worse, as if I was eating the filth. "Shallow breaths." This last bit of instruction did not help much either. The sewer water swirled ankle-deep, soaking through my boots and stockings, and the icy wetness against my skin caused me to shiver.

The stranger lit a carbide lamp and the light licked the rounded walls, illuminating a half-dozen strange, scared faces around me. Closest stood two men, one about my father's age and the second appeared to be his son and maybe twenty or so. They were dressed in the yarmulkes and black clothing of religious Jews. "Yids," Papa would have called them before the war came and we were all lumped together. He did not mean it unkindly, but rather as a sort of shorthand to refer to the religious Jews. They had always seemed so foreign to me with their own customs and strict observance, and in some ways I felt I had more in common with Gentile Poles than these other Jews.

Behind them stood another family, a young couple with a little boy of two or three sleeping in his father's arms, all wearing nothing but pajamas beneath their coats. There was a stooped elderly woman, too, though she stood apart and I couldn't tell which of the families she belonged to. Perhaps neither. I did not see any other girls or children close to my age.

As my eyes adjusted, I looked around. I had imagined the sewer, if I considered it at all, as pipes running beneath the ground. But we were in an immense, cavernous passageway with a rounded ceiling at least twenty feet across, like a tunnel that a freight train might pass through. The middle of the tunnel was filled with a swift current of black water, wide and deep enough to be a river. I had not imagined that such a vast body of water was rushing endlessly beneath our feet. The sound as it echoed off the high walls was almost deafening.

We stood on a thin lip of concrete not more than two feet wide that ran along one side of the river and I could just make out a second ledge running parallel on the far side. The current was strong and seemed to pull me in as I clung to the narrow path. I had read a book on Greek mythology once about Hades, lord of the underworld; now I seemed to find myself in just such a place, a kind of strange, underground world I had never thought of or known to exist. I stared dizzily at the water, my fear rising. I could not swim. No matter how many times Papa had tried to teach me, I could not bear to put my head beneath the water, even in the calmest lake in summer. I would never survive if I fell in here.

"Come," the man who had popped through our bathroom floor said. He was broad-shouldered and stocky, I noted now that I could see all of him. He wore a simple cloth hat and high boots. "We can't stay here." His voice echoed too loudly in the rounded chamber.

He started walking along the ledge, holding the lamp aloft in front of him. Despite his boxy frame, he moved easily along the narrow path with the ease of one who worked in the sewer, spent his days here.

"Papa, who is he?" I whispered.

"A sewer worker," Papa replied. We followed the worker single file, using the rounded slimy wall to balance ourselves. The tunnel stretched endlessly into the darkness ahead. I wondered why he had chosen to help us, where we were going, how he would ever get us out of this wretched place. Except for the rushing of water, the air around us was silent and still. The awful noises of the Germans above were muted, nearly gone.

We reached a place where the wall of the tunnel seemed to bow outward away from the water, forming a small alcove. The sewer worker motioned us inside the wider space. "Rest, before we go on."

I peered doubtfully at the small black rocks that covered the ground, wondering where we were meant to rest. Something seemed to move on top of them. Closer, I could see that they were thousands of tiny yellow maggots. I stifled a yelp.

My father, seemingly not minding, sank down to the rocks. His back rose with great breaths of exhaustion. He looked up for a moment and I saw something, worry or fear maybe, cross his face in a way it never quite had before. Then noticing me, he held out his arms. "Come." I lay across his lap, allowing him to shield me from the filthy, maggot-infested ground.

"I will come back for you when it is safe," the worker said. Safe for what? I wanted to ask. But I knew better than to question the person who was trying to save us. He stepped out of the alcove, taking the lamp with him and casting us into darkness. The others settled onto the ground. No one spoke. We were still beneath the ghetto, I realized, hearing the Germans above once more. The arrests seemed to be complete now, but they were still combing the buildings, looking for anyone who might be hiding and picking through the meager belongings people had left behind like vultures. I imagined them going through our tiny apartment. We had almost nothing by the end; it had all been sold or left behind when we moved to the ghetto. Still, the idea that people could go through our property, that we had no right to anything of our own anymore, made me feel violated, less human.

All of my fears and sadness welled up anew. "Papa, I don't think I can do this," I confided in a whisper.

My father wrapped his arms around me and the feeling was so warm and comforting we might have been back home. I buried my head against his chest, taking comfort in the familiar mint and tobacco scent, and trying to ignore the sewer stench that mixed with it. Mama settled by his side and rested her head on his shoulder. My eyelids grew heavy.

Sometime later, Papa shifted, waking me from sleep. I opened my eyes and peered in the semidarkness at the other families, who were scattered around us sleeping. The younger man from the religious family was awake, though. Beneath his black hat, he had gentle features and a small, trim beard. His brown eyes glittered in the darkness. I moved carefully away from Papa, and crawled gingerly across the slippery floor toward him. "Such an odd thing to do, sleeping among total strangers," I said. "I mean, winding up here, who could have imagined?" He did not answer, but eyed me warily. "I'm Sadie, by the way."

"Saul," he replied stiffly. I waited for him to say something more. When he did not, I retreated back across the floor toward my parents. Saul was the only one in the whole group close to my age, but he seemed to have no interest in being friends.

A short while later, the worker returned, re-illuminating the alcove with his lamp and waking the others. He gestured silently that we had to keep going, so we stood up stiffly and assembled single file to follow the path along the wide river once more.

A few minutes later, we reached a juncture. The worker led us off the main channel, turning right into a narrower tunnel that took us farther from the raging sewer river. That path soon ended at a concrete wall. A dead end. Had he lured us deliberately into some sort of a trap? I had heard stories of Gentiles betraying their Jewish neighbors and turning them in to the police, but this seemed an odd way to do it.

The worker knelt with his lamp and I could see that lower on the wall there was a small metal circle, a kind of cover or cap. He pried it open to reveal a horizontal pipe, then stepped back. The entrance to the pipe was only about twenty inches in diameter. Surely he didn't mean for us to go through it. But he stood, waiting expectantly.

"It's the only way," he said, a note of apology in his voice that seemed to be directed mostly at my mother. "You have to go on your stomach. If you put your head and shoulders through, everything else will follow." He handed Mama something, then climbed into the pipe, and it seemed impossible that his stout frame would fit. He had done this before, though. He slid in, and a moment later he disappeared.

The religious family went first and I could hear them grunting and straining with the effort of making it through. Then the family with the small child climbed into the tunnel. Only Mama, Papa and I were left. When it was my turn, I knelt in front of the pipe, which reminded me of the dusty attic crawl space where Stefania and I had played in our old apartment before the war. I could make it through on my belly. But what about my mother?

"You next," Mama said. I hesitated, doubtful she would be able to follow. "I'll be right behind you," Mama promised, and I knew I had no choice but to believe her.

Papa nudged me and I started to shimmy through, trying

to ignore the trickle of damp water on the bottom that seeped unpleasantly through the front of my clothes. The pipe surrounded me, viselike on all sides, encasing me in a watery tomb. I stopped, suddenly paralyzed by fear, unable to move or breathe. "Come, come," I heard the stranger call from the far end, and I knew I had to keep going or I would die here. The pipe was about ten meters long, and when I reached the other side and climbed out onto another ledge, I turned and listened. Surely Papa was too big to make it through, and Mama in her present state as well. I was seized with fear at the notion I might be left alone on this side without them.

Five minutes passed and no one else appeared through the opening. The sewer worker took a rope from the ground and fed it through the pipe, crawling partway back in to make it go through. He began tugging on it gently, pausing every few seconds. Through the pipe, I could hear Mama's soft groans. When she finally appeared through the pipe with the rope tied around her, she was covered in some sort of grease, which the worker must have given to her to help her slide through. Effective to be sure, but humiliating. With her blackened dress and disheveled hair, she looked nothing like her usually elegant self and she kept her eyes low as the stranger helped her out. Papa followed, shoving himself through with sheer will. I had never been so glad to see him in my entire life.

But my relief was short-lived. At the very place where we had come out of the pipe, there was a sewer grate just above our heads. We were still beneath the ghetto, I could tell, hearing German voices like the ones that had woken us from our beds just hours earlier, barking orders once more. A flashlight's beam licked the edge of the manhole cover and spilled over. "We must keep going," the worker whispered.

We followed him from the smaller tunnel where we had come out of the pipe back to the main tunnel and the wide rushing waters of the sewer river. The concrete ledge disappeared and we were forced to walk along the stony bank of the sewer, our feet in several inches of water. The rocks were slippery and slanted and I feared falling into the river with every step. Something sharp beneath the water cut through my boot and into my skin. I grabbed my foot, fighting the urge to cry out. I wanted to stop and check my injury, but the sewer worker was moving faster now, and I sensed that if we didn't keep up, we would be left behind for good.

We came to a junction where the river of sewage we had been following intersected with another torrent of water, equally wide and fierce. The rushing of the sewer water grew to a roar. "Careful," the worker cautioned. "We have to cross here." He gestured to a series of boards that had been loosely connected to form a bridge over the rushing water.

My breath caught with fear at the idea of crossing the river. Behind me, Papa put a hand on my shoulder. "Easy, Sadie. Remember when we waded in Kryspinów Lake? The stepping stones? It is just like that." I wanted to point out that the waters at Kryspinów, where we often picnicked in summer, were calm and gentle, and filled with small tadpoles and fish—not teeming with the filth of the entire city.

Papa nudged me forward and I had no choice but to follow my mother, who despite her rounded stomach had begun to cross on the boards with her usual grace, as if she were playing hopscotch. I started forward. My foot slipped off one of the boards and Papa reached out to steady me.

I turned around. "Papa, this is madness!" I exclaimed. "There has to be another way."

"Darling, this is the way." His voice was calm, expression certain. Papa, who had always kept me safe, believed that I could do this.

I took a deep breath, turned and started forward once again. I crossed one board, then another. I was in the middle of the river now, far from either shore. There was no turning back.

I took another step. The board beneath my foot gave way and started to slip sideways out from under me. "Help!" I cried out, my voice echoing through the tunnel.

Papa lurched forward to steady me. As he did, he lost hold of the small satchel Mama packed, which he had been carrying for her. The bag, containing what little we had left in the world, seemed to sail slow motion through the air, hovering above the water. Before it could fall in, Papa tried to snatch it. He grabbed the bag and flung it back to me, then tried to right himself. But he had reached too far and he flailed off balance.

"Papa!" I cried as he fell into the dark sewer water with a mighty splash. The worker spun around and raced swiftly onto the boards, pulling me to safety. Then he tried to reach for my father. But as his hand neared Papa's, the strong current pulled my father away and he was drawn under. From the far bank, my mother screamed.

Papa reappeared above the surface. He emerged like a phoenix, his entire torso and most of his legs lifting above the water, defying it. Hope rose in my throat. He was going to make it. The water seemed to seize him then, a giant hand reaching out to pull him under. It dragged him, head and all, in a single swoop beneath the icy blackness. I held my breath, waiting for him to reappear, to fight back and emerge once more. But the surface of the river remained unbroken. The bubbles of air he had left behind disappeared into the current and then he was gone.

4

Sadie

Stunned, we stared at the unbroken surface of the sewer river. "Papa!" I cried again. My mother made a low guttural sound and tried to fling herself in the water after him, but the sewer worker held her back.

"Wait here," he instructed, racing farther down the path and following the current. I grasped Mama's hand so that she would not try to jump in again.

"He's a strong man," Saul offered. Though he meant it comfortingly, my anger rose: how did he know?

"And a good swimmer," Mama agreed desperately. "He might have survived." I wanted to cling to hope as much as she did. But recalling how the current had tossed him around like a rag doll, I knew even Papa's sure, burly armed swim stroke would be no match for the river.

Mama and I huddled together for several minutes in silence, numb with disbelief. The sewer worker returned, his face grave. "He was caught underneath by some debris. I tried to free him, but it was too late. I'm sorry, but I'm afraid there's nothing to be done."

"No!" I cried, my voice echoing dangerously through the cavernous tunnel. My mother's hand clamped down over my mouth before I could speak again, her skin a mixture of vile sewer water and salty tears on my lips. I sobbed against the warm filth of her palm. Papa had been here just minutes earlier, keeping me from slipping. If he hadn't reached for me, he would still be alive.

A moment later, my mother released me. "He's gone," I said. I leaned against her, feeling like a small child. My father had been a gentle giant, my protector, my closest confidant and friend. My world. But the sewer had swept him under and away like so much trash.

"I know, I know," Mama mouthed through her tears. "But we must be quiet or we will be done as well." Making too much noise could cause us to be detected by the police on the street above, and none of the others would suffer that risk. Mama slumped against the wall of the sewer, looking vulnerable and helpless. This whole escape had been Papa's plan—how were we ever to manage without him?

Saul took a step toward me, his brown eyes solemn. "I'm sorry about your father." His voice was friendlier now than it had been when I'd tried to speak with him earlier. But it didn't matter anymore. He touched the brim of his hat and then moved back closer to his father.

"We must keep going," the sewer worker said.

I stood stubbornly, refusing to move. "We can't leave him." I knew Papa had been pulled downstream, yet some part of me believed that if I stood right here, in the very spot where he disappeared, he would resurface and it would be as if none of this had happened. I reached my hand out, willing time to stop. One moment Papa had been here real and firm in the space beside me. Now he was gone, the air empty and still.

"Papa is dead," I said, the reality of it sinking painfully into my bones.

"But I am here." Mama cupped my face in her hands, forcing me to look into her eyes. "I am here and I will never leave you."

The sewer worker walked over and knelt in front of me. "My name is Pawel," he said gently. "I knew your father and he was a good man. He trusted me with your safety and he would want us to keep going." He stood and turned away and continued on, leading the others down the path.

Mama straightened, seeming to gain strength from his words. Her rounded belly protruded even more. "We will make it through this, somehow." I stared at her in disbelief. How could she even think—much less believe—that now, right as we had lost everything? For a second, I wondered if she had gone mad. But there was a calm surety to her words that I somehow needed to hear. "We are going to be fine."

Mama began pulling me forward. "Come." She had always been deceptively strong for her slight size, and now she tugged so hard I feared that if I resisted I might slip into the water and drown as well. "We must hurry." She was right. The others had kept going without us and were now several meters ahead. We had to follow or we would be left lost and alone in the strange, dark tunnel.

But I hesitated once more, looking fearfully at the churning dark river that ran alongside the path. I had always been terrified of the water, and now those fears seemed validated. If Papa, a strong swimmer, could not manage the murky current, what chance did I possibly have?

I looked down the dark path ahead. There was no way I could do this. "Come," Mama repeated, her voice softer now. "Imagine that you are a warrior princess and I, your mother, the great queen. We will travel from the halls of Wawel Castle down to the dungeon to slay the dragon Smok." She was referring to a make-believe game we had played when I was little. I was too old for such childish things, and the memory of such games, which I had most often played with my father, caused my sorrow to well up anew. But my mother's ability to put the best face on any situation was one of the things I loved most about her, and her willingness to make believe, even now, reminded me that we were in this together.

We caught up with the others and continued along the sewer path, which seemed to go on forever. Pawel walked in front, followed by the young couple and then the religious family with the old woman, who, despite looking close to ninety, moved with surprising speed. Surely we must be nearing the city limits, I thought. Perhaps there was some route to freedom ahead, maybe to the forest on the outskirts of the city where I'd heard of Jews hiding. I could not wait to breathe fresh air once more. Pawel led us to the right into a smaller offshoot of the main tunnel and the path seemed to incline upward, as if we were nearing the outside. My heart lifted as I imagined feeling the morning sunlight on my face and leaving the sewer behind forever.

Pawel turned again, left this time, and led us to a concrete chamber, without windows or any other source of light. Maybe four by four meters, it was just smaller than the single-room apartment I had shared with my parents in the ghetto. The sewer waters lapped at the slanted entranceway like waves on a shore. Someone had put some narrow boards across cinder blocks to form makeshift benches and there was a rusty woodstove in the corner. It was almost as if we were expected here.

"This is where you will hide," Pawel confirmed. He gestured around the chamber. I realized then that Pawel had not been leading us through the sewer pipes to get somewhere else. The sewer was the somewhere.

"Here?" I repeated, forgetting Mama's earlier warning to be quiet. All heads turned in my direction. Pawel nodded. "For how long?" I could not imagine spending another hour in the sewer.

"I don't understand," Pawel said.

Mama cleared her throat. "I think what my daughter is asking is, where will we be going from here?"

"Fools," the old woman snapped. It was the first time I had heard her speak. "This *is* where."

I looked at my mother in disbelief. "We're meant to live here?" My mind whirled. We could survive here a few hours, a night maybe. When Papa had bade me to go through the hole in our bathroom into the sewer, I had understood it to be transit, a passage to safety. And as we made our way through the filth and despair, I told myself it was necessary to escape. Instead, it was the destination itself. For all of my wildest nightmares, I could not have imagined that we would be staying in the sewer.

"Forever?" I asked.

"No, not forever, but…" Pawel glanced at Mama uncertainly. People living through the war did not have an easy way of speaking of the future. Then he looked me in the eye once more. "When we first made plans, we assumed we would get you out through the tunnel where it ends at the river." I could tell from the catch in his voice that the "we" he was talking about included my father. "Only now the Germans have that exit guarded. If we go forward, we will be shot." And if we returned to the ghetto, the same, I thought. We were trapped, with nowhere to go. "This is the safest choice for you all. The only hope." There was a note of pleading in his voice. "There is no other way out of the sewer, and even if there was, the streets are too dangerous now. All right?" he asked, as if needing me to agree. As if I had a choice. I didn't answer. I could not imagine saying yes to such a thing. Still, Papa would not have brought us here unless he believed it was the only option, our best chance of surviving. At last I nodded.

"We can't stay here," a voice said behind me. I turned. Across the chamber, the young woman with the toddler was speaking to her husband, repeating my protest anew. "We were promised a way out. We can't stay here."

"Leaving is impossible," Pawel said patiently, as if he had not just explained the whole thing to me. "The Germans have the end of the tunnel guarded."

"There's no other choice," her husband agreed.

But the woman took her son from her husband and started for the entrance to the chamber. "There's a way out ahead, I know it," she insisted stubbornly, pushing past Pawel and heading in the opposite direction from where we had come.

"Please," Pawel said. "You mustn't go. It's not safe. Think of your son." But the woman did not stop and her husband followed. In the distance, I could hear them still arguing.

"Wait!" Pawel called in a low voice from the entrance to the chamber. But he did not go after them. He had all of us—and himself—to protect.

"What will become of them?" I asked aloud. No one answered. The couple's voices faded in the distance. I imagined them walking toward the place where the sewer met the river. Part of me wished that I had fled with them.

A few minutes later, a sound like firecrackers rang out. I jumped. Though I had heard gunfire several times in the ghetto, I had never gotten used to the sound. I turned to Pawel. "Do you think...?" He shrugged, unable to say whether the shots had been aimed at the family that had fled or had been fired on the street above. But the voices in the corridor had gone silent.

I moved closer to Mama. "It will be fine," she soothed.

"How can you possibly say that?" I demanded. "Fine" was the furthest thing from describing this hell we had entered.

"We'll be here a few days, a week at most." I wanted to believe her.

A rat walked by the entrance to the chamber and eyed us not with fear, but contempt. I yelped, and the others glared at me for being too loud.

"Whisper," Mama admonished gently. How could she be so calm when Papa was dead and rats were staring us down?

"Mama, there are rats. We can't stay here!" The idea of staying here among them was more than I could take. "We have to leave now!" My voice rose to near hysterics.

Pawel marched over to me. "There is no back. There is no out. This is your world now. You must accept it for yourself and your mother, and for the child she is carrying." He looked me in the eye. "Do you understand?" His voice was gentle but firm. I nodded. "This is the only way."

Behind him, the rat still stood in the tunnel outside the entranceway, looking at us defiantly, somehow knowing that it had won. I never liked cats. But oh, how I wished for that old tabby that lingered in the alley behind our apartment now to take on this creature!

Mama turned to Pawel. "We will need plenty of carbide, and matches, of course." She spoke calmly, as if she had accepted our fate and was trying to make the best of it. It seemed to me she should be asking and saying please. But she spoke in that special firm tone she used on occasion that always seemed to make people do as she wished.

"You'll have it. And there's a leaking pipe down the path we can tap for fresh water." Pawel spoke kindly again now, as though trying to reassure us. Then he shifted awkwardly. "You have the money?"

Mama faltered. She had no idea that Papa had agreed to pay him, or how much. And most of the money we brought had surely sunk to the bottom of the sewer river with Papa. She reached in her dress and held out a crumpled note. A look crossed Pawel's face and I could tell it was not as much as he had been promised. What would happen if we couldn't afford to pay him? "I know it isn't much." Mama pled with her eyes for him to let it be enough. At last he took it. The religious man, who had been standing in the corner with his family, passed Pawel some money as well.

"I'll bring you food as often as I can," Pawel said.

"Thank you." Mama looked over his shoulder at the other family. "I don't believe we have been properly introduced." She walked across the chamber. "I'm Danuta Gault," she said, offering her hand to the father.

He didn't take it, but nodded formally, as if meeting on the street. "Meyer Rosenberg." He had a salt-and-pepper beard that was yellowed around the mouth with tobacco stains, but his eyes were kind and his voice melodic and warm. "This is my mother, Esther, and my son Saul." I looked at Saul and he smiled.

"Everyone calls me Bubbe," the elderly woman interjected, her voice raspy. It seemed odd to use such a familiar name for this woman I had just met.

"A pleasure to meet you, Bubbe," my mother said, respecting the older woman's wishes. "And you, Pan Rosenberg," she added, addressing him with the more formal Polish term for mister. Then she turned back toward me. "I'm here with my husband... That is..." She seemed to forget for a second that Papa was no longer with us. "That is, I was. This is my daughter, Sadie."

"That other family," I could not help but ask. "The one with the little boy. What happened to them?" Part of me wished I hadn't. I wanted to imagine they had made it to the street and found somewhere to hide. But I had never been any good at pretending or looking away. I had to know.

Pawel looked uncertainly over my head at my mother before answering, as if asking whether he should lie to me. "I don't know for sure. But they were most likely killed at the entrance to the river," he said finally. Shot, I thought, remembering the gunfire. We would be, too, if we went that way. "Now you understand why it is so important that you stay here, out of sight and silent."

"But how can we stay here?" Bubbe Rosenberg demanded. "Surely now that the others were caught, the Germans will know there are people down here and come looking." Saul moved closer to his grandmother and put his hand on her shoulder as if to offer comfort.

"Perhaps," Pawel said mildly, unwilling to lie to comfort us. "I saw some Germans at one of the grates when I left you earlier and went up to the street. I told them there are rats so they wouldn't come. They wanted to send the Polish police to look in their stead, but I told them that it is impossible for anyone to survive down here." I wondered if perhaps that was right.

"Still, they're bound to patrol the sewers at some point," Saul said solemnly, speaking for the first time. His brow wrinkled with worry.

Pawel nodded gravely. "And when they do, I will have to lead them." A gasp circulated through the group. Would he betray us after all? "I will take them down other tunnels so they don't see you. If they insist on coming this way, I will swing my lantern in a wide circle ahead of me so you have time to hide." Looking around the barren chamber, it was impossible to imagine where.

"I have to go now," Pawel said. "If I don't turn up for work, my foreman will ask questions." It must be morning, I realized, although the light did not reach us here. He rummaged deep in his pocket and pulled out a package wrapped in paper. He opened it to reveal meat of some sort and broke it into two halves, then handed one piece to my mother and the other to Pan Rosenberg, splitting the meager rations evenly between our two families. "It's *golonka*," my mother whispered. "Pork knuckle. Eat it." Though I had never had it before, my stomach growled.

But Pan Rosenberg looked at the meat Pawel offered and wrinkled his nose in disgust. "It's *trayf*," he said with distaste at the notion of eating something that was not kosher. "We can't possibly eat that."

"I'm sorry. It was all I could get on short notice," Pawel said, sounding truly contrite. He held it out once more, but Pan Rosenberg waved it away. "For your mother and son, at least?"

Pawel tried again. "I'm afraid there won't be anything else for a day or two."

"Absolutely not."

Pawel shrugged and brought the extra meat to Mama. She hesitated, caught between wanting to feed us and not wanting to take more than her share. "If you're sure…"

"It shouldn't go to waste," he said. Mama took a small piece of the pork for herself and gave the rest to me. I ate it hurriedly before Pan Rosenberg could change his mind, trying to ignore the baleful eyes of his son. The elderly woman hung closely behind her family, not complaining, but I wondered guiltily if she would have liked some. I looked at the Rosenbergs in their strange dark clothing. What had they done to earn the saving graces of the sewer worker? They were so different from us. Yet we were all to live here together. We had been spared the indignity of sharing an apartment in the ghetto. But now hiding in this small space together with these strangers was our only hope.

And then Pawel was gone, leaving us alone in the chamber. "Here," Mama said, pointing to one of the benches. She pointed to a spot so dirty and wet she would have scolded me a day earlier for sitting there.

My foot throbbed as I sat, reminding me of my earlier wound. "I cut my foot," I offered, though it seemed silly to mention in light of all that had happened since. Mama knelt beside me, the already filthy hem of her skirt dipping into the vile water. She lifted up my right foot and removed it from the soaked shoe, then patted it with a dry bit of her dress. "We must keep our feet dry." I didn't understand how she could think of such things at a time like this.

She reached for the satchel she had packed, the one Papa tossed to me just before he fell in the water. What was in the bag that my father had paid for with his life? Mama opened it. Medicines and bandages, a blue-and-white baby blanket, and a spare pair of socks for me. I crumpled into a little ball, grief crushing me anew. "Socks," I said slowly, my voice heavy with disbelief. "Papa died for a pair of socks."

"No," Mama said. "He died to save you." She drew me close. "I know it is difficult," she whispered, her eyes shining with tears. "But we must do what is necessary in order to survive. It's what he would want. Do you understand?" She wore a steely, determined expression that I had never seen before. She leaned her head against mine and the soft curls of hair around her ear still smelled like the cinnamon water she had sprayed after her bath the previous day. I wondered how long we would be down here before that glorious scent would be gone.

"I understand." I let her put salve on my foot, then changed into the clean pair of socks she had given me. As I reached down, I glimpsed on my sleeve the armband with the blue star that the Germans had made us wear to identify ourselves as Jews. "At least we don't need this anymore." I tugged at the armband and the fabric tore with a satisfying rip.

Mama smiled. "That's my girl, always seeing the bright side." She followed suit and tore off her own band, then gave a satisfied chuckle.

As my mother went to close the satchel, something small and metallic fell from it and tumbled to the sewer floor. I hurried to pick it up. It was the gold chain my father had always worn under his shirt, with a pendant bearing the Hebrew word *chai*, or life. Jewelry was not common among men, but the necklace had been a gift to my father from his parents at his bar mitzvah. I had assumed he was wearing it when he fell, that it was lost to the sewer river as well, but he must have taken it off before we fled. Now it was here with us.

I held it out to my mother. But she shook her head. "He would want you to have it." She fastened the clasp around my neck and the *chai* lay on my chest, close to my heart.

There was a clattering outside the chamber. We stood up, alarmed. Had the Germans come so soon? But it was only Pawel once more. "The light," he said, pointing to the lone carbide lamp that hung from a hook. "It's giving off steam on the street above. You must turn it off." Reluctantly, we abandoned the only source of light we had and the sewer went cold and dark once more.

5

Ella

April 1943

Spring had always come slowly to Kraków, like a sleepy child unwilling to get out of bed on a school morning. This year, it felt as if it might not come at all. Dirty snow still covered the base of the bridge as I made my way from the city center toward Dębniki, the working-class neighborhood on the southern bank of the Wisła. The air was frigid, the wind sharp. It was as if Mother Nature was personally protesting the Nazi occupation as it dragged through a fourth year.

I hadn't expected to find myself on an errand to this remote part of the city on a Saturday morning. An hour earlier, I had been in my room, composing a letter to my brother, Maciej. He had lived in Paris for nearly a decade, and although I had not had the chance to visit him, the city came alive through the dancing script and detailed description and wicked humor of his letters. I wrote him back in the most general of ways, mindful always that our letters might be read. *The Falconess has been hunting*, I said at one point. The name was our code for Ana Lucia and her love of wearing animal carcasses as clothing, "hunting" a reference to the times when she was being particularly wretched. *Come to Paris*, he had urged in his last letter and I smiled as I heard his acquired French affect jump off the page in his words. *Phillipe and I would be overjoyed to have you.* As if it were that simple. It was impossible to travel now, but perhaps when the war was over, he would send for me. My stepmother would not care if I left, as long as the trip didn't cost her anything.

I had just finished sealing the letter with a bit of wax when I heard the commotion down in the kitchen. Ana Lucia was yelling at our maid, Hanna. Poor Hanna was often the target of my stepmother's wrath. We'd once had four full-time house staff. But the war had meant sacrifices for everyone, and in my stepmother's world that meant making do with one servant. Hanna had been our maid, a tiny waif of a girl from the country with no family of her own—she was the only one willing to take on the work of the entire household staff and so she was the one who stayed, gamely managing housekeeper and butler and gardener and cook duties all at once because she had nowhere else to go.

I wondered what the subject of my stepmother's wrath was today. Cherries, I learned when I went downstairs. "I have promised Hauptsturmführer Kraus the best sour cherry pie in Kraków for dessert tonight. Only we have no cherries!" Ana Lucia's cheeks were flushed hot pink with anger, as if she had just stepped from the bath.

"I'm sorry, ma'am," Hanna said. Her pockmarked face bore a flustered expression. "They're out of season."

"So?" The practicalities of the situation were lost on Ana Lucia, who wanted what she wanted.

"Perhaps dried cherries," I offered, trying to be helpful. "Or canned."

Ana Lucia turned toward me and I waited for her to reject my suggestion out of hand, as she always did. "Yes, that," she said slowly, as though surprised I had a good idea.

Hanna shook her head. "I tried. There are none to be had at market."

"Then you go to other markets!" Ana Lucia exploded. I feared my suggestion, though well-intentioned, had just made the poor girl's situation worse.

"But with the roast to cook…" Hanna's voice sounded helpless, aghast.

"I'll go," I interjected. They both looked at me with surprise. It was not that I wanted to help my stepmother appease the appetite of some Nazi pig. To the contrary, I would sooner shove the cherries down his throat, pits and all. But I was bored. And I wanted to go out to the post office to deliver my letter to Maciej, so I could do both in one trip.

I expected my stepmother to protest, but she did not. Instead, she passed me a handful of coins, vile reichsmarks that had replaced the Polish zloty.

"I heard there might be some cherries to be had in Dębniki," Hanna offered, her voice full with gratitude.

"Across the river?" I asked. Hanna nodded, pleading with her eyes for me not to change my mind. Dębniki, a district on the far side of the Wisła, was at least thirty minutes by tram, longer on foot. I had not planned on going so far. But I had said I would go and I could not abandon Hanna to my stepmother's wrath a second time.

"The pie has to be in the oven by three," Ana Lucia said haughtily, instead of thanking me.

I put on my coat and picked up the small basket I often used for shopping before starting from the house. I might have taken the tram, but I welcomed the crisp, coal-tinged air and the chance to stretch my legs. I followed Grodzka Street south until I reached the Planty, crossing the now-withered swath of parkland that ringed the city center.

My route beyond the Planty going south toward the river took me along the edge of Kazimierz, the neighborhood southeast of the city center that had once been the Jewish Quarter. I'd seldom had reason to visit Kazimierz, but it had always seemed exotic and foreign with its men clad in tall, dark hats and Hebrew writing in the shop windows. I passed what had once been a bakery and I could almost smell the challah they used to bake. It was all gone now since the Germans had forced the Jews to the ghetto in Podgórze. The shops were abandoned, their glass windows broken or shuttered. Their synagogues, which for centuries would have been filled with worshippers on a Saturday morning, were now empty and still.

I had hurried past the ghost town uneasily and now stood at the base of the bridge that spanned the wide stretch of the Wisła. The river separated the city center and Kazimierz from the neighborhoods of Dębniki and Podgórze to the south. I gazed over my shoulder at the hulking Wawel Castle. Once the seat of the Polish monarchy, it had presided over the city for nearly a thousand years. Like everything else, it was part of the General Government now, taken by the Germans as the seat of their administration.

As I looked at the castle now, a memory loomed of a night not long after the invasion when I had taken a walk. As I had reached the high embankment over the river, I saw boats clustered around the castle. Large crates were being carted from inside and carried up a ramp onto a boat, the heavier ones wheeled. A heist, I thought, my childhood imagination working overtime. I imagined summoning the police, being hailed as a hero for foiling the plot. The people who were taking things did not look like criminals, though. They were museum workers, stealthily slipping our national treasures from the castle in order to save them. But from what? Plunder? Air raids? The paintings were being rescued, yet we were being left behind to face whatever fate awaited us under the Germans. I knew then that nothing would be the same.

On the far side of the bridge sat Dębniki, the neighborhood

where Hanna thought there might be cherries to buy. Its sky-line was a mix of factories and warehouses, another world from the elegant churches and spires of the city center. I paused on Zamkowa, a street close to the river's edge, to get my bearings. I had not been to Dębniki on my own before and it had not occurred to me until now that I might get lost. I hesitated, looking at the low building on the corner, which seemed to be a loading site for crates onto a barge that was docked at the river's edge. It was not the sort of place I was comfortable asking directions. But there were no passersby whom I might ask and so it seemed my best option if I wanted to get to market in time to get the cherries and save Hanna. I steeled myself and started forward toward a group of men who stood smoking by a loading dock.

"Excuse me," I said, and I saw in their faces just how out of place I was here.

"Ella?" I was surprised to hear my own name. I turned to find a familiar face: Krys' father. His strong brow and deep-set eyes were a mimeograph of his son's. Krys had been raised in the working-class neighborhood of Dębniki. His father was a stevedore, and his family utterly unsuited to ours, Ana Lucia had reminded me more than once. I had been to Krys' house just a few times to meet his parents. Though he would never admit such things mattered to him, some part of him, I suspected, had been embarrassed to show me the small house on a plain street where he had been raised. I had been charmed, though, by the simple warmth of his family, and the way his mother doted on her "baby" even though he was a strapping twenty-year-old who towered over her by nearly a foot. I had loved spending time in their home, which was as welcoming as my own was now cold.

Of course, their house was still now, too. Krys' parents had sent three sons to the war, and the older two had been killed and one was still gone. His father looked older than I remembered him, the lines in his face more deeply etched, broad shoulders stooped, hair mostly gray. Guilt rose in me. Even though I had not been close to Krys' parents, I should have checked in on them since he had left.

But his father showed no recrimination as he stepped toward me, eyes warm but puzzled. "Ella, what are you doing here?" I started to tell him that I needed directions. "If you are looking for Krys, he will be back soon," he added.

"Back?" I repeated the word, certain that I had heard him wrong. Had he received word from Krys? My heart skipped a beat. "From the war?"

"No, back from lunch. He's expected within the hour."

"I'm sorry, I don't understand. Krys is still away at war." I wondered if the older man was confused, if the grief and loss had teased his mind.

But his eyes were clear. "No, he's been back for two weeks. He has been working here with me." His voice was sure and certain, leaving no doubt. I froze, stunned silent. Krys was back. "I'm sorry," Krys' father said. "I thought you knew."

No, I hadn't. "Please, do you know where I can find him?"

"He said he had an errand. I believe it was to the café on Barska, the one where he went often before the war." He pointed up the street that led away from the river. "Second street on the right. You might find him there."

"Thank you." I set off in the direction of the café, mind racing. Krys was back. Part of me was overjoyed. He was just steps away, and in a matter of minutes, I might see him. But the man I was supposed to marry had returned from the war—and had not bothered to tell me. I suppose it made sense; after all, he had broken up with me before leaving. I was just a girl from his past, an afterthought. Still, to not even tell me that he was back and safe, to leave me worrying and wondering, was outrageous. Surely he owed me more than this. I considered my options: go after him, do nothing. If he had not come to see me, I should not lower myself to chasing him. But I needed to know what had happened, why he had not come back to me. Propriety be damned. I started toward the café.

Barska Street, where Krys' father had sent me, was near the center of Dębniki. As I made my way through the neighborhood, I noticed that the buildings here were close-set, their facades tinged with soot and pockmarked. I soon reached the café. This was not some elegant restaurant on the market square, but a simple café, where people grabbed a black ersatz cup of coffee or a quick poppy seed or sweet cheese roll before heading back to work. I scanned the patrons who stood around the few high tables on the far side of the window. I had imagined seeing Krys more times than I could count over the past few years. Occasionally, I had even thought that I caught a glimpse of him on a passing trolley or in a busy crowd. Of course, it was never him. I did not see Krys now either, and I wondered if his father was mistaken. Or perhaps Krys had been here and I had missed him.

I walked inside the café and the warm smell of coffee and cigarette smoke filled my nostrils. I weaved my way between the close-set tables. At last, I spotted a familiar figure seated in the very back, facing away from me. It was Krys. My heart rose and then quickly fell again. Seated across from Krys was a stunning, dark-haired woman a few years older than me, watching him with a rapt expression as he spoke.

I stared at him, as if facing an apparition. How was it possible? I had dreamed and thought of him endlessly. At first, I had pictured him off fighting. As his letters slowed, I imagined him dead or wounded. But here he was, sitting in a café, a cup of coffee before him and another woman by his side, as if none of it had ever happened. As if *we* had not happened.

For a second, I was relieved, even glad to see him here and safe. But as the reality of the situation crashed down upon me, my anger flared. I marched across the café. Then I stopped, floundering momentarily, unsure what to say. The woman who was with Krys noticed me approaching and her expression turned to confusion. Krys turned, and our eyes met. The entire room seemed to stand still. Krys whispered something to the woman across from him, then stood, coming toward me. I started away and made it outside, feeling as though I was gasping for air. I kept going.

Krys quickly followed. "Ella, wait!" I wanted to run, but he caught me quickly with his long-legged gait, reaching for me before I could dodge. His fingers wrapped warm around my forearm, stopping me in his sure but gentle way. His touch filled my heart and broke it again, all at the same time. I looked up, awash in anger and hurt and happiness. Standing so close, I wanted to reach for him, to lay my head upon his chest and have the whole world fade away as it always had before. Then over his shoulder I saw the woman he'd been sitting with looking at us quizzically through the café window. My warm feelings faded.

"Ella," Krys said again. He leaned in toward me. But the kiss he attempted was aimed at my cheek, worlds away from the passionate embrace we had shared when I last saw him. I pulled away. A hint of his familiar scent wafted by my nose and waves of painful memory rushed over me. An hour ago, the man I loved was still mine in my memories. But now he stood before me—really here yet a stranger.

"When did you return?" I asked.

"Just a few days ago." I wondered if that was true. His father had said two weeks. It wasn't like Krys to lie—but I never thought he would keep his return from me either. "I was coming to see you," he added.

"After your date at the café?" I shot back in retort.

"It isn't like that. I want to explain, but I can't do it here. Will you meet me later?"

"What's the point? It's over between us, isn't it?"

He looked back into my eyes, unable to lie. "Yes. It isn't what you think, but it's true. We can't be together anymore. I'm sorry. I told you as much before the war."

He had, I admitted silently. I recalled our last conversation before he left, me more certain than ever that we should be together, him pulling away. But I hadn't wanted to hear it.

"You must believe that I would never do anything to hurt you." His eyes were pleading. "That this is for the best."

How could he possibly say that? I considered arguing with him. I wanted to remind him of all that we had been to one another and all that still could be between us. But my pride rose up, preventing me. I would not beg for someone who didn't want me anymore. "Goodbye, then," I said, managing not to let my voice quiver.

Without speaking further, I turned and started away, nearly colliding with a man unloading crates from a horse-drawn wagon. "Ella, wait!" Krys called, but I kept running, eager to put as much distance between myself and the pain of seeing Krys again yet realizing we could not be together.

When I was several blocks away, I turned back, half hoping that he had followed me. He had not. I continued onward, walking more slowly now, letting my tears fall. My relationship was over. My future was dead. I didn't understand it. When I looked into Krys' eyes, I felt the same as I always had. But he stared back at me stonily, as if we were strangers. How could he not remember? Even as I thought about him angrily, warm memories flooded my brain. There had been a kind of desperation when the war broke out, a sense that each time we were together might be the last. It made me feel heady, alive. But it also made me do things I would not otherwise have done. I had slept with Krys just once before he left, instead of waiting until our wedding or even until we were formally engaged, a desperate attempt to hold on to what we had a bit longer. I had assumed that it meant as much to him as to me. Only now he had left me for good.

A few minutes later, I looked up and saw my reflection in a butcher shop window. My eyes were red and swollen from crying, my face puffy. Pathetic, I scolded myself, wiping away my tears. Still, I could not stop thinking of Krys. I imagined him returning to the woman at the café and continuing his conversation with her as though nothing had happened. Who was she? Had he met her while he was away? Despite everything, I knew that Krys was an honorable man and I could not imagine that she had been in his life when we were together. But he seemed like a stranger, and the pieces between when he left for the war and now were behind fogged glass, obscured from view.

I could not stay in Kraków, I decided. There was no future for me here anymore. Kraków was the biggest small town, my friends and I had often joked. We were forever running into one another. I would have to see Krys, and even if I didn't, the city would be laden with painful memories. Paris, I thought suddenly, as my brother's face appeared in my mind. More than once in his letters, Maciej had urged me to come. I would rewrite my letter to him, ask him to send for me as soon as he was able. The war might make it difficult, even impossible, but I knew Maciej would try. I took the letter that I had planned to mail to him from my basket and threw it in a nearby trash bin, intending to write another one after my errand.

I looked up at the sky. The sun was high now, signaling that it was almost midday, and I still had done nothing to get the cherries that Hanna needed. I started in the direction of the Rynek Dębnicki, the neighborhood's main market square where vendors brought their wares to sell on Saturdays behind the simple wooden stalls. As I neared the market, I marveled that it was still open—there was almost nothing for sale anymore after years of rationing and deprivation. There was no meat for sale and hardly any bread, and what little produce there was had already begun to rot. Sequestered in my world of privilege and protection, I didn't often see the hardships that the ordinary people were facing during the war. Now as I watched the locals scurry between stalls to see what was available and whether they could afford it, our differences loomed large. The shoppers here were thin and their cheeks hollow. They seemed unsurprised by the lack of food available for purchase, but rather took what they could get and left with their baskets and satchels largely empty.

I walked toward the nearest produce vendor, scanned the meager offerings at the stall, mostly potatoes and some rotting cabbage. "Dried or canned cherries?" I asked, already knowing the answer. Cherries grew plentifully on trees outside the city in early summer. If properly preserved last year, they should not have been scarce. But the Germans had stripped Poland of so much of its natural bounty, from crops to herds of cattle and sheep. Surely they had taken the cherries, too. Still I asked the man in case he had some that were not displayed for sale that he might be willing to part with for a price. I half wanted the vendor to tell me he was out of cherries so that Ana Lucia would be unable to make her special treat for the German. But that would just give my stepmother another chance to crow about my failures.

He shook his head, cap bobbing atop a deeply lined face. "Not for months," he answered through tobacco-stained teeth. I was annoyed to have come all this way for nothing and that Hanna had been wrong. The vendor looked remorseful to have lost out on the sale. Impulsively, I pointed to a bunch of chrysanthemums he was selling. His face brightened. "You might want to try the *czarny rynek* around the corner on Pułaskiego Street," he added, as he took the bright red flowers and wrapped them in fresh brown paper. He handed me the flowers and I put a coin into his leathery palm.

I was surprised that there would be two markets so close together. But when I rounded the corner, I discovered that the location he had sent me to was not an established market at all, but rather a narrow alleyway along the back of a church where a dozen or so people were clustered. I understood then. *Czarny rynek* meant black market, an unlicensed place where people sold goods that were forbidden or scarce for a higher price. I had heard of such places, but had not actually known they existed until now. The few sellers here had no stalls, but splayed their wares on old blankets or tarps on the ground, tenuous stands that could be picked up in an instant if one had to flee the police. There was a mix of everything, from hard-to-get foods like chocolate and cheese to a contraband radio and an antique gun so old I wondered if it would actually work.

I considered turning away. The black market was illegal and one could be arrested for buying or selling on it. But I could see a fruit seller halfway down the alley with considerably more produce than the actual market had. I started forward. Here there were dried cherries, at least some, splayed on a soiled tarp on the ground. I took all there were and paid the toothless proprietor, using most of the remaining coins my stepmother had given me. I popped one of the cherries into my mouth for good measure, trying not to think of the dirty fingernails of the merchant who had just handed them to me. The sour sweetness caused my jaw to tingle. I sucked on the pit as I walked, then spit it into a nearby sewer grate.

I stepped over the grate, taking care not to catch the heel of my shoe. From below there came a rustling that startled me. I jumped. Probably just a rat, I told myself, like the ones that came out at night to feast on whatever they could find. But it was daytime now, and I would not expect the vile rodents to be about.

The noise came again from below, too loud to be a rat. I looked down. Two eyes stared back at me. These were not the beady eyes of an animal, but dark circles ringed with white. Human. There was a person in the sewer. Not just a person—a girl. At first I thought I imagined it. I blinked to clear my vision, expecting the sight to have faded like some sort of a mirage. But when I looked again, the girl was still there. She was skinny and filthy and wet, staring up. She had stepped back a bit, as if afraid to be seen, but I could still make out her eyes in the darkness, searching. Watching me.

I started to remark aloud about her presence. Something stopped me, though, a fist that seemed to clench my throat, silencing my breath so that no sound would come. Whatever had forced her into that awful place meant that she did not want to be found. I should not, could not say anything. I gasped for air, willing the tightness to ease. Then I looked around, curious if anyone else had noticed, seen what I had just seen. The other passersby carried on heedlessly. I turned back again, wondering who the girl was and how she had come to be down there.

When I peered into the sewer again, she was gone.

6

Sadie

We were back in our apartment on Meiselsa Street, Papa whirling Mama around the kitchen to the tinny piano music that came through the floor as if it was one of the grand ballrooms in Vienna. When they had finished dancing, Mama breathlessly called me to the table where a fresh, delicious *babka* sat cooling. I picked up a knife and cut into the moist pastry. Suddenly, there was a rumbling beneath my feet and the floor began to crack. Papa reached across the table for me, but his hand slipped through mine. I screamed as the ground gave way and we fell through to the sewer below.

"Sadele." A voice roused me from sleep. "You must be quiet." It was Mama, softly but firmly reminding me that we could not cry out in our dreams, that we must be silent here.

I opened my eyes and looked around the damp, smelly chamber. The nightmare of falling into the sewer had been real. But my father was nowhere to be found.

Papa. His face appeared in my mind as it had in the dream.

He had seemed so close, but now that I was awake, there was no way I could reach him. Even after a month, his death was still a constant pain. A knife shot through my heart anew every time I woke up and realized that he was dead.

I closed my eyes once more, willing myself to return to sleep so the dream of home and my father could come again. But it had slipped beyond reach. Instead, I pretended Papa was lying there beside Mama and me, that I could still hear the snore I used to complain about.

My mother gave me a reassuring squeeze, then rose and walked across the chamber to the makeshift kitchen in the corner to help Bubbe Rosenberg, who was shelling beans. Though the dimness of the chamber remained unchanged, I could tell from the noises on the street above that it was nearly dawn.

A few days, Mama had said. *A week at most.* That was more than a month ago. Once I could not have imagined staying in the sewer for so long. But there was simply nowhere to go. The ghetto had been emptied, all of the Jews who lived there killed or taken to the camps. If we went onto the street, we would be shot on sight or arrested. The sewer, which ran beneath the length of the city, opened at the Wisła River, but the entrance was guarded by armed Germans. I felt certain that Papa had not meant for us to stay and live in the sewer like this. But he had taken whatever plan he had for our escape with him to his watery grave. We were, quite literally, trapped.

I looked out from the corner where we slept. We had taken one side of the chamber as a sleeping area and the Rosenberg family the other, leaving the area in between for a kind of makeshift kitchen. Pan Rosenberg sat across the chamber, reading. I looked around for Saul, but he was nowhere to be found.

I sat up on the wood planks that formed my bed a few inches above the ground, bones aching in a way that reminded me of the pains my grandmother used to complain about. I thought longingly of the eiderdown quilt that had once covered my bed in our apartment, a far cry from the thin piece of burlap Mama had found for me here. I reached for my shoes at the foot of the bed. Mama still insisted, as she had the day we arrived, that we keep our feet dry, instructing me to swap between the two pairs of socks I had daily. I came to understand why: the others, who were less careful, developed infections, sores and pain from the dirty water that constantly seeped through our shoes.

I brushed my teeth, using a bit of the clean water from the pail and wishing for some baking soda to make them fresher. Then I walked to where Mama was preparing breakfast. The day after Pawel had left us, the others sat around, as though waiting for him to come and take us from here. But Mama set about making the chamber as inhabitable as possible. It was as if, despite her promise to me that it would be only a few days, she knew we were going to be here much, much longer.

My mother kissed me on the top of my head. We had become closer in the weeks since coming to the sewer. I had always been Papa's girl, "little Michal," Mama teased, referring to how much like him I was. But it was just the two of us now. She smoothed my hair. Mama brushed her hair and mine every single night in the sewer. "We must keep up appearances," she said determinedly, and the glint in her eyes revealed a hope for the life we would live after. As a child, I had always been a tomboy, resistant to grooming and looking nice. But here I did not fight her. Despite her efforts, staying clean was a constant battle. The filth of the sewer continually soiled my clothes and hair to a point even I could not stand. I was grateful that we did not have a mirror.

As she pulled away from me, her much-rounder stomach brushed against my arm. I imagined the baby (still too unreal to call brother or sister) who would be born without a father, who would never know the wonderful man that Papa had been. "We'll read after breakfast," Mama said decisively, referring to the school lessons she insisted on giving me each morning. She tried to keep a certain order to our lives here, breakfast, then cleanup and lessons on a small chalkboard Pawel had given her as if I were not nineteen but still a child in school. We took long naps in the afternoon, though, trying to pass the day.

Breakfast this morning was dried cereal, less than usual because we were waiting for Pawel to make his semiweekly visit with more food. Mama had divided it equally into five portions, three for the Rosenbergs and two for us. Bubbe came and collected their bowls wordlessly and retreated to their corner of the chamber. The Rosenbergs had their own routine, too, which seemed to revolve around daily prayer.

Each Friday evening, the Rosenbergs invited us to join them for Shabbos. Bubbe would light two stubs of candles and pass around a bit of wine in a kiddush cup they'd smuggled with them. At first, I had thought their traditions were stubborn, perhaps even foolish. But then I realized that these rituals gave them structure and purpose, like Mama's schedules, only more meaningful. I found myself wishing I had a bit more tradition myself to mark the days. They had even fashioned a makeshift mezuzah on the door frame of the chamber to mark it as a Jewish home. At first Pawel had fought it: "If someone sees, they will know that you are here." But the truth was that if anyone got close enough to find the door to the chamber we were done for anyway—there was nowhere to hide. It was April now and in just a few days it would be Passover. I wondered how the Rosenbergs would comply with the requirements of not eating bread or leavened things when sometimes that was all Pawel could manage to bring us.

I reached for the ledge above the stove, feeling for the extra bit of bread I had saved from the previous day's rations and stowed to add to our meager breakfast. In the beginning, I had tried keeping food beneath my bed, but when I had tried to retrieve it, something snapped at my hand. I drew back and looked beneath. Two beady eyes appeared. It was a rat, its stare defiant, belly full. I never left food in a low place again.

I held up the bread to my mother. "I'm not hungry," I lied. Although my stomach rumbled, I knew Mama, paper-thin except for her belly, was supposed to be eating for two and needed the calories. I watched her face, certain that she would never believe me. But she took the bread and ate a bite, then handed the rest back to me. Lately she seemed to have lost interest in eating. "For the baby," I pressed, holding it up to her lips and coaxing another bite. Now that Papa was gone, I had to take charge and care for my mother. She was the only family I had left.

Mama retched, spitting up the bit of bread she'd managed into her palm. She shook her head. The pregnancy had not been easy on her, even before the sewer.

"Do you regret it?" I blurted out. "I mean, having another baby like this…" The question came out awkwardly and I wondered if Mama would be angry.

But she smiled. "Never. Do I wish he or she were being born under different circumstances? Of course. But this baby will be a piece of your father, like you, more of him that lives on."

"It won't last forever," I offered, meaning to reassure her that the pregnancy and the ways in which it taxed her body would end in a few months' time. But Mama's face grew darker at this. I had imagined Mama would want to be done with the oversized bulk, which looked so uncomfortable. "What is it?" I asked.

"In my womb," she explained, "I can protect a child." But out here, she could not. I shivered, a part of me wishing I could be in there as well.

"You'll understand someday, when you have children," Mama added.

Though I knew she didn't mean to be hurtful, the words stung a bit. "If it were not for the war, I might be starting a family of my own right now," I pointed out. It was not that I was anxious to get married. To the contrary, I had always dreamed of college and a career in medicine. A husband and children would have made such things impossible. But the war had left me trapped, first in the ghetto and now here, in a kind of no-man's-land between childhood and adulthood. I was eager for a life of my own.

"Oh, Sadele, your time will come," Mama said. "Don't rush time away, even here."

There was a clattering outside the entrance to the chamber, followed by a splashing noise, the sound of thick boots moving through water. Everyone jumped instinctively, preparing for the worst. We relaxed once more as Pawel came through the opening bearing a satchel of food. "Hallo!" he greeted brightly, as if meeting us on the street. He visited us twice a week on market days, Tuesdays and Saturdays.

"*Dzień dobry,*" I replied, genuinely glad to see him. Not long ago, we were unsure if Pawel would return at all because Mama had run out of money.

Each week Mama paid Pawel for the food he would bring us next time. But a few weeks earlier, I found her searching for-lornly through the satchel. "What is it?" I had asked.

"The money, it's all gone. We have nothing left to pay Pawel." I was surprised by her bluntness. Usually she kept problems from me, sheltering me like I was a child and not nineteen years old. I soon understood why she had told me. "We need to give him the necklace," she explained. "So he can barter it for money or melt down the gold."

"Never!" My hand rose instinctively to my neck. The neck-lace was the last piece of my father I had, my last link to him. I would sooner starve.

I quickly realized that the sentiment was a childish one. Papa would have given up the necklace in a heartbeat to feed us. I reached around my neck and loosened the clasp and put it in Mama's hand.

When Pawel came that day, she held the necklace out to him. "Take this for the food."

But Pawel refused. "That was your husband's."

"I have nothing else," she admitted to him finally. Pawel stared at her for several seconds, wrestling with the news. Then he turned and left.

"Why did you tell him that?" Bubbe demanded. The Rosenbergs, it seemed, were out of money as well.

"Because there is no way to hide having no money," Mama snapped, returning the necklace to me. I refastened it around my neck. Each night, I lay awake with my stomach grumbling, worried that he had left us for good.

The next Saturday after Mama told Pawel we had no money, he had not appeared at his usual time. An hour passed, then another, the Rosenbergs finishing their Shabbos prayers. "He's not going to come," Bubbe declared. She was not mean, just a grouchy old woman who did not bother to mute her opinions— or suffer others' when she thought they were foolish. "We will all starve." The notion was terrifying.

But Pawel had come, albeit late, still bearing food. No one had mentioned money again since. We were his responsibility and he had not abandoned us, but rather somehow kept finding food. He handed the satchel to Mama now and she unpacked it, placing the bread and other items in a canister she'd managed to hang from the ceiling of the chamber to keep it dry and away from the rats. "I'm sorry to be late," he offered contritely, like a deliveryman who had been expected from the shops. "I had to go to an extra market to get enough." Feeding all of us with the limited food supply on the streets and not enough ration cards was a constant challenge for Pawel. He had to scramble from market to market across town buying small bits at each so as not to attract attention. "I'm sorry there isn't more."

"It's wonderful," Mama said quickly. "We're so grateful." Before the war, Pawel would have been a street worker, barely noticeable. Here, he was our savior. But as she pulled a loaf of bread and a few potatoes from the bag, I could see her calculating how to stretch it to feed so many mouths in the days before Pawel brought more.

Sometimes Pawel would linger a bit to talk to us and share news of the outside world. But today he left swiftly, saying that he had been away too long shopping and was needed at home. His visits were always a bit of light in our dark, dreary days and I was sorry to see him leave.

"We need water," Mama said when Pawel had gone again.

"I'll go," I said, even though it wasn't my turn. I was eager to escape the too-close chamber, even for a few minutes. Before the war, I had always been on the move. *"Shpilkes,"* my grandmother would say in Yiddish, the fondness in her voice making my restlessness sound like a compliment when otherwise it surely was not. When I was a child, I loved to play outdoors with my friends, chasing stray dogs down the street. As I grew older, I channeled my energy into walking the city and finding new corners to explore. Here, I was forced to do nothing but sit. My legs often ached from the lack of motion.

I thought Mama would say no. She forbade me from leaving the chamber unless it was absolutely necessary, fearful that the narrow walkways beyond these walls would spell certain doom for me as they had Papa. "I can do it," I pressed. I longed for space and privacy, a few minutes away from the watchful stares of others.

"Take the trash as well," Mama said distractedly, surprising me. She held up a small bag, which was to be sunk to the base of the riverbed with stones. It always seemed strange to me that one could not leave garbage in a sewer. But there could be no sign that we were here.

Outside the chamber, I gazed longingly down the tunnel in the direction the water flowed, away from our hiding place. I desperately wanted to escape the sewer, fantasized every day about running away. Of course, I would not leave Mama. And the truth was that as awful as things were down here, they were a million times worse above. Many times we had listened in horror as screams rang out from the streets and then there were gunshots followed by silence. Death hung like a scepter above, waiting for all of us if we were captured. We didn't want to be trapped underground—yet everything hung on our making it work.

Farther along the tunnel, I heard a noise. I jumped back instinctively. No SS or police had come into the sewer during our time here, but the threat of being discovered was ever-present. I listened for the sound of growing footsteps and, hearing none, I ventured forward in the tunnel once more. As I rounded the place where the tunnel curved, I noticed Saul, crouched on the ground.

I moved closer. When we first came to the sewer, I had been curious about Saul. He was the only one here close to my age and I hoped that we might be friends. At first, he had been standoffish. Though soft-spoken and kind, he didn't talk much and his nose was often buried in a book. I could not blame him—he didn't want to be here any more than I did. "It's his religion," Mama had told me once in a low voice, after witnessing my failed attempt to talk to him. "The boys and girls stay separate among the more observant Jews." But as the weeks in the sewer passed, he had grown a bit friendlier, offering a word or two of conversation when the moment presented itself. More than once, he had looked across the chamber with his kind, dancing eyes and smiled at me, as if commiserating in the ridiculous awfulness of our situation.

Saul was often missing from the chamber and several times I had woken at night to find him gone. A few weeks earlier when I saw him creeping out, I had followed him from the chamber. "Where are you going?" I asked.

I expected him to be annoyed by my question. "Just exploring," he said simply. "Come with me if you'd like." I was surprised by the invitation. He started down the tunnel without waiting to see if I would accept. Saul walked ahead of me at a swift pace, and I struggled to keep up as he turned this way and that down a dizzying path through tunnels I had never explored. I could not have found my own way back if I wanted to. The waters had slowed to a trickle and there was a kind of eerie silence as we traveled through the pipes.

Finally, we reached a raised alcove, much smaller than the one where we lived. Saul gave me an awkward boost to help me into the space, which was just big enough for the two of us. Moonlight streamed through a broad grate, illuminating the alcove. It was high up and close to the street. Coming here in daylight would have been impossibly dangerous. Saul reached into a notch in the wall, searching for something, and I wondered what he had hidden. He pulled out a book.

"You've been here before," I remarked.

"Yes," he admitted sheepishly, as if I had discovered a dark secret. "Sometimes I can't sleep. So I come here to read when the moonlight is good enough." He fished out a second book, *With Fire and Sword*, and handed it to me. It was a historical Polish story and not a book I would have chosen for myself. Here, though, it was like gold in my hands. We dropped to the floor and sat side by side, reading in silence, our shoulders inches apart.

I walked to the alcove with Saul many nights after that. I didn't know if Saul wanted my company, but if he minded, he didn't complain. Our first business was always reading, but when it was cloudy or the moon dropped too low to illuminate the chamber, we would talk. I learned that Saul's family was from Będzin, a small village near Katowice to the west. Saul and his father had decided to flee to Kraków after the occupation, thinking things would be better here. But Saul's older brother, Micah, a rabbi, had stayed behind to be with the Jews who remained in the village and had been forced into the smaller ghetto the Germans had created in Będzin.

Saul had a fiancée. "Her name is Shifra. We're to be married after the war. When my father and I had the chance to get out, I begged her to come with me. But her mother was too sick to travel and she refused to leave her family. I learned from a letter from Micah after we left that she was forced into the ghetto as well. I've had no word from her in some time, but I can only hope…" He trailed off. Hearing the warmth in his voice as he talked about Shifra, I felt an unexpected pang of jealousy. I imagined a beautiful woman with long dark hair. One of his own people. Saul and I were friends; I had no right to expect more. I realized in the moment both that I felt affection toward him and that my feelings were completely one-sided.

Back in his village, Saul had trained to be a tailor. But he wanted to be a writer and he told me stories he had written from memory, eyes dancing beneath his black hat. I loved hearing all of his ideas about the books he wanted to publish after the war. Though I had once planned to study medicine, I had tucked that idea away long ago. I had not known it was possible for people like us to have such big dreams, especially now.

Saul had become the closest thing to a friend I had found in the sewer. But now as I found him crouched low against the wall in the tunnel, he did not smile. His face was serious, eyes pained.

"Hello," I ventured, moving toward him. I was surprised to see him here; he and his family seldom left the chamber on Shabbos. He did not answer. "What's wrong?"

He held up his leg, and as I moved closer, I could see below the rolled cuff a deep gash on the back of it, oozing blood. "I was walking and something sharp was jutting out from the tunnel wall that cut me," he explained.

"The same thing happened to me when we first arrived." Only my wound had not been nearly as bad. "Wait here," I instructed. I raced back to the chamber and grabbed Mama's bag of

salves, leaving again before she could see me. When I returned
to where Saul sat, I uncapped one of the tubes and squeezed out
a bit of salve. I knelt and reached for his leg, but he reared back.
"You don't want it to get infected," I said.

"I can do it myself," he insisted, but the spot was on the back
of his calf and difficult to see. I understood his hesitation. A religious Jew, he was not permitted to touch women outside of
his family.

"You can't see the spot or reach it properly," I pointed out.

"I can manage," he insisted.

"At least let me guide you so you dress the right spot." He
reached behind his calf awkwardly with the salve. "A little to
the right," I said. "Rub it in a bit more." He tried to place the
bandage over the wound, but one of the ends slipped. Before
he could protest, I moved to press it into place, then pulled my
hand back hurriedly.

He stepped away. "Thank you," he said, clearly flustered. He
studied the dressing before rolling his pants leg down. "You did
a good job."

"I want to study medicine," I blurted, instantly embarrassed.
The idea sounded too big, foolish.

But Saul smiled. "You'll do well at it." The certainty in his
voice reminded me of Papa, who had never expected me to be
any less than my dreams. My insides warmed.

"You shouldn't wear that," Saul said, gesturing to Papa's *chai*
necklace around my neck, which dangled as I stood up.

"Hah! You're one to talk." How could someone who wore a
yarmulke and tzistzis, whose family put a mezuzah on the door
to the chamber, tell me it was unsafe to wear a simple necklace that identified me as a Jew? The truth was that if we were
caught, we would have worse problems than what we wore.

He shook his head. "Mine is a requirement of the faith. Yours
is jewelry."

"How can you say that?" I replied, stung. "It belonged to my father." Papa's necklace was so much more than that, a connection to him and my last bit of hope. I turned away.

"Sadie, I'm sorry. I didn't mean it that way. I didn't want to hurt you. It's just that I worry about you." He looked away, a note of embarrassment in his voice.

"I can take care of myself. I'm not a child."

"I know." Our eyes locked and held for several seconds and a jolt of electricity went straight through me. I liked him, I realized suddenly. I had not given much thought to boys before the war and it caught me off guard now, the idea foreign and strange, especially given our circumstances. Of course, it was just a crush. Saul had Shifra waiting for him, and anything else was completely imagined on my part. I turned abruptly away.

I picked up the trash bag and water jug and started down the tunnel on my original errand. Water and garbage were tasks that always fell to me or Saul, especially garbage because it involved climbing through one of the forties, a forty-inch-diameter pipe too narrow and awkward for the older folks. We had to place the garbage at a spot where the bag would sink unseen, Pawel explained early on, and not be carried to the sewer entrance and give our presence away. I took the filthy bag and clutched the water jug between my teeth and began crawling through the pipe, pushing the bag of garbage and water jug in front of me.

When I emerged from the forty, I continued along the tunnel, feeling for the wall in the semidarkness and ducking so as not to bump my head. I reached the juncture with the larger pipe and put the trash bag into the water, trying not to think of the river below that could take me as easily as it had my father. I saw that moment over and over again. If only I had reached for him. What had become of his body? He should have had a proper burial.

Turning away from the river, I started in the other direction and crawled back through the forty. I passed the entrance to the chamber and started toward the place on the other side where we gathered clean water from a leaking pipe. A few meters from the chamber, I stopped once more beneath a slatted sewer grate. Our hiding place was not far from the main market square in Dębniki, a working-class neighborhood on the south bank of the river, just a few kilometers west of Podgórze, where the ghetto was located. Today was Saturday, a market day, and I could hear the sounds of the vendors hawking their wares. I stood listening to the customers placing their orders, smelling the roasted meats and salted fish, and remembering a time when I was a part of it all.

I continued on a bit farther and stopped beneath the leaking pipe, which ran just above my head along the sewer wall. I fashioned a cloth as my mother had shown me so the water would trickle into the jar. As the jug filled, I listened for the sounds of the market. I had come to know the rhythms of the city from its sounds in a way I could not have imagined living above ground: the predawn scraping of the carts, the walking of pedestrians as morning broke to noon. At night the streets fell silent as everyone returned to their homes before curfew. Our chamber was just below the St. Stanisław Kostka Church and on Sundays we could hear the parishioners singing, the sound of the church choir filtering through the grate.

Capping the jug, I started back. A bit farther along, I reached the sewer grate once more. Sunlight shone through the slats, creating bars of light on the wet sewer ground. They reminded me of days by the stream with Papa not so many years ago. We would always climb Krakus Mound, the high hill outside the city, on Sundays at dusk. First he carried me on his shoulders, and later when I was older and my legs strong enough, we walked hand in hand. The red rooftops of the city seemed to shimmer amidst the pale gray domes and spires. In autumn the falling leaves turned the hill to copper and we would try to pile the leaves to jump in before the rains or street sweepers took them.

I tried more than once since coming to the sewer to share my memories with Mama, but she stopped me. "We're the only family we have now," Mama would say, drawing me close to the roundness of her stomach. "We must concentrate on surviving and staying together, not on the past." It was as if the thoughts were too painful for her to bear.

Feeling as if I might drown in the memories as easily as the sewer water, I forced the images from my mind and looked up at the grate, picturing the street. I often pretended that when we'd fled to the sewers, time above had stopped. But I felt it now, the way the people still stopped and cooked and ate, children still went to school and played. The whole city had carried on without us, not seeming to notice that we were gone. The people above passed by me heedlessly. They could not possibly imagine that beneath their feet, we breathed and ate and slept. I couldn't blame them; I certainly hadn't given the world below a second thought when I lived above. I wondered now if there might be other unseen worlds, in the earth or the walls or the sky, that I hadn't considered either.

I knew I should stay out of sight. Still, I stood on my tiptoes, wanting to see more of the world above. The grate opened up into a side street or alley. Beyond the edge, I could make out the high stone wall of a church. Although the bit directly above the grate was not the main market, I could still hear people above, bartering and trading.

A trickle of water came down through the sewer grate. I moved closer, curious. It was different than the water we siphoned off the pipe, warmer and smelling of soap. I peered above the grate. There was a laundry nearby, I guessed, the water running off from the wash. I had dreamed of bathing these many months. But in my dream, the waters always turned brown and threatened to take me away. Now the warm, soapy water beckoned. Impulsively, I took off my shirt and moved to stand under the trickle of water. It felt so good to wash the filth from my skin.

A close noise above startled me. Someone was coming. I pulled my shirt back on hurriedly, not wanting to be caught half-naked. The noise came again, the plink of something small falling through the grate and hitting the sewer floor. Curious, I moved closer to the grate, though I knew that I should not. I saw a young woman, close to my own age, a year older maybe, standing alone. My heart rose with excitement. The girl looked so fancy and clean she could not possibly be real. Beneath her tam hat, she had hair a color I had never seen, bright red, brushed until it was luminous and secured in the back by a single bow with perfect ringlets flowing in a ponytail beneath. I bowed my head slightly, feeling the knotting of my own hair despite Mama's care and remembering when it wasn't tangled and filthy. The girl wore a crisp light blue coat. What I envied most was the coat's sash, white as snow. I hadn't known that such pureness existed anymore.

I noticed that the girl held something in her right hand. Flowers. She had been buying flowers at market, red chrysanthemums, the kind the sellers always seemed to have, even though they were not in season. Envy shot through me. Down here we barely managed to eat and stay alive. Yet there was still a place in the world where beautiful things like flowers existed and other girls could have them. What was wrong with me that I didn't deserve the same?

For a second, I thought the girl looked familiar. She reminded me a bit of my friend Stefania, I realized with a pang, except Stefania had dark, not red hair. I had never seen this girl before in my life, though. She was just a girl. Yet I desperately wanted to know her.

A hand touched my shoulder. I leapt, startled. I turned, expecting to see Saul again. This time, it was Mama. "What are you doing here?" I asked. She almost never left the chamber anymore.

"You were gone long. I was worried." She had gotten up from her resting place with effort and was supporting her back with one hand, reaching for me with the other. I expected her to scold me for standing in the open beneath the sewer grate and risking detection. But she stood beside me, hidden in the shadows, not moving. Her eyes traveled to the girl above.

"Someday," Mama whispered, "there will be flowers."

I wanted to ask how she could say that. The idea of a life outside the sewer with nice, normal things sometimes felt like a nearly forgotten dream. But she had already started her slow amble back toward the chamber. I started to follow her. She stopped and turned me around firmly by the shoulders. "You stay there and feel the sun on your face," she instructed, seeming to know what I needed more than I did. "Just keep out of sight." She disappeared into the chamber.

I returned to the grate, but hung back farther now, heeding Mama's warning. I suddenly realized how vulnerable I was, how easily I might get caught. It would be foolish to get any closer. The girl was not Jewish, I reminded myself. Despite the fact that we had lived among the Poles for centuries, many were glad to be rid of the Jews and turned them in to the Germans. There were even stories of small Polish children telling the Germans where escaped Jews were hiding, pointing them out as they tried to run in exchange for a piece of hard candy or a simple word of praise. No, even a nice-looking girl my own age was not to be trusted. I could still see the girl, though, and found myself curious about her.

The girl looked down. At first, she seemed not to see me in the darkness beneath the grate. It was as if the pitch-black of the sewer had somehow made me invisible to her. Then, as her squinting eyes adjusted to the darkness below, she found me. I tried to step back from the light, but it was too late—surprise flickered across her face as our eyes met. She opened her mouth, preparing to say something about my presence. I started to dart back into the shadows. Then I stopped. I had spent so long scurrying in the darkness, like some kind of sewer rat. I was not going to do it again. Instead, I closed my eyes, bracing for certain discovery and imagining all that would come after. When I opened them again, the girl had looked away. She had not said anything about me after all.

I exhaled, still standing frozen. A few seconds later, the girl looked back and smiled. It was the first honest-to-goodness smile I had seen since coming to the sewer.

Our eyes met, and even though we did not speak, the girl seemed to read all of my sorrow and loss. As I watched the girl, yearning broke over me. She reminded me of friends, of sunlight, of everything I'd once had that was now gone. I desperately wanted to go and stand alongside her. I reached my hand up. She did not come closer, but looked at me with an odd mix of pity and sadness.

There was another sound behind her, footsteps made by loud boots. The girl might not tell anyone else about me, but surely others would. Terrified, I slipped back into the darkness and ran from the grate to the safety of the chamber once more.

7

Ella

Just as well, I thought after the girl beneath the grate disappeared and I started back with the cherries. If someone was hiding in the sewer, it was for no good reason. The last thing I needed was to get involved in someone else's problems.

But as I crossed the bridge back into the city center, an image appeared in my mind of Miriam, a dark-haired girl I had known in Lyceum, the high school I had attended before the war broke out. Miriam was quiet and studious, the pleated skirt of her uniform always meticulously pressed, bobby socks perfectly white. I had not known Miriam before high school; she was from a different neighborhood and not part of the circle of girls whom I'd called friends. She sometimes loaned me her eraser, though, and helped me with math at recess and we grew close over our four years in school together. Many days, I sat with her at lunch, her quiet, thoughtful humor a welcome change from the noise and gossip of the other girls.

One day not long after the war began, the teacher called

Miriam abruptly to the front of the class and instructed her to go to the director's office. Miriam's eyes widened with fear and she looked toward me with worry. There was a ripple through the classroom. Going to the office meant you were in trouble. I could not imagine what solemn, mousy Miriam had done.

After Miriam had left the room, I asked for a pass to go to the toilet. In the hall, a trickle of pupils were leaving their classrooms, other students being summoned to the office. They were all Jewish. I saw Miriam walking down the corridor with her head low, alone and scared. I wanted to say something or reach out to her, to protest the unfairness of these students who just wanted to learn like everyone else being taken. But I silently returned to class.

The Jewish pupils did not come back to school after that day. When I told Krys what had happened, he clenched his fists angrily, but did not seem surprised. "They are taking the Jews' rights and privileges," he told me. "If we don't stop them, who knows what they will do next?" For me, this was not about politics, though, but the friend I had lost. Miriam's departure from school left a much greater void than I could have imagined. I'd thought of her many times since, curious what had become of her. Sometimes I replayed that day over several times in my head. What would have happened if I had said something in protest, tried to help her? It would not have changed anything. I would have gotten in trouble and they would have expelled the Jewish students just the same. But Miriam would have known that someone cared enough to speak up for her. Instead, I had done nothing.

The girl in the sewer was a Jew like Miriam, I realized. She must be hiding from the Germans. I wondered if there was something I should have done to help her—and whether or not I could have managed it if there was.

The truth was, I was not a brave person. I would never help the Germans—of that much I was certain. But I had not been courageous enough to stop them from expelling Miriam, and I was wary of trying to help this strange girl now. Keep your head low, that was the lesson I had learned from the war. Tata had fought for his country and it had gotten him killed. Stay out of everyone's way and you might have a chance of coming out on the other side.

Yet as I neared Ana Lucia's house (I had long stopped regarding it as home) I kept thinking about the girl beneath the grate. Ana Lucia was out when I returned, so I gave the cherries to Hanna. "It's only half enough," she said, not ungrateful but afraid of Ana Lucia's terrible wrath.

"I'll keep looking for more," I promised. Of course, by the time I might find any more cherries, it would be too late for tonight's dessert.

Hanna thanked me, which was more than my stepmother would have done, and set about making her pie. I considered what to do with the rest of my day. It was Saturday and I might have gone to the shops or even to see a film at the one cinema that still admitted Poles. I didn't want to run into any of my old friends, though, or worse yet, Krys. So I climbed the stairs to the tiny garret on the fourth floor of our house, which used to belong to Maciej. It was a narrow space with a sloping roof that required me to stoop not to bump my head. But it was the quietest part of the house and the room farthest from Ana Lucia's, with a view of the Old Town cathedral spires across the weathered rooftops of our street. I claimed it as my bedroom after my brother left and spent much time there painting. Oil colors were my favorite medium and my teacher Pan Łysiński commented more than once that I might study at the Academy of Fine Arts. Of course, that felt like a long-forgotten dream.

Today I was too distracted to paint. I looked across the river in the direction of Dębniki, thinking again of the girl in the sewer. I wondered how long she had been down there and whether she was alone. Later as night fell and the sounds of Ana Lucia's dinner party carried on, I curled up in the old chaise lounge that occupied most of the space in the garret, wrapped in an old quilt my brother had left there. I was tired from the long walk across the river and back and my eyes grew heavy. As I drifted off, I pictured the girl. How did she sleep in the sewer? Was she cold? My house, which I had always taken for granted, suddenly seemed like a palace. I slept in a warm bed, had enough to eat. These basic things now felt like treasures. I knew then and there that, despite my fears and hesitation to get involved, I would go see the girl again.

Or at least I would try, I decided the next morning, after I woke, stiffly unfolding myself from the chaise lounge, where I had spent the entire night. I would return to the sewer grate, but there was no guarantee she would be there. I dressed and went down to breakfast, planning my secret return to the place where I had seen the girl. I thought of a half-dozen excuses I could give Ana Lucia if she asked where I was going. But her party had carried on deep into the night and she did not come down to breakfast at all.

I put on my coat and hat and prepared to leave, then stopped again. I should bring something for the girl. Food, I decided, remembering how pale and thin she had looked. I walked to the kitchen. Recalling the smell of Hanna's sumptuous cherry pie baking, I hoped there might be some left over from dinner the previous night. Hanna kept the kitchen spotless at my stepmother's insistence, though, and there were no bits of food or leftovers lying around at all. I reached into the bread bin and opened a tightly wrapped loaf, ripping off as big of a piece as I dared and shoving it in my pocket. Then I started from the house.

Outside, the sky was heavy and gray with clouds, the April air still more winter than spring. This time I took the tram since I did not have an excuse to be out as long as I had the previous day when looking for cherries, and I did not want Ana Lucia to find me gone and start asking questions. As the tram clacked

along the bridge over the Wisła, I looked at the unfamiliar, industrial neighborhood on the far bank. My doubts renewed:
why go back and see the girl at all? I didn't know her and to do
it meant risking everything. I would be arrested or worse if I
was caught. Yet for some reason, I could not turn away.

I arrived at the Dębniki market just before ten. The few locals
who still dared were making their way to church. It was more
than an hour earlier than I had come the previous day after my
run-in with Krys. I should have waited a bit longer, I scolded
myself. Going to the grate at the same time would surely offer
the best chance of seeing the girl again. I walked the market
square, browsing idly to buy some time. But it was Sunday and
most of the stalls were closed. I couldn't be gone from home
too long, so fifteen minutes later, I started around the corner
toward the sewer grate.

I peered down, seeing nothing but darkness. I waited uncertainly, hoping that the girl might appear soon. I saw a few
churchgoers peer curiously into the alleyway as they passed,
noticing me. My nervousness grew. I dared not stand over the
grate looking down for too long in case someone witnessed my
unusual behavior and asked questions or pointed me out to the
police that seemed to linger on every corner.

Several minutes passed and the church bells pealed, signaling the start of Sunday mass. The space beneath the grate was
still empty. Dejected, I prepared to leave. But a moment later,
a bright circle appeared in the darkness behind the grate. The
girl was here. Excitement rose in me. The vision in my mind,
which I had imagined since the previous day, was suddenly real.

The girl stared up at me for several seconds, two dark eyes
blinking like a scared animal trapped in lights. I could see her
more closely now. She had a smattering of freckles on her nose
and one of her front teeth was chipped at the bottom. Her skin
was so pale it was almost translucent and her veins seemed to

form a map beneath her skin. She looked like a china doll that might break at any second.

"What are you doing down there?" I asked. The girl opened her mouth, as if to answer. Then, seeming to think better of it, she looked away. I tried again. "Do you need help?"

I wasn't sure what else to say. She didn't seem to want to talk, but remained there, staring up at me. *Give her the bread and go*, I thought. I reached in my pocket and pulled it out, then kneeled close to the grate.

I started to reach down and then hesitated. An image popped into my mind from a few years earlier when I had found a stray dog in the street. I had brought it home proudly, but Ana Lucia scowled. My stepmother hated animals and mess and I was certain she would make me turn it out once more. To my surprise, she did not. "You've taken it on now and you'll have to take care of it." As awful as my stepmother was, she felt duty bound and she made me feed and walk it until, months later, it died.

It was the worst thing to compare this poor girl in the sewer to an animal. But I knew that if I helped her now, she would somehow become my responsibility and that terrified me.

Still, I pushed the bread through the grate. "Here!" The girl was several feet below me, and as the bread sailed too far to the left of her, I feared she would miss it. But she moved with surprising speed and scrambled to catch it in her hand. Realizing that it was food, her eyes widened with delight. *"Dziękuję bardzo." Thank you very much.* She smiled with her whole face and the joy she found in the tiny piece of bread broke my heart.

I expected her to gobble it down, but she did not. "I have to share it," she explained, as she put it in her pocket.

It had not occurred to me before that there might be others below ground with her as well. "How many of you are there?"

She hesitated, as if unsure whether to answer. "Five. My mother and I, plus another family."

I noticed then the tear on her sleeve, a line that went evenly around the circumference where stitches of fabric had been pulled out. My breath caught. Sadie had worn a band with a blue star, just as my classmate Miriam had. "You're Jews." She lowered her chin in confirmation. Of course, some part of me had known that already. Why else would one hide in the sewer?

"Are you from the ghetto?" I asked.

"No!" she snapped, taking offense. "The ghetto was a place where we stayed for a few awful months; it was not my home. I'm from Kraków, just like you. We lived in an apartment on Meiselsa Street before the war."

"Of course," I replied quickly, chastised. "I only meant, was the ghetto where you came from before here?"

"Yes," she said softly. My eyes traveled above the alleyway to the east. The Germans had built a high-walled ghetto in Podgórze, a neighborhood just a few kilometers east along the riverbank from here, a few years earlier and forced all of the Jews from Kraków as well as from the surrounding villages to move there. Then, just as improbably, they had emptied the ghetto and sent all of the Jews away. "When the Germans liquidated the ghetto, we were able to escape to the sewer."

"But that happened more than a month ago." I recalled hearing the news that the Germans had taken the last of the Jews from the ghetto in Podgórze. I did not know where they had been sent. But I understood now that it was the very reason the girl was hiding. "You've been in the sewer ever since?" The girl nodded. A chill ran through me. Living in the sewer sounded horrid. Wherever the Jews were being taken, though, must be even worse. Going underground had undoubtedly spared her that fate.

"How long will you stay there?" I asked.

"Until the war is over."

"But that could be years!" I blurted.

"There really isn't anywhere for us to go." Her voice was calm, accepting of her situation. I admired her bravery; I did

not think I could last an hour in the sewer, if our situations were
reversed. Pity rose up in me. I wanted to do something more to
help her, but I didn't know what. I pulled a coin from my pocket
and pushed it through the grate. It clattered to the ground and
she scampered to pick it out of the mud.

"That's very kind, but I've no way to use it down here," she
said.

"No, of course not," I said, feeling foolish. "I'm sorry, I don't
have more food."

"Can you see the sky from your window?" she asked abruptly.

"Yes, of course." The question seemed an odd one.

"And all of the stars?" I nodded. "How I miss that! I can see
just a tiny little sliver of the sky from down here."

"So?" I didn't mean it unkindly, but given her situation, it did
not seem the thing to worry about. "Aren't they all the same?"

"Not at all! Each one is its own picture. There is Cassiopeia
and the Big Dipper..."

She was smart, I could tell, in a way that reminded me of my
friend Miriam. "How do you know so much about the stars?"

"I love all the sciences, and astronomy is one of my favor-
ites. My father and I used to go onto the roof of our apartment
building to see them." There was a look of sadness in her eyes.
She had a whole life before the sewer, now gone.

"Your father, he isn't with you in the sewer?"

She shook her head. "He died right after we escaped the
ghetto. He drowned in the sewer waters shortly after we fled."

"Oh!" I had not imagined water wide or deep enough to
drown in beneath the ground. "How awful. My father died
during the war, too. I'm sorry to hear about yours."

"Thank you, and yours as well."

"Ella?" a voice called behind me.

I turned, stumbling as I tried to stand back up quickly. I had
not expected to hear my own name in this faraway part of town.
I froze, praying the girl had scampered from view.

Then I turned to see Krys.

"Krys." I was caught off guard by the unexpected meeting and a dozen emotions seemed to cascade over me at once. Happiness and the rush of warmth I always felt when I saw him. Anger and sadness as I remembered how he had broken up with me, all that was no longer between us. And surprise: how had he found me here?

Krys helped me to my feet. He looked more handsome than ever, a bit of stubble lining his strong jaw, blue eyes twinkling beneath a low-brimmed cap. His hand lingered awkwardly on mine, sending a current of electricity through me. Except we weren't that way at all anymore, I remembered. The rejection washed over me anew. I took a step back. I had left the house hurriedly for my errand. My hair was not at all what it should be, my dress soiled at the hem from where I had knelt. I looked away, not meeting his eyes.

"This is an odd part of town for you," he remarked. "What on earth are you doing here?"

"I could ask you the same thing," I said, stalling for time. Then I remembered my errand from the previous day. "I came for some cherries my stepmother needed." The excuse was implausible since it was Sunday, but it was the best I could do.

"Doing Ana Lucia's bidding?" He smiled. "That's odd." My dislike for my stepmother had been a joke between us many times. Now it seemed too personal, not his place.

"I was just trying to be helpful," I said coldly, not wanting to laugh with him anymore.

"I can help you find some," he offered.

"That isn't necessary. I'll manage," I said, holding together my pride. "Thank you." There had been a time when I could have accepted his help, but now that seemed like another life.

He looked down, shuffled his feet. "Ella, about yesterday… I wish you would let me explain."

"That's all right," I said quickly, cutting him off. "I'd rather not." The last thing I wanted was a long list of excuses as to why his new life no longer included me. Krys had not changed his mind. Rather, he was just trying to justify his decision not to be with me anymore. Discussing it further was a pain I didn't need.

We stood looking at one another for several seconds, neither speaking. His eyes traveled over my shoulder. Following his gaze, I could see that there was a Polish policeman on the corner, watching us. "You need to take care, Ella," Krys said. "Things are dangerous on the streets and getting worse." He was still concerned about me; that much was clear. But not enough to want to be together.

"We should go," I said.

"Ella..." he began. But what else was there to say?

"Goodbye, Krys." I turned away from him, not wanting to watch as he left me behind once more.

8

Sadie

When the man appeared above the grate and started talking to the girl on the street, I jumped back into the shadows. *Ella*, he had called her. The name rolled off my tongue like a musical note. I was not able to hear the rest of their conversation, but I could tell from her expression and the way that they stood close to one another that she knew him well and liked him—or once had anyway.

As I watched them, my eyes fixed on the cross around her neck, which marked her as a Catholic Pole and magnified the differences between us. I remembered then the exact moment as a child that I realized we were not like everyone else. I had been five and shopping with my mother at Plac Nowy, the open-air market that served both the Jewish and non-Jewish residents of Kazimierz. It was late April and the third day of Passover. We had cleared the *hametz*, the bread and other leavened foods that were forbidden during the eight days of the holiday, from our kitchen. As we passed the bakery, though, fresh *bułeczki* sat temptingly in the window. "But it's Pesach," I had remarked, confused as I eyed the rolls.

Mama explained to me that only a small percentage of the Polish people were Jewish. "The others, they have their own holidays and customs. It's a good thing," she added. "Imagine how boring the world would be if we were all the same." But I wished I could be like the other children my age and eat pastries whenever I wanted, even during Passover. It was then I understood for the first time how very different we Jews were from the rest of the world, an early preview of the lesson I would learn all too well when the Germans came. Now as I stood in the sewer, staring up at beautiful Ella With The Cross, I felt that otherness more than any other time, even during the persecution and suffering of the war.

Finally, the man walked away. A few minutes later, after glancing around cautiously, Ella looked down once more, searching for me. I stepped closer to the grate and into the light so that she could see me.

She smiled. "There you are. I thought maybe you had gone." She might have walked away, too, I realized, once she had finished her conversation with the man on the street. It would have been safer for her to leave and pretend she had never seen me. But she had not.

"I'm Sadie," I offered. Some part of me knew it was better not to give my name, but I couldn't help it.

"Ella." Her voice was lyrical, reminding me of a sparrow's song. Her pronunciation was different than mine, the way she closed the end of each word more refined. But it was more than just speech—her accent spoke of good schooling, a grand house, perhaps holidays abroad and other wonders I could not begin to imagine. This, more so than the fancy dress or the cross, confirmed that she was not like me and set us apart.

"I know. I heard that man say your name. Who was he?" I

berated myself for the question, which was too nosy and personal for someone I barely knew.

She swallowed. "Just a boy I used to know." There was a note of pain in her voice. Clearly, he had been something more to her. "What's it like down there?" she asked, changing the subject.

How could I explain the strange, dark world below ground, now the only one that I knew? I tried to find the words to describe it, but could not. "It's awful," I said finally.

"How do you survive down there? Is there food?" Her questions came rapid-fire, in a way that reminded me of myself.

I paused, again struggling to find an answer. There was no way I could mention Pawel without risking his safety. He would face much trouble if the Germans found out he was hiding Jews. "We get by."

"But how can you stand it?" she burst out, and I saw for the first time a tiny crack in her elegant demeanor.

I had never considered the question. "Because I have no choice," I said slowly. "At first I did not think I could bear it a minute. Then a minute passed and I did not think I would last an hour. Then a day and a week and so on. It's amazing what you can get used to. And I'm not alone. I've got my mother and soon I will have a little brother or sister." For a second, I considered mentioning Saul as well, but I felt silly doing so.

"Your mother is pregnant?"

"Yes, she's due in a few months' time."

Her face registered disbelief. "How can she possibly have a baby in the sewer?"

"Anything is manageable if you can stay with the ones you love," I replied, trying to convince myself as well as her. Ella's expression saddened. "What is it?" I asked, hoping I had not said anything to offend her.

"Nothing," she replied quickly.

"Where do you live?" I asked, changing the subject.

"Kanonicza Street," she said, a tinge of embarrassment in her voice at giving the grand address. "It's off Grodzka."

"I know where it is," I replied, a bit irked that she thought I would be unfamiliar with the ancient streets of the city center. I had walked the posh neighborhood many times. Even before the war, the well-appointed street, with its large, well-manicured row houses close to the market square, was like a foreign country, worlds away from my own modest upbringing. Now that I was in the sewer, such a place seemed like the stuff of storybooks, nearly unfathomable. A picture appeared in my mind of a study with shelves overflowing with books, a sparkling kitchen filled with the finest food. "It must be lovely." I could not keep the note of longing from my voice.

"It isn't really," Ella said, surprising me. "My parents are both dead and my brother and sisters gone. The only one left is my stepmother, Ana Lucia. She's truly awful. And then there's my former fiancé, Krys."

"The man you just saw on the street?" I asked.

She nodded. "Yes. My former boyfriend, really, since we were never formally engaged. He broke things off with me before leaving for the war. I was certain we would get back together, but then he returned without telling me. And I've got no friends anymore either." I understood then her pained look a few minutes earlier when I spoke of being able to survive anything with loved ones. Despite her fine living conditions, Ella was completely alone.

"It could be worse. You could be living in a sewer." For a second, I feared that my joke was distasteful. But her face broke into a smile and we laughed.

"I'm sorry," she said. "It was petty of me to complain with everything you are going through. I've got no one to talk to."

"It's all right." The sewer was filthy and horrible. But at least I had my mother to love me, and Saul for company. Ella had no one. She was trapped, I could see, in a kind of prison of her own. "You can always come talk to me," I offered. "I know it isn't much, visiting a dirty girl in a sewer."

"It's plenty." Ella reached her hand down through the sewer grate. I stood on my tiptoes, trying to touch her fingers. But the space between was too much, the inches an ocean, and our hands floundered separately in the air.

"I can help you," she said, and for a second my heart lifted. "Perhaps I can try to find some way to get you out, ask someone…"

"No!" I exclaimed, petrified by the notion that she might reveal that we were here. "You must never speak of me," I added sternly, trying to sound much older and more authoritative than I was. "Or you will never see me again." The threat felt like a hollow one. Surely it didn't matter to her.

Ella nodded. "I swear it," she said solemnly, and I could see that she wanted to come back to the sewer and see me again, too. "But don't you want to escape?"

"No… That is, yes." I tried to think of a way to explain. "It's awful down here, but the sewer is the safest place for us right now. There really isn't anywhere else for us to go." Although I sometimes wondered if that were true, I had to trust in Pawel, who protected us, and my father, who had brought us here in the first place.

"I can only stay a minute more today," she added. "My stepmother will expect me back."

"I understand." I tried to keep the disappointment from my voice. I had known, of course, that at some point she would have to be on her way. But there was something about speaking with Ella that was like being reunited with an old friend, even though we had just met.

"Wait here," she said, standing and disappearing from view. A minute later, she knelt again and pushed something else through the grate. I leapt to catch it before it fell into the sewer water beneath my feet. It was an *obwarzanek*, one of the poppy-covered pretzel rings that Poles sold on the street. "A bit more food," she offered.

"Thank you." I tucked it into my pocket to share with my mother.

"I have to go," Ella said a moment later.

I couldn't help but be disappointed she was leaving. "Will you come again?"

"I will, if I can get away. I'll try to come next Saturday and bring more food." I wanted to tell her that she didn't need to bring me things; all I wanted was her visits. But the words stuck in my throat and then it was too late. She was gone.

I stood alone in the cold and dark once more. It was as if I had imagined Ella. But the piece of bread and the pretzel were there in my pocket and the coin in my palm, reassuring me that she was real. I prayed she would have the chance to come again.

"Sadie!" a voice whispered urgently behind me in the darkness. It was Saul, who must have been out walking. Or maybe he had come looking for me. Normally I would have been happy to see him, but now I was startled. His eyes traveled up to the grate and then back to me. Had he seen Ella?

"Sadie, no!" He grabbed me by the arm and pulled me back into the shadows, his eyes deep with concern. "You can't let anyone see you. I know you are lonely. But the Poles are not to be trusted," he added forcefully.

"Surely not all Poles."

"All of them." His face grew stony and in the resoluteness of his voice I heard the horrors of stories he had lived but not shared with me.

"What about Pawel?" I asked. "He's a Pole and he has helped us."

He did not answer. "Promise me you won't go again." There was a note of tenderness in his voice.

"I promise." I knew even as I said the words that they were a lie. I would go to the grate again to see Ella. There was something about her that told me I could trust her, even if Saul could not see it.

Saul took the water jug and we started back down the tunnel. As we neared the chamber, Bubbe stood, blocking our path. "What's that?" she cried, pointing to my pocket where the edge of the pretzel peeked out. Our relationship with the Rosenbergs had become close during our weeks in the sewer, and despite the difficulty of living together in such close quarters, moments of acrimony between our two families were few. But elderly Bubbe seemed to grow more grouchy and irrational over time, as if the strain of living here was wearing on her.

"It's mine," I said, trying to step around her through the entranceway.

Bubbe shifted sideways in the same direction, unwilling to be deterred. "Thief!" she cried, seeming to think I had taken the pretzel from our food stores. I opened my mouth to tell her that such a thing was impossible. We didn't even have *obwarzanki* here; it wasn't a food that Pawel brought, so how could I have stolen it?

Before I could speak, my mother appeared behind her in the entranceway to the chamber. "How dare you?" she demanded of Bubbe, having heard the exchange in the tunnel. Mama had grown sullen and drawn these past few weeks, as her pregnancy and our time in the sewer dragged on. Now she seemed to find strength in defending me.

"She's got extra food," Bubbe accused, pointing her gnarled finger close to my face. "Either she's stealing it or she's going up to ground without our knowing."

"That's ridiculous!" Mama snapped. Though my mother was usually respectful and deferential toward the older woman, she would not suffer her accusing me. But her eyes traveled to my pocket and, as she saw the bit of pretzel, widened. I watched as she remembered seeing me looking at the girl on the street and realized that was how I had gotten it. Concern, then anger, crossed her face.

Still Mama defended me. "Leave my daughter alone." She walked over and stepped in between Bubbe and me. She pushed the old woman's finger away. Bubbe's anger grew and she grabbed Mama's wrist roughly.

"Stop it!" I protested too loudly, heedless of who might hear. How dare she put her hands on my pregnant mother like that? I reached out and tried to pull Mama's wrist away from Bubbe's grip, but it was surprisingly tight. Mama freed herself and jerked backward. Her foot slipped and she fell to the ground in a heap, yelping like an injured animal. Hurriedly I helped her to her feet. "Mama, are you okay?" She did not answer, but nodded, face pale.

Saul placed himself between me and his grandmother. "Sadie didn't take anything. Go back to the chamber, Bubbe." His voice was gentle, but firm. The old woman muttered something and started back.

"I'm sorry about that," Saul said in a low voice as we followed his grandmother toward the chamber. "She doesn't mean any harm, but she's almost ninety and getting a bit confused. It's hard to watch people you love grow old."

"And hard not to," I replied, thinking of my father and wondering what he might be like as an old man if he had been given the time. I would never really know.

I started to follow Saul into the chamber, but my mother, who had been walking behind us, stopped me outside the entrance. "Promise me," Mama said. There was strength in her voice that I had never heard. "That you will never go again." I turned to her, surprised. She had not seemed angry when she found me at the sewer grate. But now she had drawn up her tiny frame to its full height. She loomed over me so close that the roundness of her belly pressed against mine. "Promise me you won't go to see her again, that you won't let yourself be seen or talk to her."

Her words were an echo of Saul's. "I know that you are lonely here. But it's too dangerous."

I thought of Ella and the hopeful feeling she gave me. But Mama was right; it was irresponsible of me to compromise our safety. "Okay," I said at last, chastised. Breaking my promise to Saul was one thing, my mother quite another. I saw the image of my new friend fade and disappear.

Pawel appeared in the tunnel then. "Hello," I said, surprised to see him. It was Sunday, not one of his usual visiting days, and he had just been here the day before. But he had not brought much food yesterday, and seeing his satchel now, I was hopeful that he had found more.

He nodded, not answering my greeting. His usually cheerful face was drawn tight and somber, the warmth missing from his eyes. I wondered if he had heard our quarrel and was angry. He followed us silently into the chamber and handed us the satchel of food.

"What is it?" Mama asked, instinctively knowing it was bad news.

Pawel turned away from us and toward Pan Rosenberg. "I'm afraid I have word from Będzin and it isn't good," he said. At the mention of his village, Pan Rosenberg stiffened. "The small synagogue in the ghetto…the Germans burned it."

A knot of dread formed in the pit of my stomach. I recalled Saul telling me proudly how his brother, who had stayed behind, had created a makeshift synagogue out of a small shop in the ghetto, so that those who were forced to live there had a place to worship. Going to such lengths just to pray had seemed incredibly foolish to me at the time. Surely God could hear you from anywhere.

I looked at Pan Rosenberg, whose face had turned white as a sheet beneath his shaggy beard. "The Torah," he said, aghast. An uneasy feeling overcame me. The destruction of a synagogue was, of course, an awful thing. But the darkness in Pawel's eyes spoke of so much worse than just prayer scrolls. Beside me, I felt Saul tense with understanding. I reached for his hand. For a second, he hesitated and started to pull away, caught between the restrictions of his faith and the need for comfort. His hand went slack and he did not protest when I curled my fingers around his, bracing for what would come next.

Pawel continued, "I'm afraid it's more than that. You see, there was a young rabbi who tried to stop the Germans and he struck one of them. In reprisal, the Germans came and locked the remaining Jews in the synagogue and set it on fire."

"Micah," Pan Rosenberg cried, stumbling. Bubbe let out a sharp wail. Saul broke away from me to catch his grandmother before she fell. Saul led Bubbe to his father, her son, and the three of them huddled, clutched in an embrace. I stood watching their grief, powerless to help.

"My fiancée…" Saul said, looking up. "She was in the ghetto, too, and often at my brother's shul."

Pawel bowed his head.

"I'm sorry, but my understanding is that everyone who was at the synagogue at the time was killed." Saul's knees buckled and I thought he would fall as his grandmother had, but he willed himself to remain standing.

"Come," Mama said softly to me and Pawel. "They need time alone with their grief."

I faltered, wanting to stay and comfort Saul. Then I reluctantly followed Mama into the tunnel. "I didn't know whether to tell them," Pawel said sadly.

"You did the right thing," Mama reassured. I nodded. Even in the sewer, the truth could stay buried for only so long.

"Pawel…" I hesitated. These days it was better not to ask so much. But there was a question that had been nagging at me, so many answers lost now that I did not have my father to ask. I sensed that soon there might not be time. "How did you come to help us? That is, how did my father find you?"

Pawel smiled, the first light I had seen in his eyes in any of his recent visits. "He was such a friendly man. I often passed him on the street and he would always say hello, not like the other gentlemen who ignored a simple pipe fitter." I smiled, too, knowing what he meant. My father had been kind to everyone, regardless of stature. "We talked occasionally about this and that. Once he told me about a work site that needed laborers and gave me a reference. Another time, he gave me some money to run an errand. He was helping me out, you see, for no other reason than I was a fellow man. But he always did it in a way that made it seem as though I was helping him. He didn't want to hurt my pride."

He continued, "Then one day I noticed him wearing the armband and seeming troubled. I struck up a conversation and he was asking not so directly about warehouses and such, places a family might hide. Those places would never work, I knew. So I told him about the sewer and later, after you all had gone to the ghetto, we began to construct the entrance."

"And the Rosenbergs?"

"As the ghetto was being liquidated and I was racing to meet your father, I saw them on the street. It was a bad day and others dressed like them were being rounded up and beaten and shaven or worse." He stopped, as if some things were still too awful for my young ears. "I told them to come with me and they did." Moments of chance that had saved us while so many others suffered and died. He continued, "Then just before we reached the sewer, we spotted the young child with the couple fleeing. I thought I could save them as well." There was an unmistakable note of sadness in his voice.

"Were you always a sewer worker?" I asked.

"Sadie, so many questions!" Mama scolded.

But Pawel smiled. "I don't mind. Before the war, I was a thief." I was surprised. He seemed so good, when in fact he was a common criminal. "I know it's awful. But for so long there were no jobs for pipe fitters and I had to feed my wife and daughter. And then you all came along and I knew, after all of your father's kindnesses, what I was meant to do. Saving you is my life's work." I saw it then. Rescuing us had become his mission, his chance at salvation.

A short while later, Pawel left and Mama and I returned to the chamber. I wanted to go to Saul and see how he was doing, to try to offer whatever comfort I could. But he stayed close to his grandmother, who wailed inconsolably, and to his father, who simply prayed. Later that night, Saul lay beside his father, one hand across his back. I felt certain he would not go walking. But when his father's breathing had stilled, Saul stood and started for the door. I followed. "Do you mind if I come with you?" I asked, wondering if he would prefer to be alone. He shook his head. We walked together, the silence between us heavier than usual.

"I'm sorry about your brother," I offered, several minutes later. "And about Shifra." I wanted to comfort him in his grief about her, too, but it seemed I was the wrong person to do it.

He kept walking, not speaking. I tried again. "I understand. When my father..." Then my voice trailed off. I wished that my own sorrow and loss might have given me some wisdom, something I could say to ease his pain. Each person was an island in grief, though, isolated and alone. My sorrow could not help Saul any more than Mama's sorrow could help mine when my father died.

We reached the annex. Saul did not reach for a book, but stared off into the distance. "Tell me a story," I started. "About your brother."

He looked at me, puzzled. "Why?"

"I think talking helps. So often since my father died, I have wanted to share memories of him. But my mother never speaks of him. I think it would help if she did." I hadn't been able to share that part of me after Papa died. But I could do this for Saul now.

Saul didn't say anything at first and I wondered if he wouldn't or couldn't talk about his brother. Perhaps it was too soon. "He was the least likely of us to become a rabbi," he said finally. "He was always getting into trouble. One time when we were little he decided that we should clean rocks with bleach. All over the house. Our mother was fit to be tied." He smiled in spite of himself. "He could have left, you know, come with us. But he stayed in the village to help those who could not leave, to be with the women and children and offer religious comfort. Only now he's gone." His tears, the ones that he couldn't shed while comforting his father and grandmother, began to fall. I reached out and put my arm around him, hoping he wouldn't mind. He tensed for a second, as if to pull away, but did not. I drew him close, as if trying to shield him from the grief and pain that coursed through him, or at least share the burden so he wouldn't have to carry it alone. I could not, of course, mourn for him. Being there, that was all I could do.

Saul talked on and on through his tears, telling stories of his brother, as if pressing the memories of his brother between pages to preserve like dry flowers. I listened quietly, asking a question or two when he paused and squeezing his hand when the saddest parts came. Usually after a while, when the moon dropped too low to light the annex, we stopped reading and returned to the chamber.

"We should go back," I said after a while.

He nodded. Our families might wake and worry if they noticed us gone. Neither of us moved, not wanting to leave this quiet place where we could be away from the world. "And then there was the time that my brother fell in the creek," Saul said, beginning another tale. He went on, his voice growing hoarse and cracked, pouring forth his memories in the darkness. When at last there was nothing more to say, he tilted his head toward mine and we closed our eyes and slept.

9

Ella

Two weeks after I had first spoken to Sadie, I set out from our house on a Sunday morning to see her. I stepped onto the street and inhaled the fresh air gratefully. It was nearly May now, and the breeze was warm and perfumed with the fragrance of flowering linden trees as I crossed the Planty. More people seemed to be out today than I had seen since the start of the war, running errands or visiting friends or family. They still walked swiftly and kept their eyes low, not greeting one another or stopping to chat, as they once might have. But there was a kind of defiance in their steps, the way they lifted their chins, even briefly, to admire the way the sunlight bathed Wawel Castle in gold. It was as if to say to the Germans, *You will not steal this beautiful day in our city from us.*

I had gone to see Sadie the previous week on Saturday as promised at the same time, bringing with me a bit of sheep's cheese I'd managed to sneak from our kitchen. But she had been late and seemed nervous. "I can only stay a few minutes," she said. "I'm not supposed to come see you. I promised I wouldn't." She, too, had others who might notice and mind if she was missing.

"If you can't come anymore, I understand," I said, feeling a surprising tug of disappointment. The first time I had returned to the sewer out of curiosity about the girl, the second because I felt bad for her and she seemed to need my help. If she couldn't meet me again, it really shouldn't matter to me at all. Yet somehow it did. I liked helping Sadie and even the little bit I had done made me feel as if I were doing something that mattered.

"Of course I will come again," she said quickly. "Sundays would be better," she added. "The other family, the Rosenbergs, they stay in the chamber where we live all day on Saturdays to observe the Sabbath, so it's more obvious when I am not there."

"Sunday, then," I agreed. "I'll try to come every week, even tomorrow, if you'd like."

"I would," she said with a smile. "Meeting up, even for a bit, well, it makes the rest of the time down here just a little easier to bear. Does that sound silly?"

"Not at all. I enjoy coming here, too. I'll come tomorrow. But you'd best go back now." I didn't want her to get in trouble and not be able to come anymore at all.

But the next morning, Ana Lucia decided it was time to spring-clean the house. In addition to running Hanna ragged, my stepmother enlisted me, too, with a thousand small chores that made it impossible to get away. It was as if she knew my plans and had devised the impediment deliberately. So I had not been able to go see Sadie that day at all. I imagined her, standing at the grate, disappointed and wondering why I had not come.

Today, though, a week later, I was determined to make it back to Dębniki to see her. I had left early and slipped down the stairs quietly, not wanting to wake Ana Lucia. I reached the base of the river and started for the bridge. The footpath was crowded with pedestrians and I tried to navigate between slow-moving *babcias* and the mothers bearing too many parcels, their squalling children in tow. The sky had grown dark to the west now, a thick sheet of clouds rolling in and eclipsing the sun unexpectedly. I had not thought to carry an umbrella on such a pleasant morning.

As I neared the middle of the bridge, the flow of people walking stopped suddenly. The man in front of me came to a halt so abruptly that I bumped into him. *"Przepraszam,"* I said, excusing myself. He did not respond or move, but continued chewing on the end of his cigar. The bridge was not just crowded, I realized, but blocked. The police had barricaded the bridge at the midpoint, preventing anyone from going in or out of Dębniki.

"What's happening?" I asked the man I had bumped into. I wondered if the police had set up an impromptu checkpoint, as they often did, to inspect *Kennkarten*. They would not question mine, with the special stamps Ana Lucia had procured from her German friends giving us free transit across the city. But getting through such checkpoints could take hours, and I didn't want to be delayed in getting to Sadie. The sky was dark gray now, more twilight than midday. From a distance came the low rumble of thunder.

"An *aktion*," he replied without looking back.

"Here?" I stiffened with fear. I had assumed that the mass arrests he referenced occurred only in the Jewish neighborhoods.

He removed the cigar from his mouth. "Yes, the ghetto was in Podgórze, the next neighborhood over."

"I know, but the ghetto was emptied."

"Exactly." He sounded annoyed, as if the point was an obvious one. "They're looking for those who might have escaped. Jews in hiding."

Hearing this, I grew worried for Sadie. The police had cordoned off the neighborhood around the sewer, looking for Jews who had escaped arrest when they emptied the ghetto. I pushed my way to the front of the crowd. Down the street, I could see that German military and police vehicles lined all four sides of the Rynek Dębnicki. There was a lone truck as well, which under normal circumstances looked as though it might carry cattle to market. Strangely now it had benches for people to sit on in the back. The police were combing the neighborhood, going from house to house and business to business with their awful dogs, trying to sniff out those in hiding. A cold sweat broke out on my skin. Surely they would search the sewer as well and find Sadie and the others.

I looked around desperately, wondering if there was another way to cross the river so that I could get to Sadie and warn her. But I was blocked by the crowd to the side and behind.

A sudden scream cut across the bridge, ringing high above the Germans shouting orders and dogs barking. On the street at the base of the bridge, the police dragged a woman in her twenties from a building. Her once-fashionable A-line skirt was torn at the hem and her white blouse was soiled. On the upper sleeve of her blouse she wore a white armband bearing a blue, six-pointed star. I could tell from her clothes and matted hair she had been hiding somewhere dirty. For a second, I wondered if the woman was one of the people with Sadie. But the woman was not wet, nor as filthy as she would have been coming from the sewer.

The woman was holding two children, an infant in one arm and a toddler in the other. She did not fight the police as they led her toward the back of the awaiting truck. But as she neared the truck, one of the Germans waiting there tried to take the children from her arms. The woman reared back, refusing to let go of them. The German spoke to her in a voice too low for me to hear, but I imagined him telling her why the children had to go separately—an explanation that no sensible person would believe anymore. He reached for the children once more, but the woman shook her head and pulled away. The German's voice rose, ordering her now to obey. "No, please no!" the woman begged, clinging desperately to her children. She broke away from him and started running toward the bridge.

But the bridge was barricaded by the police and choked thick with people. There was nowhere for the woman to go. One of the Germans pulled out a pistol and leveled it at her. "Halt!" Around me, there was a collective gasp from the onlookers.

"No!" I cried aloud. A bullet could kill not just the woman, but her children. I prayed that she would stop and do as the German ordered.

"Shh," the man who had been in front of me scolded. He had dropped his cigar and it now lay squashed and smoldering on the bridge. "You can't do anything. You'll get us all killed." The man was not concerned for my safety, but his own. German reprisals against the local Polish community were swift and severe, and dozens might be killed for a single act of protest or defiance.

The woman kept running toward the bridge. But her gait was slow and awkward as she carried the children, like an animal already wounded yet still trying to flee. A shot rang out and several people around me ducked, as though the shot had been aimed at them. The woman was not hit. Had the German fired off-target as a warning or actually missed? The crowd around me stood silently, as if mesmerized by the macabre spectacle. The woman started across the bridge. Then, seeing that the way forward was blocked by barricades and the crowd, she turned to the wall of the bridge and started to climb over. The German aimed again and I could tell by the intensity of his expression that this time, he did not intend to miss.

The woman did not look back, but flung herself without hesitation off the edge of the bridge with her children. There was a collective gasp from the crowd and a sickening thud as the woman and her children hit the water several meters below.

For a minute, I wondered if the Germans or police would

go in after them. Seemingly satisfied that the woman and her children could not have survived the leap, the officials turned away and the crowd began to disperse. However, the barricades remained, with several police remaining to form a makeshift checkpoint, leaving the bridge unpassable. I knew I would not be seeing Sadie today. Even if I could get across the bridge, it would not be safe to go to the grate now. I started sadly back toward home.

Thick raindrops began to fall as I recrossed the city center, pelting the cobblestones, which gave off an ancient, earthy smell. The pedestrians and shoppers scurried home now beneath umbrellas, a sea of bobbing black mushrooms. My hair and dress grew soaking, but I was so shaken by what I had seen that I scarcely noticed. I pictured the woman and her children as they jumped from the bridge. Had they died upon impact or drowned? Some part of me imagined them swimming to safety and coming out of the river to freedom farther down the banks. But the truth was that, in the broad daylight of a spring morning, a woman had just killed herself and her children in front of my very eyes, rather than be taken and separated from them by the Nazis. And I, along with dozens of other people, had stood by and watched.

I had been out longer than I expected on my failed trip to see Sadie and it was nearly noon when I returned to our house. Ana Lucia was entertaining again, this time a smaller gathering for Sunday lunch. I had skipped breakfast that morning in my hurry to get to Sadie, and as I imagined the buffet spread of meats and cheeses, my mouth watered. But I would sooner eat dirt than join them.

I tried to slip through the foyer and up to my room unseen to change out of my wet clothes. But as I neared the stairs, a German officer stepped from the toilet into the hall and blocked my way. *"Dzień dobry, fräulein,"* he said, his greeting a clumsy mix of Polish and German. I recognized him as Oberführer Maust.

He was a high-ranking SS colonel who had recently transferred to Kraków, I'd heard Ana Lucia tell one of her friends a
few weeks earlier. Drawn to his power and influence, she had
quickly ingratiated herself to him, and he had become a regular fixture by her side.

And not just at her lunches and dinner parties—the previous
night when I had gotten home, Ana Lucia's dinner party had
ended but one guest had remained behind. I had heard him follow her up the stairs to her bedroom. He said something low and
cajoling, and my stepmother had giggled, a sound too young and
unseemly for someone her age. I was repulsed. It was one thing
to entertain the Germans, quite another to have one sleep in
the bed she had shared with my father. I never hated her more.
That morning as I had passed Ana Lucia's bedroom I could hear
from the corridor two sets of snoring, hers thick and bubbling,
another unbroken and deep.

Her new friend. I studied the beast. He looked like the rest of
them, thick-necked with ruddy cheeks, except that he was taller
with a paunchy middle and hands like bear paws. He looked
down at me now like a snake about to devour a mouse.

Before I could respond, Ana Lucia appeared from the dining
room. "Fritz, I was wondering where you..." Seeing him talking to me, she stopped and frowned. "Ella, what are you doing
here?" she asked, as though I had wandered in from the street
and not come into my own home. Her dress, this year's latest
fashion from Milan, was too tight on her thick frame. Pearls that
had once been my mother's strained against her neck.

"Your daughter is quite charming," the German said. "You
never mentioned."

"Stepdaughter," Ana Lucia corrected, wanting to put as much
distance between herself and me as possible. "My late husband's
child. And she's soaking wet."

"She should join us for lunch," he said.

I could see the conflict in Ana Lucia's eyes, wanting to accede to the wishes of her Nazi guest, yet wanting me gone even more. But Colonel Maust's tone made clear that my joining them was not a request. "Fine," she said at last, compliance winning out over spite.

"I'm sorry, but I really can't," I said, trying to think of an excuse.

"Ella," my stepmother said through clenched teeth. "If Oberführer Maust is good enough to invite you to join us, then that is what you will do." I could tell from her eyes that if I embarrassed her by refusing, the consequences would be severe. "You will change and join us."

Ten minutes later, I walked into the dining room reluctantly in a fresh blue dress, hair still defiantly wet. There were four other guests, two men in German military uniforms and one in a suit, plus a woman about Ana Lucia's age whom I did not recognize. They did not look up from their conversations to greet or acknowledge me as I entered. Seeing these strangers sitting around what had once been our family table and using my mother's wedding china and crystal, I felt physically nauseous. I took the only empty seat, beside Colonel Maust and close to my stepmother. Hanna served me a plate of *szarlotka*, a warm apple pie grander than any I had seen since the war started. But the thick pastry stuck in my throat.

I set down my fork. "I saw a woman jump off the Dębnicki Bridge today," I blurted out. If I was going to have to be here, I might as well make it interesting. The other conversations around the table stopped and all heads swiveled toward me. "The police were trying to arrest her and she jumped with her children." The lone woman beside Ana Lucia and me covered her mouth with her napkin, looking aghast.

"She must have been a Jew," Colonel Maust said dismissively. "There was an *aktion* to try to root out the last few in hiding." He had known about the very arrests that were taking place while he sat in our dining room, eating cake.

"Hiding?" the other woman at the table asked.

"Yes," Colonel Maust replied. "There were a few Jews who managed to escape when the ghetto was liquidated, mostly to the neighborhoods along the river."

"That close to where I live!" the woman gasped. I understood then that her horrified look had not been out of concern for those arrested, but rather her own well-being. "How dangerous!" One would have thought from her voice that she was talking about hardened criminals.

A mother with two children, I wanted to say. *A danger to the very existence of our city.* Of course, I did not. "What will happen to them?" I asked instead.

"The woman who jumped? I assume that she and her children will feed the fishes." Colonel Maust laughed at his own cruel joke and the others joined in. I wanted to reach over and slap his fat face.

I swallowed back my anger. "The Jews who are arrested, I mean. The ghetto has been closed. So where will they go?"

Ana Lucia shot me daggers for continuing to raise the subject. But one of the Germans at the far end of the table answered. "The able-bodied may go to Płaszów for a time," he said between mouthfuls of apple pie. He was a slim, sinewy man, with dark beady eyes and a face like a ferret's. "It's a labor camp just outside the city."

"And the others?"

He paused for a beat. "They will be sent to Auschwitz."

"What's that?" I was familiar with the town of Oświęcim, about an hour west of the city. I had heard mention of a camp there called by the Germanic name of the town, whispered references to a place for Jews more awful than the rest. Only no one could confirm the rumors, people said, because no one ever returned from there. I looked the German in the eye, daring him to acknowledge the truth in front of everyone.

He did not hesitate. "Let's just say they won't be coming back to dirty your neighborhood again."

"Even the women and children?" I asked.

He shrugged indifferently. "They are all Jews to us."

He met my eyes without blinking, and looking into the darkness there, I saw everything that he had not said, of imprisonment and death that awaited the Jews. The woman on the bridge had sooner jumped than abandon herself and her children to such a fate.

Ana Lucia flashed daggers at me. "Enough questions." She put her hand on Colonel Maust's arm. "Darling, let's not speak of such things in polite company and ruin our lunch. My stepdaughter was just leaving."

"I must be going as well," Colonel Maust said, folding his napkin.

"Must you?" Ana Lucia asked, seeming to deflate.

"Excuse me." Not wanting to witness their farewell, I stood abruptly and pushed my chair back from the table so hard that the coffee cups rattled. I hurried from the room and up the stairs to the garret. There was a strange ringing in my ears as I processed what the German had said. The Jews were being taken to camps—all of them. What had I thought? I berated myself. I knew the ghetto had been emptied. Still, it had been easier to tell myself that the Jewish occupants had simply been "relocated" to live somewhere else—or to not think about it at all. Now the truth was laid before me impossible to ignore. The Jews were being imprisoned and used as slave labor, or worse.

Sadie flashed into my mind. She had fled the German liquidation of the ghetto, as surely as the woman I had seen jump from the bridge. And the same horrors that the German had described awaited her if she got caught. Though I had met her only a few weeks earlier, I felt like I had gotten to know Sadie and I did not want anything bad to happen to her. She had been through so much already and I could not stand the thought that she might be captured and taken away.

Sometime later, I heard the lunch gathering wind down, the wretched remaining guests make their way out onto the street. But I stayed upstairs for the rest of the day, wanting to avoid Ana Lucia's wrath. Looking across the rooftops toward the far bank of the river, I pictured Sadie and prayed that she was safe. It would be a week before I could go to her again and know for sure.

The next morning when I went down to breakfast, Ana Lucia was already seated at the table. It was a rare occurrence that we met in the morning; I usually made it a point to be up and gone long before she came downstairs, which wasn't hard, since she seldom awoke before noon. Neither of us bade the other good-morning as I sat down at the far end of the table.

"Ella," Ana Lucia said, once Hanna had served me coffee and toast. I could tell from her tone, even more disapproving than usual, that the topic was not a good one. Was it the fact that I had left her lunch party so swiftly the previous day or asked too many questions? Perhaps it was something else entirely. I braced myself for her tirade.

"What were you doing at the Dębniki market?" she asked suddenly.

A lump formed in my throat. "Getting cherries for your dessert, remember?"

"No, I mean the second time." I stiffened. Ana Lucia knew I had gone to Dębniki more than once. She continued, "My dinner party with the cherry pie was weeks ago on a Saturday. But someone saw you there after that." Ana Lucia often appeared clueless. But her memory was razor sharp now. I realized I had underestimated her. Her eyes bore down on me, demanding answers. Our poor maid, Hanna, slipped from the room with a terrified look on her face.

"Well, you may remember I couldn't get enough for the

party," I said, struggling to speak in an even voice. Ana Lucia smiled as she watched me squirm, caught in her trap. "But the seller said he would have some cherries coming in soon, so I decided to go back, in case you wanted Hanna to make the pastry again." My voice was weak, the excuse implausible.

"You need to mind your ways," she said, an unmistakable note of menace in her voice. "I don't know what you're up to." I breathed an inward sigh of relief. "But I won't tolerate anything out of line that would jeopardize our position." She loomed over me now, eyes flaring, temper unleashed. "You interrupted my party yesterday uninvited." I wanted to correct that her German friend had asked me in, but I didn't dare. "And then you ruined it by talking about the Jews."

"How can you stand it?" I burst out. "What they are doing to those poor, innocent people."

"The city is better off without them." She gazed at me unblinkingly. I recalled then how Austria, Ana Lucia's native land, had welcomed the Anschluss, its annexation with Germany. Ana Lucia was not just consorting with the Germans for a social life, or to gain their favor. She actually agreed with them.

Sickened, I rose from the table. As I left the room, my mind raced. Ana Lucia knew I had gone back across the river. Thankfully, she did not seem to know why—at least not yet.

Upstairs, I looked across the rainy skyline at the drab, gray neighborhood on the far side of the bridge. I should not go back to the sewer. With Ana Lucia suspicious, she would be watching me more closely than ever. I did not know Sadie all that well. I had spoken to her only a handful of times, and it made no sense to risk everything for someone who was practically a stranger. Yet even as I thought this, I knew I would return to the grate. There was nothing to be done for that woman on the bridge—I had stood by helplessly as she took her life and those of her children, just like I had done nothing when Miriam and the other Jewish students had been kicked out of school. But Sadie was still safe, and in some small way, I could help her. I swore to myself then and there that, unlike the others, I would not let her down.

10

Sadie

I listened one Sunday morning as the voices at Kostka Church above the sewer rose in prayer, the priest intoning the now-familiar mass and parishioners, fewer each week it seemed, giving the response. Though I did not have a watch or clock, I could tell from the part of the mass they chanted that it was a quarter past ten, nearly time to go meet Ella. My anticipation rose and I pushed it down, trying not to get too hopeful. Ella had promised to come every Sunday and mostly she did, but there had been a few Sundays in the six weeks since we met that she had not appeared.

"I'm going to get water," I announced when I judged it to be just before eleven.

Mama gestured toward the full jug. "Saul already went. We have plenty."

I looked around the chamber, hoping to find some garbage that needed disposal. I found none. "I'm going for a walk, then," I said, expecting Mama to object. She didn't answer. I studied her face, wondering if she was suspicious. The first few weeks after making me promise not to go see Ella, she had watched me like a hawk. But she seemed distracted now, weary from her growing belly and the struggle of keeping us going in the sewer. She did not protest as I started hurriedly from the chamber. My discussion with Mama had made me a few minutes late, and as I neared the grate, I hoped that Ella had waited for me.

"Fool!" a voice hissed behind me, just as I approached the grate. I turned to see Bubbe Rosenberg, who must have seen me leave the chamber and followed me. Or perhaps she had just been walking the tunnels aimlessly. She seemed increasingly confused lately and prone to wandering. More than once, Saul had followed after her when she strayed from the chamber at night and led her back. He often lay beside her, holding her as he slept, so that she didn't get lost, or fall into the sewer river and drown like Papa. "You'll get us all killed," she said now. I wondered if she had seen me talking to Ella before or if Saul had told her. "Go to the grate again and I'll have you tossed out." I wasn't sure if she could do that, or even what she really meant. But I didn't want to find out.

"Enough," I said rudely. My mother, if she had heard me, would have been mortified at my rudeness. But I simply couldn't take it anymore.

Bubbe muttered something unintelligible. I hoped she would return to the chamber. She lingered in the tunnel, though, still talking to herself. So I remained in the shadows, close to the grate, not daring to violate her order. I did not want her to create a scene and alert the others to what I was doing. I imagined Ella on the street above, waiting for me.

When the old woman finally left, I hurried to the grate. "Hello?" I called softly. I did not see Ella. I wondered if she had been there and gone because I had taken too long, or whether she had not come at all. Perhaps she had forgotten about me. That seemed unlikely; Ella was always so helpful and kind. The

street above was strangely quiet, though, and I did not see anyone else either. In the distance, I heard the wailing of a police
siren long and low. Something was wrong, I sensed uneasily. It
was not safe to wait here any longer.

Rain began to fall then, thick drops falling through the grate
and puddling on the already wet sewer ground. I started back
sadly.

As I neared the chamber, Mama appeared in the entranceway. "Oh, thank goodness," she said in a low voice. Her face
was more somber than usual. I wondered if Bubbe had told her
about my going back to the grate. "I was just about to send Saul
to look for you. You must come now."

"What is it?" Mama did not answer, but led me back into the
chamber. She tilted her chin upward. The sound of the parishioners had gone silent, but there was another noise, louder and
more ominous, of doors opening and slamming shut, male voices
speaking German. "They are searching for Jews," Pan Rosenberg whispered ominously from across the chamber.

It was not, of course, the first time I had heard of such things.
Still, my panic rose at the realization that they were searching
for Jews so close to our hiding place. "Are they coming for us?"
I asked.

Mama shook her head. "They are looking for hiding Jews on
the streets and in the houses. They don't know about the sewer,
at least not yet." She drew me close and we sat down on our
bed. From across the chamber, Saul's eyes met mine, his expression a mix of warmth and concern. We had grown closer in the
weeks since he learned the awful news about his brother and
Shifra and I had comforted him. Living together in such tight
quarters made everything more intimate and familiar, too. I
knew the ways that he ate and slept, could tell from his expression whether he was angry or sad or worried.

Mama wrapped her arms around me and we tried to make
ourselves as small and silent as possible. But it was useless. If the

Germans searched the tunnels and discovered the chamber, we would have nowhere to hide. *We should go*, I thought, not for the first time. Better to leave than be caught in the chamber like trapped animals. But without Pawel to lead us, we simply had no way out.

We sat in silence for what seemed like hours, listening to the sounds above, waiting for the footsteps in the tunnel that would spell our doom. At one point, I heard a woman's voice cry out and wondered if someone had been caught. The rain began to fall heavier now, muting the sounds of the police hunting their prey.

Eventually the voices faded, although I didn't know whether the Germans had been deterred by the rain or given up looking. The searching sounds were replaced with a rhythmic thundering, like marching boots as the rain teemed heavier. Outside the chamber, the pooling water began to run in a great stream. "Spring floods," Bubbe said ominously.

I looked up to see the shadow that passed across Mama's face. The notion was nearly as scary as the idea of the Germans looking for us. We always knew that heavy spring rains, when they finally came, were going to mean trouble. It had rained often the past few weeks and the river was swollen, the levees full. Whenever rain fell on the streets above, the sewer waters in the big tunnel would rise, pushing water into the narrower pipes and causing small waves to lick at the entrance to our chamber. Usually the rain stopped after a while and the waters receded.

But today it did not stop. Sheets of water fell above. I imagined a torrent of water pouring through the sewer grate where I went to look for Ella that morning and backing up in the pipes. Now that the Germans had ceased searching on the streets above, we unfolded ourselves from the place where we huddled. We tried to carry on with our day, Mama preparing a late lunch of reheated potato soup. The rain continued all day, and as evening fell, the water began to swirl at the entrance of the chamber. I fell asleep beside Mama and dreamed of the waters rising and carrying our plank bed away like a toy boat.

It was not entirely a dream, I discovered the next morning. "Sadie, wake up." Mama roused me from sleep. The water was ankle-deep in the chamber now. We put on our sodden shoes, then collected our other belongings hurriedly and moved them to higher ground. Mama waded across the chamber to salvage our food stores. Across the chamber, I glimpsed Saul doing the same. I wanted to get his attention but could not. Water from the tunnel entered the chamber and began to fill it. Soon the swirling water around our ankles became a torrent, reaching my knees. As the water rose, everything around us began to float, jars and bottles and plates, resembling a bizarre underwater tea party.

"What will we do if it doesn't stop?" I asked.

"It will stop," Mama replied, not answering my question. She led me to the highest end of the chamber in an attempt to keep as much of us dry as possible. But it was futile. The rains continued to pound and the floodwater filled our living space like a giant bathtub. The water was soon past our midsections and our clothes were soaked through. It was as if we were swimming in a cold, filthy pool or lake that we could never leave.

I looked across the chamber at Saul, who was helping his grandmother reach a higher spot without slipping. His eyes caught mine and held. For a second, it seemed that he wanted to come to me as much as I did him. Then he turned back to focus on aiding his family once more. I wondered if we should have left the chamber to find higher ground. Of course, that was impossible now. As the swollen sewer river had risen, it would have eclipsed the thin ledge we always used to navigate its banks. If we dared try to go, we would surely be swept away. And the same high water and current that kept us from leaving prevented Pawel from coming here and rescuing us as well.

The water level neared my mouth dangerously. I lifted my

head higher, struggling to breathe. My panic rose. In a few minutes, the water would be too deep to stand. I had always been like a frightened animal in the water; my limbs were clumsy and ineffective when I tried to swim. How would I possibly survive if we had to swim?

I reached up on the wall and found the makeshift shelf where we usually kept the bread. Clinging to the ledge, I raised myself so that I was a few feet higher, my head close to the roof of the chamber. That bought me a few minutes and some extra air. But it would not solve the problem if the water continued to rise.

I held my hand out to my mother, who was treading water now beside me, wanting to help her. She had always been an excellent swimmer, though, and even now with her extra girth, she seemed to bobble effortlessly on the surface. Across the chamber, I could see Saul, supporting his grandmother with one arm and his father with the other as they struggled to stay afloat.

The flood seemed to go on forever. My arms began to burn from clinging to the ledge. I couldn't hold on forever and I had no chance if I had to swim. Finally, I let go, preparing to drown and let the water carry me to Papa. My mother caught me by the collar, holding me afloat. But my weight was too much and we both began to go under. I tried to shake her off, but she held fast, unwilling to let me go. Her blond hair fanned out about her like a halo. As the water rose, I inhaled, taking a deep breath, which I planned to hold as long as I could once my head submerged beneath the water.

Suddenly there was a mighty creak in the distance, and although the rain continued to pound just as steadily above, the water in the chamber seemed to slowly stop rising. "A levee," someone said. "They must have opened another path for the water to flow." I was too weary to process the good news or to care if the explanation was true. Surely it would take days, if not weeks, for the water to recede and I couldn't possibly hold on for that long.

"Hang on," I heard Mama say, but her voice sounded far away now as I began to slip beneath the surface. I struggled, gasping for air, then slid under once more. Water filled my mouth and nose, causing me to cough and gag. My eyelids were heavy now, as though I was going to sleep at night. The chamber went dark around me and I knew no more.

I awoke sometime later on the ground a short distance from the wall where I had clung. "What happened?" The waters were gone; they had receded even more quickly than they came, leaving the black silt floor sodden and strewn with our wet belongings. But the last thing I remembered was the chamber filled with water, me gasping for a few last gasps of air.

"Sadele!" Mama sat on the ground beside me. "Thank heavens you're all right. When the water rose too high, you passed out. I tried to keep you afloat myself, but I couldn't manage it. Saul held you up until the waters receded."

Saul. I looked across the chamber to where his father and grandmother sat trying to recover from the flood. But I did not see him. "I'm right here." I turned to find him crouching just inches from where I lay. Our eyes met. Knowing that he had saved me seemed to bring us closer.

"Thank you," I said.

"I'm glad you are all right." His hand reached in the direction of mine and I wondered for a second if he might touch me. But with the others here, he could not. He stood and started back across the chamber to his family.

"He wouldn't leave your side until he knew you were safe," Mama said in a low voice. I felt myself grow warm inside. "Now let's find a way to dry ourselves." I tried to stand, but my clothes, heavy and soaked with icy sewer water, seemed to weigh me down. "Come," Mama said, making it to her feet before me despite the bulk of her stomach. She held a hand out to help me. There was a steely look of determination in her eyes. She was not going to let this beat us either. Slowly we began to put the chamber back together.

As we worked, I thought about all that had happened the previous night. The flood had come suddenly, without warning. If the waters hadn't receded, we would have all drowned. And that was not the only danger; as long as we stayed in the chamber, without another hiding place or way out, we were vulnerable, trapped. I remembered the night we came to the sewer, the labyrinth of tunnels Pawel had led us past or through. There had to be other places we could hide if things got bad—or perhaps even a way out.

I looked over at Saul, wanting to share my thoughts with him. He had walked the tunnels more than I and perhaps he had seen other places that might be useful. But there was little chance to be together during the day with our families constantly around.

That night as the others prepared to sleep in their still-damp beds, Saul gestured to me and nodded toward the tunnel. After Mama was asleep, I slipped out of the chamber to find him waiting for me. We started down the tunnel in silence.

"Saul, I wanted to talk to you about something." I hesitated, unsure how to introduce the subject. "The floodwaters...they almost killed us."

"It was terrifying," he agreed.

"It's more than that. We have to find a way out of the sewer in case we ever need to escape."

"Out?" He looked at me as though I was out of my mind. "But here in the sewer we are safe." His jaw set stubbornly. He had been so scarred by the loss of his brother and fiancée that he could not imagine surviving anywhere but here.

"For the moment, yes. But what if the rains come again? Next time, they might not stop. Or if the Germans search the tunnels." He did not answer. "We are trapped here, sitting ducks. Things are only getting worse. We aren't going to be able to stay here forever."

"You want us to leave?"

"No," I relented. In truth, I was not ready to leave the sewer yet either—mostly because I could not envision anywhere safe that we could go. "Not exactly. Not right now. But we need to know how to get out, where to go if something worse happens." We were fighting a war of hunger and flooding and a battle against time and being detected—and the sewer was winning. "There has to be a way out. We should know so that if we ever need to flee we can find our way."

"Maybe if we ask Pawel..." Saul offered.

I shook my head. "Pawel is doing enough for us already. He isn't going to help us leave." Pawel had given almost everything just to get us here and keep us hidden. He believed the sewer was the only way to keep us safe, that if we tried to leave we would bungle it and get caught like that family who had fled the first night we came here. He wasn't going to start showing us ways to leave and risk our own lives—and his. "And what if Pawel can't get to us, like he couldn't yesterday in the flood? We need to know what our options are just in case and we need to find out ourselves."

"Where would we go if we did get out?"

I hesitated. "I don't know," I admitted finally. "We should at least look. So that we know a way if it comes to that. If the worst happens..." I tried to imagine what the worst might be, but found that I could not. "Saul, we can do this, but I need your help."

I expected him to argue further with me, but he did not. "Fine," he relented.

"You're going to help me?" I asked.

He nodded reluctantly, not meeting my eyes. "I will go with you tomorrow night and we will see if there is a way out." Leaving went against everything Saul wanted and believed in, but he was willing to look for a way for me. "But only to check in case we need somewhere to go in an emergency. We are not leaving." His voice was firm.

The next night he met me outside the tunnel. "What about the grate above the annex where we read?" I asked.

He shook his head. "It's welded shut."

"You tried to open it? I'm surprised."

He smiled. "There are a great many things about me that might surprise you, Sadie Gault." Then his expression grew serious again. "But I did pass another tunnel once when I went past the annex." He started in that direction and I followed him, our arms bumping into one another occasionally as we navigated the narrow tunnel side by side. "I think there may be a path here." He led me down a pipe, but it was a dead end, walled off.

"We have to follow the water," I said.

We tried a different tunnel, but it was a circular route and led us back to the chamber. Another failure. Finally, we followed the tunnel to where it grew wider, the water rushing more fiercely. I saw for the first time since we had come the slatted boards across the water where Papa had fallen and drowned. I stopped, tears filling my eyes.

Saul walked up beside me and put his hand on my shoulder, seeming to sense my pain. "Your father, he would have been very proud of you," he offered. "The way you have managed in the sewer and taken care of your mother." I did not answer. We stood for several seconds, neither speaking. "Come," he said at last. "I think the river is this way." I thought for a second that he meant the sewer river, which made no sense—we were already standing on its banks. But as he led me in an unfamiliar direction and the water began to flow harder and faster, I realized he meant the Wisła River and the outside world.

As I continued on, the path became more familiar. We were retracing the steps we had taken the night Pawel had led us here, only in reverse. I saw the low, capped pipe we'd had to shimmy through and hoped we would not have to do that again now.

Thankfully, Saul led me away from the narrow pipe. "Look, there's another way over here." He pointed to a path almost too narrow to fit through, more of a crack in the wall than an actual tunnel. We had to go through single file and I went first, wedging myself into the tight space. It sloped upward as though reaching the street. At last we could see a wide opening where the sewer pipe dumped into a branch of the river, the vast sky beyond. The sight of so much open space, more than I had seen since we had gone into the sewer, was tantalizing. I took a step forward, eager to see the stars that dotted the now-clear sky. We could go, I realized. Saul and I could just keep walking and reach freedom.

Suddenly there was a loud clattering noise ahead. Saul caught me in his arms and pulled me back away from the opening. We heard the barking of German shepherds on the riverbank, followed by voices giving them stern commands to search. I froze. Had the Germans detected us? Saul pulled me into a crevice in the tunnel wall, pressing me so tightly to him I could feel his heart beating through our clothes. We did not move, barely breathed.

A few minutes later, the barking subsided. Still, Saul continued to hold me close. A wave of warmth shot through me. I liked him, I realized more fully than I had before, in a way I had never felt before about a boy. For a second, feeling his heartbeat against mine, I wondered if he might feel the same. Even as I thought this, I was more certain than ever that it was impossible. He could not possibly be drawn to me like this, amidst all of the dirt and filth and fear. I could not help but feel, though, that something had changed between us, with the flood and now this, bringing us closer. He released me and we started back to the chamber in silence.

"So you see," he said when we were well away from the opening, "there is no way out but the river, and we cannot possibly…"

I raised my hand, silencing him. I heard an echo ahead, coming from a small tunnel off to the right that I had not noticed before. "This way." I motioned for him to follow me. It led to a deep chamber, more of a concrete basin really, the bottom a good six feet down. The basin was empty now, but I could tell from the dampness it was a reservoir that would fill when the water in the pipes overflowed. On the far wall, there was a high opening to another pipe. "Come on," I said, scampering down into the basin.

"Sadie, wait. What are you doing? You'll never get back up."

But I continued across the basin, not listening. "I have to try."

"Of course you do." There was a note of fondness in his voice as he followed me.

"I need you to boost me to that pipe on the far wall to see if there is a place for us to hide or escape." He looked at me as if I was out of my mind and I thought that he would protest, but he followed me across the basin. "Help me," I said. But he hesitated. Then reluctantly, he put his hands on my waist just enough to lift me to the high pipe on the far side. He pulled away quickly, but the warmth where his hands had been lingered.

I peered down the pipe. There was a narrow crawl space and a tunnel leading upward. At the end of it I could make out daylight. I could not make out any buildings or people here, just open sky and a bit of the castle looming over the river. "There's another path outside," I said breathlessly. "It's a steep climb, but perhaps we could make it if we had to." Though still dangerously visible, the opening here would not be as crowded with people as the one by the market where I met Ella.

"Let's hope that it won't come to that." Saul clung stubbornly to the belief that if we just stayed where we were, everything would be fine. But I had seen it too many times, the war taking all of the things we knew, destroying the ground under our feet until it was no longer there.

Saul helped me down from the ledge and we stood in the basin too close for a second, his hands lingering around my waist.

Then he pulled away abruptly. "I'm sorry," he said. "Touching like this…"

"It isn't allowed. I understand."

"It isn't just that. You see, Shifra…"

"Of course." I pushed away my hurt. His heart was still with his fiancée, gone just over a month. I had no right to mind that. "It's too soon."

"No, you must understand. Shifra and I were betrothed by our parents, that is, arranged to be married from a very young age."

"Oh." I had heard of such traditions, but I had not realized they actually still existed.

"So we didn't really know each other well at all. She was a lovely person and I assumed that we would get to know each other, to feel affection grow over the years. When I left, we were still largely strangers. And now, to be here with you… I like you, Sadie, and I shouldn't. The way that I feel about you, how close we have become, it just isn't permitted, even here." He faltered. "Shifra was my fiancée, and she suffered and died. I should have stayed above ground to protect her instead of hiding like a coward."

"No, you left your village to protect your father. You thought Shifra was safe. No one could have imagined such things would happen to the women and children."

"Does it matter?" He shook his head stubbornly. "No, in the end, she is dead, and I am here with you. But I don't deserve happiness, not after all that has happened. So you understand why we can't be together."

I nodded, overwhelmed by two feelings at the same time, the joy of knowing Saul felt the same way that I did and sadness that it could go no further. "I understand," I said finally. We started walking once more.

We reached the entrance to the chamber. "At least we know now a place we can go if we have to," I offered.

"Hopefully it won't come to that. Promise me, Sadie, that you won't try to get out." His voice was heavy with concern. "We are safe here together." To him, the sewer was our only hope.

"For now," I replied. In my heart, I knew that the sewer would not protect us forever.

"Then for now, let that be enough." In spite of what he had said earlier, he took my hand, lacing his fingers through mine. We walked silently back into the chamber that was both our prison and our salvation once more.

11

Ella

One Sunday morning in late June I awoke early, eager to go see Sadie and make sure she was all right. Ana Lucia was not at home, I gathered from the stillness of the second floor as I made my way downstairs after washing and dressing. She had been out at a cocktail party the previous night with Colonel Maust and I assumed she had stayed at his apartment, but did not know for sure.

I ate quickly, then picked up my basket and walked into the kitchen, looking for something I could bring Sadie. Taking her bits of food each week seemed like a meager gesture; I felt as if I should be doing more. But she needed food and seemed glad to have it. And it was really all I could do.

I peered into the icebox. There was a plate of freshly cut salami and cheese, neatly arranged. There was no way to take any of that without it being noticeable, though. On the shelf below was the remainder of a quiche from Ana Lucia's lunch party the previous day, typical of the pretentious French cuisine she loved to serve. I pictured Sadie's delight in having some of the special treat. Just a bit off the edge, I decided. I reached in and pulled up the wrapping, which crinkled loudly. I cut off a piece of quiche and wrapped it in wax paper, then put it in my basket. As I replaced the dish, I heard footsteps behind me. I shut the icebox and turned. Standing there was Hanna.

"Hanna, I didn't hear you. I was just…" My voice trailed off as I searched for an explanation, but found none. "I was still hungry," I finished lamely. Hanna's eyes traveled to the basket where I had placed the food. My heart pounded. Hanna worked for Ana Lucia, and despite my stepmother's awfulness, she was still the one who paid the girl. Surely Hanna would tell.

But Hanna stepped around me wordlessly and reached into the icebox. She pulled out the cheese tray, took several pieces off and wrapped them in wax paper. She rearranged the cheeses on the tray so it was not as obvious that some of the pieces were missing and put it back in the icebox. Then she handed the wrapped package to me.

I hesitated before taking it. "Hanna, no." I wasn't sure if she knew what I was doing and wanted to help or simply thought I wanted food. If Ana Lucia found out, she would fire Hanna and put her out into the streets.

Then, thinking of Sadie, I relented. "Thank you. I will take this with me and eat it for lunch." Hanna continued to stare at me, not believing. Then she turned and walked from the kitchen.

Outside on the pavement, I paused as I always did before setting out to meet Sadie. Though it had been a few weeks since Ana Lucia had voiced her suspicions about my going to Dębniki, I was still afraid she might be on to me. But she was not home, and even if she was, she would not follow me herself to the distant, working-class neighborhood. I promised Sadie I would come again and I wanted to bring her food and make sure that she was all right.

Forty minutes later, I stepped off the tram on the corner of Rynek Dębnicki. I made my way around the corner of the square toward the grate. As I reached the top of the alleyway where the grate was located, I froze, stopping dead in my tracks.

Standing over the grate where Sadie and I met were two German soldiers.

They had found her.

I froze with panic. I had imagined it before, picturing the grate pulled back, soldiers marching Sadie and the others out with their hands up, arresting them as they had tried to arrest the woman with the two children I had seen jump from the bridge. I often wondered what I would do if Sadie was caught. Would I step in and try to save her, or stand silently by as I had with Miriam at school, and again the woman and her children?

Easy, I thought now, my heart pounding. Closer, I could see that the two Germans were just standing in the alleyway, talking. The grate was still intact. They had not yet discovered that there were people in the sewer. One of the soldiers was kicking the grate with his foot as they spoke, though, lifting the edge with his toe where it opened. He looked down, said something to his companion. I could not hear him, but I imagined that he was remarking about the fact that it was loose.

Sadie was surely on her way to meet me and any minute now she would be here. The soldiers were standing just over the grate and Sadie had no idea. If she wasn't careful, she might unwittingly step into view. I had to distract them.

Steeling myself, I walked into the alleyway in the direction of the Germans, forcing myself to smile. The younger of the two, who had close-cropped blond hair beneath his hat, noticed and stepped toward me. *"Dzień dobry, pani,"* he said, mangling the Polish language in his attempt. He gave me an appraising look and smiled, revealing a wide gap between his front teeth. I channeled Ana Lucia, batting my eyes at the soldier and feeling sick at doing so.

"Dzień dobry." I smiled in the direction of the other German in hopes that he would walk over as well.

But he remained firmly planted above the grate. *"Ja,* what do you want?" he asked rudely, clearly in no mood for pleasantries. I could tell by the stripes and medals on his uniform that he was the more senior of the two.

"It's such a lovely day," I offered, thinking of something to say to these beasts, stalling for time. Food and fighting, I'd heard Ana Lucia tell one of her friends once, were the things men liked. "I'm looking for a good café for coffee and dessert," I said.

"You won't find any in this part of town," the younger soldier offered.

"No?" I feigned ignorance about the city where I had lived my entire life.

"You have to go to the main market square in the Old Town. The restaurant Wierzynek has a *sachertorte* that is almost as delicious as the one back home in Heidelberg."

"I would love to try it." Sadie had to be close to the grate now, so I spoke a bit louder than normal, willing her to hear my voice and stay hidden from sight. "Perhaps you could take me for a coffee." I didn't want to go with him, of course, or leave Sadie, but I wanted to draw these two men away from her hiding place.

The younger soldier smiled, seeming flattered by the suggestion. But the older man beside him glowered. "We don't have time for this, Kurt."

"Perhaps later, then," I said. My eyes darted to the grate. Sadie had not appeared. I prayed that she had heard the exchange and kept away. "I should be on my way." I inched back from the Germans. I still wanted to see Sadie, but as long as the soldiers lingered here, that was impossible.

The older German's eyes dropped to my basket. "What are you carrying?"

"Just some food for my family. I bought it at the shops." I instantly recognized my mistake. It was Sunday; the shops were closed.

"Let me see," he demanded. As he reached for the basket, I panicked.

"Darling!" someone called behind me. Even before I turned, I recognized Krys' familiar voice. He moved closer and swiftly took the basket from me. Then he produced an identification card and ration book and handed it to the older officer. "We were getting so worried. My fiancée's mother is sick and she had to get food for all of us while I cared for her," he said to the Germans, lying smoothly. Even in my panic, Krys' calling me his fiancée tugged at my heart. For a moment it felt like things between us were as they had once been. But of course it was a ruse to fool the Germans.

"My mother, Ana Lucia Stepanek, is a good friend of Ober-führer Maust," I added, hoping the name of my stepmother's consort might buy some goodwill.

I was right—their expressions changed instantly. "Of course, *fräulein*," the older man said, now contrite. He returned the ration book to Krys. "So sorry." The men moved back to let us pass. But as I began to step around them and go, I glimpsed a familiar face in the sewer. It was Sadie. She had come looking for me and unwittingly stepped into view. I willed her to duck back. But she stood motionless, her face frozen with horror. Any second they would see her.

"Come," Krys urged, not understanding why I had not started away with him. I was paralyzed, uncertain what to do. I heard a scraping below then, Sadie's footsteps echoing in the sewer as she scuttled away. I coughed loudly to try to mask the sound.

One of the Germans looked over his shoulder. "What was that?"

"Pardon me," I said. "Spring allergies." I let Krys lead me away, praying that the Germans would not question further.

"Wait!" the older German called. I froze. Did he suspect something? I turned back to see him staring strangely at Krys.

"You look familiar," he said.

"I make deliveries," Krys said, keeping his voice neutral. "You've probably seen me around town." He turned to me. "Come now. Your mother is waiting." As he led me away, I forced myself not to look back reluctantly at the grate.

My heart pounded as we walked. I could still feel the eyes of the Germans on us as we went, and I half expected them to come after us and detain us for questioning, or worse.

But they did not. "You again," I said to Krys when we were well away from the alley. I tried to sound annoyed. "Are you following me?"

"Hardly," he replied. "I work in this neighborhood, at the dock with my father and a bit at the café in exchange for the flat above it where I'm staying. This isn't your part of the city, though. Cherries again?"

He was trying to be humorous, but I did not smile. "Something like that. I come to the market sometimes for errands."

"You shouldn't," he replied bluntly. "Wandering the city, it's dangerous. You have to be more careful," he scolded, as though talking to a child.

I stopped walking and turned to face him. "Why should you care?" I flared. He stepped back as if genuinely surprised by my outburst. "You left me. You didn't even tell me you were back." I hadn't meant to confront him, but now that the words had come out, I wanted answers. "Why?"

"Shh. Not here." He took my arm and led me down the busy street, away from the shops and the houses, in the direction of the industrial buildings and warehouses by the river. "I've wanted to come see you," he said at last when we were alone on the banks of the Wisła and could not be heard. "I tried to explain when I saw you here a few weeks ago, but you ran away."

I turned to face him, put my hands on my hips. "I'm here now. So tell me."

He looked over his shoulder before speaking, as if even here on the riverbank, which was deserted but for some disinterested ducks, someone might be listening. "Ella, I wasn't gone all of that time because of the army. At least not the army you know."

"I don't understand." Had he been lying about everything?

"I really did enlist and go off to fight." In my mind, I saw him at the rail station Kraków Główny the day he left, so proud and hopeful in his new uniform, winking at me before boarding the train. "But then Poland was defeated and something else happened. Have you heard of the Home Army?" I nodded. It was rumored early in the war that a group of Polish men had organized to fight the Germans and I had since heard claims that they engaged in acts of sabotage. But as the occupation continued undaunted, resistance seemed surreal, the stuff of fairy tales or legends.

"You see, when it became clear that Poland was going to lose in combat, another soldier told me about an underground army that was forming," Krys said. "I heard about the work they were going to do, and I knew I needed to be a part of it. There was nothing more to be done on the battlefield; secret operations were our only hope. So I started working with a small group to fight the Germans. Later we joined forces with other similar organizations to form the Polish Home Army."

I still didn't understand quite what it all meant—or how it had kept him from coming back to me. "What do you do, exactly?"

He shook his head. "I can't say. It's terribly dangerous work, though, fighting the Germans in many different ways. That's why I had to stay away from you, even after I came back. You see, most people who are a part of this don't live very long."

"No…" I said, stung by the notion that something might happen to him. I moved closer to Krys and he put his arm around me.

"I didn't want to cause you pain. And I didn't want to put you in harm's way. I'm not worried for myself. But if I were caught, they would go after everyone I loved. I didn't come back because I needed to protect you. I still care about you more than anything. But I cannot see you hurt. So you see now why we couldn't be together."

"And why we still can't." I straightened, pulling away from him.

He nodded grimly. "It's the only way."

"Do you think you can defeat the Germans?" I asked incredulously.

"I don't." His tone was blunt. "We are no match for their weaponry or their numbers."

"Then why do it?" He was throwing away his future—and ours together—for an impossible chance. How could someone give their whole life to a fight that at the end of the day could not possibly make a difference?

"Because when people look back on the history of this time, at what happened, they should see that we tried to do something," he said with determination. I tried to imagine this awful time as a moment in the past, after the world had restored order, but found that I could not. "We can't sit here and wait for the outside world to do nothing while thousands die." His eyes grew dark and stormy. "It's so much worse than everyone thinks, Ella. Thousands upon thousands of people have been arrested and imprisoned in labor camps."

"You're talking about the Jews." I saw Sadie's face in my mind.

"Mostly, yes. But it isn't just them. They've arrested priests and professors and Roma and homosexuals." My heart cried out, thinking of Maciej. Surely things couldn't be that bad in Paris as well. But once I had thought the same about Kraków, and after all of the horrible things I'd witnessed these past few months, I knew that nowhere was safe. Krys continued, "They aren't really just being sent to labor camps, like the Germans say. They're being shot in quarries and forests, or sent to death camps right here in Poland where they are being killed in large numbers with gas." I inhaled sharply. I'd seen the cruelty with my own eyes when I witnessed the woman jumping from the bridge with her own children, heard about the camps from one of the Germans at Ana Lucia's lunch. But that had not prepared me for the horrors Krys now shared.

"But surely the Allies will stop them." For so long, we had heard about the advancing armies from the east and south, racing to our aid. *Just hold on*; that had been the message.

He shook his head. "They're trying. But we need help here faster than they can manage. So many die while we wait. And what if they don't succeed?" The thought, which had come to me more than once in the dark hours of the night, was more than I could bear. I could not imagine living this way forever.

"We have to do something," he finished. A steely look formed in his azure blue eyes and I could see that he had found his true purpose, a newfound strength. I hated how it had taken him from me, but I knew that he was doing the work he was meant to do. I looked up at Krys with admiration. He would not have let Miriam and the other Jewish students be taken from his class. He would have done something to help the woman on the bridge. And he would help Sadie now. I wanted to tell him about her, but the words stuck in my throat.

"Now are you going to tell me what you were doing in this neighborhood again?" he asked, changing the subject back to me without warning.

I hesitated. He had confided so much. I should be honest with him as he had been with me. But Sadie's secret was not mine to tell. "Just running an errand," I insisted. He looked at me skeptically and I could feel the distance grow between us once more.

"Now that you know about my work, you could help us," he said.

"Me?" I was surprised.

"Yes. Women are very useful to the Home Army because they can act as couriers and go more places without suspicion. There are errands in the city and beyond. Or we might be able to use Ana Lucia's closeness to the Germans to get information for the Home Army. You could make a real difference, Ella." I was flattered that Krys might think of me that way.

"You said it was too dangerous."

"It is dangerous," he admitted. "That's why I tried to keep away from you and not tell you about my work. But you know now. And the Home Army needs help more than ever. Perhaps we could work together," he added. "What do you say?"

I desperately wanted to say yes, to be in his life once more. But something held me back. I wasn't brave, like Krys. Part of me was afraid. Slipping some food to help someone in hiding was one thing, but risking my life for the Home Army quite another. I didn't dare risk my stepmother's wrath, any more so than I already was by going to see Sadie. "I can't," I said finally. "I wish I could. I'm sorry."

Krys' face fell. "Me, too. I understand how terrifying this all must sound. Still, I thought you would say yes. I thought that you were different." I *was* different now, I wanted to say, with secrets of my own. But I could not explain without betraying Sadie. I felt the distance rise up and solidify between us again like an iceberg, the moment of closeness gone. "It's all dangerous, Ella." His words were pointed and I wondered if he knew about Sadie after all. "We might as well stand up and be counted." I did not answer. "I should be going," he said.

"Goodbye, Krys," I said. I wished we were not parting poorly again, but he had his reasons for what he was doing and I had mine. I turned and started up the riverbank before he could, wanting to be the one to leave.

I did not go home, though. I pretended to start for the bridge. But when I looked behind me and Krys was no longer there, I slipped away and into Dębniki once more. As I made my way toward the square, I thought about all Krys had told me. He had found his purpose, but in a world that would not let us be together. I walked a long loop around the neighborhood and then doubled back to the alleyway, checking to make sure that Krys had not followed me and that the Germans had gone. Then, despite everything that had happened, I returned to the grate.

It was more than an hour past when Sadie and I usually met. Yet miraculously, she was there, waiting for me. "Hello," I said brightly. For all that had happened that day, I was still glad to see her. Then, taking in her solemn face, my concern grew. "Are you all right?"

"Yes, fine. Only you can't come here again," she said, and I knew then she had seen the Germans and heard our exchange. "It's too dangerous, you coming to the grate in the middle of the day with so many people around. Someone will see you."

"Yes," I agreed. She was right. Standing over the sewer grate and talking to Sadie in broad daylight was too risky for both of us. Even if I had not encountered the Germans, people could see me looking down and they might even notice Sadie if they passed by too closely. I recalled what Krys had said about the awful things that were being done to the Jews. Sadie's very life depended upon her remaining hidden and out of sight.

A flicker of sadness crossed her face. "Your visits are just such a bright spot."

"I know. I like coming, too. But it's hardly worth it if I cause you harm." She looked as if she wanted to disagree, but could not. No, I couldn't come here anymore, but I couldn't abandon her either. There had to be another way. I thought of the sewer, which Sadie had once described as a labyrinth of tunnels. It ran beneath the entirety of the neighborhoods that lined the southern bank of the river. Surely there had to be another place where it came to the surface that we could meet.

"We have to find somewhere else, close to the river, maybe?"

Sadie's face brightened as a light seemed to dawn in her eyes.

"There is," she said. "I found it when Saul and I were walking."
She had not mentioned Saul before and I wondered who he was.
I could tell from the way she said his name that she was fond of
him. "There's a ledge that I can climb that will bring me out on
the riverbank. I'm not quite sure of the specific location, but it
is in Podgórze, close to where the ghetto was located."

"I will find it," I promised. "Let's try meeting there next
time." My spirits brightened at the prospect of an alternative
place to meet, and a way not to stop coming to see Sadie. She
was not just some poor girl I was trying to help anymore. At
some point, we had become friends.

"It might not be safe for you there either," she fretted.

"For me? I'm worried that it might not be safe for you." We
laughed softly at the irony. "Aren't you afraid?" I asked, serious
now. The police nearly discovering the grate had made the peril
of her situation all the more real. "I mean, not just about coming to the grate, but all of it, living in the sewer…"

"And worrying that, at any time, I might get caught?" she
asked, finishing the sentence that I could not. I nodded. "Yes,
of course. But what choice do I have? To live with fear or grief
or any emotion constantly would be paralyzing. So I put one
foot in front of the other and I breathe and I string the days together. It isn't enough," she continued, gaining force behind
her words. "I want more for my life. But this is the reality."
Her face saddened.

"For now," I added, admiring her courage. I regretted my
question, which seemed to make her feel worse, and quickly
changed the subject. "We will try the other grate next time."

"I don't know if it's a good idea," Sadie said, her brow wrin-
kling, seeming to second-guess her own suggestion. "When Saul
and I found the other grate, there were Germans with dogs near
the river. But it's a quieter spot, and if you wait until there are
no people around, it may be possible."

"I'll manage it," I said, not at all sure how. The riverbank was open, exposed. We couldn't possibly meet there during the day when my actions could be easily seen. "Why don't we try meeting at night instead?"

"Do you think it will be any safer?" she asked doubtfully.

"Maybe." I was not at all sure that was true. I would have to sneak out and break curfew. But I had to try something. "I'll have to wait until next Saturday," I said, thinking of Ana Lucia. Slipping out at night would not be easy and I needed to go when Ana Lucia was either out or entertaining, and would sleep heavily from the alcohol. "Ten o'clock?" I asked.

She nodded somberly. "That should work."

"I will be there, trust me."

"I do," she said solemnly. "Wait for twenty minutes," she said. "If you don't see me, it means that it wasn't safe to come." None of this was safe, I realized, for her or for me. Fear rose up in me then. I wanted to tell her that it was a bad idea, that we couldn't possibly do it.

But it was too late. "I will meet you there," Sadie said, her eyes brimming with hope.

"Be careful," I added, my concern for her deeper now. A moment later, she disappeared into the sewer. I started for home, overwhelmed. Now seeing Sadie meant sneaking out at night and breaking curfew—not to mention the fact that today, I had very nearly been caught. How had all of this happened? Once I had kept my head low and planned to ride out the war without being seen. Now life was getting more dangerous by the day and there was no going back. I couldn't abandon her now.

12

Sadie

After leaving Ella, I started back toward the chamber. Earlier, after the Germans had appeared on the street, I thought that she might not be able to come and see me at all anymore. She was intent on trying at the new location, though. She had not given up on me—and for that I was grateful.

As I rounded the corner, there was a sudden clattering. Someone was in the tunnel. I leapt back. Then I recognized Pawel's familiar voice. I relaxed slightly. It was Sunday, not Pawel's usual day to come see us, but occasionally he visited unannounced, bringing an unexpected bounty of apples or cheese that he had found. Who was he talking to? I wondered. I heard an unfamiliar voice demanding answers, followed by Pawel trying to explain.

I peered around the corner. Pawel was surrounded by three Polish policemen. My heart stopped. They had found him coming into the sewer to help us.

"Where are you going with that food?" one of the officers asked.

"It is just my lunch," Pawel insisted, though the size of the satchel he carried made that impossible. The policemen kept barking questions, but Pawel refused to answer. I wanted to go help him, but that would only make things worse. He saw me over the shoulders of the police and his eyes went wide before he signaled silently for me to get away.

I jumped back around the corner. I needed to run to the chamber to warn the others, but there was no way to slip past the police and I didn't dare risk detection. Instead, I pressed into a crack in the wall, willing myself to become invisible.

The police continued interrogating Pawel and I heard a sickening sound as one of them struck him. He would not give us up, I realized. I was seized with the urge to race to him, to protect him as he did us. There was a scuffling sound, followed by Pawel's cry of protest as the police started to drag him from the tunnel. I knew in that moment we would never see him again. I bit my lip, struggling not to cry out.

As the police forced Pawel to go with them, the satchel of food he had been carrying fell from his hands into the river with a splash. I did not know if the police had taken it from him, or if Pawel, in his desperation to help us, had thrown the bag, hoping it might land close to me. But it was in the water now, floating on the current, contents scattering. I wanted to reach for the bag, but even if I dared step from my hiding place, it was too far gone to catch. I watched with a sinking feeling as the last potato disappeared around a corner.

After the tunnel went silent, I stood motionless in my hiding place, overcome with sadness. My heart screamed, as it had the night Papa had drowned. Pawel, our savior, had been arrested. Dread rose in me then, mixing with my sorrow. Pawel had not just given us sanctuary, but had brought the food that sustained us. We could not possibly survive without him.

Devastated, I returned to the chamber. I considered not telling the others the terrible news at all to spare Mama from losing even further hope. But I could not hide the fact that Pawel would not be coming with food again. "Pawel was arrested!" I cried. Bubbe, who had been napping in the far corner of the chamber, stirred.

Mama looked aghast. "Are you certain?"

I nodded. "In the tunnel, just now. I saw it with my own eyes."

Pan Rosenberg stood from the place where he had been sitting. "There are Germans in the tunnel?" His face paled.

"It was the police actually, not the Germans."

My clarification was of little comfort. "They've come for us. Pawel warned us this might happen."

"They've left," I said, trying to soothe him despite my own worry. "They don't know about us."

"But they might find out," he panicked, eyes darting back and forth. "We have to go, now, before they come back." His voice rose higher, nearly cracking.

"Pawel won't tell anyone about us, Papa," Saul said, his voice echoing with doubt. There was fear in his eyes like I had never seen before.

"I'm sure he won't," Mama agreed quickly.

"Pawel did not give us up," I confirmed. "We are safe here." Pan Rosenberg's entire body sagged with relief. But over his shoulder, Saul's eyes met mine, questioning if that was really true. Pawel was loyal to us and strong. But who knew what the Nazis might do to him, or whether or not he would break?

"We will have no food." Bubbe, whom I had not known was listening, bolted upright on her bed. Though her voice was not as panicked as her son's, her eyes were wide with worry. "Without Pawel, how are we to survive?" Her question hung unanswered in the air among us.

The police did not return. But as the next few days wore on, our uneasiness grew. Even if we were still safe here, our only source of food was gone. We ate even less than usual. We shared the crumbs as if they were a feast, each person careful not to take more than his or her share.

But despite our efforts to conserve, three days after Pawel was arrested, the last of our food was finished. "What are we to do?" I asked.

"We will have to think of something," Mama said, trying to force the worry from her voice. "We will have to find another way to feed everyone ourselves."

"But how?" I asked.

Pan Rosenberg rubbed his fingers against his beard, thinking. "When we were in the ghetto, there was a rumor of a man in our building who kept potatoes behind a wall."

"If you tell me exactly where, I can go find it," I offered without thinking.

"Go to the street?" Mama asked with disbelief. Her expression was horrified.

"We need food, Mama. I can do it."

"Never," Mama replied with all of the force she could muster. "None of us, especially not my daughter, is leaving the sewer to look for food. We will have to think of something else."

That day wore on, and the next, we grew hungrier. We drank small drips of water to ease our stomach pains. I even imagined the tiny baby in Mama's womb, crying silently as he or she waited in vain for nourishment that did not come.

Another night fell with no food. Saul and I started from the chamber, though I was nearly too weak with hunger to stay up and read. "My father is right," he said when we neared the annex. "There is food hidden in the ghetto cellar. Not just potatoes, but cured meats. You remember how in the ghetto they sometimes gave us dried pork?" I nodded. It was the Germans' idea of a cruel joke, giving the Jews food that was not kosher. "We couldn't eat it, but I stored it away, just in case of an emergency. There are a few sacks of potatoes there, too, that might be salvageable. It is in the apartment building where we lived at Lwowska Street, number twelve, behind the basement wall. If only there was a way to get to it."

"Maybe my friend Ella can help find it," I said, before I could think better of it or stop myself.

"The girl on the street? You've continued to speak with her?" He sounded horrified. I did not answer. "But, Sadie, you promised me."

"I know." I searched for a justification for what I had done, but found none. "I'm sorry. If I ask, perhaps she can help get the food."

"I don't like it. We can't trust her."

"I think we can. She has known about me for weeks and hasn't told anyone. Why would she betray us now?" He did not answer. I knew he would agree, or see Ella as a friend like I did. "Anyway, there's really no other choice."

"All right," Saul relented. "If I tell you exactly where the food is hidden, you can send her."

I considered the idea. I tried to picture Ella, who had spent most of her life in the posh city center, attempting to navigate the ruins of the liquidated ghetto. She would never be able to manage it. "She would stick out," I said. "And she wouldn't know her way around. If I could get onto the street, I could go myself."

Saul's eyes widened. "Sadie, you can't be serious." The sewer was our only hope to stay alive. To consider going to the street was to risk capture and death.

"It's the only way," I said.

"I could go," Saul offered. Yet even as he said it, we both knew that it was impossible. With his yarmulke and beard, he would be detected immediately. I loved him for offering, but he couldn't possibly go. I was our only hope.

Still, he would not hear of it. "Promise me you won't go,"

he said, his voice somewhere between a command and a plea. I wondered why he would trust my word when I had broken it by talking to Ella. His brow furrowed deep with concern. "I can't let anything happen to you." He reached up and touched my cheek. I saw then how his feelings for me had grown, the depth of affection in his eyes. We had known each other such a short time; it hardly seemed possible that we had grown so close. But life seemed to move at a different speed during the war, especially here, when any moment might be our last. Everything was intensified.

I nodded. Saul leaned back, seemingly satisfied by my promise. But my mind still worked. I knew every bit how dangerous it would be to go to the street. If I didn't, though, we were all going to die, Mama, my unborn sibling, the Rosenbergs and me. There was no other choice.

The next night, I waited anxiously, planning to slip from the chamber. I did not tell Saul, or anyone else, that I was going to see Ella. The skies beyond the grate had been gray earlier and I hoped it would be too cloudy and there would not be enough light for Saul to go read at the annex and invite me to go with him. But as the others were getting ready for bed, he approached me. "Do you want to come with me?" He sought me out more often these days for company, sometimes sharing stories from his youth as we made our way through the tunnels, other nights just ambling beside me in thoughtful silence.

The invitation, which I normally would have welcomed, filled me now with dread. "I'd love to, but I'm exhausted," I said, hating that I had to lie to him. But it was not entirely untrue; we all had less energy from not eating.

Surprise, then disappointment, crossed his face. "Then I won't go either."

Inwardly, I exhaled. "Tomorrow night?"

"Gladly." Saul touched the brim of his hat and retreated to his side of the chamber. Watching him go, I felt a pang of regret. I looked forward to our walks and it hurt to say no and reject him now.

I waited until the others were asleep. Mama tossed and turned restlessly, made uncomfortable by her pregnancy, and I feared that by the time she fell asleep it might be too late. At last when her movements stilled and breathing went to its heavy, even snore, I crept from the chamber.

I walked down the tunnel, feeling my way in the darkness. The path to the exit Saul and I had found was the farthest I had traveled through the pipes since the night we arrived. As I made my way through the underground crypt alone, silent but for the running of the sewer water, it seemed I might be apprehended at any second. My skin prickled. I saw ghosts of my father, then Pawel. They did not haunt me, though, but rather seemed to guide me, creating faint light in the tunnel just ahead.

At last I reached the basin Saul and I had found. The pipe leading to the street sat high on the far side. There was no way to hoist myself up, I realized. Last time Saul had helped me, but I had not considered how I would be able to manage the high wall to the pipe without him to boost me up this time. I scrambled down into the basin. My eyes had adjusted now, and in the semidarkness, I could make out some boards on the ground. I collected them and made a pile against the wall I needed to climb, hoping that it would be enough. I reached high above me for the pipe. I missed and fell, sending the boards scattering. I looked up. There was simply no way for me to reach the pipe on my own. But if I didn't get up there, I would not see Ella, nor be able to get the food we needed. I restacked the boards and tried to heave myself up the wall with sheer force and determination. My limbs were weak from hunger and it seemed impossible. I took a deep breath and summoned every last ounce of strength I had as I leapt for the top. My hands grasped the edge of the pipe and I pulled myself up, scraping my knees against the rough metal edge.

I crawled through the pipe and, a few seconds later, reached the end. I peered through the grate here that was rectangular and bigger than the one had been on the street in Dębniki. I did not see Ella. I wondered if she had been unable to get out. Perhaps she might not show at all. My anxiety rose. When we had planned to meet here, I had simply hoped to see her. But now, with Pawel and our food supply gone, I needed her help. I could not get out of the sewer pipe without her. Without the food stores Saul had mentioned, we would all starve.

At last, I heard footsteps above the grate, growing louder. I slipped back into the shadows, in case it was someone else. But a minute later, Ella appeared.

Through the grate, I could see Ella's face, her expression expectant and grave as she searched for me. "I'm here," I whispered.

Ella smiled. "You managed it!" I moved closer. The space beneath the grate was shallow and I had to half sit, half lie down just to fit in it. "It worked," I said.

My satisfaction faded as I looked in her hands to see if she had any food, but saw none. "I had to sneak out quickly," she said, reading my thoughts. "So I couldn't go to the kitchen. I'm sorry."

"It's no matter," I replied, though my empty stomach burned.

"How are you?" she asked.

I paused uncertainly. I often worried that if I told Ella of my troubles, she would find me boring and not want to come see me anymore. But my hunger loomed, too large and menacing to deny. "Honestly, not well. We have nothing left to eat. The sewer worker who had been helping us was arrested." I saw concern flash over her face, as if realizing fully for the first time the dangers she might face as a consequence of helping me. "I need to find more food." I hated to even ask. She had done so much for us.

"I'll see what I can do to get more," Ella replied quickly.

"No, no, that's not what I meant. You've given me so much

and I don't mean to sound ungrateful. But there are five of us in the sewer. We need to find a larger store of food to hold us over until…" I faltered, not sure what we were holding on for: Pawel to come back to us? The war to end? Neither seemed terribly likely at the moment. "Until things change," I finished weakly.

"I don't have anything," she said. "If you can give me a few days, I'll try some of the markets outside the city."

In my mind I saw Mama, who had been so weak with hunger that she had nearly fainted earlier. "I'm sorry, but that won't be soon enough," I said bluntly. "That is, I really appreciate all that you have done, but if we wait longer to find food, it might be too late. We're out of time."

"What is it that you want me to do?"

"I know of some food left in the ghetto. I need to get to it."

"If you tell me where, I'll go look," she said without hesitation. Despite the danger of what I was proposing, she was willing to try.

"I can't just tell you. It will be hard to find and dangerous for you to go on your own." I took a deep breath, bracing for the audacity of what I was about to say. "I need to find it myself and I need your help getting out of here so I can do it."

"When?"

I swallowed. "Now."

She paused. "When we first met, you said it was too dangerous for you to be on the street."

"It is. Still, we need food and if there is a chance that I can get it, I must try. There's no other choice." The risk of being arrested was real. But the threat of starvation felt so much worse right now. "Please, help me get out and do this."

I expected her to say no. But she nodded solemnly, willing to do what I asked. A second later, she began tugging at the sewer grate. It stuck, seemingly rusted shut. My heart sank. I would not be able to get out this way. I began pushing as she pulled. At last, the grate released. Ella lifted it with effort and heaved it back. Then she reached for me, her hand floundering in the dark space between us. Our fingers locked, touching for the first time, and she tugged on me with more strength than I would have thought she possessed. I unfolded myself and straightened, freed from my hiding spot.

Just like that, I was out of the sewer.

I inhaled deeply, drinking in the air in great gulps and it was so fresh and cold it burned my lungs on the way down. We were standing on a gentle slope of grass that led down to the embankment by the river. My eyes traveled immediately to the night sky, a carpet of stars above Wawel Cathedral. It was the first time in months that I had seen the view I had shared dozens of times with my father as a child on our walks, which let us see so much more than we could from the narrow windows of our apartment. Once I had taken for granted that the stars would always be there. Then they had been stolen from me, as surely as Papa had. I looked up now, drinking in the magical view, even more brilliant than I had remembered.

I was out of the sewer. I wanted to dance, to run, to scream. Of course, I did not. We were standing on a bit of riverbank close to the concrete embankment that led up to the street. Though deserted, the riverbank was exposed. We might be seen by the Germans or the police at any moment. "We can't stay here," I said.

"No," Ella agreed.

I stood upright beside her, noticing for the first time how much taller than me she was. She was staring at me, and I wondered if it was my bedraggled appearance. "What is it?" I asked.

"It's just so strange to see you at eye level," she replied, and we both laughed softly. "You should wipe the dirt from your face," she added more seriously. She looked around for something I could use and, finding nothing, pulled off her fine silk scarf and handed it to me. I could feel my own filth seeping through and soiling her scarf. She did not complain. I handed it back, wishing I had a way to wash it before I returned it to her. She used the edge of it to wipe clean a spot on my cheek that I had missed. Then she wrapped the scarf loosely around my head like a shawl. "There you go." She smiled brightly, as though that had fixed everything.

"Thank you." A wave of gratitude washed over me, and impulsively, I hugged her. I thought she might pull back, repulsed by my smell. But she did not. Instead, she squeezed me back tighter. We stood embracing, not moving, for several seconds.

When we pulled apart, my necklace caught on the top button of her dress. I disentangled it carefully. "What's that?" she asked, pointing to the charm.

"It was my father's."

"It's lovely. But what does it mean?"

I traced my finger over the Hebrew letters, gold and glittering in the moonlight. My father had done this when I was a child as he explained the meaning and I could almost feel his hand on mine now, guiding me. "*Chai*. It stands for life."

"It's beautiful. But you'll have to take it off." I recalled Saul warning me about the necklace, too. In the sewer, I could disregard his concerns. But wearing it up here on the street and revealing that I was Jewish could mean detection and death. I unclasped the necklace and put it in my pocket.

"Now come," Ella said.

We started east along the riverbank toward Podgórze, the neighborhood where the ghetto had been located. The streets looked bigger than I remembered and everything seemed more ominous and menacing. I should not be here. I was seized with the urge to crawl back into the ground.

We made our way toward the ghetto, taking the alleys and hugging the shadows of the buildings. I cringed at the sound of our shoes scratching too loudly against the cobblestones. Even being out at this hour was a crime, and if seen, we would be detained and questioned. I would never see my mother again. I walked tentatively, afraid that each step might be my last. Ella, though, moved through the streets with a surety that I envied. Resentment rose up in me unexpectedly. This was my city as much as hers, or at least it had been. But now I was an outsider, visiting only by her good graces. I pushed down the feeling. The only thing that mattered now was finding the food. I thought of the others back in the sewer who were counting on me, what would happen to them if I failed to find food or did not return.

We soon reached the Rynek Podgórski, the neighborhood's main market square, which sat just outside the ghetto walls. It was deserted now except for a few rats searching the trash bins for food. We skirted the edge of St. Joseph's, the immense neo-Gothic church at the head of the square, and reached the ghetto wall. Although there was no one to keep inside anymore, the ghetto gates were still closed. We followed the perimeter of the high brick wall until we found a section that had been knocked down, then stepped gingerly over stones and rubble to get inside. The devastation was so much worse than I had heard about or realized from below, building after building burned out, the windows smashed, just shells of where people had once lived. I looked at Ella, who had stopped walking. I knew the ghetto all too well, but this was the first time that she was seeing it and her face was twisted with dismay as she saw the awful way we had lived—and how it had all ended.

"Come," I said, urging her onward. Now I had to lead the way, weaving through the ghetto streets toward the house on Lwowska Street that Saul had told me about. The air was tinged with coal and something more acrid, perhaps the smell of garbage burning. At the corner of Józefińska Street, I paused, looking in the direction of the building where we had once lived. The ghetto had not been my home—we had been forced there, and before the sewer, it was the worst place I had ever known. Still, this was the last place my parents and I had really been together, and I found myself assaulted by my memories and a kind of nostalgia I had not expected. More than a small piece of me wanted to go and see our apartment once more.

But there was no time. We pressed onward. Amidst the destruction, there were several houses that had been refurbished, with new glass in the once-broken windows or, in a few cases, newspaper held in place with tar to cover the gap. The ghetto was inhabited, I realized with surprise. Not by Jews anymore, but most likely lower-class Poles, who had either been assigned the housing by the General Government or taken the vacant residences for themselves. Part of me wanted to be angry at them. These were not wealthy Poles exploiting the property of Jews for their own gain, though, but rather local people just seeing an opportunity and doing what they needed to and providing for their families. No one who had a choice would have come to live here.

Still, they would surely tell the police if they saw us. I considered turning back. We had expected the ghetto to be deserted. It wasn't safe for us to be here. But we needed the food. The address Saul had given me might be occupied now as well, I thought as we turned onto Lwowska Street. I didn't know how we would look for the food if that was the case.

As we neared number twelve, I could see the windows were still punched out and the walls charred by a fire I prayed had not destroyed the food stores in the basement. Though Saul had told me that he and his father had come to the ghetto briefly after leaving their village, I had not pictured him living here, just blocks from me, until now. I took in the house, which was so much smaller and more run-down than the building my parents and I had occupied, imagining how they had managed with a half-dozen other families, crowded into shared rooms.

I tried the front door. Despite the decimated condition of the house, it was locked. I was afraid we would have to navigate the broken glass and climb through one of the windows. "Let's go around back and look for a cellar door," Ella suggested. We slipped through an alleyway between the houses, crouching low so no one would see us. In the rear, we found a cellar door and pried it open. I crept down the ladder into the cellar first, praying the rotted rungs would hold. Ella followed. I stopped, caught off guard by the dirty, too-close ghetto smell that had filled my lungs all of the months we were here, and which lingered now still. After breathing the stench of the sewer for so long, it was almost pleasant by comparison.

Hurriedly, we walked to the cellar wall that Saul had told me about and felt for the hidden compartment. There was a panel that slid back, just as he promised, revealing a cavernous empty space, meant for hiding things. Only the place he had described was empty.

The food he had promised was not there.

13

Ella

Standing beside Sadie and looking down into the empty space where the food should have been, my heart sank. "I'm sorry," I said, feeling the weight of her disappointment wash over us. Sadie did not answer. She stood still, her eyes sad and hollow.

"We should go," I said after a few minutes had passed. It wasn't safe for us to linger in the ghetto building.

Sadie shook her head. "It has to be here. I can't go back without it."

What now? My mind raced. "We can look around," I said, although I really had no idea where. Despite the war, Ana Lucia did not keep extra food stores in the house because she feared attracting mice. Instead, she trusted that her money and contacts would always allow us to have enough to eat. So I could not steal what Sadie needed from her. Krys appeared in my mind. We had not parted well and I was unsure he would help me. But he was my only option and deep down I knew that he would not refuse me if there were something he could do. "I have a friend who might be able to help." I instantly regretted my offer. I had no reason to think he could manage to find food in such a short amount of time. But I had to try.

Krys had said he was staying in a flat above the café, I recalled. "Come with me." We slipped from the cellar of the apartment building, through the charred rubble. As we made our way among the ruins that had once been the ghetto, I walked faster, wanting to get Sadie away from her painful memories of this place.

I led her along the riverbank away from Podgórze in the direction of Dębniki. Though I was unfamiliar with the neighborhoods that blended without a clear border, I knew that Dębniki was just a few kilometers to the west of Podgórze along the industrial southern banks of the Wisła. As we neared Dębniki, we turned away from the riverbank and climbed the road toward Barska Street and the café. I looked up at the apartments above the café, wondering how I could figure out which one was Krys'. It was after eleven and the café was supposed to be long since closed for the curfew. But behind the smudged glass window, I could see that a few patrons still lingered. I did not see Krys, but perhaps if I asked, someone might know where to find him.

I started for the door. Then, looking at Sadie, I stopped again. She could not go inside the café. Her soiled clothes and emaciated, ghost-pale appearance would surely attract attention. There was an arched passageway between the café and the adjacent building leading from the street to the alley behind. I led Sadie there and hid her behind some trash cans. "You need to wait here."

"You're leaving me?" She looked terrified.

I patted her hand. "I'll be just a few minutes." Before she could protest, I walked from the alleyway into the café, which was deserted except for a table of older men playing cards to the rear. As my eyes adjusted to the dim lighting, I recognized a familiar figure behind the bar. I stopped short. It was the woman

I'd seen Krys with the day I had found him here. My insides recoiled and I was seized with the urge to turn and leave. But I had to find Krys.

I walked toward her with determination. "Hello, I'm looking for Krys Lewakowski," I said bluntly, waiting for a sign of recognition on her face. But her expression remained unchanged. "I saw you together," I added. "I know you know him. He said he is staying here."

"He isn't here," she replied coldly.

"I need to find him. It's important." She stared at me for a beat, then turned and disappeared into the back of the café. He wasn't here, I realized with disappointment. I contemplated what to do next, whether to try his parents' house at such a late hour.

"Ella?" Krys appeared suddenly through the door behind the bar. The woman had been lying; he was here. He hurried toward me. "What is it? Is everything all right?" I had worried that he might still be angry from our last meeting. But his expression was a mixture of surprise and concern.

"Yes… That is, no." I paused, trying to figure out the best way to tell him the secret I'd been keeping. I lowered my voice. "When they cleared the ghetto, some of the Jews managed to escape and go into hiding."

He nodded. "I've heard rumors of such things."

"A few escaped to the sewer."

"The sewer? But even if that were possible, where would they go?"

"They didn't go anywhere. That is, they're still in the sewer, close to the Dębniki market. I've been helping one of them, a girl."

His eyes widened. "So that's why I kept seeing you there?"

"Yes. But now their main source of food is gone. I need to help her find some food to take back to the others."

Remembering how I had refused to help him with his work

for the Home Army, I thought he might say no. "How many people are with her?"

"Four I think." I watched as he processed the information. "I'm sorry I didn't tell you sooner." I expected him to be angry with me. He ran his hand along the back of his head, seeming to think.

"When do you need it?"

"Tonight. Can you help?"

"I don't know. There's so little food now in the city, Ella."

I nodded, acknowledging the truth of what he said. The faces of the people at the market seemed more gaunt by the day as they left with their baskets still largely empty. "Surely through your army contacts, you can manage to find something."

"I'll try, but it is very difficult. The Home Army is complicated. It's big and it's got a lot of people with different aims. There is this one black marketeer, Korsarz, who sometimes helps the Polish Army get what it needs."

"Korsarz," I repeated the code name, which in Polish meant pirate. "Do you think he can help?"

Krys shook his head grimly. "I don't know, but I'd rather not find out. He's an unscrupulous character and he'll deal with anyone—including the Germans—for a price."

"If it's a question of money…" I began, picturing Ana Lucia's grand belongings and wondering which I could steal that would be most easily pawned for cash.

"It isn't that. Korsarz has done some awful things and I won't deal with him, at least not if I can help it. I'll try to find another way. I need to reach out to my contacts and find a way to get extra food without attracting attention. It will take a few days, a week at most."

My shoulders slumped. "We don't have that kind of time. They need food now and I need to get Sadie back to the sewer." It was the first time I shared her name and it felt somehow vulnerable.

"She's out?" I nodded. Alarm crossed his face. "Where is she?"

"I hid her in the alleyway."

"Do you want me to get her out of Kraków?"

I considered the idea. Sadie was out of the sewer now, and this could be her only chance for freedom. The offer was a big one, I knew. Getting a Jew out of Kraków now would not be easy and I was grateful to Krys for suggesting it. But I knew Sadie would never accept. "I'll ask her, but I doubt she'll agree. Her mother is down in the sewer. She has to go back. Either way, she won't abandon the others to starve. I just need to get her food."

"Just? I wish it were that simple."

"If you can't do it, I understand." I struggled to keep the disappointment from my voice. Krys didn't owe me anything anymore. "Thanks anyway." I started away, thinking about how I was going to tell Sadie I had failed her.

"Wait," he said. I turned back. "Let me see what I can do."

"Really?"

"No promises, but I'll do my best." A wave of hope and gratitude rose in me. Despite our quarrels and the difficulty finding food, Krys was willing to try. I could see his mind working, trying to figure out how to make the impossible happen. "Give me a few hours."

I looked up at the night sky, trying to calculate how much time we had. "She has to go back before daybreak."

"Where does she go underground?"

"There are concrete steps down to the river near Podgórze. About twenty feet to the east of there, you will see a sewer grate. Do you want me to come with you to get the food?"

"Yes," he said bluntly, an unmistakable note of affection in his voice. The woman who had summoned him for me was behind the bar again, and though we were too far away for her to hear our conversation, I could feel her watching us. "But I don't think that's our best plan. You go with your friend and hide her somewhere safe. I will meet you by five o'clock by the grate with whatever I have—if I can find anything at all."

Before I could thank him, he turned and walked through the door behind the bar. I started out the front door to find Sadie.

When Sadie saw me emerge from the café and step into the alleyway, she straightened from behind the garbage cans. "Any luck?" I could see her searching my arms for the food she so desperately needed. "You don't have it," she said, crestfallen.

"It's coming," I promised quickly, and her face brightened. "Or at least, my friend Krys is going to try," I corrected, not wanting to get her hopes up in case he failed.

"You told him about me? But, Ella, you promised."

"I know. I'm sorry. It was the only way. He can be trusted."

But her panic did not lessen with my reassurance. "He could tell someone. I have to go back and warn the others."

I took both of her hands in mine. "Sadie, stop. You trust me, don't you?"

"Yes, of course," she said, without hesitation.

"Then you can believe me now. Krys isn't going to say anything. He's part of the Polish Home Army," I added, betraying Krys' secret as well in my effort to reassure her. "He is fighting against the Germans. He isn't going to tell, I swear it. And he can get what you need." Or at least, I hoped he could.

The explanation seemed to calm her. "How long?"

"He needs a few hours. Let me get you back to the sewer and I will bring you the food as soon as I have it."

"All right," she said, seeming to agree. We started from the alleyway. "Wait." She stopped again. "If it's only going to be a few hours, why can't I stay out of the sewer while we wait for the food?"

"Oh, Sadie, I don't know…" I was caught off guard by her request. "That would be so dangerous."

"I know it's not a good idea, but it's been months since I was above ground. I just want to be here for a bit longer, breathe the air. I'll be careful, stay out of sight."

I hesitated, not answering right away. I could see how she drank in her freedom and was desperate to stay. "It's just so dangerous. And it might take Krys longer than a few hours."

"I'll go back before dawn," she said, almost pleading now. "Whether he has the food or not."

She watched my face as I considered it. Staying above ground was foolish. She might be caught at any time. I could see, though, how badly she needed this. I was happy to have her company, too, and not eager to have her go back so quickly. "Fine," I relented. "But not here." The Dębniki neighborhood where the café was located was not far from the former ghetto and thick with police patrols.

We started from the alleyway and toward the river. The streets were deserted and our footsteps echoed too loudly on the pavement. As we neared the bridge, I spied a police car parked by the base. "Hide!" I whispered, pulling Sadie behind the low retaining wall that ran along the riverbank. We huddled close, not moving. We were pressed so closely I could feel her heart beating against mine. I hoped the police were not setting up a checkpoint on the bridge, which would force us another way across the river. Beside me, Sadie was rigid with fear. She did not have papers to show if she was stopped; she would be arrested immediately. I wondered then if I had made a mistake giving in to her request, whether I should have insisted she go back to the sewer immediately. It was too late now. I laced my fingers with hers, determined to see her safely through the night.

Several minutes later, the police car drove away. As we rose from our hiding spot, Sadie grabbed my arm. "Where are we going?"

"My house," I said, before immediately second-guessing myself. Going there meant a long walk through the city streets after curfew, risking detection or worse. But Ana Lucia was out for the night, I recalled. She had gone to dinner with Colonel Maust at a restaurant on the far side of the city, closer to his apartment, and would not be back until the morning. My house was the best option for hiding Sadie. There was nowhere else.

Sadie stared at me in dismay. "How can we possibly?"

"It's safe," I said, forcing certainty into my voice. "I promise."

Sadie looked as though she wanted to argue further. But if she wanted to remain above ground while Krys went for the food, there was really no other choice.

As we crossed the bridge toward the city center and my house, Sadie looked upward, staring so intently that she forgot to look where she was walking and nearly stumbled. Taking her arm so she would not fall, I followed her gaze. At first I thought she was trying to see Wawel Castle, which sat high on its hill, partly obscured by the riverbed. But her neck was craned beyond that, her eyes locked on the night sky. "They look almost blue to-night," she said, her voice filled with marvel.

I remembered then how on the day we met, one of the very first things she asked me was about the stars. "Which constellations can you see?"

"There," she said eagerly, pointing to the north. "That's Ursa Major, or the great bear. My father used to say as long as you could find it, you would never be lost." Her words spilled out in a great tumble. She spun around. "And over there, that long triangle with a tail is called the Chamaeleon." I tried to follow her finger as she drew lines in the air, connecting the stars, but I could not see the images.

We walked swiftly from the bridge toward the Old Town. Sadie did not speak, but as we neared the city center, I could see her drinking in the familiar streets, which had been hidden from her view for months.

Several minutes later, we turned onto Kanonicza Street. "You live here?" Sadie asked with disbelief as I led her around the back of the house.

"Yes." I saw our house from Sadie's eyes then, realizing how grand it must look after the awful places she had lived. For a second, I wondered if she might resent me for it. But there was no time to worry. I put my finger to my lips to signal that she should be quiet so the neighbors would not hear us. At the back of the house, I unlocked the door and let her inside.

I started up the servants' staircase, but behind me, Sadie stopped. "Ella, it isn't safe for me to be here," she whispered, too loudly.

"My stepmother is out for the evening," I reassured her, urging her up one flight of stairs and then two more to the garret.

"Have a seat," I said. Sadie hesitated, looking awkwardly around my room, and I realized she did not want to stain anything with her dirty clothes. I laid a throw blanket across the soft chair where I liked to draw and read. "There." I noticed then how pale and tired she looked. "When was the last time you ate?" She did not answer, and I wondered whether she could not remember or did not want to say. "I'll be right back." I scampered back down the stairs to the kitchen and pulled a plate of meat and cheese from the icebox, too rushed now to care if Hanna noticed them missing, and carried them back upstairs.

Sadie had moved the chair close to the window and was looking at the sky once more. "You have a lovely room," she remarked. "It's the view I admire the most. You paint?" she asked, noticing my art supplies in the corner. A canvas sat propped up against the wall, a picture of the city skyline I had started working on some time ago but had not finished.

I shrugged. "A bit." Embarrassed, I tried to block the canvas from view, but she moved closer to see it. "That's wonderful, Ella. You've got real talent."

"It's so hard to think about art with the war now. I've sort of given up."

"Oh, you shouldn't! You should paint now more than ever.

You mustn't let the war steal your dreams." A sad look crossed her face. "But who am I to talk?"

"What do you want to be?"

"A doctor."

"Not an astronomer?" I teased, remembering how captivated she was by the stars.

"I like astronomy, all of the sciences, really," she answered earnestly. "But it's healing people that interests me the most, which is why I wanted to be a doctor. I still do." She looked at me unblinkingly. "If I can find somewhere to study after the war." I was awed by the scope of her dreams, unmuted by all that had happened.

"You will," I said, wanting to encourage her ambitions as much as she had mine. I set the plate of food on the low table beside the chair. "For you."

She did not take any, but stared at the plate. "That's very nice china."

I considered the flower-edged dish for the first time. It was one of our everyday plates and I had never given it a second thought. Seeing it through Sadie's eyes now, I remembered that the plate was part of a set my mother had gotten as a wedding gift from her parents—a connection to a lost world. "You should eat," I said.

Still, Sadie did not. "The others… I should take this back to the sewer and share it," she said guiltily.

"There will be more for them. You are going to need your strength to carry food back. Eat," I urged.

Reluctantly, she took a piece of cheese and put it in her mouth. "Thank you," she said as I handed her more food. She turned toward the portrait on my desk, my parents, siblings and me by the seashore. "Your family?"

I nodded and pointed to the baby in my mother's arms. "That's me. And that," I added, pointing to Maciej, "is my brother, who lives in Paris. I'm hoping to go live with him."

"You're leaving?" Her voice was tinged with a note of sadness and surprise.

"Not now," I said quickly. "Maybe after the war."

Sadie reached out and pulled another photo from behind my
family portrait. "That's Krys, yes?" I nodded. I had meant to
put away the photo of Krys in his army uniform, taken just before he left for the war.

"We were almost engaged before the war. He left to fight,
and when he came back, he didn't want me anymore." Though
Krys had told me about the real reason he had stayed away, the
rejection still stung.

"I'm sorry," Sadie said, putting her hand on mine. It felt silly,
pathetic even, to have her comfort me when she was the one
who was suffering. But it was the first time I'd really been able
to confide my feelings in anyone since it had all happened. "I'm
sure that can't be true," she added.

"He says it isn't," I sniffed, seeming mollified. "He told me
he is doing some work to fight the Germans and that he must
stay away because it is dangerous."

"See? He's just trying to protect you. I could hear him on the
street that day and he sounded so concerned. When the war is
over and the danger is passed, he'll come back to you and you
can be together." We both knew that promises of life after the
war were too uncertain to mean much, but she was trying to
offer whatever comfort she could.

"I've never had a boyfriend," Sadie admitted.

"No?"

She shook her head. "Honestly, I've always been awkward and
felt more comfortable around my books than boys."

"Surely there's someone…"

"Not at all!" she protested, but I could tell by the catch in her
voice that the opposite was true.

"Saul?" I pressed, recalling the name she had mentioned.

"Yes," she admitted. "But it isn't like that."

"It is exactly like that. I can tell by your face," I teased, and we both laughed.

"No, really." Her cheeks flushed. "His family is more religious and he's a few years older and he doesn't think of me that way. It's just a crush on my part. He was engaged before the war and his fiancée was killed and he is in mourning. I'm nothing more than a friend to him. It can never be."

"Never say never."

"I'm sure he doesn't see me like that."

"You must see yourself as you want others to see you," I said, recalling Ana Lucia's words from when I was younger. It was one of the few useful things she had ever told me. I walked to the armoire and pulled out a freshly ironed dress. "Here, try this on."

"Now? Oh, Ella, I couldn't possibly! I wouldn't want to soil it."

"Then wash." She looked surprised by the suggestion. "Why not? We have time. Come, freshen up." I led her down to the bathroom on the third floor. "You can wash in there." Sadie looked longingly at the claw-foot tub. "Go on. I'll wait right here. There's time for a bath if you don't take long." I closed the door to give her privacy. A second later, I heard the water begin to run from the faucet.

As I stood outside the door, my thoughts turned back to Krys. I wondered how he would be able to get the food, prayed that he would be able to get it. I was curious, too, why he spent so much time at the café. Did it have something to do with his work or was it simply because he had a room upstairs? Or was he there so often because of the woman with the dark curls?

A few minutes later, Sadie stepped out of the bathroom, scrubbed clean and wearing the dress I had given her. It was too big and she looked a bit uncomfortable, as though she was wearing some sort of a costume. "You look beautiful," I said. She really did. Cleaned of dirt, her pale skin was luminescent. Her brown eyes were bright with happiness.

She smiled, rubbing her hands against the fabric. "I feel wonderful. Thank you."

I led her back up to my room. "Let me brush your hair," I offered, and she sat down in the chair willingly. She sat perfectly still as I styled her dark hair into a high knot and then patted her nose with powder. "There, ready for a night at the opera." We both chuckled. "You look like a different person." The words came out not at all as I intended. "That wasn't what I meant."

She smiled brightly. "I understand. It just feels so good to be clean. Of course, it won't last, once I go back."

"Don't worry about getting the dress dirty," I said. "Keep it. It's yours."

"Thank you, but I'm not just talking about the dress. All of this tonight, it's like a dream. A dream that has to end." Her time here was just a momentary reprieve from the sadness and suffering. She reached out for my hand and squeezed it.

"I'm happy to do it. It's really nice, having you here." It really was, even if in a short while she would be gone. "You still need shoes." The boots she had been wearing were nearly disintegrated from the constant wetness.

"I've been wearing them since we left the ghetto. They're too small," she acknowledged. "But I can make do."

I reached into my armoire once more, suddenly mindful of the dozens of shoes I'd cast in there over the years without a second thought. I pulled out a pair of black, patent leather shoes. "They might be too big," I fretted.

"They're perfect," Sadie said after putting them on, and whether that was true or she was just saying it to be polite, I could not tell. They were warm and dry, though, and Sadie looked at them as if she had never felt anything finer. "Thank you," she said again.

Just then, there was a commotion from below, the sound of

a door opening. My heart stopped. "What is it?" Sadie asked, seeing my expression.

I shook my head, barely able to speak over the lump that had formed in my throat. "Ana Lucia is home."

14

Ella

"My stepmother," I explained in an urgent whisper. "She's back." Her plans must have changed. And she wasn't alone, I judged, hearing a second heavier set of footsteps as they started up the stairs. I didn't mention that part, not wanting to panic Sadie.

But it was no use; Sadie's face paled with terror. "You said no one was home, that she was out for the night."

"That's what I thought. You have to hide."

"But where?"

I opened the door to my room a crack and listened. Hearing Colonel Maust's voice as well as Ana Lucia's, I shut it again just as quickly. "You must be very quiet. My stepmother has company." There was no way to avoid the truth any longer.

"Ella, is your stepmother's guest German?" Sadie whispered.

I wanted to lie, but Colonel Maust's accent was unmistakable. "Yes." My heart stopped. "You must understand, I'm not like that at all. I hate that she socializes with the Germans, in my father's house no less. I certainly didn't expect them to be here tonight. And I didn't have anywhere else to hide you."

But my explanation was of little comfort. "You shouldn't have brought me here." There was a note of accusation in Sadie's voice.

"I'm sorry. It was wrong of me. I was trying to help. I never meant to put you in any danger." I searched desperately for a place to hide her. "In here," I said, gesturing to the armoire. She stood frozen. "It's the only way. Just until they fall asleep. Then I can get you out of the house." Sadie climbed into the armoire and I covered her with some clothes.

Just then, there was a knock at the door. "Ella, is that you?" a slurred voice in the hallway called. I was flooded with alarm; Ana Lucia never ventured to the fourth floor.

"Yes, Ana Lucia." I tried to make my voice sound normal.

"I thought I heard voices."

"I was just playing the gramophone. I'll stop now."

Without saying good-night, Ana Lucia turned and stumbled down the two flights of stairs, nearly falling. I heard the door to her bedroom close. Still, I did not dare open the armoire door. Through the pipes came the awful sounds of Ana Lucia and the colonel in bed. Mortified, I prayed Sadie could not hear them in the closed armoire.

After a while, the bedroom below went silent. I waited until I was sure that they were asleep. Then I opened the armoire door and helped Sadie out. She looked angry and afraid. She opened her mouth as if to speak, but I clamped my hand over it so she would not wake Ana Lucia or her wretched guest. "Shh," I said. "Not now." I led her quickly from my room and down the back steps. The floorboards creaked, threatening to betray us with every step.

At last we reached the ground floor. "Is it time to go back?" Sadie asked as we stepped from the alley behind my house onto Kanonicza Street.

I shook my head. "We have another two hours at least." It was the middle of the night and I didn't know of another place where we could wait or hide.

"Can we walk a bit?" she asked. "I'd like to see the city one more time."

I started to say no. We should head straight toward the river and find a place to hide close to the sewer grate. Being out and about was not safe; we were out breaking curfew and would be arrested if caught. But she already knew that. "Please, Ella. I'm free just for a bit more. Who knows when I will have a chance like this again?"

I saw it then from her point of view. These were cherished moments of freedom to her, maybe the last she would have. I started toward the shadowy streets below the Rynek, assuming that she wanted to see the Old Town, planning to lead her as I always had. But Sadie caught my arm, tugging in a different direction, taking the lead and guiding me south toward Kazimierz, the neighborhood that had once been Kraków's Jewish Quarter—and her home.

Though I had passed by the outskirts of Kazimierz several times on my way to the bridge, I had not walked through the neighborhood since the start of the war. It was a cluster of narrow streets, packed with more than a dozen synagogues. Once it had bustled with Jewish shops and merchants, more Yiddish spoken on the streets than Polish. The Jews were all gone now, the buildings burned and windows broken. But the remnants were still here, Jewish writing etched on a shard of broken glass, the faint outline of a mezuzah where it had once hung on a door.

We walked the deserted streets without speaking, the silence broken only by the shards of glass that crunched beneath our feet. I watched Sadie out of the corner of my eye. Her expression grew sadder with every passing block. This was the first time she had seen what had become of her neighborhood and I wondered if she regretted coming. "We can turn back," I offered.

"Go another way." Seeing what was no longer would surely only bring her more pain. But grim and determined, she pressed on.

Sadie turned down a smaller street and stopped before a row of town houses. They did not seem to have been as badly destroyed as some we had passed. It looked as if people might live there. Sadie did not speak as she gazed up at the building, lost in memories.

"Yours?" I asked.

She nodded. "Our apartment was on the third floor." They had lived in only part of the building, I realized, not the whole house as we did. Sadie's home had been a simple one, but I could tell from the way her eyes danced with memories that it had been filled with warmth and love.

"You'll come back here," I said. I slipped my hand into hers and laced our fingers together. "After the war." Though I meant it kindly, we both knew it was a lie. The war had shattered her life into too many pieces to be put together the same way again. Whatever life held for her after the war, it wouldn't be here.

Sadie stood motionless for so long that I feared she would not leave at all. I prepared to coax her away, but she took a last look at the house and turned to me. "I'm ready," she said at last. Together we walked slowly back toward the river to Podgórze.

As we neared the bridge, I scanned the far bank for Krys. He wasn't there, of course. It was too early, more than an hour before we were supposed to meet. Still, I worried about all of the bad things that might have happened—that he had not been able to get food, that he had been arrested.

"Krys isn't here yet," I said.

"You still like him," Sadie said. "I can hear it in how you say his name."

I shrugged. "Perhaps. But we can never be together, so what does it matter?"

"Never say never," she said, flinging my own words from earlier back at me. We laughed for a moment, our voices carrying too far with the wind. "Love always matters," she added, her voice earnest now.

We rounded the corner near the bridge. Just then, there came the sound of a car engine ahead. It was a police car like the one we had seen earlier, now patrolling the riverbank. We leapt back around the corner, pressing ourselves flat against one of the buildings to stay out of sight. Beside me, Sadie trembled. I braced for our discovery, tried to think of an excuse to explain our being out at this hour. The police car snaked slowly by on the road that ran along the river.

"We can't wait here," I said when the police car had passed.

"What should we do?" Sadie asked, still shaking with fear. I considered the question. We could not go back to my house, but it wasn't safe to stay on the street. "We need to find somewhere out of sight."

"Where?" she asked.

I did not answer, but studied the row of houses that ran along the river, searching desperately for some sort of hiding place. My gaze stopped at a house that looked abandoned, with a set of steps leading up to the front door. "There," I said, pointing to the space beneath the stairs, which was empty but for a handful of crates.

Sadie followed me to the house with the stairs. As we pulled the crates out of the way, a stale odor billowed out from the crawl space. I took shallow breaths and tried not to gag, but Sadie climbed into the tiny space without hesitation, seeming not to notice the smell. I didn't know if people lived in the adjacent houses, whether they would notice us under the stairs or mind. But it was all we had and it would have to do.

I crawled in carefully and Sadie blocked the entrance with the crates to protect us, though they would not stop anyone who tried to get in. We huddled together in silence. "It's my birthday today," I realized suddenly aloud. With all that had happened, the way the days blended together, I had nearly forgotten.

Sadie sat up straighter. "Oh, Ella, happy birthday!"

It was hard to believe I had forgotten my own birthday. I was the youngest child in my family and my parents had always made a great fuss, with parties and presents and balloons, and a trip to the zoo if the weather was nice. Now there was simply no one to remember. "When is your birthday?" I asked Sadie.

"September 8. Maybe this will all be over by then and we can celebrate together."

"We shall," I said, wanting to cling to the improbable vision of the future she offered. Seemingly exhausted, Sadie leaned her head on my shoulder. She began to shiver, and I wasn't sure if it was from cold or fear or something else. I moved closer for warmth, then took off my sweater and placed it around her, pulling her close. Then warmth enveloped me, and in this most improbable of places, we slept.

Sometime later, I awakened. Sadie had turned away from me and was curled into a tiny ball.

"Sadie, wake up!" I berated myself for being so foolish as to let myself doze off. In the distance a bell chimed five. "We're late! We have to go!"

Hurriedly we climbed from the crawl space beneath the stairs and raced back toward the river. Daylight was beginning to dawn in the eastern sky as we crossed the bridge, the fine cracks of light that split the dark clouds widening and shining through. I scanned the far bank, searching for Krys at our meeting place. He was not there. I wondered if he had already come and we had missed him. It was nearly morning. Soon workers would appear along the riverbank and the chance to return Sadie beneath ground unseen would be gone. I braced myself to tell her that she would have to go back without the food. I could bring it to her later, but that would not be the same. She needed it now.

At last, I saw Krys, speeding toward us from the other direction, crossing the riverbank with great strides. "Hurry," I said to Sadie, then raced to meet him. He carried a sack in his arms, much larger than I expected.

"Just potatoes," he said, breathless from running. "That's all I could get." There was a note of apology in his voice.

"That's wonderful." Potatoes, Sadie had told me, were like gold because of how long they kept.

"This is all I can get for now. I will try to find more."

"Thank you," I said. Krys and I stood looking at one another for several seconds, feeling anew the connection we had once shared.

I turned toward Sadie, who hung back, several meters away. "It's okay," I said. "This is my friend."

"I'm Krys," he said, walking toward her and extending his hand. She did not take it. "Nice to meet you," he added. I could tell from his eyes that he was taken aback by her appearance, how thin and pale she was. I had gotten used to it, but seeing her for the first time must have been something of a shock.

"Sadie," she said, and I could see how much it took for her to trust him enough to share her name. "Thank you for the food."

"I have to go," Krys said, and I didn't know whether that was true or he was just giving us a last minute alone. He passed me the sack of potatoes and our fingers brushed. His eyes met mine.

"Thank you," I said.

"Ella, I wanted to tell you…" He faltered.

Just then, there was a clattering from beneath the bridge. I pivoted in that direction, fearful it was the police once more. But it was just a dockworker, unloading goods from his truck. "I have to help Sadie get back," I said apologetically.

"Of course." Disappointment flickered across his face. "Will you meet me later?" he said. "There is a room above the café on Barska where I'm staying, on the top floor."

I should say no, I thought. It wasn't proper, meeting Krys at his apartment. I didn't know whether he meant to talk or something more. Things were too far gone between us for all of that now.

But something stopped me from refusing. "I'll try," I said, unwilling to promise more.

Seemingly satisfied, he started away.

"Krys!" I called, and he turned back. "Everything you did... for me...for Sadie... I really appreciate it." There was so much more I wanted to say to him, but now wasn't the time. He tipped his hat and was gone.

I handed the sack of potatoes to Sadie. "He doesn't like you at all," Sadie said. Her voice dripped with sarcasm.

I decided to ignore her teasing. "You have everything you need?"

"Yes." She ran her hand over the sack of potatoes. The potatoes were a temporary solution, and might buy Sadie and the others a few weeks at most, not save them from starving. But they seemed to give her hope. "Because of you."

"And Krys," I added.

"Yes, of course," she replied. "I'm very grateful for what he did, too. It's just that trusting others, it doesn't come easily now."

"I understand." We reached the sewer grate. "Wait," I said. She looked at me expectantly. "You know, if you don't want to go back, there are ways."

She shook her head. "The others need me. I could never leave them."

"I know," I said, admiring her loyalty. "I guess I'm just not ready for you to leave yet." I tried to make my words light but failed. Sadie was my friend now, and I hated sending her back into the sewer.

"It's all right," she said, comforting me when it should have been the other way around. "I'll see you next week."

"Yes, of course." It felt, though, like something was irrevocably changing. "Sunday morning, though, if that's all right, so I don't have to break curfew."

"I'll be here," she replied. In the distance, I could see more workers headed to the riverbank. It was not safe for Sadie to be here anymore. I opened the sewer grate. "You have to go now."

"Thank you," she said, then hesitated. "I really don't want to go back under."

"I'll get you out again, I swear it," I vowed.

Sadie paused, then pulled the *chai* necklace from her pocket.

"You should wait until you are below ground to put that back on," I said. Instead, she held it out to me. "I don't understand."

"This belonged to my father. It is the only piece of our family left, and if I don't make it out..."

"Don't say that," I interrupted. I knew, of course, that Sadie's life in the sewer was dangerous, and that at any moment she might be caught. We were friends now, and I couldn't stand the thought that something might happen to her.

She shook her head, unwilling to deny the likely truth. "If I don't make it out, it needs to be kept safe."

"You'll make it out," I promised, even though I could not possibly know for sure. "I'll hold on to it for you until you do." I took the necklace from her reluctantly, its weight feeling heavier than it should have in my hand. Jewish valuables were contraband and required to be turned over to the authorities. If I was discovered, I would pay with my life. But I took it. "I promise to keep it safe."

Seemingly satisfied, she started to lower herself into the watery prison, clutching the potato sack. "Be careful," I urged. I hung on to her as long as I could, and was nearly pulled underground myself. Then when I could hold on no longer, I released her back into the earth once more. She turned her face upward to me one last time.

"Thank you, Ella." And then she was gone.

15

Sadie

I lowered myself sadly into the sewer, Ella watching from above. She replaced the grate and the wall formed between us once more. As I fell back into the darkness of the earth, it seemed like I was reliving the night that we had first gone into the sewer. Only this time, Papa was not here to catch me.

I made my way through the basin. Dirty water splashed around my feet, soiling the hem of the dress Ella had given me. I started down the tunnel, carrying the sack of potatoes. As I walked, I imagined Ella returning to her home, which was grander than anything I had ever seen. One day after the occupation had begun, Papa and I had walked past a fine apartment building (nowhere near as nice as Ella's house) overlooking the Planty, the ring of parkland that separated Kazimierz from the city center. I was surprised to see a well-dressed woman walk from an elegant black car into the building carrying several shopping bags. "How do they still live like that?" I marveled. Papa explained later that the only people who still lived like that were those who collaborated with the Germans. Ella's family were those people. Her stepmother was seeing a Nazi. Her family had stood by while we had been taken, perhaps even profited from it. I should hate her, I thought angrily.

But I was also confused: Ella was the same girl who had come faithfully to the sewer almost every Sunday, bringing food and gifts and, more importantly, talking to me. She had risked her own safety to hide me and help me, to help my mother and the Rosenbergs. Without her, we all would have starved. Despite her family and the differences between us, she was a good person—and my friend.

As I neared the chamber, I walked more quickly, the potato sack bumping awkwardly against my leg. It was not just that I was eager to share the spoils of my mission with the others. It was morning now; in another few minutes, Mama would wake up and find me missing.

As I neared the entrance to the chamber, Saul appeared. "Sadie!" he cried, too loudly. My heart warmed. I had missed him during my short absence and I hoped now that he might have felt the same. But as he raced toward me, his expression was one of alarm. "I'm so glad I found you! When I discovered that you weren't here, I went looking, but I couldn't find you. I was so worried." In his relief, Saul's words came out in a quick tumble. "I need to tell you that—" He abruptly stopped speaking, clearly taking in my new clothes. "What were you doing?"

I held up the potato sack proudly. "Getting these." I handed it to him and he set it down by his feet.

"Thank God you are all right," he said with relief. "And it's wonderful that you found food. But, Sadie, you must come right away. Something's happened."

"What?" I asked apprehensively.

"You're here!" a voice crackled, interrupting us before Saul could answer. We turned to find Saul's grandmother standing behind us with her hands on her hips. I waited for her to berate me for having been out. "Your mother," Bubbe said instead. "She's in labor."

"What?" A rock seemed to form in the pit of my stomach. "But she isn't due for another month."

"I was just about to tell you," Saul said. "She slipped and fell."

"When she was looking for you," Bubbe said, not mincing words. "She fell in the tunnel and her labor began. The baby is coming."

The baby is coming.

I prayed I had heard Bubbe wrong. The baby was not due for another month. We had done nothing to prepare for him or her, not that I was sure there was anything we could actually do to get ready for a baby in this horrific place.

Guilt and panic flooded me as I raced into the chamber. Mama was on the floor beside the bed, as if she had fallen. I knelt quickly beside her and tried to help her up, but she remained curled in a tight ball. "Mama, are you all right?" She did not answer. I put my arms around her once more and tried to lift her to the bed. But the pregnancy weighed her down and I could not. "Mama, please. You can't stay here. You have to get up." She seemed to rouse slightly and I put my arm around her waist, helping her to her feet.

She looked up, seeming to see me for the first time. "Sadele?"

"I'm here." Her face was pale and covered in faint perspiration and her breathing labored.

Her face contorted and I thought she was having a contraction. "You went to see that girl again, didn't you?" she panted, anger mixing with her pain.

I hesitated, not wanting to answer and cause her further distress. "I found food, Mama. I'm sorry I broke my promise. You can be mad at me later, but right now, let me help you."

She looked as though she wanted to scold me further. But her face contorted with pain and she fell sideways into me. "The baby is coming."

I helped Mama into our bed. I saw then that her legs were wet, not with the sewer water, but something else, dark and thick. Blood. I had heard about babies being born dozens of times in the ghetto and I was pretty sure there should not be blood, or at least not so much. I looked around desperately for Bubbe, but she had disappeared. Before the war, there was a hospital near our apartment where Mama might have gone to deliver a child. In the ghetto, neighbors who were doctors or midwives came to the aid of women who were in labor. Here, we did not even have a clean sheet or towels. I wished my father, or at least Pawel, was here to tell me what to do. I looked in the direction of Saul and Pan Rosenberg, but they would be no use.

At last, Bubbe reappeared in the chamber. Though she was grumpy and usually angry at me, she was my only hope. Without my asking, she walked over and rolled up her sleeves. "There's blood," I said, my voice nearly breaking.

Bubbe nodded curtly in acknowledgment, but did not explain what that might mean. "Lay her down," she ordered. "Quickly!" she barked when I did not obey. "We need to elevate her legs, get them above her heart to slow the bleeding. Do you want to lose her or not?" A cold chill ran through me. I had heard of women dying in childbirth, yet it had not occurred to me until just now that having this baby could kill Mama.

I touched my mother's shoulder. "Mama, lie down, please."

Still doubled over, she shook me off. "The baby. It's too soon."

The old woman shooed her son and grandson from the chamber for privacy, then returned with our lone jug of drinking water and a towel that was not nearly as clean as it should have been. "I assisted the midwife in our neighborhood a few times," the old woman said, guiding Mama gently into a lying position. "I can do this. You stay by her head and hold her hand." I did not know whether her experience would be enough. But there was no other choice.

Mama let out a wail that ricocheted through the chamber.

"Shh!" the old woman admonished. I knew that childbirth was painful. I had heard it through the thin walls of the ghetto, the screams and wails that came with bringing a new life into the world. Here, though, Mama could not cry without giving us away to the Germans above. The old woman found a piece of wood and placed it between Mama's teeth. Mama bit down on it hard, her face going red, then pale.

A moment later, Mama lay back, seemingly exhausted. "Are you all right?" I asked, leaning close and blotting her forehead with a cloth.

"Let her rest," the old woman instructed. "She needs to gather her strength in between contractions—before it gets bad." I stared at her in disbelief. I had assumed this was the bad part. I could not imagine it getting any worse.

But it did get worse. The pattern continued, each burst of pushing and pain seemingly longer and more intense than the last. In between, Mama lay resting, barely conscious. An hour passed, then another. The contractions grew closer together and Mama's agony intensified.

After one particularly awful bout, Bubbe examined Mama, then straightened, her expression grim. "You should go," she said, trying to shoo me away suddenly.

"Why? What's wrong?"

Bubbe shook her head. "She's lost a lot of blood. If the baby doesn't come soon..." She did not finish the thought.

Terror ripped through me like a knife. "No!" Mama lay still now, her eyes closed. I felt under her nose to make sure she was still breathing. Then I placed my head close to hers and took her hand. "You can do this, Mama. Please. We need you." I was speaking for myself and my brother or sister who had not yet been born.

Mama seemed to draw strength from my voice. She opened her eyes and began to push again. This time she let out a wail so loud it was surely heard on the street above. Her nails dug hard into my palm, drawing blood, but still I held fast. I would not leave her.

The baby came into the world determinedly with a loud cry that gave no doubt as to its health. As the wail cut defiantly through the sewer, a dark look crossed Bubbe's face. "Give the baby to me," Mama said, her voice hoarse. Bubbe passed the baby to Mama, who put the baby's head to her breast in an attempt to silence the squall. Her milk had not come in yet, though, and the baby's face turned purple with frustration. Mama drew the baby close to her breast, nearly suffocating the child to muffle its cries.

"A girl," the old woman pronounced. I wondered if my mother would have preferred a son to remind her of Papa. I hurried to our things to fetch the baby blanket we had brought with us when we fled. Even though it had been soaked in the flood like everything else we owned, it was still white with two blue stripes at each end. I passed it to Mama.

Mama's head tilted back suddenly and her arms slackened, nearly dropping the baby. The old woman moved with surprising speed to catch her. "Hold her," she ordered, passing the baby to me without warning. I had never held a baby before and my hands fumbled awkwardly around the strange, squiggling bundle.

"Mama!" I called, too loudly. "What's happening?" Bubbe did not answer, but concentrated on reviving her. I held my breath. Mama was the last piece of my world. I could not lose her.

A second later, Mama's eyes fluttered open. She blinked for several seconds before focusing on me holding my little sister. She smiled faintly.

"She'll be all right," Bubbe declared. "She's weak, but at least the bleeding has stopped."

I looked down, studying the baby. I hadn't been sure how I was going to feel about having a little brother or sister. Bald and round, babies had always looked the same to me. Gazing now at the child with the same stubbed nose as my own, a wave of love broke over me and crested. I would do whatever I could to protect my sister.

"What's her name?" I asked, hoping she might choose a feminine version of Papa's name, Michal. Mama shook her head. I wondered if she was too weak to decide now. Or perhaps naming a baby born in such hopeless circumstances was more hope than she could bear.

A moment later, the old woman took the baby back from me and handed her to Mama to try nursing again. I walked out of the chamber into the tunnel to tell the others the news. "It's a girl," I said.

"Mazel tov," Pan Rosenberg offered without emotion.

"A child is a sign of life, of hope," Saul said, taking a step toward me. I thought for a second he might take my hand, but of course he could not. "Your mother, she's well?"

"Yes, thank you. She seems to be."

The baby's squalls grew louder, spilling from the chamber into the tunnel. The lines in Pan Rosenberg's forehead seemed to grow deeper with worry. "How will you keep her from crying?" he asked. I had no answer. I had been so worried about how Mama could have the baby in the sewer, making sure she and the baby both came through it safely. But now that the baby was here, the question loomed large. The sewer required us to be silent, especially during the long daytime hours when people walked the streets overhead and entered the cathedral. Surely the cries of a baby would be heard. How would we ever manage?

I turned back toward the chamber, my stomach heavy as lead. We faced so many obstacles living here: hiding from the Germans, getting enough food, staying healthy in these awful conditions, dangerous floods. Now it seemed that a tiny little baby would become the biggest problem of all.

16

Ella

After Sadie disappeared back into the sewer, I hurried from the riverbank, starting in the direction of Dębniki. Daylight had fully broken now and street sweepers cleaned debris from the pavement. When I reached the café on Barska Street, I did not go inside, but instead walked through the door next to it and up the stairs that led to the apartments on the floors above. The building was old and dank. No one had bothered to replace the lights in the stairwell that had burned out and the whole place smelled of pipe smoke.

I reached the top floor and knocked on the lone door. There was no answer. "Krys?" I called softly. Silence. I waited a few seconds, confused. He had asked me to come find him after Sadie returned to the sewer; this was surely the right place. I turned the knob and pushed the door open a few inches and peered inside. It was a bare attic space, not much bigger than Maciej's garret, with a straight ceiling instead of sloped. Heavy curtains had been drawn to keep out the early-morning sun.

As my eyes adjusted to the dimness, I could make out Krys sitting on a bare mattress on the far side of the room. He leaned motionless against the wall with his head tilted back. "Krys?" He did not respond and for a moment I worried that something had happened after he left me on the riverbank. Had he been hurt—or worse? As I moved closer, though, I could see that his chest rose and fell with long, even breaths. He was simply asleep. Watching him, I felt a tug of longing. I wondered when he had last rested in a comfortable bed or had a full night's sleep at all.

I had not slept either, other than the short while when I'd hidden with Sadie beneath the stairwell. I was suddenly exhausted from the long night of hiding Sadie and walking the city with her. I dropped down softly beside Krys, trying not to wake him. As I watched him, a mix of affection and desire arose in me. I wished more than ever that things between us might be as they had been before the war, and that it wasn't all so complicated now. He shivered in his sleep. Even though it was spring, a chill from the night air lingered in the unheated room. Krys had no blanket, but a coat was flung on the floor not far from the mattress, so I retrieved it and covered us both. Then I leaned my head softly against his shoulder.

He seemed to sense my presence and his eyes flickered open. "Ella, you're here. I'm so glad." He put his arm around me and I moved closer, feeling like everything that had happened since he left for the war had been a bad dream.

"I let myself in," I said. "You should lock the door."

"I left it open for you. Anyway, if they want to come for me, a lock isn't going to stop them."

He was talking about the Germans, I realized, shuddering inwardly. Krys' work for the Home Army made him a wanted man. Suddenly it seemed as though they might burst through the door at any second. Even this simple moment together was fragile, fraught with danger.

He reached around the far side of the mattress, then pulled

out a small wrapped parcel and handed it to me. "Happy birthday," he said.

"Thank you," I said, touched. I had not expected Krys to remember my birthday; I had nearly forgotten myself. Inside the parcel was a piece of Polish honey cake, dusted with powdered sugar.

"It isn't much, but I didn't know until last night that I would be seeing you. It's the best I could do on short notice."

"It's perfect." We did not have forks, so I broke the piece of cake in two and passed him half. Eating the sweet dessert with our hands at such an early hour of the morning felt strange, yet somehow right. "A new tradition," I added. Then I felt my cheeks go warm. I had not meant to suggest that we might carry on together.

"A new tradition," he repeated, his gaze holding mine. He reached out to wipe a smudge of powdered sugar from my lip.

"You live here?" I asked.

"Not exactly. This is a safe house and a good place to rest when I'm working."

"What about your parents?" I asked, puzzled. "They're nearby."

He nodded. "I still leave my things with them and go there to wash. But I stay away as much as I can to protect them. I can't put them in danger any more than I can you."

I saw then that his keeping his distance from me these past few months was not an excuse. He really had been trying to shield me from the dangers of his work. I drew closer to him. "Well, I'm not staying away anymore. I don't want to."

"Good." He wrapped his arms around me. "I was trying to keep you safe by staying away. But I see now that was a mistake. None of us are safe, Ella. The best way to protect you is by keeping you close."

He turned to me and his lips met mine with more intensity than they ever had before. Something was different now, the layers of distance between us stripped away. We fell into each other's arms. I kissed his lips, let his hands travel to the places they had only gone the night before he left for the war. "I've missed you so," he said as he rose above me, and I could tell by his pent-up desire that there had been no one else for him either in the time that we had been apart. I let myself be swept away, blocking out the voices that said this was wrong because he had left me and we were no longer really together. We had found each other once more. It was a moment of rare joy in a sea of danger and darkness and I took it greedily.

After, we lay in one another's arms, letting our breath subside and not speaking. I rested my head on his chest.

"You returned Sadie underground safely?" he asked finally.

"Yes," I said, grateful to talk about something other than us and what had just happened. I remembered the look on her face as she disappeared below the earth. "She seemed so sad to go back. But grateful for the food," I added quickly. "How did you even get it?"

He smiled and brushed away a lock of my hair that had fallen into my eyes. "I have my ways." Then his expression turned serious. "Someone owed me a favor." He pressed his lips together and I knew he would say no more about it.

"Well, I'm beyond grateful. If there is ever anything to do to repay you…"

"There is," he said quickly, surprising me. He paused for several seconds, as if debating, and I could not imagine what he would ask. Was he planning to ask me to help with his work once more? "There are supplies, guns and weapons, that are critical to our work. I need to find a place to hide them for a bit."

"But where? Surely you don't mean for me to store them in my house with Ana Lucia constantly bringing her German friends around."

"No, of course not. But you have the perfect place: the sewer."

I sat up, covering myself. "You can't be serious." But his solemn eyes told me otherwise. "No, I can't do that."

"Just ask Sadie. For all that you have done for her, I'm sure she would say yes."

Of course, that was the problem. Sadie was grateful and she would be only too willing to help. But she was barely surviving down there. I couldn't ask her to do something that would jeopardize her even further.

I looked at Krys, half lying beside me, and suddenly what had taken place between us seemed altogether something else. "Is that why you asked me to come here, because you needed help?" I reached for my dress.

"No, it isn't like that. I wanted to be with you, Ella, just like I always have. But this is a critical moment in our fight against the Germans and we must strike with everything we have. The hiding place you have in the sewer, it's too perfect."

I shook my head. "I'm sorry." Even for Krys and the important work he was doing, there were some things that were too much to ask.

"Why does Sadie mean so much to you?" Krys asked.

I hesitated. Krys had a point. I had met Sadie only a little while ago. She was no one to me. I should not care about her so much. But somehow in the short time since I had known her, we had become friends and I wanted to help and protect her. I felt certain that she would do the same for me.

But Krys understood none of this. All he saw was some strange girl in the sewer whom I barely knew—and that I was putting her before him.

"I can't explain it," I said at last. "There's just a connection between us. I care for her. She's my friend."

"And what does that make me?"

"You know what you mean to me," I replied quickly, unwilling to let him make my feelings for him a point in his favor. "But you have other options for hiding the munitions."

"No," he said sharply. "I don't." I had no idea if that was true. "If I did, I wouldn't be asking."

"The sewer is Sadie's last hope," I explained, desperate to make him understand. "If she's caught, she'll be arrested or killed."

"You think I don't know that?" Krys exploded. His voice was so loud that I was sure that whoever was in the apartment below could hear. "That's why we are doing all of this."

"That's not true," I countered. "The Home Army is fighting to liberate Poland. Most Poles care nothing for the Jews." I understood that for Krys, it was about the bigger fight, not a lone Jewish girl and her family. But to me, Sadie mattered.

"So you won't help?" he asked.

"Not in this way. I'm sorry." I looked away, unable to meet his eyes. The one thing he asked of me was the very thing I could not give.

"Me, too." He slid away from me and stood up. "I thought you understood," he said.

"I could say the same thing."

"This is war," he said tersely as he tucked in his shirt. "Every one of us has to make compromises." I realized then that Krys had come back from the war changed. He belonged to the cause now, to his work. Not to me.

I wanted to tell him I would help him hide the munitions. But I couldn't betray Sadie's safety. "I want to help you," I said. "I'll carry packages or whatever you need me to do. We can place the munitions in Ana Lucia's house, if need be." I knew even as I said it how ridiculous the suggestion was. "But don't ask me to compromise Sadie's safety again," I said, pleading now. "I can help you find another place."

He shook his head stubbornly. "There's no time and there's nowhere better. You know, I don't need your permission, Ella. I could ask her directly, or even just go into the sewer myself." It was a calculated bluff, designed to make me acquiesce.

We sat in silence, neither speaking. "You should go," he said a moment later. I stood, stung by his coldness. I searched for the right words to fix our quarrel. I did not want to part in anger. But the gulf remained between us, too wide to breach.

"I need to do this," Krys pressed, trying one more time to persuade me. He was headstrong, unaccustomed to being told no.

But so was I. "If you go near the sewer, I will never speak with you again." I turned and walked from the room.

Back on the street, I started for home, shaken. It was a bright and sunny morning now, the sidewalks crowded with people who had already begun their day. It felt as if everything was crashing down upon me and my head swirled with confusion. Krys and I had come back together, so perfectly that it might have been a dream. Now with the moment between us faded and the distance between us returned, it seemed as if it had never happened. I had trusted Krys, told him the truth about Sadie and the others hiding in the sewer. Now he was threatening to risk their safety for his own ends. I wondered with regret whether the price of getting the food Sadie needed had been too high a price to pay.

When I reached Kanonicza Street, it was after nine o'clock and there was no hope of sneaking into the house. Smoothing my hair, I started through the front door. Ana Lucia was seated at the far end of the breakfast table. As she took in the soiled, wrinkled dress I still wore from the previous day, I braced for her interrogation. But she asked me nothing. "There's kiełbasa," she said mildly. Hanna brought me a plate, and though I was not that hungry, I took a sausage. Of course, Ana Lucia made no mention of my birthday. She never remembered it at all.

"So, Ella," she said a moment later. I looked up from my breakfast to find her staring at me, eyes narrowed like a cat's.

My breath caught. Did she know about Sadie being in the house last night? "You'll be glad to know that I'm feeling better."

I looked up. "You were ill?" Her complexion was ruddy, eyes clear. She did not appear unwell to me. "I had no idea."

"That's not what you told the Germans in Dębniki." I froze, remembering the soldiers I had encountered when I had tried to go see Sadie the previous week and the excuse I had given them for my basket of food. "You said that your mother was sick and that you were bringing me food. They told Colonel Maust." Of course they had. "You used my name, Ella. You lied about me and made me look a fool. For what?"

I searched my mind for an explanation, but found none. "The Germans stopped me and I couldn't find my *Kennkarte*," I lied. "They wanted to know what I was doing. I was scared and I made up the excuse, I'm sorry."

"What *were* you doing there?" she pressed. I had unwittingly walked right into her trap. "You had no business going to Dębniki again. And Fritz said the officers told him you were with a young man." She paused, thinking. "It's that awful boy again, isn't it?" Ana Lucia's lip curled with distaste. She had never liked Krys, considered his family far below us. It had always infuriated me.

But now I accepted the excuse she provided willingly. "Yes."

"You need to stop chasing him around that filthy neighborhood. You're not to go there again."

"Yes, Ana Lucia," I said, trying to sound duly chastened.

By agreeing with her too readily, though, I had overplayed my hand. Her eyes widened. "You're up to something," she said slowly, predator circling her prey.

"I have no idea what you're talking about," I lied, willing my voice not to shake.

"Careful, little girl. You are playing a dangerous game and you are going to lose. This is my house now and you are only in it by my good graces. You know that, don't you?" I did not answer, but finished my sausage in silence, then got up from the table. Feeling her eyes still on me, I tried to walk normally and forced my breathing to be calm as I left the room. Ana Lucia was suspicious, but she did not know about Sadie—at least not yet. I would have to be more careful.

As I started up the stairs, I noticed an envelope on the table in the foyer. It was addressed to me and I wondered when it had come, whether Ana Lucia had forgotten or deliberately neglected to give it to me. A letter from Paris, I realized, taking in the French stamps. Perhaps a birthday greeting from my brother. But the handwriting was not Maciej's long, familiar looping script. I tore it open.

Dear Ella,
We have not met, but I've heard so much about you from your brother that I feel we have. I am your brother's friend, Phillipe.

Friend, I reread the word. It was a euphemism, carefully censored code for so much more. I knew from Maciej's earlier letters that he and Phillipe cared for one another deeply and it seemed a great pity that society did not permit them to acknowledge their feelings and call their relationship what it was. Quickly, I read on.

I'm afraid I write with the terrible news that Maciej was taken by the police during a raid of a cabaret we sometimes frequent.

My heart stopped. My beloved brother had been arrested.

There were rumors that the police might raid the cabaret and I begged him not to go out, but he would not be dissuaded.

Of course not. Maciej had always been stubborn and defiant— it was partly what had destroyed his relationship with my father and sent him fleeing to Paris in the first place.

> *I have worked my every contact in an attempt to get informa-*
> *tion about his well-being and secure his release. I am told that he*
> *is fine and will soon be freed.*

I exhaled slightly. Still my heart screamed for my gentle brother, forced to endure such circumstances.

I finished reading the letter.

> *Before he was arrested, Maciej applied for a visa for you, which*
> *recently came. I am enclosing it here. Please come when you are*
> *able and we would very much like to have you live with us.*
> *Yours,*
> *Phillipe*

I looked in the envelope and pulled out a second piece of paper. It was a visa for me to travel to France.

I held the visa in my hand, contemplating it. It was a pass to freedom. So many people would kill to have it. Once it was all that I had wanted. But that dream, which I had held so dearly just a short while earlier, felt like a relic from another life now. Still, I should take it, go to Paris and make sure Maciej was all right.

Then Sadie appeared in my mind. She needed me in a way few people ever had, was counting on me for food to survive. I thought of the times I had stood by helplessly, first with Miriam and later when the woman jumped from the bridge with her children. Then, whether by circumstance or choice, I had done nothing. Here, I could make a difference. The easy thing would be to leave, but the brave thing to do was stay. I could not go, at least not now. I folded the envelope and tucked it in my pocket.

17

Sadie

Mama huddled in the corner of the chamber, trying to nurse the baby. Some days, I knew, her milk didn't come, but thankfully today her breasts were swollen and full. As I moved to shield her from the view of the others in the chamber, I could see how thin and drained she was. A nursing mother should have good, rich food. All we had were the potatoes Ella had helped me find, and even those would not last forever. What would we eat then?

Pushing my concerns aside, I looked at the baby, whom we still had not named three days after she was born. She turned her head away from Mama's breast and stared back at me with her clear, unblinking gaze. Babies weren't really supposed to be able to see you the first few months, Mama said. But whenever I drew near, my sister's eyes found mine and held. We had an instant connection. I was the one who could soothe her when she was tired and cranky, or when Mama tried to nurse her but was dry.

I studied my mother. Despite the difficult childbirth, Mama

had seemed to draw strength from the baby after she was born. She was filled with purposefulness at taking care of her. She moved through the routines of feeding and changing the child, as though we were back at home and not in a sewer where she had to wash the same two dishrags that served as diapers over and over again.

While Mama finished nursing, I walked from the chamber. Saul had gone for water a bit earlier and I hoped now that I might see him returning. But the tunnel echoed with emptiness. It had rained heavily the previous night, but the storm had been mercifully short so we didn't have to worry about another flood. I could not imagine how we would survive such an ordeal again, with a baby to keep afloat on top of everything else. The rain had stopped entirely now, and the early-morning clouds had cleared. Sunshine came through the slats in the sewer grate, causing the stones that lined the tunnel to sparkle like the beach at low tide that I'd seen just once when Papa had taken us to the Gdańsk seaside on holiday. It was not Ella's day to visit and I wondered what she was doing, and if she was glad to be free of her obligation to me.

Inside the chamber the baby began to cry, her wails echoing through the tunnel. I raced back inside to help. Mama walked the floor, swaying from side to side, trying to soothe my sister, who had grown colicky after eating. I took her from Mama and held her close. Even through the stench of the sewer, her sweet baby scent endured. Her weight filled my arms. She gazed up at me, seemingly soothed. She might have been my own child; I was old enough. I drew her close and whispered to her. I told her about our old life and about the things we would do after the war. I would take her to the places Papa and I had gone and breathe light into the city for her the way he had me. She listened, seeming to understand my words.

Cradling the baby's neck gently like Mama had shown me, I shifted her to my other shoulder. As I did, the receiving blanket we'd put her in when she was born slipped away and fell to the ground. "No!" I cried as it landed in a puddle of water by the chamber door. I reached for it quickly, but it was too late. Filthy brown water seeped into the fabric. The corner of the blanket was stained brown now. Mama took the blanket and tried to wring it out, but it was stained forever. I waited for Mama to berate me, but she did not. Instead, she looked at the blanket, resigned. Then she began to cry, great heaving sobs, as all of the pain of losing Papa and the birth and everything else came out at once. I felt guiltier about soiling that blanket than I had about almost anything in my entire life.

But there was no time to worry about the blanket. The baby opened her mouth and it was as if she was trying to tell me something. Then she let out a bloodcurdling wail and her cries ripped through the sewer, seeming to reverberate against the walls.

"Here, let me," Mama snapped, taking my sister from me. Suddenly I felt as if I had done something wrong and caused the baby to cry. "Shh," she soothed, a note of urgency in her voice. Across the chamber, Pan Rosenberg watched us with a grave expression. I remembered his somber mood the night my sister was born. A crying baby, especially times like now when we most needed to be silent, made it more likely that we would be discovered and brought danger to us all.

Wanting to help, I reached out to stroke the baby's head to soothe her. Usually she loved my touch. This time, though, her face turned purple and she began to scream. "Don't," Mama snapped, yanking the baby away from me. I stepped back, stung by her rebuke. Still, I could tell that she was not angry with me, just tired and frustrated and scared. She sank down to the edge of the bed, still trying to calm the baby. My sister cried heedlessly, knowing no need but her own.

Mama and I were so busy trying to quiet the baby that we didn't hear the footsteps until they were right next to us. I looked up. Bubbe was standing above us. She knelt down and took Mama's hand.

"She can't stay," Bubbe said gravely. The three words cut through the chamber. "The baby has to go."

"Go?" I stared at her in confusion, certain that the old woman, who had seemed more confused of late, had finally lost her mind. My sister was three days old. Where did she expect her to go?

Pan Rosenberg walked over and I expected him to contradict his mother, or at least soothe her. "You are risking all of our safety," he said, agreeing with his mother. "This cannot continue." I could not believe that the Rosenbergs, who had become our close allies and, I thought, friends, were saying such things. I looked for Saul, but he was nowhere to be found.

"There isn't anywhere to go," Mama protested, shaking off Bubbe's hand. "You can't possibly expect us to leave."

"We're not asking you to leave," Pan Rosenberg said, and for a moment I hoped this was all a misunderstanding. "But a child in the sewer. Surely you didn't think you would be able to keep her here." Clearly, he and Bubbe had discussed this already. I stiffened. Did he mean for us to send her somewhere? There were stories when we were in the ghetto of Jewish families hiding their children away with Catholic Poles. Mama would never let my sister go, though, not for a moment. The baby's wails rose, as if she herself was protesting.

"Something has to be done," Bubbe insisted.

Just then, Saul appeared at the chamber door, filled water jug in hand. I ran to him. "Saul, you have to do something! Your family, they're trying to make us leave." For a second, I wondered if he had been part of their earlier conversations, too. But I could tell from his expression that he was genuinely dismayed.

"What?" Then his expression turned from surprise to anger. He hurried across the chamber toward the others. "How could you say such a thing?" he demanded of his father. He was clearly caught off guard by the idea as well.

"That child is a curse," Bubbe spat, any pretense of civility gone now. "She's going to get us all killed."

Aghast, Saul turned to me. "She doesn't mean it," he said quietly.

But his grandmother overheard. "I certainly do mean it. I lost one grandson and I won't lose another because you can't keep the baby quiet. You have to be practical and do what is best for all of us. It's not for myself I say this," Bubbe added, her voice softening as she turned back toward Mama. "I'm an old woman and my time is nearly done. But I have my grandson to think about, and you have your daughter." She gestured toward me.

"What am I to do?" Mama asked, her voice cracking with desperation. "Perhaps it would be more merciful..." Her hand traveled to my sister's mouth and I knew she was thinking of the Kleins, a family in the ghetto who had been hiding in a wall during an *aktion* when their infant began to cry. The mother had covered the child's mouth to muffle its cries and avoid detection. But she smothered the child for too long and it had suffocated and died.

"Mama, no!" I reached for her hand and she moved it away from my sister's mouth. Mama had barely survived the day in the ghetto when she thought I had been taken. She would never hurt one of her children.

"Then there's no choice but for you to go," Bubbe persisted.

"No," Mama said firmly, standing and facing Bubbe directly. "We're not leaving." We had all been here since the beginning. What right had she to tell us to leave? Mama's spine straightened and I saw that glimmer of her strength of old. I prayed for her to reclaim all of it as she stood up to this woman.

"At least think of your other daughter," Bubbe shot back, gesturing in my direction. "Do you want to get her killed?"

Mama did not reply for several seconds, seeming to think about what Bubbe had said. "She's right," Mama said to me in a low voice. "We can't possibly keep a baby quiet down here."

My sister, who had finally gone quiet in Mama's arms, cooed in seeming agreement.

"What other choice do we have?" I asked.

"I won't risk your safety," Mama said, not hearing or ignoring my question. "Not after everything we have been through."

She looked over my shoulder at the others. "I'll go," she said suddenly. "I'll take the baby out of here. But my daughter stays."

I stared at her in disbelief. Did she really mean to leave me behind? "Mama, no!"

"We'll leave you two to discuss it," Pan Rosenberg said, leading his mother away by the arm. He and his family retreated to their side of the chamber, Saul watching me with sad, apologetic eyes.

"You can't go," I said to my mother when we were alone. My voice broke, an almost sob. "How can you even think about leaving without me?" My sister, exhausted from her earlier crying, now slept peacefully in Mama's arms. "Please. I lost Papa. I can't lose you, too."

"But what other choice is there?" she asked desperately. "You heard them: we can't keep a crying baby here."

"Let's leave here together," I begged. I had no idea where we might go. I could ask Ella to help us. But even as I thought this, I knew that it was too much. She had barely been able to hide me for a night. There was no way she could manage to find a place for three of us permanently.

"Pawel mentioned some time ago a place we might take the baby when it was born," Mama said unexpectedly, surprising me. "He spoke to me about it several weeks ago before the baby was born. He told me about a doctor at the Bonifratrów Hospital who takes Jewish children and hides them with families." The Bonifratrów Hospital was a Catholic hospital on the edge of Kazimierz, run by a monastic order. I had not imagined that they had taken in Jewish children—or that Pawel and Mama had contemplated such a thing.

I was stunned. Why had she not mentioned such a thing before? "Mama, no!" I protested. She could not mean to send my
baby sister away.

"It's the only way," she said quietly, resignation in her voice.
I studied her face, wondering whether it was the stress of giving
birth that had somehow clouded her mind. But her eyes were
clear. "If I take her there, I can come back to you." She would
be abandoning my sister to return to me.

"You can't give up the baby," I protested. The thought was
nearly as terrible as losing my mother.

"It would only be for a time," she said, her eyes growing dark.

Still, something told me that if she went, we would never be
together again. "The three of us have to stay together," I insisted. "It's the only way."

"Please." She raised her hand. "Let's not speak of it anymore
right now." She gestured to my sister, who slept peacefully in
her arms. I wanted to press Mama, to make her swear not to
leave. Her face was pale now, though, and I could see how the
whole ordeal had drained her.

My baby sister was quiet and calm for the rest of the day and,
to my relief, no one spoke more about leaving. Still, the notion
ricocheted around my brain, painful and stunning: Mama could
send the baby away. She couldn't possibly mean it. She would
never abandon her own child. I did not bring it up again, hoping that she would not say more about it.

That night, I slept restlessly. In the middle of the night, I
awoke with a start. I immediately sensed that something was
different, felt the stillness in the air beside me. Even before I
reached over, I knew that Mama was gone.

I sat up, alarmed, trying without success to see her in the
blackness. Neither she nor the baby were there. "Mama!" I
called, not caring about the others sleeping or about being too
loud. Then I leapt to my feet and raced out of the chamber.

Mama was not outside the door. Had she really gone? I ran

down the tunnel to the larger pipe. There I found her standing in the dark, holding the baby, not seeming to feel the cold water that seeped ankle-deep into her stockings. At first I wondered if she was sleepwalking, but her eyes were open and clear. She had left the chamber on purpose.

"Mama, what are you doing?" She did not answer. "Were you trying to leave?" She did not have her satchel, I noticed.

She stared off blankly into the space before her. "I was looking for a way out." I started to protest that she did not know the path. She was not talking about escaping just the tunnel, though, I realized, but this whole impossible situation that bound us. I wondered where she would have gone or what she might have done if I had not come and found her.

For the rest of the night, I lay with my body half atop Mama's to keep her in place, my cheek pressed firmly against her delicate shoulder. I slept lightly, if at all, waking at her slightest move. I needed to make sure that she did not try to slip out from under me.

But the next morning, I woke late, tired from poor sleep. Mama was no longer beside me, yet whether I had rolled away or she had slipped from beneath my grasp intentionally, I did not know. I sat up with a start. I saw her across the chamber, preparing breakfast as she always did while cradling my sister in one arm. My body slumped with relief. Perhaps she had forgotten or given up on the notion of leaving.

Then I saw something sitting at the foot of the bed. It was the satchel, neatly packed. Mama was leaving.

I leapt up just as she crossed the chamber toward me. "What are you doing?" I demanded.

She passed me the thin piece of potato that was my breakfast, then tucked a second piece into the satchel. "Taking the baby, like we discussed yesterday." Her voice wavered.

"No!" How could she possibly send my sister away? Bubbe Rosenberg was right, though. It was only a matter of time before the Germans heard my sister crying and discovered us. She could not stay here. The hospital was at least a chance. "But with Pawel gone, how are you to get the baby there?"

"I will take her myself."

"Mama, you can't possibly. You're still weak from giving birth. At least let me take her. I have been above ground. I can find my way."

She shook her head. "I need to take her myself. I have to see with my own eyes that she's safe."

My mind reeled back to two nights earlier when I had awoken to see Mama doubled over the sleeping baby, as if in pain. "What is it?" I had asked, alarmed. "Are you feeling unwell?" I wondered if she was having complications from the labor and whether I should wake Bubbe to help her. "You should eat something." She needed more food than we had to sustain herself and the baby she was nursing. She shook her head and waved me off. Then she began to cry, sobbing into the crook of her arm so as not to make noise. I had never seen my mother cry, not when we came here or when we lost my father. Seeing her at her weakest scared me more than anything else had.

A moment later, her sobs eased. She brushed her tears away and forced a smile. "It's nothing, really. I'm just tired. All of this is so much. And sometimes after having a baby, women get weepy for no reason at all. I'm fine, really." I had desperately wanted to believe her.

Remembering that moment now, I understood: Mama had known that this would come, that we could not all stay together, even before Bubbe had demanded that she take the baby from the sewer. She had been crying at the knowledge that she would inevitably have to part with her child.

Mama slung the satchel over her shoulder and picked up the baby, as if preparing to go. Did she really mean to leave me without so much as a goodbye? "You said you'd never leave me," I said, reminding her in my desperation of her words the night we had come to the sewer and lost Papa.

"And I won't," she replied, her words sounding so sure that I almost believed her. "I just need to take your sister to the hospital and then I'll come back straightaway." Her words were of little comfort. Mama would not abandon me forever, I had to believe that. She meant to return as soon as she could. But what if she didn't make it?

"You can't go." Leaving the sewer meant certain death. "If you leave, you'll be killed." There was nothing left for Mama, though, if her children were not safe. She kissed me on the forehead, and in the strength of her lips, she seemed to return for just a second. But when I looked up, her eyes were hollow and dark, a stranger's. "Please don't." I began to cry.

Saul stood and walked from where he had been sitting with his family toward me. He tried to put his arms around me, but I shook him off. "Please, tell her not to go!" I insisted. I waited for someone, Pan Rosenberg or his mother maybe, to point out the foolishness of my mother's plan and prevent her from leaving. My father would have stopped her, if he were here. I turned to Saul. "How can you let her do this? She won't survive up there. There's nowhere she can go that is safe."

"Because it is the right thing to do," Saul said quietly. I was stunned. "My grandmother is right: if the baby stays here, we are all dead. And I won't lose you, Sadie, not if I can save you." I knew he was thinking of Shifra, and the ways in which he had failed her. "You can't stop her," he added in a low voice, gesturing with his head toward my mother. "She is determined to leave. The only thing you can do now is help her to go safely."

I took in all that he had said, numb with disbelief. He was right. None of us could stop her from going. But I could not stay here without her. "Take me, too," I begged. "I will come with you," I insisted. "I know the way out. I can help carry the baby."

Mama shook her head. "No, you must stay here. Together we

would be more easily spotted. I can move more quickly alone.
I will be back in a few hours, a day at most." She forced certainty into her voice.

"If you wait until my friend Ella comes, I can ask for her
help." I didn't know how Ella could possibly help hide a baby,
but I was stalling for time, anything to keep Mama from going.

She shook her head. "I can't wait. Every time the baby cries,
it puts us all at risk. We can't count on anyone else now. Just
let me get her to safety and I will come back to you, I swear."

So it was decided. My sister would go. Mama would take her.
And I would be left here alone.

Mama set down the satchel and passed the baby to me while
she reached for her coat. Then she hesitated. The coat sleeve still
bore the white armband with a blue star that we had been ordered to wear. "Here, take this," Bubbe Rosenberg said, walking across the chamber with her own dark cape.

"Thank you." Mama took the cape and put it on. I saw then
how Mama's blond hair had begun to turn to gray and her once-
rosy skin was pale and withered like tissue paper. The sewer had
aged her, seemingly overnight. She took the baby back from me.

Bubbe put her hand on Mama's shoulder and then touched
the baby's head. I wanted to smack her hand away. How dare she
feign kindness after what she had done? "We will keep her safe
until you return," she said, nodding her head in my direction.
I was confused. Mama said she would not be gone more than a
day, but Bubbe's words made it seem like so much longer. An
uneasy feeling balled like a fist in my stomach.

Mama picked up the satchel once more and walked to the entrance of the chamber with the baby. "Come," she said to me.
"I need you to show me the way." My stomach twisted. Was
she really asking me to help her leave?

"Take her to the grate," Saul urged in a low voice. "Otherwise, she might get lost."

He was right; Mama would need my help to get out. "But how can I help my own mother leave?" I protested.

"I can guide her, if you want," Saul offered.

I shook my head. "I have to do this myself."

He put his hand on my arm. "I'm sorry, Sadie. I can't even imagine how hard this is for you. I'll be waiting here for you when you come back." His words were little comfort.

Reluctantly, I followed my mother into the tunnel. She started toward the grate where I had first seen Ella. I took her arm to stop her. "This way," I said, guiding her in the opposite direction. The grate near the river, where I had come out to find food, was the safer option.

As we started down the tunnel, doubts flooded me. Nothing about this plan made sense or was all right. There had to be another way. I wanted to argue once more. But Mama's steps were dogged now, her jaw set with grim determination. She would not be dissuaded. I had no choice. I had to lead her safely to the street or she would try to find her own way—and she would never make it alone.

A few minutes later, we reached the basin. "The exit is on the far side," I explained. I saw the doubt in her eyes, not just about being able to climb from the well, but about her entire plan to bring my sister to safety. I went first, then helped her down into the deep basin. We made our way across. On the far side, she handed me the baby and attempted to climb the wall to the ledge without success. I tried to help her while holding my sister, but I could not do it with one hand. I looked around and found a dry spot on the ground and placed the baby gently on it. I put my hands around Mama's waist. She was featherlight as I lifted her and helped her up the wall and onto the ledge.

Then I picked up the baby once more. I leaned down to kiss my sister goodbye, a lone tear splashing against the soft, warm skin of her forehead. "I'm sorry," I said. If only I had been stronger and could have done more to keep her with us.

"Quickly," Mama said. I handed my sister up to her, feeling the warmth fade from my hands as I let go of her. I climbed up the wall of the basin to join them and we crawled through the last bit of pipe in silence.

When we reached the grate, the space above was deserted. "The grate will let you out on the riverbank and then you can walk across the bridge." I faltered, knowing that our time together was quickly drawing to an end. "You must stay close to the buildings and take the backstreets and alleys." I thought of the distance and the danger that stood before her. It would have been nearly impossible under normal circumstances. How would she ever manage it in her weakened state with a baby?

I wrapped my arms around Mama as though I was a child, tucking my head under her chin. I clung to her waist, not wanting to let her go. She held me firmly for several seconds, rocking the way she once had when she wanted to soothe me and humming a familiar lullaby under her breath. I wanted to stand frozen in that moment forever. My childhood, all of the memories we had shared, passed between us, slipping through my fingers like the tide receding. Between us, my sister cooed.

I looked down at the baby, caressed the top of her head, which had become as familiar as my own in such a short period of time. I had only just found her and grown to love her and now I was going to lose her, maybe forever. The three of us were the very last family we had. "It will be a few months tops," Mama said. "Then the war will be over and we can go get her right away." I wanted to believe it would be that simple. But I had seen too much of the war.

"Mama, she still needs a name," I said.

"God will name her," she said, and I knew in that moment that she did not believe we would get my sister back.

Then Mama disentangled herself and turned to face the grate. I pushed it open for her and she climbed out, holding my sister.

Still I could not let her go. "Wait, I'll come with you," I

said, grasping her ankle so hard she nearly stumbled. I started to climb out after her.

"No," she replied firmly, shaking off my grip. I knew that there would be no convincing her. "You must stay here. I'll come back to you, I swear." Mama's voice was strong and sure. "I love you, *kochana*," my mother said as I helped her replace the grate with effort. Her face lingered for a moment before disappearing. I stood motionless, listening for the sounds, anything to know that she was still there. But I heard only her footsteps, growing fainter as she walked away. I was seized with the urge to climb out and follow, beg her not to go, or at the very least keep her safe while she did.

There was a scraping noise from above. My breath caught. Mama had returned! I waited for her to realize her mistake, to come back and say she would never leave me, that we would find a way together. But a pigeon appeared, pecking at the grate. It looked down at me sorrowfully before flapping its wings and flying away, leaving me alone.

18

Sadie

And just like that, my whole world was gone.

After Mama disappeared onto the riverbank with my baby sister, I remained by the grate, waiting. Some part of me expected her to realize the foolishness of her own plan and return.

"Mama!" I called, louder than I should, just in case she was still within earshot. It was dangerous—I might be heard by a patrol or passerby overhead and give us all away. But I didn't care anymore.

After listening for a response and hearing none, I started back toward the chamber, dejected. As I neared the entrance, I stumbled forward and tripped, falling into the shallow water on my hands and knees. Water soaked into my clothes. "Mama!" I cried like a helpless child, not getting up.

Bubbe appeared at the entrance to the chamber and helped me to my feet. "Your mother's gone," she said without emotion.

"Mama," I said again, as though calling her name over

and over would somehow bring her back. But my voice was weaker now.

"You must be quiet," Bubbe admonished as she steered me back to the chamber. "Someone will hear you and we'll all be done for."

Inside the chamber, I slumped against the wall. Mama was lost and on her own with the baby. How could she manage, alone and weakened from giving birth just days earlier? Exposed on the street without a place to hide or even a clean set of clothes, she would surely arouse suspicion and might be quickly caught.

Saul came and wrapped me in a dry blanket, then put his arms around me. As I nestled my head under his chin, I could feel his father's puzzled stare as he watched the two of us together. It was more than just our physical contact, which normally would have been forbidden. He was also realizing for the first time how close his son and I had become. For Pan Rosenberg and his mother, this had to come as a shock. Despite his fondness for me, he would never understand nor approve his son being with someone like me, who was not an observant Jew.

Heedless of what the others might think, Saul led me to the corner of the chamber Mama and I shared. "Sit," he said, still holding me. I did not argue, but dropped to the edge of the bed. His embrace, which I usually welcomed, was little comfort. My mother had left me. The entire chamber seemed cavernous and empty.

Bubbe crossed the chamber and handed me a cup of watery tea. I wanted to hate her and her son now. They were the ones who had said the baby could not stay and who had all but forced my mother to flee with her to the street. But in reality, they had just stated the obvious, given voice to the truth we had all known but had not wanted to admit. The decision to leave with my sister—and to leave me behind—had been my mother's and hers alone.

"Your mother is fair-skinned and doesn't look like a Jew,"

Pan Rosenberg offered, trying to be helpful. "She might be able to fit in on the street." The idea was so ridiculous I might have laughed. Mama was gaunt and ghost-pale after months in the sewer, with filthy, torn rags as clothes. I should have given her Ella's dress, I realized. I had been too distraught at her leaving to think of it at the time. That would not have made a difference, though. None of us could pass for normal people anymore.

That evening, I sat among the Rosenbergs for dinner, feeling the void where Mama should have been. "She's coming back," I told the others as we finished eating.

"Of course she is," Bubbe replied, not sounding at all like she meant it. I calculated in my head how long it would take Mama, slowed by the weight of the baby and her own weakness from giving birth, to get to the hospital and return. Several hours maybe; a day at most.

Night came and still Mama didn't appear. "Do you want to read?" Saul asked. I shook my head. Although I would have liked to be alone with him, I was too tired and sad to manage the walk. "I'll be close by if you need me," he said, his voice heavy with concern as I climbed into bed. Of course, he could not comfort me here.

After he walked away, I lay alone in bed on my side of the chamber, the space beside me now cold. Mama's words rattled around over and over again in my head: *I'll come back to you, I swear.* Her intentions seemed clear—deliver the baby safely to the hospital, then return swiftly to me. I wanted to believe her. But so much could have gone wrong.

I replayed in my mind the moment my mother left. I thought, too, back to that day in the ghetto when the German police had come and I'd hidden in the trunk. Mama, thinking I'd been taken, had been ready to jump and end her own life. Then, she would have sooner died than lived without me. Now she'd willingly left me behind. What had changed?

The baby, of course, was what had changed. Still, I could not resent my sister. In fact, I longed for her, too. I missed the tiny baby who had lain between us in bed for months in Mama's belly and then for just a few nights outside. For a moment I had a sister and then she was gone. Once I had not wanted her at all. But she had come and I loved her and the loss was cavernous and vast. I had not imagined that the absence of something so tiny could feel so immense.

I slept with my arms flung over the emptiness where Mama usually lay. I half expected her to slip in beside me during the night and warm me with her tiny frame as she always did. I tossed restlessly, dreaming that she had come back, still holding my sister. "I just couldn't leave her," she said, passing the baby to me once more.

When I awoke, it was morning and Mama had not returned. But the dream was so real, I could almost see her beside me and feel the baby warm in my arms. Then the cold dampness jarred my bones. I lay still, overwhelmed by the wholeness of my loss. First Papa, then my mother and sister. My family had been taken from me piece by piece until there was simply nothing more left. My heart screamed.

The second day after Mama was gone stretched long. After breakfast, I retreated to our bed and curled up into a ball. "What are you doing?" Bubbe scolded when several hours had passed and I lay in bed still. "This is not what your mother would have expected of you." She did not force me to get up, though. Instead, she brought me meals when it was time, potato mash for lunch and again for dinner. I tried to eat a little, but the thick starchy mixture stuck in my throat.

Saul came to comfort me several times throughout the day, bringing me water and a bit of food. He suggested a walk, but did not push when I declined. As the day wore on and I still did not get up, his concern grew. "Is there anything I can do?" he asked.

Turn back time. Bring my mother and sister back. For all of his good intentions, he was powerless to help. I shook my head sadly. "There's nothing."

Nighttime fell. Mama should have been back by now. Something had happened. I needed to go after her. But even if I could make it onto the street, I had no idea where to find her. She had surely reached the hospital where she was taking my sister by now, if all had gone well. Where she had gone after, though, and why she had not returned were mysteries.

Three days without Mama became four and then five. I stayed in my corner of the chamber for the most part, venturing away only for food or when it was my turn to fetch water. The days seemed endless. Mama had insisted on a routine in the sewer, at least before the baby was born: get up and fix our hair, brush our teeth after breakfast. She had created lessons and simple games to pass the time. But without her, the order she had established disappeared. I napped often, looking for my family in my dreams. I tried to imagine what the next lesson would have been, if Mama were still here to teach it. I did not dare to write on the little chalkboard Pawel had given us that contained the very last of my mother's handwriting, wanting to hang on to that bit of her forever.

"Get up!" Bubbe snapped again one morning. Nearly a week had passed and I still spent most of my days sulking in bed. "What would your mother think?" she demanded. She was right. The tiny living area that Mama and I shared, which she had kept so neat, was a mess now, the few belongings I owned strewn about. My hair was unkempt, clothes dirty.

"Does it matter?" I cried. Overcome with sadness, I stood and ran from the chamber into the tunnel to the main pipe where the water ran fast and deep. I looked down at the rushing water, wishing that the river would carry me away to safety far beyond the sewer and the war. I could step into it and be swept away to Papa. I imagined a reunion with him, though I could not picture where. I reached my foot toward the water and dipped it in, the iciness seeping through my shoe. I pictured darkness too thick to see through, felt the water filling my lungs. Could I simply let go or would I fight until the last? Or I might be carried downstream to where the sewer met the outside river and be shot. Any which way would be an escape from this hellish prison.

I leaned farther forward. But I could not do it. There was a sudden shuffling sound behind me. I turned to face Pan Rosenberg. He saw me near the water and his face seemed to crumple with understanding. "Sadele, no." The nickname, one my mother used for me, brought tears to my eyes.

I tried to think of an explanation for what I had been doing so close to the edge. "You need to do better," Pan Rosenberg said before I could speak. He pointed upward. "Up there, almost no more Jews live." He did not bother to spare me from the truth the way my parents and others had when I was younger. There was no safety in hiding things anymore. "We are the last of our kind and down here we are alive. You owe it to your parents to go on."

"But what is there left to go on for?" My voice was plaintive as I spoke these words of despair aloud for the first time.

"You must go on for your mother," he replied. "After all, she left for you."

"How can you say that?" I demanded, feeling the full rush of pain and loss behind my words, which came out rudely. "She abandoned me."

"No, no," Pan Rosenberg said. "She left to save you. Your mother didn't leave because she didn't care. She left because you and your sister were the only thing she had left to care about, and she thought leaving was her best chance to save you both. You don't want that to be for nothing."

He continued, "You are the only one of your family. You have an obligation to go on." He was right. Though my heart ached with pain, I needed to be strong and do what was right for Mama's sake—just as she had tried to do for me.

"My mother..." I still could not let go of the fact that she had abandoned me—or ignore the danger she was likely in right now. "Where is she?"

"I don't know. But you owe it to her to survive, no matter what."

"But what if she doesn't come back?"

For a second, I hoped that he would protest that wouldn't happen and deny the possibility that Mama might not return. But he would not lie to me. "Then you owe it to her to live in a way she would have wanted. To make her proud."

He was right, I realized. What would Mama think if she could see me now, messy and undisciplined, all of her hard work undone? I vowed that I would start a routine after that, and force myself to walk for exercise, to study and to keep myself clean.

Pan Rosenberg led me back inside and went to his corner of the chamber. A moment later, he returned and handed me a book. "I carted as many books as I could from our home to the ghetto."

I nodded. "Like my father." The two men were so similar in that way; despite their outward differences, they might have become good friends if they'd had the chance.

I had known about Pan Rosenberg's books—it was where Saul got the ones we read each night. His father, Saul had explained, simply couldn't bear to leave them, and insisted on grabbing the few he could when fleeing. "He guarded his books in the ghetto and only once, when we were nearly freezing to death and there was no wood, did he let us burn one for kindling," Saul had explained. It was one of the few times, Saul said, that he had seen tears in his father's eyes.

In all the months in the sewer, though, Pan Rosenberg had never personally offered any of his precious books to me—until now. I accepted the book, a collection of stories by Sholem

Aleichem, eagerly. I opened to the first page, struggling to see the words in the dim light. "It's too dark in here," he said apologetically. "You probably have to go to the place beneath the grate to read with Saul." I was surprised he knew about that.

"I always wanted a daughter," he added. "I hoped that my wife and I might have had one if we had been blessed with more children. Or a granddaughter if my son Micah had lived to have children." His voice cracked as he saw the full spectrum of his loss splayed before him. He cleared his throat. "Anyway, I'm glad you're here with us."

"Thank you," I said, surprised and touched by his words.

"You must find little bits of light, things like this to help you go on," he added as he straightened.

"But how?" Mama had given me hope, and my sister, too. Both of them were gone.

"Find the things that give you hope and cling to them. That is the only way we will make it through this war."

That night, I waited eagerly until the others went to bed, wanting to go to the annex and read the book that Pan Rosenberg had given me. I hoped that if I escaped into the story, I might find a brief respite from my constant worry about Mama.

After a while, a shadow appeared over my bed. It was Saul. He held out his hand to me, indicating I should come with him. I picked up the book Pan Rosenberg had given me and carried it along. We set out in silence, fingers intertwined. Normally I found our quiet walks together soothing. But nothing could ease my panic about my mother.

"I have to go after my mother," I said when we reached the annex and settled into our close reading space.

Saul shook his head. "Impossible. There is no way to find her. You have to stay and live. It is what she would have wanted." His words were a refrain of his father's earlier. "Anyway, I need you here." I turned to him, surprised. "That sounds selfish, I know. I didn't know how much I missed you until you were gone that

night to find food. Without you to walk beside me, I was lost."
He touched my cheek. "This is love, Sadie." I stared at him in
stunned silence, wondering if perhaps this was all a dream. "I
know that now. I'm only sorry it took me so long to realize it."

Impulsively, I leaned toward him and our lips met. I expected
him to pull away. Our being together was wrong. For Saul, because of his lost fiancée. For me, because I did not believe that
I could possibly be a woman he could love under these circumstances, or maybe at all. I had just lost everything. How was it
possible to feel so much sorrow and joy at the same time? But
both of us were swept away, powerless to stop the feelings that
had grown between us.

Several seconds later, we broke apart. "But how can we possibly?" I blurted out. "I'm not religious."

"Does that matter here?" He smiled. I wanted to ask what
would happen to us if we made it out. Neither of us dared speak
of a future, though. The moment would have to be enough.

I moved closer, taking comfort in the warmth of his affection. But my thoughts quickly turned back to my mother. "I'm
just so worried."

"Your mother would never leave you for good," he said. "Not
by choice. Something must have stopped her from coming back."

The notion was not a comforting one. "She could have been
arrested or hurt or worse," I fretted. I waited for him to argue
with me, and reassure me that it hadn't happened. But he could
not. "I never should have let her go," I berated myself.

"You couldn't have stopped her."

I nodded, acknowledging the truth of what he'd said. "I just
feel so powerless. Trapped down here, I can't do anything to
help her."

"Maybe your friend can help."

Ella, I remembered suddenly. The previous Sunday, in my
sadness and shock after Mama left, I had not gone to see her. I
was surprised that Saul had suggested I go to her now. He did

not trust Ella and, under normal circumstances, asking her for help was the last thing I would have thought he'd suggest. "You made me swear not to go to her."

"Yes. I was worried about you and wished you hadn't gone, but she's the one person who might be able to help."

I considered the suggestion. In my worry, I had not considered asking Ella for help. The last time I had seen Ella had been nearly two weeks earlier. I had missed our regular visit and I didn't know if Ella had given up or stopped coming. But I would try.

It was only Wednesday, I realized. I would have to wait another four days to see Ella. The days between passed slowly. At last, on Sunday morning, I set out from the chamber while the others were still asleep. In the tunnel, I stopped again, seeing a shadow ahead. Someone blocking my path. Panic rose in me. Bubbe, I realized, taking in the hunched figure. I relaxed somewhat. I had not noticed that she was not in her bed.

"What are you doing out here?" I asked.

"I was just going to fetch water," she replied.

"I can do that for you." I took the empty jug, puzzled. It was always the younger people, me or Saul, who went for the water. She could not have crawled through the forty, nor managed the weight of the jug when it was full. Why did she think she had to do it now?

"Thank you," she said when I returned with the jug a minute later. It was heavy and I walked alongside her carrying it. "I want to make soup and I didn't have enough water for five bowls."

"Four," I corrected gently. That we were one less without Mama was like a dagger in my heart.

"Yes, of course, four," Bubbe agreed. There was a confusion that lingered in her eyes.

A realization came over me. "Bubbe, are you feeling okay?"

"Fine, fine," she snapped. "I'm an old woman. I forget things. That's to be expected."

Uneasiness rose in me. Bubbe had seemed to change during our time in the sewer, growing angrier and sometimes not remembering things. I had attributed it to the terrible conditions and her being ill suited to handle them due to age. But I could see it clearly now: this was more than just the forgetfulness or grumpiness of old age. Bubbe was not well. Illness or age or the madness of the sewer, or maybe some combination of the three, was slowly taking her mind. Perhaps her body, too, I thought, seeing for the first time how frail and wizened she had become, compared to the woman who had navigated the tunnels so heartily the night we first arrived. I wondered if Saul had noticed, and decided not to say anything to him yet. He had already been through so much and more bad news might be more than he could bear.

"Come," I said gently. I led her back to the entrance of the chamber. "Go inside and rest." More than once Bubbe had forbidden me from going to the grate because of the risk. I waited for her to stop me. I prayed she would not quarrel or insist that she come, too.

When she had retreated inside, I started down the tunnel once more. I approached the deep basin and climbed down into it. Then I climbed up the far side, quicker this time because I knew how to manage it.

I reached the grate. It was Sunday morning and Ella should have been there. But she was not. Of course. I had missed the previous week and she probably assumed I wasn't going to come today either. She may well have given up on me entirely by now.

Seeing the daylight beyond the grate, something broke open in me then. Even without Ella, I needed to go to the street, to find Mama and see if she was okay. I could get out on my own.

I reached for the grate, then stopped. *It isn't safe up there*, a voice seemed to say. It sounded like Pawel. Pawel, God love him, had kept us here because he thought it was the only way to protect us. But Pawel was gone and my mother would be, too, if I didn't do something. We had to save ourselves.

Of course, if I went onto the street without Ella, I would have no help and no hiding place. I would be nearly as vulnerable and exposed as Mama had been. But I could not stay down here and wonder. I had to try.

I pushed on the heavy grate. It didn't budge. I tried again. I was confused. It had opened just days earlier when I let Mama out. I wondered if someone had come and sealed it shut. There was a stone, I could see, that had somehow wedged into the narrow space by the edge of the grate, sealing it shut. A tiny stone, standing in the way of me getting out and finding my mother. It was all suddenly too much. My frustration rose to a boil, bubbled over. I rattled the grate noisily, pounded on it so loud that anyone passing by might have heard. But the grate remained stuck.

Defeated, I turned and started back through the tunnel. I could not get out, at least this way. The Dębniki grate, I remembered. That was how Ella and I had seen each other in the first place. As I started in that direction, my doubts bubbled anew: the grate was high up and just off a busy street. I didn't know if I could reach it, and even if I did, I might be spotted. If I wanted to find Mama, though, it was my only hope. I had to try.

I retraced my steps, through the tunnels and past the chamber. At last I reached the other grate. I looked up, wishing I might see Ella's face above as I so often had. Of course, the space was empty. She wasn't expecting me here. I looked around dubiously. Then I noticed notched metal ledges along one of the walls. The workers must use those for climbing in and out of the sewer. I put my foot on the first one and reached up, but the walls were slimy and I struggled not to slip. I climbed slowly to the second ledge, then the third. Gingerly, so as not to fall, I reached up and pushed on the sewer grate, praying it would not be stuck shut as the other one had been.

The grate slid sideways. I peered above ground in both directions to make sure that no one was in the alley to see me.

Then, using all my effort, I hoisted myself from the sewer and onto the street.

I was above ground once more. Only this time I was on my own.

19

Ella

Sadie had disappeared.

Or at least that was my fear as I made my way toward the river one warm morning in July. It had been two weeks since I had seen her. The previous Sunday, a week after we went in search of food together and she had returned underground, I went to the sewer grate by the river at our usual meeting time. When Sadie didn't appear that day, I assumed that she had been delayed and waited as long as I could. The grate looked slightly ajar, as if someone had moved and replaced it. I wondered if I had left it that way the night I'd helped her return to the sewer. I remembered placing the grate squarely back atop the hole, though, and checking it to make sure it looked untouched so no one on the street would notice. No, it had been moved again. As I had straightened the grate, I prayed that someone from the street had not gone down below. There was simply no way to tell.

As I drew near the bridge, the crowd of pedestrians grew thicker, the normal flow of morning foot traffic somehow impeded. Ahead, the police had erected some sort of barricade, forcing the crowd into a queue. I prayed it was not another *aktion* like the time I had seen the woman jump from the bridge with her children. But the police did not seem as urgent as they had that day, their movements perfunctory and efficient. A checkpoint, I realized as they began checking the papers one by one of the people attempting to cross the bridge. The notion was only slightly less worrying than the *aktion*. Since the start of the war, the police had set up checkpoints across the city at random, inspecting the papers of ordinary Poles, questioning any irregularities. But it happened with greater frequency now, and the reasons people might be detained for questioning seemed more arbitrary and frequent.

The man in line in front of me shuffled forward and I followed, pulling out my identification card as I neared the checkpoint. *"Kennkarte?"* the policeman asked me. As I handed the card to him, my heartbeat quickened. My papers were in order and the stamps Ana Lucia had procured from the Germans enabled me to walk freely throughout the city. But that would not stop the police from questioning the purpose of my going to Dębniki.

The policeman looked up from the card, appraising me. I braced for the interrogation that would surely come. Then he handed it back just as quickly. "Move on!" he barked, gesturing for the person behind me to step up and be checked. I hurried on, fighting the urge to run.

A few minutes later, I reached the far riverbank. I looked back uneasily at the checkpoint, afraid that the police might be able to see the sewer grate. But the vantage point was thankfully obscured from view. There were a few children playing by the water's edge, though, feeding the ducks, and I had to wait several feet away until they moved on. At last I started toward the entrance to the sewer. It was almost eleven thirty now, our scheduled meeting time had passed, and as I neared the grate, I expected to see Sadie, looking up, her brown eyes hopeful and expectant. She wasn't there. My uneasiness grew. One missed visit was an aberration; there might be any number of reasons that she could not get away. Twice in a row meant something was wrong.

I knew how important our visits were to her. She wouldn't just stop coming. More to the point, she needed me for food, I thought guiltily, regretful that there had been nothing I could sneak from home that morning without being noticed.

Sadie had not come. Something was wrong. A dozen awful scenarios swept through my brain. She could have been arrested or drowned like her father. Of course, it might not be that bad, I realized. She might be caring for her mother or someone else underground. There was no way to know.

Unless I went into the sewer. I knelt by the grate, my stomach churning as I tried to see beneath. But the space was shrouded in darkness. I did not know how Sadie did it, day after day. It wasn't that bad, she had said more than once. The sewer was a refuge to her, salvation. She had gotten used to the awful conditions. As I stared into the hole, though, I could not imagine going down there for a single second. It was not the filth, nor the raging sewer waters she had described sweeping her father to his death, that scared me the most.

Rather, I was afraid of tight spaces. "Claustrophobia," my brother, Maciej, had called it.

My mind reeled back to a childhood nightmare of being trapped. It was more than a nightmare, I realized suddenly, the memory snapping clear into place. When my father was on business trips, Ana Lucia could be unfathomably cruel. She didn't hit me, but she had other ways, like forgetting to feed me for a day and a half. Olga, our cook at the time, slipped me scraps when my stepmother wasn't looking so I didn't grow faint with hunger. Once when I had gotten dirty playing outside, Ana Lucia locked me in an armoire, packed full with a dozen fur coats. Stuck among the pelts of those dead animals, I could not breathe. I cried out, but the coats muffled the sound of my voice. I imagined the air disappearing and me slowly suffocating while nobody knew. I tried the door but it was locked. It was four hours before Olga realized where I was and freed me and I came out sweaty and hysterical. Ana Lucia had gone to town and there was no telling how long she would have left me there if my Olga had not come.

After that day, I could not bear to be in a close space again. And I could not go into the sewer now. I stepped back, ashamed of my cowardice.

In the distance, a clock chimed half past eleven. It was too late for Sadie to come now. I started away from the riverbank, then hesitated. The bridge was still choked thick with pedestrians at the checkpoint, so there was no point in starting back home now. I looked up the road toward the square in Dębniki and the spires of the Kostka Church which loomed above it. The other grate, I remembered suddenly. I had not returned to the sewer opening behind the church since Sadie and I had decided to meet by the riverbank. The grate in Dębniki was closer to where Sadie lived underground; perhaps if I went there, I might be able to find her. It was unlikely, but there was no other place I might look for her. I started up the riverbank and toward the industrial neighborhood, which had become more familiar to me since I had started coming. I reached the alleyway and, after making sure that no one was watching, walked to the grate. But the place beneath was dark. Sadie was not there.

Of course not. We had decided not to meet here anymore. Dejected, I left the alley. I neared the market square and looked in the direction of the café. Part of me wanted to go see if Krys was there, but after how poorly we had parted the last time, I could not. Instead, I started back toward the bridge. It was going to take a while to get through the checkpoint and I debated whether I should take the time to walk to another bridge. As I skirted the edge of the Rynek Dębnicki, I spied a familiar figure.

Sadie.

I blinked twice, not quite believing what I was seeing. Sadie was on the street.

I raced toward her. What was she doing here? I had gotten here not a moment too soon. She was standing in the middle of a crowd of ordinary people in broad daylight, looking around, as if to get her bearings. The dress I had given her when we last met was now soiled and wet from the sewer. She sorely stood out with her gaunt frame and dirty clothes. People steered wide around her, giving her odd looks, and any moment now someone was going to realize what was going on—and possibly alert the police. I raced toward her.

"There you are!" I said, forcing normalcy into my voice. I kissed her cheek as though nothing was amiss, trying not to cringe at the sewer smell. "We're late for your doctor's appointment. Come." Before she could protest, I led her away from the square and onto a side street.

"Doctor's appointment?" she asked when we were far enough away that no one else could hear.

"I was just trying to think of an excuse why you were standing on the street in such a state. What on earth are you doing here?" I was torn between happiness at seeing her and concern at the same time.

"The grate by the river was stuck and I had to get out. I need to find my mother."

"Find her?" I stopped walking and turned to Sadie. An uneasy feeling rose in me. "What do you mean?"

"Right after I last saw you, my mother went into early labor. She had the baby, a girl. But we couldn't keep her in the sewer because she was crying too loudly. So my mother brought her up to a hospital, the Bonifratrów Hospital in Kazimierz, because Pawel said someone there might shelter a child. Or at least that is what she was trying to do. It's been over a week and she hasn't come back yet."

"Oh, Sadie…" My mind whirled, trying to process all that had happened to Sadie in the short time since I had last seen her.

She continued, "So I came looking for you to see if you would help me. Only you weren't there."

"I'm so sorry. There were children playing near the grate and I had to wait until they left." I omitted the part about the checkpoint, not wanting to alarm her needlessly. "But, Sadie, you can't do this. It isn't safe for you to be up here."

"I came out of the sewer before."

"That was different." Sneaking around at night to find food was one thing. Walking the streets in broad daylight, though, and asking questions was quite another. If she spoke to the wrong person, she would be arrested and it would all be over. But she didn't care anymore. With her mother and sister gone, there was simply nothing left to lose. "Sadie, think. You won't be able to help them at all if you are caught." She remained silent, unwilling to acknowledge the truth of my words. Her jaw set stubbornly.

"Last time you helped me come up," she said finally.

"We planned it. It was nighttime. And things are more dangerous now," I added.

"How?" she demanded. There was a hardness to her. She was less trusting—even of me.

I hesitated. "There are more police on the street, even SS, stopping people and questioning them. There was even a checkpoint on my way here today where I had to show papers," I added, telling her the truth now in my attempt to make her understand. Sadie's eyes widened. "So you see, it is not entirely safe for even me to be out, much less you." Sadie, in her wild, despairing grief, looked even more out of place than she had before. No amount of clothes or makeup would help her fit in.

No, there was no way for Sadie to walk the streets safely now. "I don't know if I can protect you."

Sadie's face turned to a mixture of anger and disappointment. "Then don't." She did not mean it rudely, I knew. She was just determined to find her mother at any cost. "If things are more dangerous, then it is even more important that I find my mother quickly and bring her back to the sewer safely."

"If you get arrested, there are others who will pay as well." I was not thinking only of myself, but of Krys, who had helped me. "Coming up in the middle of the day is dangerous and foolish."

"I'm sorry," she said, sounding genuinely contrite. "I had to look for my mother. I couldn't wait any longer."

"If you had asked me, we could have made a plan. I would have helped you. And I will now." I wrapped my arms around her, caught between wanting to help her and protect her at the same time. I didn't think I could do both. Helping her was risky for me as well. I had intended to be gone on my errand to see her for only a few hours. This would surely take much longer, causing Ana Lucia to ask questions about my absence and whereabouts. Despite the danger, though, I could not turn my back on Sadie. "I will go ask at the hospital for you. But you have to stay hidden while I do."

"I won't go back without her," she said, her eyes resolute.

"Come." I didn't know where to take her. I did not dare hide her in Ana Lucia's house a second time. "Krys," I said suddenly aloud. "Perhaps he can help." Then I stopped again. We had not parted well last time I saw him. He might not want to see me at all. But I had to try. Swallowing my pride, I started toward the café. At least he might be able to hide Sadie while I went in search of her mother.

"Have you seen Krys?" Sadie asked as we walked. "Since that night on the riverbank, I mean."

"Yes. But I almost wish I hadn't."

"Why? How can you say that?"

I hesitated. Though I had wanted to tell Sadie about Krys, it seemed ridiculous to talk about my troubles now when Sadie was suffering so. "After you went back underground, I went to see him. At first, things were good between us, the way they used to be. I almost thought we could be together again. But then we quarreled."

"About what?"

"You," I admitted. Her eyes widened. "That is, about the sewer. He wanted to store munitions there for the Home Army. But I told him it was too dangerous."

"I'll store them if you want," she said meekly, fear in her eyes. "It's the least I can do."

"No," I said quickly. "I won't let you do that. It's very good of you, but I can't let you endanger yourself or the others. We will find another way." But the point gnawed at me as we made our way toward the café. I had refused to do what Krys wanted and we had parted angrily. Did I really dare ask for his help now?

"Saul kissed me," Sadie blurted abruptly. "That is, we kissed. You were right. It turns out he is fond of me as well." As she confided in me, her cheeks flushed.

"Oh, Sadie, I told you so!"

"I know it's awful. I shouldn't be thinking about such things right now, much less talking about them. But I had to tell you."

"I'm glad you did. I'm so happy for you." Anything that gave Sadie the slightest bit of hope right now seemed a blessing.

We reached the café and I led Sadie to the same archway where she had hidden the last time we had come here. I walked into the café and stopped. I had expected to see the girl with the dark curls. Instead, an unfamiliar man with an auburn beard stood behind the bar, drying glasses. "Excuse me," I said. "I'm looking for the young woman who usually works here."

"Kara?" he asked, and I nodded, hoping that was right. It was the first time I had heard her name. "She's in the cellar bar."

He gestured down a flight of stairs on the right side of the café that I had not noticed before. I walked carefully down the uneven brick steps. At the bottom, I was surprised to find a lively *piwnica*. Redbrick cellar bars were not uncommon in Kraków; at least a dozen ringed the main market square. But I had not known about this unmarked one here beneath the café. An off-license, I realized, a business running without the knowledge or permission of the Germans. I was surprised how crowded it was for late morning. A mix of young people, students and workers, filled a half-dozen or so tables hewn from rough wood, drinking beer from large mugs. They were almost all men and a few shot me curious looks as I reached the bottom of the stairs.

Kara stood behind the bar, pulling on a long tap on a wooden barrel to serve beer. I walked to her and her eyes flickered with surprise, then annoyance. "You again." She put a mug in front of me. I fished a coin from my bag and placed it on the bar, but she didn't take it. I had never liked beer and I didn't want to drink it at this hour of the morning, but I could tell from Kara's expression that she was trying to keep up appearances. I took a sip from the mug, the bitter froth tickling my lip.

"Krys isn't here," she said.

"Where is he?" I asked.

"Out of the city." She lowered her voice. "He's away on an errand for Korsarz."

"The black marketeer?" She nodded. "But Krys would never work with Korsarz." Krys hated the man and all he stood for. "Not unless he had to." I thought back to the potatoes Krys had managed to get for Sadie—and his reluctance to say how he had procured them so quickly. He claimed someone owed him a favor, but I realized now that he had gone to Korsarz to help Sadie—and me even, though it meant working with the despicable man to repay to debt.

"When will Krys be back?" I asked.

"I have no idea. Do you want to leave a message for when he returns?" Kara asked, pushing a napkin across the bar.

I shook my head. But suddenly I was filled with remorse. Krys had helped me, even as I refused to do the same for him. Thinking better of it, I scribbled a note.

I'm sorry. I will help with whatever you need. E.

I debated putting some sort of affectionate sign-off and decided against it.

But still I had no way to hide Sadie. Krys, I realized, was not the one who could help me now. I handed Kara the note and took a deep breath. "I need your help."

"Me?"

I nodded. "I have a package I need you to store." Kara looked confused. "She's outside."

Her jaw tightened. "No. Absolutely not. We can't shelter fugitives here."

"She isn't a fugitive, just a girl trying to stay alive."

Still, Kara refused. "If the police come looking, we'll be shut down." I could tell by her voice that she was not concerned about the business of the *piwnica* itself, but rather its use as a front for the work of the Home Army.

"Please. She's got nowhere else to go."

"That's not my problem."

"Krys is also helping her," I added. It was only partly a lie; he had found food for Sadie. "She has a hiding place that he thinks may be of use to the Home Army for storing things. But not if she's caught."

Kara's expression softened. "There are cellar doors around the corner behind the building. Take her and I will meet you there."

I sprinted back up the stairs and outside to the archway where Sadie hid. "Follow me." I led her around the back of the building. There were wide metal double doors in the ground, the kind

used to unload beer and other provisions. One door opened and
Sadie climbed down the ladder into the cellar. I started behind
her, but Kara stopped me. "You don't need to be here," she said
coldly. "Go take care of your errand." She might have agreed
to help, but she still didn't like me.

Sadie looked back up at me, seeming dismayed that I was not
staying with her. "I'll be back for you," I promised. "You need
to stay out of sight."

"But I have to look for my mother." Despite everything I had
explained to her, she still wanted to go.

"I will look for her," I added, putting my hand on her shoulder. "I'll go to the hospital and check for you. But only if you
promise to stay here." Her expression remained doubtful. "You
believe me, don't you?"

"Yes," Sadie replied. "But please be careful. Helping me get
food was one thing, but going to the hospital and asking questions is much more dangerous." Her brow furrowed.

"Don't worry," I replied, touched by her concern for my
safety. "I'll go quickly and come straight back, all right?" Seemingly satisfied, Sadie turned away.

"Wait," I said. "What's your mother's name?" I had only just
realized I didn't know it.

"Danuta," she said sadly. "Danuta Gault." She disappeared
into the cellar.

"I'll be back for her as soon as I can," I said to Kara. "She
could use something to eat, if you can manage it."

"I can. She needs to be gone by nightfall."

"I swear it. And thank you." Without speaking further, Kara
closed the cellar door, leaving me on the street alone.

I hurried from Dębniki toward the bridge that connected the
south bank to the city center. As I walked, I processed all Sadie
had told me. I knew little about having babies, but I could not
imagine what Sadie's mother had been through, giving birth in
the sewer. And to be forced to leave her other daughter behind;

it was unimaginable. Sadie seemed so hopeful that her mother and sister might be all right. Part of me did not want to know what had become of them, to have to tell her the awful truth if I found out. But I had promised Sadie—and so I had to try.

I crossed the bridge and soon reached the Bonifratrów Hospital, a mammoth building on the edge of Kazimierz. Though I could tell it had once been well-tended, its redbrick facade was pockmarked and stained with soot, sidewalks cracked, the untended bushes and shrubs outside withered and brown. The front door to the hospital, set back in an archway, was locked, so I rang the buzzer beside it. A minute later, a nun appeared. The hospital was owned by a monastic order, I recalled, with a church and rectory just around the corner.

"I'm sorry, but we're closed to visitors," she said, looking down at me through crooked spectacles.

"I'm looking for a woman called Danuta Gault."

A guarded look crossed the nun's face. "I don't know any such person."

I was confused. Sadie had seemed so certain of her mother's destination. Had she been wrong or had something happened to change her mother's plans once she was above ground? "Are you sure?" I pressed. "She is a petite woman, quite beautiful, with very light hair," I said, recalling how Sadie had once described her mother to me.

The woman shook her head firmly. "There is no such person here." I felt a tug of disappointment. Sadie's mother was not here. I had nowhere else to look. I was going to have to return to the *piwnica* and tell Sadie I had failed.

"She was traveling with a newborn child," I said then. In my haste, I had forgotten to state the obvious. "She was trying to find a safe place for the child."

Something seemed to shift in the nun's eyes and I could tell that Sadie's mother had been here. "I can't help you." Though her expression remained unchanged, there was fear in her voice now.

"She's my mother," I lied, hoping she would be more willing to help me if the person I was searching for was immediate
family. "I have to find her. I'm worried something might have
happened to her," I said, feeling Sadie's sadness and fear as if
they were my own. "Please. She's the only family I have left. If
you could just let me in. I'll only stay a minute."

The nun hesitated, then opened the door a crack further.
"Inside, quickly." She led me into the hospital. I followed her
down a long corridor, with at least a dozen rooms on either side.
There came a beeping sound from a machine in one room, a
low moan from another. A metallic smell assaulted my nose.
My mind reeled back to when I was a small child, visiting my
mother in the hospital. My father had lifted me up to kiss her
papery cheek because she was too weak to hold me herself. It
was the last time I had ever seen her.

Pushing the memory aside, I focused on the nun who walked
briskly ahead of me and led me into a small office. I studied the
picture behind her desk, a framed oil painting of Jesus at the
crucifixion. Although I often wore the small cross around my
neck that Tata had given me for sentimental value, we were not
a religious family and I had not been to mass since my mother
died. The nun cleared some papers from a chair and gestured
for me to sit.

"You can only stay for a minute. We're under a no-visitors
order from the General Government. I would be in grave trouble if anyone found out I let you in."

"I'll go quickly," I promised. "But first, can you tell me if
you have seen the woman I asked about?"

"She isn't your mother, is she?" the nun asked sternly.

I lowered my head. "No. I'm sorry. She is my friend's mother."
I had lied to a nun. I felt as though lightning might strike at any
moment. I wondered if she would be angry, insist that I leave
without helping me.

"The woman you mentioned came here. One of our priests

found her on the street and brought her in for care. When she arrived here, she was very weak. She had a high fever, an infection from giving birth. She had lost a great deal of blood." I was surprised; Sadie had not mentioned that her mother was so sick. Perhaps she had not known. "We offered her a bed. At first, she did not want to take it. She said she had to get back, to where or whom, she would not say. But she had no choice—she was simply too weak to leave. So we tended to her, gave her what little food and medicine we had."

My heart raced with excitement. I had found Sadie's mother. "Where is she now?" I asked. I could reunite them, or at least let Sadie know that her mother was safe.

Her face grew stony. "The Germans came. Usually they avoid the hospital, not wanting to get sick themselves. But this time, they entered and interrogated the staff. They'd received reports of a strangely dressed woman who had nearly collapsed on the street." The nun's words sank deep into my bones. Someone had seen Sadie's mom and reported her. "We could not stand up to the Germans and risk the other patients and the work we are doing here." Something in her voice told me that their mission went beyond medical care and I wondered if the hospital itself played a role in resisting the Germans. "But we were not about to let them take her. They surely would have killed her as they did the patients at the Jewish hospital." She paused. "So we gave her mercy ourselves, a simple injection. She did not suffer or feel pain."

Mercy. The word reverberated in my mind. Sadie's mother had died. My heart ached for my friend, who had already lost so much.

I swallowed down my sadness, looked up at the nun. "When?"

"A few days ago."

I shuddered. I was too late. If only I had known, come sooner. But even as I thought it, I knew that I could not have saved her. "And the child, what became of her?"

The nun looked confused. "I'm sorry, I don't understand."

"My friend's mother had an infant with her."

She shook her head. "She didn't. She came here alone."

"But you said she had a baby."

"No, I said that she had given birth. We could tell that much from her condition. And she kept talking about a child. Such things are not uncommon with women who have lost a child or are in a kind of denial. But there was never a child here with her." She stood. "I'm sorry, but I've told you all that I know. Now for the safety of our patients, I must ask you to leave." She walked me from her office and let me out of a side door to the hospital.

I turned away, sickened and stunned by all I had learned. I stopped at the fence outside the hospital, leaned on the railing for support. Sadie's mother was gone, her baby sister nowhere to be found. I felt the pain of losing my own mother so many years ago, as sharp and real as if it was yesterday. But when my mother died, I still had Tata and my siblings to comfort me. Sadie had no family left at all. How was I ever going to tell her?

When I reached the café, I went around back and knocked softly on the cellar door. Kara opened one of the doors and led me to a corner where Sadie sat. Seeing me, her face brightened expectantly. "Any news?" Over Sadie's shoulder, Kara's eyes met mine. "My mother," Sadie said. "Did you learn anything?"

I faltered. *Tell her nothing*, a voice inside said. Revealing the truth would only destroy her. What harm was there, really, in allowing her to keep hope? But I had never been any good at keeping secrets. I recalled the long, excruciating months when my father was missing at the front, before we had known his fate. Hope had been almost crueler than grief. I took a deep breath.

Then I stopped. I couldn't do it.

I tried to tell Sadie that her mother had died. But the words stuck in my throat. Her mother had been the very last part of her world, the thing that had kept her going. Now I had to take

that last bit of family away from her. I remembered how I felt
the night I learned my father was killed, like there was no one
left. I would be doing the same thing to Sadie, under circumstances a million times worse. I would be taking away her very
last hope, her reason to live. It was, quite literally, signing her
death sentence.

What was the harm, really, in letting her cling to hope for a
few more days? Perhaps I could even search further for Sadie's
baby sister. Even as I thought that, I knew it was futile. But it
gave me hope—and a reason not to tell her just yet.

"Nothing so far." The lie came out before I could stop myself.

Sadie's face fell. "I can't go back without her."

"Sadie, you must. Think of Saul and his family. I will keep
looking," I added quickly. "But I can't ask too many questions
without drawing attention. Now you must come quickly. We
have to get you back to the sewer.

"Thank you," I said to Kara before starting up the ladder. "If
you hear from Krys…" Then I hesitated. I had already left him
a note. "Tell him I'll do it. I'll help, whatever he needs." We
had only this moment. Refusing to help wasn't going to keep us
safe any more than fleeing and hiding had saved Sadie's mother
and sister. Kara nodded gravely.

I led Sadie through the backstreets of Dębniki, not wanting
her odd appearance to attract attention. We walked in silence.
Every step was like lead to me. I needed to tell Sadie the truth
before we parted and she went back underground. I should have
told her back at the bar, I realized. What if she lost her compo-
sure here on the street, made a scene and cried out? At last we
reached the grate by the river. She reached down for the stone
that had caused the grate to stick, pried it open.

"My mother," she said. "You'll keep looking?"

"I promise." The lie broke my heart. I wondered once again
if I should tell her the truth. But if I did, she might not go back
into hiding—or be able to go on at all.

"Check our old neighborhood, as well as the ghetto," she said, trying to think of all of the places her mother might have gone.

I nodded. "I shall."

"Thank you." She smiled gratefully.

My guilt grew, seeming to swallow me whole. "I'm so sorry." My voice cracked and I nearly blurted out the awful truth. Then I caught myself. "I wish there was more I could do."

"You're doing everything you can. I begged my mother not to leave the sewer. If only she had listened."

"Sadie, no! That would not have been possible. If she had stayed, the baby's cries would have alerted someone and you would have all been found by now. She left to protect you."

"She's gone, isn't she?" I didn't answer, but put my arms around her. Her face was a hollow mask, as if some part of her knew the truth without my saying it. "I have no one."

"Don't say that! You have me." The words felt hollow. "I know it isn't much, and it doesn't make up for your mother not being here, or how much you miss her and the rest of your family. But I'm here." She did not respond. "Sadie, look at me." I took both of her hands in mine. "This isn't forever. I swear, I will get you out of the sewer again." How I could make such a promise, I did not know. But I was clutching at straws, anything to give her the will to press on another day.

"You don't have to go," I said, in spite of myself. I had no idea where I would hide her if she didn't. "I mean, if you don't want to go back. We could leave the city tonight, find a way." For a moment, I saw it, the two of us away from here and free.

"I have to," she said. "There are others." Even though her mother and sister were gone, she would not abandon Saul and his family.

Still, she did not go. "It's just really hard down here. The only reason I managed was because of my mother. I'm not sure I'm strong enough to do it without her." Sadie's voice broke. "I can't do this alone."

"You don't have to. Just keep coming to see me, all right? And I will come here and bring whatever I can and we will string together these awful days until the war is over." I tried to make my voice sound positive and sure.

"All right," she said, but I couldn't tell whether she really believed me or was just too sad and weary to argue. She lowered herself into the sewer. I tried to stand in front of her, to block her from view of anyone who might pass by and see the unusual sight.

"I'll be here tomorrow, okay?" I said. "And the day after that. I will come every day. You just have to get up in the morning and come see me." I had no idea how I would manage it. Getting away from Ana Lucia's prying eyes to this remote part of the city once a week was hard enough. But Sadie needed something, anything, to keep her going.

Without a word, she turned and disappeared into the sewer once more.

20

Sadie

Ella was late today. I stood in the tunnel, trying to avoid the rain that slatted through the sewer grate. Wind whipped down, sending the drops sideways, as though they were chasing me. I ducked down into the corner, trying without success to escape the wetness. For once, I wanted to run back to the chamber. But I stayed, certain that Ella would appear.

It was late July now, more than four months since we had first come to the sewer. Mama had been gone for almost three weeks. Ella had not been able to find her, nor learn anything else since I had returned underground. With each passing day it was harder to ignore the undeniable truth that she might not be coming back. Still, I clung to hope because it was the only thing that helped me get through each day. Without my mother, I would have nothing.

It was not just my sadness over Mama's absence that made things hard to bear—our living conditions had deteriorated, too. The summer weather warmed the air and caused the sewer gasses to become thicker and more foul. Our joints ached from the dampness and strange rashes would appear on our skin.

"At least it isn't cold," Pan Rosenberg said once. "I have no idea what we are going to do to survive here next winter." I looked at him with disbelief. Winter was several months away. Surely he didn't imagine we would still be here by then.

Despite the worsening conditions, I tried to do better and make Mama proud. I got up in the morning and washed and dressed, kept the chamber neat and read or studied on a regular schedule. The days passed slowly, though, and the lonely nights were even longer, filled with strange, fitful dreams. One night I dreamed I was floating in the sewer river, and that as I was carried along by the current, I was met by my mother and father. I looked for the baby in Mama's arms.

"Where is she?" I asked.

"Who?" Mama replied, seemingly not understanding. But because we had not given my sister a name, words failed me. My parents pulled me close, forming a kind of raft, and we sailed on together, missing one.

Of course, having Saul helped. We had grown closer since acknowledging our feelings. Our moments together, walking and some reading time in the annex, were still stolen ones, not much more than they previously had been. But knowing that he was close by and that he felt the same way about me as I did him made the days without my mother and sister a little easier to bear.

I looked up through the grate now, where the rain had slowed, still hoping to see Ella. She had come every single day as she had promised since the day she had searched for my mother, no matter the weather or how hard it was for her to get away. Each morning I would wait in the shadows until I saw her approaching and then move into view. We didn't dare talk too much and she would stay for only a few minutes each visit. She had still been unable to find Mama or my sister. Her visits had become a lifeline, though, the thing that kept me going from one day to the next, now more so than ever.

Ella was late today. Not just by a few minutes, but a whole hour. I wondered if she might not come at all. As the minutes passed, drawing further from our appointed meeting time, I had to accept that it might be another day until I saw my friend. If at all. Life was getting much harder for the ordinary citizens, too, on the street above as the war dragged on. I heard it all from beneath ground, the checkpoints and patrols and arrests. Although Ella did not complain or talk much about it, I saw the stress and worry that seemed to crease her beautiful face with every visit. More than once, I considered telling her not to come again. My worry rose now: what if something had happened to her?

Or maybe she was just busy, I thought, her visits with me secondary and unimportant. She had a whole life above ground full of people and hours of the day that I knew nothing about.

But a few minutes later, I saw her hurrying along the embankment, walking more quickly than usual as if to make up for lost time. Her red hair, usually so neat, was unmoored and fanned wildly about her, framed by the clearing clouds above.

"I'm glad to see you," I said. "I was afraid that something happened and you might not be coming at all."

She shrugged. "The police had the bridge blocked. I had to go back and find another way." Before we could speak further, there came noise from the road that ran along the riverbank behind her, the screeching of tires and the sound of police barking orders. Ella's head snapped in the direction of the commotion. She ducked away hurriedly. I stepped back into the shadows, wondering if she would have to go home.

A few minutes later, when the sirens and noise had faded, Ella reappeared and stood over the grate defiantly. "Things are getting worse," I said. There were no Jews left on the street, yet the arrests and reprisals against ordinary Poles seemed to grow every day.

"Yes." Her voice was blunt. "The war is not going well for the Germans." I wondered if it was true, or if she was just trying to give me hope. "The Russians are progressing on the Eastern Front and the Allies to the south." Part of me was skeptical. We had heard such rumors before and still the city remained firmly under German control. "The Germans are trying to take it out on ordinary Poles as much as possible now while they can."

"Because there aren't any Jews left to take it out on," I added bitterly. The Poles suffered, to be sure, but at least most of them were still in their homes and had not been imprisoned or forced into hiding. "You don't have to come, if it's too hard," I offered reluctantly. Seeing Ella was one of the few bright spots I had left and I would hate it if she couldn't come anymore.

Her face turned steely. "I'll be here." I thought that she was the bravest person I had ever seen. "I can't stay long today, though." I nodded, trying not to show that I minded. Even a few minutes was something, a sign that someone still remembered me and cared enough to come.

Ella passed a small loaf of sourdough bread through the grate before leaving. "Are you sure you can spare it?" I asked.

"Yes, certainly," she replied, and I wondered if that was true. She had seemed to grow thinner over the past several weeks and I suspected she was eating less to save food for me. As the war dragged on, food was harder to come by for ordinary Poles. They no longer queued at market because there was nothing to buy anymore. Even Ella and her well-to-do stepmother were feeling the pinch now. I marveled that Ella could still find food for all of us, and I tried not to complain when it was less than it had been. After all, we had fewer mouths to feed than we once had. But it was still nowhere near enough.

The cathedral bells across the river were chiming twelve when Ella left and I started away from the grate. The chamber was oddly quiet, Pan Rosenberg hunched over his prayer book in the corner. I did not see Saul. He must have gone for water, I realized. I wished that I had run into him in the tunnel, so that we could have shared a few quiet moments alone together.

Bubbe lay in the bed on the Rosenbergs' side of the chamber. She had not gotten up that morning and I had tiptoed around to prepare breakfast so as not to wake her. Her confusion had worsened to delirium the past few days and she had remained on her pallet in the far corner of the chamber, moaning and mumbling to herself nonstop. Sometimes when her suffering noises became too loud, I could not help but think that they brought just as much danger as my baby sister's cries once had.

I had tried to speak with Saul about her a few days earlier, when her deteriorating condition was impossible to ignore any longer. "Bubbe," I'd said, stating the obvious. "She isn't well." He had nodded in acknowledgment. "Do you have any idea what it might be?"

"It's a kind of dementia," he said. "Her father had it as well. There's nothing to be done."

I had moved closer, wanting to comfort him. "I'm so sorry."

"She was always such a smart, funny lady," he said, and I tried to picture the grandmother that he described, who had been largely gone by the time we had come to the sewer. "This illness, it's crueler in some ways than a physical disease." I nodded. Dementia had robbed Bubbe of herself.

Now Bubbe lay silent and still. The bowl of gruel I had tried to coax upon her that morning sat beside her, untouched. It seemed odd that at noon she was still asleep. I moved closer to check on her, hoping she had not caught another one of the fevers that seemed to bedevil only her, worsening her condition. I put my hand on her forehead to check if she was hot. To my surprise, her skin was cool. I noticed then that she lay in an odd position, her face fixed in an almost smile.

I pulled back quickly, putting my hand over my mouth. Bubbe was dead. She must have passed in her sleep. Was her death somehow related to the dementia, or had it been another illness, or simply old age? I looked over at Pan Rosenberg, who sat just feet away, unaware of what had happened to his mother. I wanted to tell him. But it was not my place. I hurried from the chamber to find Saul.

As I stepped into the tunnel, Saul rounded the corner, walking slowly with the weight of the full water jug. "Sadie…" He smiled warmly, his eyes seeming to dance as they did whenever we met. Then, seeing my devastated expression, he dropped the jug, spilling the water, and raced toward me. "What is it? Are you all right?"

"I'm fine. It's Bubbe." Without speaking, he sprinted into the chamber. I followed, but hung close to the door, keeping a respectful distance as he checked her and confirmed what I already knew. He bowed his head for a second, then stood and walked to his father, knelt before him. I could not hear the words he whispered. I thought Pan Rosenberg might wail, as he did the day he learned his oldest son had died. Instead, he pressed his forehead into Saul's shoulder and wept silently, a man too broken to give voice to his grief.

When they finally separated, I walked over. "I'm sorry," I said, trying to figure out what to say. I would have imagined that after all the losses I had seen and suffered since the start of the war that condolences would come more naturally. "I know how much you both loved her and what a terrible loss this is."

Pan Rosenberg nodded, then looked to the bed where Bubbe lay. "What are we to do with her?"

Neither Saul nor I answered. Jewish law dictated that Bubbe be buried as soon as possible in a proper grave. But we couldn't take her to the street and the floor of the sewer was impenetrable for digging. With no other choice, the three of us carried her from the chamber and into the tunnel to the juncture where our sewer pipe met up with the wider body of rushing river. We lowered her to the surface. I looked at her sadly, touched her now-cold hand. Bubbe and I had not had an easy start. But I saw

now that everything she had done was to protect her family—
and in some ways me. And despite it all, we had grown fond of
one another. As the current carried her away, I thanked her for
her help, forgave her wrongdoings toward me and my family.
She slipped around the corner before sinking unseen beneath
the surface. I imagined that my father was waiting for her.

"Should we say kaddish?" I asked. Though I did not know
much about our shared faith, I was familiar with the prayer for
the dead, which I had heard at funerals and shiva visits growing up in Kazimierz.

Saul shook his head. "You can only say kaddish if you have a
minyan, ten men." So here, with just the three of us, he and his
father would be denied this mourning ritual. Saul put his hand
on his father's shoulder. "Someday, Papa, we will stand in shul
and say kaddish for Bubbe." He sounded certain, but I wondered if he believed it. The synagogue in their village had been
burned to the ground. The ones in Kraków were gone, too, I
thought, recalling the stilled, hollowed-out shells I had seen on
my walk through Kazimierz with Ella. The few that still stood
had been desecrated by the Germans and converted into stables
or warehouses. It was hard to imagine a world where a prayer
and the house to say it in still existed.

The next few days passed sadly for all of us. Bubbe's loss was
much harder than I imagined. The chamber felt empty and cold
without her. She had been grumpy as the elderly could be and
sometimes harsh, yet she had helped my mother deliver the baby
and had comforted me after Mama left. Her death created more
of a void than I would have expected. Now it was just Saul, his
father and me. Our numbers were shrinking day by day and I
could not help but wonder who would be next—or how much
longer it would be until we were all gone.

21

Ella

One evening in early August, I sat alone in the garret, too restless to read or paint. The house below was still. Ana Lucia had not hosted any of her gatherings in more than a month. The mood of the Germans on the street had changed perceptibly as reports of their struggles in battle against the Soviets to the east, as well as Allied advances in Italy, became too frequent to doubt. I imagined that the guests who had once enjoyed my stepmother's parties were in no mood to celebrate. It was just as well. With the dwindling food supply, she would not have been able to entertain in her usual style.

My eyes traveled to the photo of Krys on my desk. More than three weeks had passed since I had gone to the café to seek his help locating Sadie's mother and found him missing. I had not heard from him since. I should not be surprised, I told myself. We had quarreled the last time we met and parted badly. I had hoped, though, that my leaving the note with Kara would have mended all of that. But I didn't know if she had even seen him since to give it to him. More than once when visiting Sadie, I had considered making the short trip from the grate by the river to the café in Dębniki and seeing if Krys had returned. But my pride always stopped me. I had pined for Krys once, waited for him, and it had backfired horribly. I would not make the same mistake again.

Instead, I passed the days by visiting Sadie, bringing her what little I could. I still had not told her the truth about her mother. It was the right decision, I tried to reassure myself more than once over my own doubts. It was growing harder to find hope in Sadie's eyes as her time in the sewer without her family dragged on. I couldn't make it worse with more bad news.

I changed into my nightgown and climbed in bed, trying unsuccessfully to sleep. Sometime later, I heard Ana Lucia and her new companion come in and traipse up the stairs to her room. Colonel Maust was gone, transferred to Munich for reasons I did not know. I had wondered if without him Ana Lucia might lose the favored status she enjoyed with the General Government. But she quickly replaced him with an even higher-ranking German, whose name I had not bothered to learn. A gruff, silent officer, he made no effort at pleasantries, stomping into the house late at night and leaving just the same before dawn instead. Hanna had whispered once that he had a wife and children back in Berlin. He was an awful sort, seeming to shout rather than talk to my stepmother. The sounds that came from her bedroom these days bordered on violent and I often wondered if I needed to go downstairs and intervene to help her.

A few days earlier at breakfast I had noticed a bruise under her eye. "You know you don't have to be with him, or to let him do that," I offered. Even though she was awful to me, I could not help but feel sorry for her. "We would be fine without a German to protect us."

Embarrassment flashed across her face. "Who are you to advise me on my personal affairs?" she flared, covering it quickly with anger. I did not push the point further.

Finally, I blocked out the noises from Ana Lucia's room below and settled down. Suddenly, a sharp rapping sound jarred me awake. I rubbed my eyes as the sound came again. A stone, then another, hit my window. I sat up. Once upon a time, Krys used to signal me that way, our covert sign that I should come down for a secret rendezvous. I smoothed my hair, wondering how long he had been back from his errand. Had Kara given him my note, or had he simply decided to come see me on his own? It seemed rather presumptuous, given our last quarrel and the time that had passed, that he would expect me to meet him now. I walked to the window.

To my surprise, standing on the street below was not Krys, but Kara.

"What is it?" I asked, equal parts disappointed and curious and annoyed. Krys had obviously told her where I lived. Why hadn't he come himself?

Kara did not answer, but gestured for me to come down to the street. I dressed and started downstairs quickly, careful not to make noise. I worried that Ana Lucia and her companion might have heard the stones hitting my window. But they snored, sleeping deeply from too much wine. I slipped outside. "Come," she said, starting to walk as soon as I closed the door behind me.

"Where are we going? Did something happen to Krys?"

"He's fine. He needs you to come right away."

"Why? Is something wrong?" I wondered if he had decided to accept my offer to help with his work. But Kara shook her head, unwilling to speak further or answer my questions on the street. She walked at a swift pace, nearly running, and despite the fact that my legs were a good deal longer, I struggled to keep up.

When we reached Dębniki, I expected Kara to lead me to the café. Instead, she started in the direction of the alleyway behind the church. She had not been to the sewer grate with us before,

I realized. Krys must have told her where it was. "Did something happen to Sadie?" My stomach tightened.

"She's fine, as far as I know."

As we neared the alleyway, I could see someone standing by the sewer grate. For a second, I panicked. But it was Krys, I quickly realized. I started toward him. Kara, who had led me to him, hurried off, leaving us alone.

Beside him on the ground were two rectangular wooden crates. "What are those?" I asked, hoping for a second that he had somehow managed to find more food and was delivering it to Sadie for me. The crates were industrial, though, stamped with large black Cyrillic letters that screamed some kind of warning. "Krys, are those the munitions?" He did not answer right away. "We already talked about this."

"Your note said you wanted to help."

"It said that *I* wanted to help. Not Sadie. Not like this."

"Ella, we have to hide these munitions. We've been expecting them for weeks and we will be able to get them where we need to go by tomorrow, the next day latest. It should not be more than one night."

"Absolutely not," I said, furious now. "I already told you, I won't endanger Sadie for your cause."

"My cause?" It was his turn to be angry now. "It isn't a cause. We're fighting for our very lives, Ella. Yours and mine, and Sadie's, too." Krys lowered his voice. "These munitions, ammunitions and explosives, are hard to come by and they are critical for an upcoming operation in Warsaw, part of the larger battle that is to come. You must understand, the sewer, it's the perfect place," he pressed. "Out of sight, impossible to find. I need to do this." This time he was not asking—the stakes were too high. "It's only for one night."

"But it's so dangerous. If the munitions are discovered or if they somehow detonate, Sadie and her friends will be found."

"That won't happen." To Krys, the notion that his plan would fail was unthinkable. Still, I knew that anything could happen.

"You can't be sure," I protested. There were so many things that could go wrong.

"I promise, no harm will come to Sadie. I will lay down my own life before I let that happen." His eyes were steely and resolute. "You said in your note that you were ready to help," he added.

"Yes, but…" I had imagined delivering a package or aiding in some way myself. If I thought he meant risking Sadie's safety, I never would have offered.

"You said you'd do anything. Now is your chance to prove it." I did not reply. "There is no halfway with this work, Ella," he said sternly. "You are either all in or you are not." Krys' eyes burned and I saw then that he was willing to sacrifice everything for the cause in which he believed.

But I was not. I squared my shoulders, prepared to tell him no and face the repercussions.

There was a rustling below the grate then and I looked down to see Sadie, who must have been drawn there by the noise. She looked up, blinking with surprise to see so many people standing over the sewer.

Fear clouded her eyes. Then, seeing me, she smiled. "Oh, hello," she said trustingly. My heart twisted. She noticed Krys behind me. "Is everything all right?"

"Yes," I replied quickly, then faltered. How could I explain to her what Krys was asking her to do?

Before I could speak further, Krys knelt close to the sewer, describing the situation to Sadie in a voice too low for me to hear. She nodded as she listened, eyes wide, taking in his words gravely.

Sadie motioned me over. "It's all right," she said meekly, accepting the reality of the situation in a way that I could not. "I can do this." Her lip quivered.

"Sadie, no…"

"I'll do it," she insisted.

"It's too dangerous. I can't let you."

"It isn't your choice," Sadie snapped. "I'm not a child, Ella," she said, her voice softer now, but still wounded. "I can decide for myself and I want to do this."

"But why?"

"Because I want to help. Once I didn't even know there were still good people like you out there. So many people have helped me, you and Krys and Kara, Pawel, the worker who brought us to the sewer. And after everything you've all risked for me, if I can help in some small way, well, I want to do it." She lifted her chin. "Since the war started, all I have done is run and hide. This is a chance for me to do something, instead of feeling helpless. I want to do my part. I can do this," she repeated, sounding more certain now.

"You don't have to do this," I persisted.

"I know, but I want to."

"We'll need help getting these below," Krys said, patting one of the crates. They looked heavy and I wondered how he had managed this far by himself. Sadie nodded solemnly. She disappeared for a few minutes and returned with a young, bearded man. Saul, I knew instantly, the boy in the sewer she'd talked about. The one on whom she had a crush. He was just a few years older than us, with the clothing of a religious Jew and thoughtful dark eyes. I could tell from the way he stood close and stepped in front of her, as if to shield her from what was going on, that her feelings were not at all one-sided.

Sadie turned to him. "This is Ella, my friend who I told you about. She's the one who has been helping us. Ella, this is Saul." I could hear the warmth in her voice as she said his name.

"Hello," I ventured. Saul did not answer or smile. To him, I was the enemy who was endangering their safety, not to be trusted. His gentle eyes hardened as he took in the situation.

"You can't seriously expect us to do this," he said to Krys, his voice low but steely. "This sewer is everything to us, the only shelter we have."

"I know," Krys replied. "And I wouldn't ask if there were any other option. But it's only for the night."

Krys pulled the sewer cover back and pushed the edge of the first crate toward it. "Stand back," Saul instructed Sadie as he tried to help Krys from below. The crate slipped and fell into the sewer with a crashing sound that reverberated loudly on the street above. I braced, praying that the munitions were stable and would not detonate or explode from the impact. Then I looked around nervously. Anyone who was within a block's radius would surely have heard the sound. Krys put his hand on my shoulder and we listened in silence for footsteps. But the street remained still. A few seconds later, Krys eased the second crate down to Saul, who placed it gently in the tunnel.

"You don't have to take them all the way in," Krys said. "Just inside the tunnel out of sight."

"Should we stand watch and guard them?" Saul asked.

"That isn't necessary. No one knows that we've got them—or that we would ever hide them here." It was impossible for most people to imagine hiding things in the sewer, I thought, much less people. Krys threw down a tarp. "You can cover the crates with this and leave them where they are for the night. Someone will be here to collect them before sunrise."

"Someone?" I demanded of Krys, turning to him. "Not you?"

"Me, if I can. If not, one of my men who can be trusted." He took both of my hands in his. "I would never do anything to endanger Sadie—or you." He looked deep into my eyes, willing me to believe him.

How could I possibly, after what he was doing now? "You already have," I said, pulling away. I walked over to the grate. I could barely see Sadie around the two bulky crates that filled most of the entranceway to the sewer. "Sadie?"

"I'm here." Her voice sounded muffled and, despite the fact that she had insisted on helping, more than a little afraid.

"You don't have to do this. You can still change your mind," I said, though in truth I didn't know how. The crates would be nearly impossible to lift from the sewer and I wondered how Krys was planning to manage it in the morning.

"I'll be fine, Ella. I can do this." In the distance, a police siren wailed. "You should go home now. It's dangerous for you to stay so long on the street." Even now, Sadie was worried about me.

"She's right," Krys interjected as the siren seemed to grow closer. "We should go."

Heedless, I lingered. I could hardly bear to leave Sadie in such awful circumstances. But there was no other choice. "I will be back at first light," I promised, certain that in leaving her, I was making the worst mistake of my life.

22

Sadie

When Ella and Krys had disappeared above the sewer grate, I turned to Saul. "What now?"

"Go back to the chamber and sleep, I suppose. Krys said we don't need to stand guard."

"I'm not sleepy," I said. It was hard to imagine simply leaving the munitions sitting in the tunnel and going to bed, as if none of this had happened.

"Me either. Shall we go read?"

"I suppose." We started in the direction of the annex. I pulled out the book I had been reading, but Saul stared off into space. "What is it?" I asked.

"I'm fine." He brushed at his eye, then waved his hand as if flicking something away. "Nothing. It's just that so much has happened the past few weeks. First losing Bubbe. Now this." Tears flowed down his cheeks. I moved closer, desperate to comfort him.

"I know it's hard," I said, moving closer. "I'm so sorry."

He wiped his face with his sleeve. "You must think me a great fool, a grown man crying about his grandmother. She had a long life, and a great deal more time than my brother and so many people are getting now. And dying in her sleep, that was a blessing, really. She raised us like her own sons, though, after my mother died. She was there my whole life."

I wanted to put my arms around him, but it didn't seem right, so I laced my fingers with his. "I understand." There had been so much loss, so much death. Bubbe had been difficult at times, to be sure, but our families had become one and I, too, felt the pain of losing her. With so little left, each loss was a grievous wound, a gaping hole in the very foundation beneath our feet.

Saul stopped crying. Still, he did not take out his book, but stared off into the distance. "Are you all right?" I asked. I wondered if he was thinking about his grandmother or the munitions, or something else entirely.

He turned to me suddenly, took my hand. "Marry me, Sadie," he said. I was too surprised to answer. I had not imagined his feelings were so strong. But he was staring deeply into my eyes now, his gaze purposeful and sincere. "I want you to be my wife. I love you."

"And I love you." I had known it for the longest time, but saying the words made it feel more true. "When we get out of here—"

"Not someday," he said, cutting me off. "I don't want to wait. I want to marry you now."

"I don't understand. Such a thing isn't possible."

"It is. Jewish law does not require a rabbi, just someone who is knowledgeable about the rituals and requirements. My father can marry us." He spoke more quickly now, gaining momentum behind his words. "I know I should be asking your mother for permission," he added apologetically. "I wish I could. What do you think, Sadie?" He searched my face, eyes hopeful.

I did not answer right away, but considered the question. I

was old enough to get married. If the war had not happened, I might already have a husband, perhaps even a child. But that world had been taken from me and the idea of marriage and a normal life was so foreign and distant I could hardly imagine it. I loved Saul, though, belonged with him. A life with him, even under these circumstances, felt right.

Still, part of me wanted to wait. Everything had happened so quickly. The sewer was nowhere to begin a life together. Yet this wretched place was all we had; there might never be anywhere else. It was now or never, perhaps our only chance to make our love for one another into something permanent and real. We could be together, not just in those stolen moments where we took more comfort in one another's arms than we should, but as actual man and wife.

"Yes," I said at last. He smiled, and it was the first real happiness I had seen in his eyes since Bubbe had died. Then he kissed me. "When?" I asked, after we broke apart.

"Now!" he exclaimed, and we both laughed. "That is, not tonight, but tomorrow." I started to say that we should wait until my mother returned. But who knew when that would be? With every passing day and week, it seemed less a hope than a fantasy. "Let's tell my father when he wakes up in the morning and he can help us get everything we need together straightaway." I nodded, wondering if Pan Rosenberg would be happy about the news. Once he would have minded that I was not observant, perhaps protested rituals that were less than in strict accordance. Still, we had all been forced to change down here, and I hoped he would welcome me warmly into his dwindling family. "We can get married tomorrow," Saul repeated.

"I want to see Ella first, if I can manage it," I said. "I would like to get married under the grate so she can be there." With Mama still missing, my whole family was gone. I needed Ella to be by my side—or at least as close as possible.

I expected Saul to protest, but he nodded. "I understand. We really shouldn't wait long, though."

We sat in silence for several minutes. Saul rested his head on mine in the way that had become familiar to us in the nights we read by moonlight. Soon I recognized the slow, even sound of his breathing. We should go back to the chamber and Saul's father, I thought, perhaps even check on the munitions on the way. But Saul needed his rest. I didn't want to disturb him, at least not yet.

My eyes grew heavy, too. I blinked several times, willing myself to stay awake.

"Sadie..." I heard a voice call. I opened my eyes, startled. We were still in the annex. I had drifted off in spite of myself. I did not know how much time had passed. Saul slept beside me, mouth agape. "Sadie!" a voice called again, more sharply now. My eyes snapped open. Krys stood at the entrance to the annex, face panicked. For a second, I was confused. It was still the middle of the night.

"What are you doing back so soon?" I asked Krys.

"I was able to arrange transit of the munitions sooner than I expected," he replied. "Where are they?"

I sat up, trying to get my bearings. "The munitions," he pressed. "What did you do with them?"

"We left them right beneath the grate," I replied. "You told us there was no need to move them any farther. So we didn't." Beside me, Saul stirred.

Krys' eyes widened. "They're gone." I leapt up and followed him from the annex, Saul closely in tow. "You must be mistaken." Krys was unfamiliar with the sewer, I told myself. He had simply looked in the wrong place.

But as we neared the spot beneath the grate where Krys had lowered the crates to us, my stomach clenched.

The munitions Krys had entrusted us to watch were gone.

"We left them, just like you said," I offered.

"You told us that there was no need to stand guard," Saul added, his voice defensive.

"Perhaps someone else moved them," Krys suggested desperately.

I shook my head. "It is only us, and Saul's father."

"He would never have the strength," Saul added. "Perhaps one of your men came."

"None were available. That's why I'm here myself." We looked at one another with a growing sense of dread. We didn't have the munitions, nor did Krys. Which left us with only one terrifying possibility.

Someone else had come into the sewer and taken them.

"Go back to your hiding place," Krys ordered.

"We have no hiding place." Only the chamber, just steps from where the munitions had been taken.

"Go back," Krys repeated, seeming not to hear me. "Don't leave, no matter what, even to go to the grate. I will go find the munitions." He sprinted off, footsteps echoing off the tunnel walls as he ran.

After he disappeared, Saul and I stood in stunned silence for several seconds. "Someone was here."

"That doesn't mean they know about the chamber or where it is," Saul offered. "That doesn't mean they know about us." The words were of little comfort. Someone else had been in the sewer. That alone was enough.

"Krys will take care of things," he said, surprising me. Saul did not trust non-Jews, and the fact that he was counting on Krys to protect us seemed the most ominous sign of all. "Try not to think about it anymore. We've got a wedding to plan," he joked, trying without success to chase the worry from his eyes.

"You still want to get married, after everything that just happened?"

"More so than ever. Each day is a gift down here, tomorrow

promised to no one." I nodded. I had not thought about it that way, but Saul was right. Even before Krys hid the munitions, our lives in the sewer were dangerous and uncertain. "Why not take this one bit of happiness, now while we can?"

"All right," I said. We returned to the chamber and slipped in quietly so as not to wake Pan Rosenberg. I climbed into my bed. I could not sleep, though, but tossed and turned. The incident with the munitions played over and over in my mind. Someone had been in the sewer. The danger felt worse, our situation unsustainable.

Hearing my restlessness, Saul crossed the chamber. He climbed in bed and lay down beside me. "Is this all right?" he asked. I could not answer over the lump in my throat. He embraced me from behind and my heartbeat quickened as I wondered if he might try to take things further than we previously had, now that we were to be married. But he simply held me tight. "One more day," he murmured in my ear, and I knew exactly what he meant. By tomorrow night, we could be together properly as man and wife. Still, it felt like forever. I imagined our life after the war, Saul writing and me studying to become a doctor. It had been so long since I believed things like that might someday be possible. I didn't know where, but we would be together. I drifted off in the warmth of his arms and slept soundly for the first time since Mama had left.

In the morning when I awoke, Saul was already gone. "He went to prepare things," Pan Rosenberg said.

Saul must have told his father the news about our wedding already. I searched Pan Rosenberg's face for a reaction. "You don't mind?"

He smiled and his eyes danced with excitement. "Sadele, I couldn't be happier!" I saw then that our marriage would be a vote of confidence, a statement that there would be a future. It would bring all of us, including Pan Rosenberg, a bit of much-needed hope. Then his face turned solemn. "I only wish that your parents were here to see it. I hope, though, that you will let me be a father to you both." I saw then that he had ripped a page from one of his books and was attempting to write a makeshift *ketubah* for us.

I didn't know where Saul had gone or what he needed me to do by way of wedding preparations. So I set about getting ready, putting on the dress that Ella had given me, which somehow had remained relatively clean, and fixing my hair as well as I was able. My thoughts turned back to the munitions and I wondered if Krys had been able to find the crates or figure out who had come into the sewer to take them.

Despite Krys' admonition to stay in the chamber, at eleven o'clock, my usual meeting time with Ella, I started for the grate. I was excited to tell her about our wedding plans and to ask her to be a part of it. But she did not arrive at her usual time, nor after. I wondered if Krys had told her what happened with the munitions and forbidden her from coming to the grate as well, and whether she would listen. How was I going to find her and let her know the news about our wedding?

An hour later, I returned to the chamber, dejected. "Ella didn't come," I told Saul, who was back now. "What if something is wrong?"

"I'm sure everything is fine," he reassured, although he could not possibly know if that was true.

"I hope so. I would still like her to be there when we get married. Can we wait a bit longer to see if she turns up?" A flash of disappointment crossed his face. "I know with the munitions and everything that has happened, it seems we should not waste a minute. But I'm sure she'll come tomorrow. I just know it."

Saul smiled. "Of course. What's one more day when we have the rest of our lives? But, Sadie, what if she does not come tomorrow?"

It was a question I could hardly bear to consider. "Then we

will get married without her." Saul was right; we could not wait forever.

The day passed slowly. "I'm going to use the time to see if I can find some scraps to make us a proper chuppah," Saul said brightly that night after dinner.

"You don't have to." The entire sewer was a kind of wedding canopy, sheltering us from the sky above. But Saul seemed so excited, I did not want to dissuade him.

"Be careful," I said. He gave me a quick kiss and then started out into the tunnel.

An hour passed, then two, and I began to worry. As night drew close, I hoped Saul had not wandered too far searching for things in his enthusiasm and run into trouble. I considered going after him, but I didn't know which way he had gone through the tunnels. By now, he could be anywhere.

"Do you think he is all right?" Pan Rosenberg asked, his voice pinched.

"Yes, definitely." I forced confidence into my voice. "He is just looking for things for the wedding." Unconvinced, Saul's father did not prepare for bed that night as he usually did, but paced anxiously back and forth.

Finally, well after midnight, Saul appeared in the entrance to the chamber. "Saul, where were you? I was so worried. Is everything all right?" My questions came out in a tumble.

He shook his head, and seeing the somber expression on his face, I felt my heart tighten. Just then, a dark shadow appeared behind him. "Ella?" I was stunned to see my friend in the sewer for the very first time. "What are you doing here?" I hoped for a second that, despite the implausibility at such an hour, he had invited her in for the wedding and that she had somehow agreed.

As I took in her expression, though, I knew nothing could be further from the truth.

"The sewer is no longer safe. I need all of you to come with me at once."

23

Ella

After Krys put the munitions into the sewer and we left the grate, I returned home. I lay awake all night, imagining the awful things that might happen. I never should have let Sadie say yes, I berated myself. I saw her face, timid yet resolved to help however she could. Neither she nor Saul were equipped for what Krys had asked them to do for the Home Army. In ordinary circumstances, it would not be all that difficult to store a few boxes overnight. But nothing about Sadie's existence was ordinary; there were at least a half-dozen ways it could all go horribly wrong and each played over in my head like a bad dream I could not escape.

The next morning, I slipped from the house before dawn, too restless and worried to wait any longer. I needed to check on Sadie and make sure she was all right. The August morning air was warm and clammy as I made my way across the deserted bridge. I went to the grate first, but of course Sadie was not there at such an early hour. I could not see anything below. From there I went to Dębniki. The café was shuttered and locked and the cellar doors to the *piwnica* were, too. I even went up to the room on the top floor where Krys sometimes stayed, but it was deserted. When I pushed open the unlocked door and peered into the bare space, it looked as if no one had ever been there, that night or ever.

My anxiousness rose. I could find no one, nor find out what had happened. Defeated, I started back toward the city center. I would have to wait hours until my scheduled meeting time with Sadie. After everything that had happened, I didn't even know if she would still come. I reached our house on Kanonicza Street and stepped inside, hoping to slip through the foyer and skip breakfast. I couldn't bear to sit across from Ana Lucia and make conversation. But when I passed the dining room, it was surprisingly still, the table cleared. I did not hear Hanna in the kitchen either. I wondered if my stepmother had already eaten or not come down yet. Perhaps she was not home at all. I started up the stairs.

As I neared the fourth floor, I heard a rustling from above. My uneasiness grew. Someone was in the garret.

"Hello?" I called. I prayed that it was Hanna, tidying up. But the footsteps were too heavy, the sound of the movements deliberate.

Ana Lucia appeared in the doorway to my bedroom, redcheeked and winded, as if from a great climb. Her face bore a triumphant expression.

"What is this?" she demanded.

In her hand, she held Sadie's necklace.

My blood ran cold. Ana Lucia had Sadie's necklace with the Hebrew letters. How had she discovered it? By snooping through my room. That did not surprise me. But I wondered what had made her go looking.

"You went through my things? How dare you?" I said, outraged.

Ana Lucia had the upper hand here, though, and she knew it—she stepped forward, undeterred. "The Jews, where are they?"

"I have no idea what you're talking about." I would never give up Sadie to Ana Lucia.

A light dawned suddenly in her eyes. "There *are* Jews, aren't there?" Although I had admitted nothing, her suspicions seemed somehow confirmed. "And you are helping them. That's why you were asking so many questions about them at my lunch a few months ago. Friedrich will be so pleased to have this information."

"You wouldn't dare!" I could see her mind working as she planned to tell her Nazi boyfriend, calculated exactly how much favor it would buy her with him.

"What a lot your father left me with! You, a Jew lover and a nosy little do-gooder. That brother of yours, the *ciota*." She used an awful term for men who liked other men.

"You leave Maciej out of this!"

"You think they are treating the gays so much better in Paris?" she asked, then smiled cruelly. My heart ached to think of my brother, who was so far away. "You're both a disgrace."

"Better than you, collaborating with that Nazi scum." I lifted my chin defiantly.

She stepped forward and raised her hand, as if to strike me. Then she lowered it again just as quickly. "You have an hour," she announced calmly.

"To do what?" I asked, confused.

"To leave. Pack your things and go."

I looked at her, stunned. I had been born in this house, spent my whole life here. "You can't do that. This is my home. It belongs to my family."

"Belonged." I looked at her blankly, not understanding. "Your father's estate papers came last week. I was going to tell you, but you are never here because you are running around with those sewer rat Jews." The papers were official notice of Tata's death, stating that his will could now be probated. "Now that he is gone, the will states that the house and everything in it goes to me."

"That can't be true." I could not believe Tata had been that heartless. Had he really been so blind to Ana Lucia's evil that he had left her everything? Perhaps it was a trick, some legal maneuver on her part. I had no way of knowing. "But where am I to go?" I panicked. For a moment, I considered pleading with Ana Lucia. If I stopped helping Sadie, or promised to anyway, she might let me stay.

"That is hardly my problem. But I would advise you not to go to your Jews. They won't be there long either."

My blood froze. The intent of her words was unmistakable: she was going to tell the Germans about Sadie.

"You didn't really think you could save them, did you?" Ana Lucia's words were mocking, cruel.

I lunged forward and grabbed her by the throat. My every instinct was to squeeze the life out of her. But that would not help me—or Sadie. A second later, I released her. She stepped back, clutching the place where my fingers had left red marks on her neck. "How dare you?" she gasped. "I should have you arrested right now."

She wouldn't, I knew instantly. The spectacle of having her own stepdaughter removed from her house by the police was more embarrassment than she could bear. "You are evil, Ana Lucia. But your time is almost over. The Allied armies are advancing. They will liberate the city soon." It was a bluff—though I had heard of the German military's recent struggles against both the Allies in Italy and the Soviets to the east, I had no idea when or if either would actually reach Kraków.

But Ana Lucia did not know that. "The Russians are nowhere near the city," she retorted. Doubt flickered behind her eyes.

I continued, "The first thing they will do after they chase the Germans out is come for collaborators like you."

She blinked several times, as if she had not entirely considered the reality of her situation until now. The fear behind her eyes deepened.

I stepped back, satisfied, and started away.

"Ella, wait." I turned toward her. Ana Lucia's face was panicked now as she processed the implications of what I had said. "Perhaps I've been too hasty. If you stop aiding the Jews, maybe we can help each other, find a way out of this." There was a note of pleading in her voice. "We could go to the South of France. I have some money stored away in Zurich. You could write to Maciej, ask him to send a visa for me as well." I had not told her about the visa that Maciej's friend, Phillipe, had sent me. I should not have been surprised, yet I realized for the first time that she had been reading my mail.

I hesitated for a beat. Once upon a time, I had wanted my stepmother's acceptance. Now she was dangling it in front of me like a carrot and part of me wanted to take it. But she was only speaking out of desperation, the fact that I might be able to give some help that she needed. Then I saw Sadie's beloved necklace crumpled in Ana Lucia's fat, greedy fingers.

"Go to hell, Ana Lucia."

I grabbed the necklace from her hand and, with only the clothes on my back, started down the stairs. At the front door, I turned back to gaze one last time at the place that held just about every memory of my family I would ever have. Squaring my shoulders, I started away, leaving my childhood home forever.

Outside, I ran through the streets heedlessly, as if Ana Lucia had already called the police and they might apprehend me at any second. My heart pounded. Then, seeing the alarmed expressions of those around me, I slowed to a walk; I could not afford to attract attention.

I crossed the bridge into Dębniki and started in the direction of the café. Then I hesitated. Just a short while earlier it had been closed. But it was morning now and I prayed that Krys, or at least Kara, would be there. Mercifully, the café door was unlocked. There was no one inside and so I walked swiftly down the steps into the *piwnica*. I found Krys behind the bar, studying a map of some sort that he had laid out across the floor.

"Ella." Seeing me, he stood. He did not smile. His face was haggard, eyes sunken and ringed with worry, as if he had not slept at all. "You can't be here." His voice was terse and I wondered if he was angry with me for quarreling about the munitions the previous evening.

But I could tell from his grim expression that his worries went much deeper than our disagreement. "What is it?" I asked. "Did something happen to Sadie?"

"She's fine." He paused. "Only the munitions…someone took them."

Dread filled my stomach like a rock. "Who?"

"We don't know. The police, we think, or maybe a German patrol."

"They went into the sewer?" He nodded. I was aghast. The very worst thing, which Krys had sworn was not possible, had happened. "Do they know about Sadie and the others?"

"I don't think so." He hesitated for a beat. "I don't know."

Alarm flooded my brain. I wanted to shout at Krys that I knew he never should have hidden the munitions in the sewer, that I had told him so. I imagined how terrified Sadie must have been to discover that someone had been there. But none of that mattered anymore.

"We're going after the munitions and whoever took them," Krys said. "There's a team searching for them and I'm going to join them now. But in any event, we're going to have to move Sadie and the others right away."

"It's probably for the best anyway," I said.

Now it was his turn to look puzzled. "Why? What do you mean?"

"Ana Lucia, she found Sadie's necklace that I was hiding for her." Krys' eyes darkened as he processed the implications of what I was telling him. I waited for him to berate me for doing something as foolish as hiding Jewish valuables, but he did not. "She put two and two together and figured out that I've been helping Jews. She doesn't know about the sewer yet, at least I don't think so. But she threw me out of the house."

Anger clouded his face, followed quickly by resignation. "I'm sorry. I know how upset you must be. But honestly, that part is for the best. When the Allies finally do liberate the city, you don't want to be anywhere near a collaborator like her."

He was right, of course. "But it's only a matter of time before she tells the Germans what I've done." I waited for him to disagree.

He did not. "We'll find you a place to go, get you out of the city," he replied instead. I watched his eyes dart about as he formulated a plan. "Your brother is in Paris, isn't he? You can go to him."

"Yes." I considered it for a moment, the notion of going to live with Maciej. Once upon a time, it had been my dream. But not anymore. "No," I said slowly. "I don't want to go to my brother."

"After we get Sadie out of the sewer, I mean. That way you can know they are safe before you leave for Paris."

"It's not just that. I don't want to leave you either." I felt the words for the first time as I spoke them. Krys and I were messy and imperfect and we quarreled often. But I loved him just as much as I had before he left for the war. Maybe more. Fate had allowed us to find one another a second time; surely it would not give us a third.

"I feel the same way," he admitted. "But with my work, we can't possibly be together now."

"Let me join you." He stared at me, as if not believing the

words. "Not just hiding things, but really join you." It was the message I had wanted to give him the day I had gone looking for him at the café and had left a note. I hadn't been able to tell him fully then, but I could now. "You said there are women in the Home Army, didn't you?" He nodded. "I want to be one of them. Not just run a few errands, but really be part of it all." I held my breath, waiting for his reaction. "Or don't you think I can do it?"

"I think there's no one finer or better suited for the job." I felt myself standing a bit taller when he said this. "But I'm afraid it's impossible. You see, the moment of truth is coming. There is to be a great uprising in Warsaw and almost all of our efforts and men and material will soon be concentrated there."

"Including you?"

"Including me."

My heart sank. "But it is even more dangerous in Warsaw."

He nodded grimly. "Which is why I must go. They need me there."

"I can't bear to lose you again." I wanted to beg him not to go. But he was determined and to do anything else would make him less than he was. My heart twisted at the thought that he would leave me once more.

"Then I'll come with you," I blurted, surprising myself.

"To Warsaw? But, Ella, it's too dangerous," he protested. "You just said as much yourself."

"Nothing is safe anymore," I replied. He looked as though he wanted to argue, but could not. "Let me join your fight." I gained confidence now, owning the words. I really wanted to do this. "At least this way, we'll be together no matter what happens."

He hesitated for a moment and I expected him to say no. "All right," he said finally, surprising me. "I love you, Ella. We can leave together." He swept me into his arms and drew me close.

"Of course, we must help Sadie first. I won't leave without doing that," I added for emphasis.

"I'll confirm arrangements for safe passage for them and run down the munitions. Then we can help Sadie and go." He made it all sound so easy.

"I'll find Sadie and the others and let them know. She should be at the grate in an hour or so."

Krys shook his head. "I'm afraid it won't be that simple. I told her to stay hidden and not come to the grate, no matter what."

I took a deep breath. "Then I have to go down and find her myself." I tried to sound confident. But my insides quivered. I had not been able to bring myself to go into the sewer there before. How was I going to manage it now?

"Ella, no. The pipes are mined."

"Mined?"

"I only just found out after the munitions were taken. The Germans have begun to mine the tunnels to fortify the city. They mean to detonate them when the Allies eventually come, but it would be all too easy to trip one of the wires ahead of time." I thought then of Sadie and the others. How many times had they walked those tunnels, unaware that they could be blown to bits at any second? "So you see why you can't go down there."

"If Sadie's in that kind of danger, I need to go now more than ever," I countered.

"At least wait for me to go with you. You can't rescue her until we have somewhere for her to go. I have to go to my team first and make sure they've found the munitions. And I have to arrange safe passage for Sadie and her friends. Let me do that and I will meet you by the grate in the alley at midnight."

"But that might be too late. We have to get to Sadie and her friends now."

"It's the best we can do. I know that you can't go back to your house because of Ana Lucia. You can stay in my room upstairs until it is time to go to Sadie."

"And then once she is safe, you and I can leave for Warsaw together. Perhaps we could even get married." The old dream flickered in my mind.

"I hope so," he said, with less certainty than I would have expected. For a second, my old doubts returned; perhaps he did not feel the same as I did. "I love you with my whole heart and I want to marry you. Everything is just so uncertain now. I won't make a promise to you that I can't keep again." It was not his feelings for me he doubted, but the future itself. "But know this, Ella: I will wait for you. I will come for you. And no matter what happens, I will never leave you again." His words meant more than any marriage vow possibly could have.

He kissed me once long and hard and then started away.

24

Ella

That night I waited by the sewer grate in the alleyway behind the church as Krys had instructed. After leaving him, I had spent most of my time in the barren room on the top floor above the café. I had wanted to try to see Sadie, or at least walk the streets of Kraków one more time before I left the city forever. But I didn't dare do anything that might risk my being seen by Ana Lucia or her associates or otherwise risk our plan.

As I hid in the shadows of the alleyway now, my heart pounded with a mix of nervousness and anticipation. Any moment, I expected Krys to appear, his strong silhouette against the moonlit sky. We would have to go into the sewer to find Sadie, which I dreaded, and rescuing her and the others would be difficult and dangerous. But once we had gotten them to safety, Krys and I could leave and start our life together.

Only he never came.

Time passed slowly as I waited for him to appear. Once I thought I saw a shadow at the entrance to the alleyway. But it was just a passing car. The clock above the church chimed half past midnight and then one—and still Krys did not arrive. I tried not to panic, to think of all of the reasons he might have been delayed. Perhaps his errand to find the munitions took longer than expected, or he was forced to find a different way to the grate to avoid the Germans, as I often had been.

As more time passed, though, my excuses became harder to accept. When the clock chimed two, I knew that something was wrong. I could not simply stand here and wait any longer. But I could not go into the sewer and rescue Sadie without Krys; I did not know his escape plan. I had to find him.

As I started from the alley, I tried not to panic, to imagine a not-terrible explanation why he had not come. He had been so certain about meeting me to help Sadie, and about our leaving together. Something had happened, something awful, I was sure of it. I had to find out.

I hurried toward Barska Street. The café was shuttered at the late hour, so I made my way around the back of the building to the *piwnica*, where Kara stood behind the bar, serving beer to a few lingering patrons. When she saw me, her expression turned guarded. I could tell from her hollow expression that something awful had happened.

"What is it?" I demanded. "What happened to Krys?" I was too loud, not discreet enough. But in my panic, I did not care.

Kara pulled me behind the bar and into the storeroom where she had hidden Sadie the day I'd gone to the hospital looking for Sadie's mother. "Krys has been arrested."

Arrested. The word reverberated around my brain like a bouncing ball. "But how?"

"He and two of our other men went on a reconnaissance mission to try to recover the munitions. They discovered the munitions had been taken by a local street thief who had happened upon them while searching for metal scraps. He was planning to sell them to the Germans. They tried to intercept him before he could hand the munitions over, but it turned out to be a trap. The wretch had been paid to lure Krys and the other men to the Germans. One of the men managed to escape, but Krys and the second man were arrested."

"We have to help him," I said, my voice rising with urgency.

"There's nothing to be done."

"Surely if you tell one of your contacts with the Home Army, they will try to do something to rescue the men."

She shook her head. "They can't risk it, not now. And we've been given orders not to attempt anything that would compromise operations. The men who were captured would not want us to save them at the expense of the larger mission. They are good men and they won't break and tell what they know. We just have to pray for them."

I tried to process what Kara was telling me: no one was going to help Krys. For all he had given, he would be abandoned to certain death. I had to do something.

"I'm going after him," I said, starting from the *piwnica*. I had no idea how I would get to Krys, but I had to try.

"Stop!" Kara grabbed me by the shoulders and spun me back toward her. "You behave like an impulsive child and it is going to get you killed. There's no coming back from where Krys went, do you understand?" I did not answer, unwilling to acknowledge the truth in what she said.

"But I can't just leave him," I protested. "I can't lose him, not now, when we finally found each other again."

Krys was lost to me forever. My heart screamed. "If you go after him and get yourself arrested, then everything he did, all of his pain and suffering will have been for nothing. Make it count for something. Go save your friend and yourself, just as you were meant to do."

My thoughts turned to Sadie. Krys would never disclose her location to the Germans. But the thief who had stolen the munitions had surely told the Germans where he had found them.

It was only a matter of time before the Germans searched the sewers to see what—or who—else might be there.

"Kara, please…" I hardly dared ask. "Krys had a plan to get Sadie and her friends out of the city."

Kara didn't answer, but I could tell in her eyes that she knew where he'd meant to take them. "Why should I help you?" she asked bitterly. "Krys and the others are gone." I saw then that her eyes were rimmed with red, and there were stains on her cheeks where tears had fallen. "It's over, Ella. None of it matters anymore."

"Of course it does. There's still the fight in Warsaw. Krys and I were going to join it as soon as we got Sadie out. That matters, and Sadie and her friends do, too. You should help them because it's what Krys would want you to do. And because if you don't, everything he has done would have been for nothing."

Something seemed to flicker in her eyes then. "All right," she relented. "Kryspinów, do you know it?" I nodded. I was familiar with the small village about fifteen kilometers from Kraków. "There's a livery behind the rail station. A truck driver there has been paid to ferry essential packages to the border for the Home Army. He is supposed to take Sadie and her friends through Poprad over the Tatras into the Slovak Republic."

"But the Slovak Republic is Nazi-occupied as well."

"Yes, they can't stay there. It isn't safe. But there is an overland route that some refugees have taken through Romania to Turkey. Our contacts will guide them and hand them off."

"That's so far," I said, picturing the route. My head swam. "Even if we can get Sadie and her friends out of Poland, their survival is a long shot at best."

Kara nodded. "I told Krys it was foolish, but he said it was the only way."

A way that would be even more impossible now without Krys. But I could not abandon Sadie. I would have to try on my own. I started from the *piwnica*. "Wait," Kara said. I turned back. "If you can get the Jews out of the sewer, I will meet you at the grate and help you get them from the city."

"Really?"

Kara shrugged. "You'll make a mess of things if I leave you to do it alone." Though her tone was dismissive, I could tell that she had come to care just a bit.

"Thank you." On the street, I stopped, the full realization of what Kara had said crashing down upon me: Krys was gone, almost certainly for good. I saw his face before me, heard his promise that he would never leave me. Yet somehow he had. We had wasted so much time quarreling since finding one another again. And in the end, none of it really mattered at all.

I pushed down my sorrow. If I was going to rescue Sadie, I had to do it now. I was going to have to go into the sewer alone.

Fifteen minutes later, I stood above the sewer grate in the alleyway once more, looking down. The sky was pitch-dark now, the clouds covering any light that the stars might have given. I could not make out anything below. "Sadie?" I called softly, hoping by some miracle she had come looking for me in the middle of the night, or at least that she was nearby. My voice echoed unanswered down the pipe. Sadie was not there. If I wanted to find her, I was going to have to go into the sewer myself.

I pried back the grate and lifted it with effort. The round opening seemed narrower than before. Even looking down into the ground made it harder to breathe. And dropping into the sewer was not the worst of it. Sadie had told me more than once about the tiny pipes that she had to squeeze herself through to get around. I could not possibly do that. Still, I needed to find Sadie and warn her in time. There was no other choice.

I lowered myself into the sewer, clinging to the sharp, wet edges of the grate. I felt for the ground with my feet. But it was still at least a meter below, I knew, from watching Sadie. I would have to let go and drop, but to me the idea was terrifying, nearly impossible. I took a deep breath and shut my eyes.

Then I released my grasp on the lip of the sewer, letting myself fall into the earth.

I hit the ground with a thud and filthy water splashed up all around me, soiling my stockings and dress. I had smelled the sewer many times from above ground. Nothing, though, could prepare me for the choking stench that filled the air here, a thousand times worse. The reality of Sadie's existence sank in then and I was horrified. How had Sadie lived like this every day for months? I should have done more, insisted on getting her out sooner.

There was no time to wonder. I had to find her. I started down the pipe in the direction from which she always came. It was not such a small pipe, I realized with relief, as my eyes adjusted to the darkness. I had imagined sewer tunnels to be narrow, like bigger versions of the pipes in bathrooms, almost too small to fit through. But this felt more like a corridor and I could see that the rounded roof was tall enough for me to walk under without bending. I put my hands out on either side for balance, grimacing as I touched the slimy walls.

Farther down the tunnel there was a divide in the path. I tried desperately to guess which way Sadie might have come from. I felt certain that if I took a wrong turn, I might never find my way back. More to the point, I could not afford to waste time getting lost.

At last I heard voices in the distance, one familiar. "Sadie!" I cried aloud. I forgot to speak softly and I was unprepared for the way my voice echoed down the pipe. I hurried toward her.

As I rounded the corner, a figure blocked my path. "Saul…" I said, recognizing him. He was carrying an odd assortment of metal poles and a tarp.

He dropped the things he had been carrying and they fell to the floor of the sewer with a clatter. "How did you find us?" he asked. Last time I had come here, I had brought Krys and the munitions and danger with me. To him, I would always be an outsider, not to be trusted.

"I knew the direction Sadie went to and from the grate," I replied. "At the end, I followed your voices."

His brow furrowed. "We should not let ourselves be so easily heard." I dreaded telling him that it was beyond all of that now, that the Germans would soon know they were here regardless of how quiet they were. "You are alone?"

I nodded. "Take me to Sadie, please. It's very important." I should tell him now that we needed to leave, but I was not sure how he would react and I didn't want to say anything until I saw Sadie.

There was a break in the tunnel wall, leading to a small alcove. Before I could walk in, Sadie's tiny frame appeared in the doorway. "Saul, where were you? I was so worried. Is everything all right?" He did not answer her. Then she saw me. "Ella?" Her voice was warm but full of surprise. "What are you doing here?"

"The sewer is no longer safe. I need all of you to come with me at once."

Sadie did not reply, but stared at me, as if not understanding. "Can I come in?" I asked. Reluctantly, she stepped aside and let me into the alcove. The dank, dirty space was smaller than my bedroom at home, not fit for one person, much less the five adults plus an infant it had once housed. An older man, whom I presumed to be Saul's father, sat huddled in the corner. All of these months I had known Sadie endured awful conditions when she left the grate. But until now, I had not realized how bad they really were. Yet there was life here, a place where Sadie and the others ate and slept and talked. I understood then that there was a whole world below ground where Sadie lived that I had not known existed.

"What are you doing here?" Sadie asked.

"I've come to get you all out."

"Out?" Sadie repeated. I saw the fear in her eyes. I had understood when Sadie had not wanted to escape before and leave the others behind. But now all of them could leave together. The others looked similarly horrified at the notion. This place, which to me seemed a wretched prison, had become their safe place. It had not occurred to me until this very moment that they might not want to go at all.

"How can we possibly?" Saul asked. "Pawel said that if we went onto the street, we would be shot on sight." They had been told by the sewer worker that hiding here was their best hope, and for so long, they believed him. Pawel had been their savior and protected them with his life. Why should they trust me more than him? Except for Sadie, they did not know me at all.

I cleared my throat. "It is true that things are very dangerous above ground," I began. "But things are changing, things that make it no longer safe for you to stay." I searched for the right way to explain. "You know that someone took the munitions. That person took them to the Germans, alerted them. There's a good chance that the police will come looking in the sewer anytime now to see what else is here."

Sadie seemed to pale. "I told you they would come," she said to Saul, her voice pinched.

"We will hide somewhere else, then," Saul countered. "Perhaps the reading annex." I had not realized they had another place.

"It's too small for three," Sadie fretted.

"We'll find somewhere else, then," Saul said, trying to soothe her. "We can go deeper into the sewers. Surely there is somewhere else." He searched desperately for another solution that would not force them to go above ground.

"That won't work," I interjected. "You see, the Germans have mined the sewer as a defensive measure. If you walk around the tunnels, you risk setting them off." Sadie's eyes widened and I could see her calculating how many times she walked those tunnels not knowing the danger.

"We'll manage," Saul insisted stubbornly. "We have before."
He glared at me. "We aren't leaving."

"I'm afraid there's something else." I turned to Sadie. "My
stepmother, she found the necklace."

"Your *chai* necklace?" Saul's eyes widened as he turned to
Sadie. "I told you not to wear it."

"It's my fault," I said, jumping in to defend her.

"No, it was mine," Sadie said, taking a step toward me. Saul
and his father looked at us reproachfully. It was as if their worst
warnings and admonitions about our friendship had all come
true. "I gave it to Ella to keep safe for me. I never should have
done that."

"And I should have hidden it better," I added. "But that
doesn't matter now. My stepmother found it and she realized I
was helping Jews. She kicked me out. So I have to leave Kraków."

"Oh, Ella." Sadie's voice was filled with remorse. "I'm so
sorry."

"After I leave, you won't have anyone to bring you food.
You can't stay here in case the Germans come and you can't go
deeper into the tunnels because of the mines. You need to leave
with me now."

"But what if, I mean when, my mother comes back?" Sadie
corrected herself, forcing a certainty that she no longer felt.
"When she comes back, I have to be here." A rock formed in
my stomach. The lie I had created weeks ago as a kindness was
the very thing that would stop me from saving her life. If Sadie
thought her mother was alive, she would never leave. I knew
then that I had no choice.

"Sadie, about your mother…"

"What is it? Is there news?" Then seeing my face, she stopped.
"Is she all right?"

I knew in that moment that I had to tell her. "I went to the
hospital where your mother had taken the baby. Only she wasn't
there anymore."

"I don't understand."

"Your mother went to the hospital where she planned to take the baby. The nuns at the hospital gave her a bed and care."

"But my mother didn't go to the hospital as a patient. She went to hide my sister."

"I know. But she was sicker than anyone realized from having the baby. She had developed a fever and an infection after childbirth. So they admitted her to try to heal her. The Germans found out she was there and came for her."

"Was she arrested?" I wanted to lie and say yes. Telling Sadie that her mother had been taken by the Germans would be awful, but at least it would give her hope.

It would also be another lie. "The hospital didn't let the Germans take her. They knew that would be a far worse fate, so they gave her a medicine that let her pass painlessly in her sleep." I walked over and put my arms around her. "Sadie, I'm sorry." I paused, taking a deep breath. "Your mother is dead."

"No...that can't be true." Her face went rigid with disbelief. Although she had suspected her mother was gone the day I had gone to the hospital, some part of her had held on to hope until now. "You're saying that just so I will leave."

"It's true." There was nothing that I could say to blunt her grief now. Her eyes widened with horror and she opened her mouth. I braced for the scream I would have made if it were me, so loud that it would bring people to the sewer and ensure her detection. She seemed to wail silently, though, her entire body shaking. No tears fell from her eyes. I stood helplessly, trying to find the words that might offer some comfort.

Finally, she stilled. "And my sister?"

"The nuns said your mother arrived at the hospital alone, without a child. I wasn't able to find out what happened. There was no sign of her."

"She is probably gone, too," Sadie said, her voice wrought with sorrow. I wanted to comfort her, but didn't know how. She straightened, pulling away from me. "You went to the hospital weeks ago. You knew this whole time about my mother. And you never told me."

"Yes." I wanted to tell her that I had only just found out, but I could not hide the truth any longer. "I wanted to spare you. I'm sorry."

"I thought you were my friend." Sadie's eyes were cold and stony. Saul stepped forward and put a protective arm around her shoulders, steering her away from me. But Sadie spun back toward me. "If you lied to me, why should I trust you enough to leave?" she demanded.

I hesitated, wrestling with her logic. "I didn't tell you because I was afraid you wouldn't survive down here if you knew the truth." I had underestimated her, I realized, and that was perhaps my biggest mistake. "I was trying to save you then. And I'm trying to save you now." I walked to her and took her hand, looking straight into her eyes. "Sadie, I'm sorry. You can hate me all you want once we are out, but don't let my mistake kill you and these good people whom you love." I was certain that she would say no. I didn't know what I would do then. They were going to get arrested or die down here, and if I stayed, I would surely die with them. I thought of Krys, wondered where he was and if we would ever know what became of one another.

Sadie did not respond. I tried again. "Please, I know that you are angry, and when we get out of here, if you never want to speak to me again, I understand. But there is no time. You must come with me now if you want to make it."

Something seemed to break in her then. "All right," she said slowly. "For Saul and his father, I'll come." Her voice was cold and I knew she would never forgive me for what I had done. Yet she was willing to leave to save the others.

But Saul, who still held on to Sadie, stood motionless, un-convinced. I tried again to reason with him. "I know that the sewer has been your sanctuary, the place that kept you safe. But it isn't anymore. Escaping, that is the only salvation now."

"Why should we trust you?" he asked bitterly, his words an echo of Sadie's.

"Because you have no other choice," I said bluntly. "I'm your only hope." Saul looked as though he wanted to argue but could not. "If you don't come with me, you are all going to die."

Sadie turned to him. "Saul, Ella is here to help us." Despite everything, some part of her still believed in me.

"We can't trust her. We can't trust any of them."

"But you trust me, don't you?" she asked, cupping his cheek with her hand. He did not answer at first. Then he nodded slightly. "Good. I'm telling you we need to go now. Please, Saul. I won't leave without you."

"But we were supposed to be married," Saul said.

"Married?" I was surprised.

Sadie nodded. "Saul asked me just last night. I was going to tell you today." She took Saul's hands and looked deep into his eyes. "We will find our wedding canopy somewhere else." She brought her hand to her chest. "In here, I am already married to you."

"By tomorrow, you can marry in freedom," I offered. Thinking of the long, difficult plan Kara had outlined for their escape, I doubted that would be true.

Saul nodded, seeming to soften toward me, as if finally seeing that I wanted the best for Sadie and for all of them. "But…" Saul looked from Sadie to his father, who was stubbornly sitting in the same spot, refusing to acknowledge the truth or to move. If he couldn't convince his father, then none of them would leave, consigning them all to certain death.

Saul dropped Sadie's hand and walked to his father. "Please, Papa. I know you brought us here because you thought it was safest. And it has been. But things are changing. You couldn't save Micah, but you can save me if you come with us now. Please give us this chance."

His father looked up and I could see him wrestling with his fear and dread of the horrors on the street above. Sadie walked over to the two men. "I promise," she said solemnly, "that no harm will come to your son." At first, I doubted he would believe her. But he reached out his hand and I could see the bond they had developed. Sadie helped him to his feet. He walked across the chamber and pulled the mezuzah from the door.

Together we started into the tunnel. I saw Sadie look over her shoulder for a second at this small, awful space that had been her home for several months, which she was now leaving forever, saying goodbye to the place that had been their sanctuary. Then she turned to me. "How? I mean, where are we going? Did Krys arrange some sort of transit for us?" I did not want to tell her the truth about Krys. I feared that if she knew he would not be there to meet us on the other side and guide us away, she might decide not to go after all.

But I could not lie to her again. "Krys was arrested," I told her at last. "Taken. He went to try to intercept the munitions and he was caught."

A horrified look crossed her face. "Arrested?" I expected her to panic. "Oh, Ella, you must be so worried." Her voice was laced with concern. "You have to go to him, to help."

"There's nothing I can do for him now," I said, willing my voice not to crack. My stomach twisted anew at the thought of Krys, arrested or worse. In that moment, I would have done anything to help him. But as Kara had said, that was not what Krys would have wanted. My place was here, rescuing Sadie. "This is what he would have wanted me to do." I hated how I spoke of him in the past tense instinctively, as if he were already gone.

"But without him, how can we possibly escape?" Her doubts seemed to double anew.

"I know the route," I said, which was partially true. "Kara, the woman from the café, told it to me and said she'd help. I can get us to safety." I tried to force confidence into my voice. I just had to get Sadie and the others out of the tunnel on my own and then Kara would help them reach Kryspinów. I could do this. "Come."

We walked through the tunnel in silence. I led the way, with Sadie right behind me. "I'm so sorry about your mother," I said. It was perhaps unwise to bring up the subject again and upset her just as we were leaving. But I felt that I needed to say something.

She sniffed. "There was some part of me, I think, that already knew when she hadn't returned after so long."

Behind her, Saul helped his father, who moved slowly. Convincing them to leave had taken longer than I had anticipated and I wanted to urge them all to hurry. The old man had been crippled by the months in the sewer, though, and could barely walk. I concentrated on the path ahead, trying not to think about the mines. I had no idea what they looked like or how we might avoid them and it seemed that every step might be our last.

We made our way toward the grate where I had first met Sadie, the one near the Dębniki market. I didn't know how we would all get out, or avoid being seen, even at night. I prayed Kara would be there to help us. *One step in front of the other,* I heard my brother Maciej's voice say, as he used to during tough times. *That is all you can do.*

Suddenly there came a rumbling sound. At first I thought it might be an air raid, but it was too close and intense. The walls began to shake. Sadie stumbled and I could not reach her, but Saul grabbed her before she could fall.

One of the mines had detonated.

"Ahead, quickly!" I cried. Perhaps just one of the mines had gone off accidentally. The Allies were nowhere near Kraków yet; surely the Germans had not set them all off. But there was another explosion and another, the first detonation setting off some kind of chain reaction. These sounds came not from above, though, but from below the ground, close and soul shaking.

There came another explosion that threw us to the ground. We all lay motionless for several seconds. I could not move and it seemed as if I was already dead. We pulled one another to our feet and brushed off the rubble. Dust and debris filled my lungs and I coughed and spat to clear them. The air was so choked with dust I could no longer see. Someone took my hand and pulled me. I recognized Sadie's delicate fingers in mine as now she took the lead. We pressed onward.

Behind us there came another mighty crashing sound as though the walls were falling in around us. Sadie stumbled, nearly taking me to the ground with her. Saul tried to help her, but she shook him off. "Help your father." She pushed the two men ahead of us.

At the end of the tunnel, I could make out faint light from the street above the grate. Krys, I thought. For a second, I imagined that his arrest had not happened and in spite of everything he would be waiting for me. Of course, that was impossible. I turned back toward Sadie. "We made it," I said. I expected her to look happy, but she did not. Instead, her eyes widened with horror as she looked over my shoulder. "Ella!" Her mouth formed my name as a loud rumbling all around us drowned out her voice. The sound was different this time, not a bomb detonating—it came from within the walls themselves. The explosions had loosened the tunnel walls, which began to come down around us, as if in slow motion, the rounded concrete cracking and starting to cave inward.

In front of us, Saul hesitated for a moment. "Go!" Sadie cried, urging him onward. Saul sprinted forward with his father, nearly carrying him. He took a long last look back at Sadie. The ceiling crumbled then and I pulled Sadie toward me, covering both of our heads so we would not be crushed. Concrete and debris and ash rained down upon us, cutting into our skin.

When I looked up, the entire pathway in front of us was blocked by rocks. The tunnel, which had once served as a bridge to connect Sadie's world with mine, had collapsed. Saul and his father and the entire world on the other side of the grate had all but disappeared, leaving Sadie and me trapped in the sewer, alone.

25

Ella

I wiped the debris from my eyes, trying to get my bearings. "Sadie?" I called. She was lying on the ground a few feet away from me where she had fallen, not moving. Hurriedly, I crawled over to her. "Are you all right?" She sat up, wincing. "Are you hurt?"

She touched her stomach. "Just a small cut." I reached for her to inspect the wound, but she swatted my hand away. "Saul?" She scrambled to her feet. "Where is he?" Seeing the wall of rock that now separated us from him, her panic rose. "Saul!" she called, louder now.

"Shh," I hushed. Even now, her cries might be heard on the street. Ignoring me, Sadie began to claw at the rocks that had fallen, separating us from Saul and his father. "I have to find him," she insisted. "We were leaving together. We are supposed to get married. I can't lose him, too." All of the grief and frustration that had been building up inside her these past few months seemed to bubble up and spill over as she dug at the rocks.

"Stop." I took her bleeding hands in mine to still them. "You'll never get through. And if you keep tearing at it, you are going to bring the rest of the tunnel down on us as well."

Her face crumpled. I would have thought that after her parents and her sister, no loss could break Sadie. But Saul was the very last person she had other than me, and the love she had only just found. The idea of losing him was more than she could bear. "We were so close to getting out together. And now he's gone."

"No, he made it safely to the other side with his father," I replied, hoping that was true.

Sadie looked around helplessly. "We'll never see each other again," she cried.

"Don't say that! We'll get out and find them."

"But they can't wait for us on the street. How will they know where to go without us? They could be caught." Even now, when we were trapped and in peril for our lives, Sadie was thinking about the others.

"Saul will manage. He is strong. And Kara will guide them to safety. All we have to do is find a way out ourselves and we can meet them." I forced confidence into my voice, making it sound much simpler than it really was.

"How?" Sadie knew the tunnels a thousand times better than me. But she was too overwhelmed to think clearly and was looking to me for answers.

"The other grate," I said. "The one that opens by the river. Can we get there?"

"I think so, if the explosions didn't collapse that tunnel as well. It's much harder to get to, though."

"We have to try," I replied firmly. Sadie took a long look at the blocked tunnel, not wanting to leave the last place she had seen Saul. "Come, we must hurry," I urged, pulling her away. Reluctantly, she led me in the other direction, walking more slowly now. Despite the fact that the explosions had not collapsed the tunnel entirely in this direction, it had still left the path in

ruins. Our progress was slow as we navigated around large cra-
ters in the floor and climbed over piles of rubble.

"The explosions," Sadie said as we made our way through
the tunnel. "What happened?"

"Some of the mines detonated. But I'm not sure why."

"Do you think the Germans set them off?"

"I don't know. I don't think so." Even if the Germans suspected people were hiding in the tunnel, it seemed unlikely that
they would have detonated mines without checking first. "Perhaps one of us stepped in the wrong place, or we set them off
with the weight of four people walking," I suggested. So much
we didn't know. "It doesn't matter. We just have to find a way
out of the sewer so we can get to the others."

Sadie turned right in the direction of what must have once
been a narrow pathway. It was blocked now, though, covered
with debris and rock from the caved-in walls. "This was the
way we were supposed to go." She paused, fretting. "Only now
it's gone."

I wondered with dread if our last and only escape plan had
failed. "What now?"

She walked back, retracing our route a few steps. Then she
looked down at the wall. "The pipe." She pointed to an opening in the wall, close to the ground, so small that I had not noticed it when we passed the first time. "I'm not entirely sure,
but I think it runs parallel to the tunnel we were supposed to
take. We have to lie on our bellies to get through," Sadie explained matter-of-factly.

I crouched low to peer through the opening, which led to
a long, horizontal pipe. "That's impossible." The pipe was not
more than two feet in diameter. She could not seriously mean
for us to go through it.

"It's not. My whole family had to do it when we came to the
sewer. Even my mother, and she was pregnant." Sadie's eyes
clouded over at the memory. "Trust me. I'll go first and pull

you through." I knelt, wondering if the pipe might have been compromised by the detonations the way the tunnels had been. But it was made of wrought iron, not rock, and remained intact. Peering into the dark, close space, I recoiled, my stomach twisting.

"What is it?" Sadie asked, noticing my reaction.

"Nothing." I shook my head. "It's just that I'm afraid of close spaces...terrified actually." The words sounded foolish as I spoke them.

"I'll help you." Sadie reached for a rope that lay on the ground. "Put this around your waist. When I reach the other side, I will pull you through." She made it sound so simple. The pipes were my worst nightmare, but to her they were second nature. "Trust me," she pled. For so long Sadie had trusted me with her safety; now she was asking me to trust her with mine.

Before I could protest, she lay down and started shimmying through the tunnel, holding one end of the rope. A few minutes later, her voice came echoing down the pipe. "I'm through." It was my turn. I stood motionless, unable to move. "Ella!" Sadie called. "Come on." She tugged on the rope. There was no other way out; I had to try. I took a deep breath, then lay down and pushed myself into the tunnel. As the close piping enveloped my body, I could not breathe. The pipe was damp and smelled strangely metallic, like blood. I heard Ana Lucia's voice taunting me, saying that I would fail here, too, like everything else in life. My spine stiffened. I was not going to let her win. I had to make it, for Sadie's sake—and my own.

I inhaled, taking as deep of a breath as I could in the tight space. Then I pushed through with my feet, straining. I could not move. I was stuck and I would die right here. For a second, the walls closed in and I thought I was going to black out. I pushed again. At the same time, Sadie pulled harder on the rope and I slid forward a few inches. We repeated this pattern, my pushing, her tugging at the rope twenty, maybe thirty more times, my progress painstakingly slow. My skin burned, rubbed raw by the rough piping. My muscles ached and I wanted to give up. But Sadie coaxed me on, her voice like a beacon. "You can do this. I promise, we're going to make it through." In the dark space before me in the tunnel, I saw Krys, imagined him urging me on. Whatever happened, I wanted him to be proud of me and to know that I hadn't given up.

Sadie's voice became gradually louder and at last I could see where there was faint light. I was almost there. I gave a mighty shove and squeezed out of the tunnel and fell to the ground on my knees. Sadie stared at me as I stood up. "You're filthy," she said. "You look just like me now." We both laughed.

There was no time for humor, though. "Come," Sadie said, pulling me down the path on which we now stood. The tunnel was bigger here, and I had to hunch over only slightly to fit. Sadie moved a bit more slowly now, her breathing labored. I wanted to urge her to go more quickly. We had to reach the outside and be well away before daylight. I felt certain that Kara would have done as she promised and rescued Saul and his father by now, if they had made it out. But I did not know if she knew about the other sewer grate and whether she would anticipate and meet us there. I was worried she might leave without us.

The tunnel sloped upward. We were getting closer to the street, I thought, allowing my hopes to rise just a little. We rounded a corner and stepped into a chamber with a deep, water-filled basin, about four meters across, and a high ledge on the far side.

"You have to cross this to get to the grate by the river?" I asked with disbelief. She nodded. The wall on the far side was sheer rock and the ledge we had to reach at least two meters high. I marveled that she had managed it on her own so many times.

"But I've never had to do it like this." She pointed into the basin below. "Usually it's empty, not filled with water. The explosions must have destroyed one of the levees." There was a loud rushing sound as water poured into the chamber we had to cross from an unseen source at great speed. In a few minutes, the whole thing would be filled.

"We'll have to swim," I said. "Come." I sat on the edge of the basin and took off my shoes, preparing to get in. But Sadie did not join me and I could tell from the doubt in her eyes that something was wrong. "What is it?" I asked.

"I can't swim," she confessed. I recalled then how she had told me once how she and her mother had almost drowned when the sewer flooded, and also how the waters had taken her father's life. I could see her reliving her fears and they paralyzed her. She was not just unable to swim, but terrified of the water, just as I had been of the close space in the pipe.

"Is there another route?" I asked, already knowing the answer. She shook her head. There was panic in her eyes. "Then we must get across somehow."

But how? I looked around desperately. Then I remembered the rope she had used to pull me through the pipe. I ran back down the tunnel and grabbed it, then hurried back to Sadie. "Here, I'll pull you." The rope that had been my lifeline in the narrow crawl space was now hers. "I am going to swim and you just have to hold on."

"But…" Sadie began.

"We have to get across," I insisted.

"I can't possibly manage it now."

"There's no choice," I said firmly. "Not if you want to reach Saul again. I'll help you." I took the rope and tied one end to me and then affixed the other end to her waist so that we were about a meter apart. It was then that I noticed the bloodstain on her dress, which was now torn. "Are you hurt?" My apprehension grew.

"Just a cut from when the mine went off and we fell. Going through the tunnel made it worse. I'm fine." There was a tightness to her voice that made me wonder if she was telling the truth.

But there was no time for further questions. I lowered myself into the icy water, then coaxed her in after me. Sadie put one foot into the water, then recoiled. "You can do this," I urged. At last, she entered the water reluctantly. Panic crossed her face and she began to flail, arms floundering. "Just relax." I held my arms out and pulled her to me. I was a strong swimmer. I had spent childhood summers in happier times at our cabin by Lake Morskie Oko in the Tatra Mountains and quickly learned to swim when my siblings threw me in the water mercilessly.

I started across the basin, pulling Sadie. She tried to swim, but her movements were flailing and ineffective. I tried to tow her. She should have been lighter in the water, but her weight was like a boulder. The rope that bound us pulled at my waist. I kicked harder, pushing onward. I had no idea how we would get up the ledge when we reached the other side. First, though, we had to get across. She grew heavier and for a moment I thought she was fighting me. When I looked behind me, Sadie had stopped moving. She was motionless in the water, as if she was exhausted or had simply given up. My frustration rose. "You have to keep trying," I said. Then I noticed that there was something red in the water. Blood, I realized.

I drew her close and lifted her to the surface to examine the wound on her stomach. "It's nothing," she said, but her face was pale as a sheet. I pulled back her dress where it had torn and was horrified to see that the injury she had described as nothing was in fact a gash, several centimeters deep, with a piece of rock buried in it. Blood oozed from it now, coloring the water around us red. The debris was wedged deep and tight in the wound; pulling it out would only make things worse. The cut was bathed in filthy water, ensuring that it would go septic.

"Hold on," I said, wrapping my arm around her waist to keep her close. I started swimming again with my other arm. Just a few feet more. I neared the far side of the basin. As I did, Sadie slipped from my grasp. She started to sink to the bottom, her weight on the rope pulling me down with her. I took a deep breath, then went under, searching. The filthy water was too dark to see through, so I tried to feel for her. My hands closed around the nothingness. I reached again and finally grasped a bit of her dress, then used all my might to pull her to the surface.

"You have to stop carrying me," she gasped.

"Never. I'm getting you out of here."

"Go now, while you can."

"I told you, I'm not leaving you." The water was rising rapidly, and once it went over the ledge and filled the tunnel on the far side, our escape would be closed. Every second that we lingered here in the chamber raised the chance that we would not make it out. But as long as Sadie was still alive, there was hope for both of us. I could not leave her.

We reached the far wall of the basin. I looked up uncertainly. Even with the rising waters lifting us, the ledge was still at least a meter above us. I could climb out, but Sadie would never manage it. I would have to lift her out. I paused, gathering my strength, while Sadie lay weakly in my arms.

Her eyes were closing now, though, her breath drawing short. "Saul," she said, longingly. She looked off into the distance, as if actually seeing him. Was she hallucinating? "He really did love me after all," she added.

"He does. He still does. He's waiting for you. We just need to get up that wall."

"Tell him…"

She was dying, I realized then. Her wound was too serious; she had lost too much blood. My heart screamed. "Sadie, no. We're going to get out of here and you are going to find Saul and tell him yourself," I insisted. She did not answer and I could see the last bit of her strength flowing from her body like her blood, as it mixed with the water. "I told you we are getting out of here."

"You have to go on for both of us."

"No." That would never be enough. "You will marry Saul. Or you can come to Paris with me. I will draw and you will study medicine and we will have a fabulous life." I was speaking quickly now, the words tumbling out in a breathless, almost non-sensical mumble, anything to keep her talking to me. "You can't leave me. You need to be strong. You owe that much to me."

But she shook her head, all of the fight in her gone. "I can't."

Sadie was not going to make it. This was the end for us. My heart broke.

"You have to let me go," she said, her voice barely a whisper. She reached down and, with her remaining strength, untied the rope that had bound us tightly together. Then she tried to pull away from me, but I held fast to her. I looked up at the ledge. The rising water had brought us a bit closer to it now. I picked up Sadie and, with great effort, lifted her above my head. She neared the ledge, then slipped from my grasp and fell back to the water, almost sinking us both. I caught her and heaved her up again. This time I managed to place her on the ledge, where she lay motionless for several seconds. She rolled onto her side and held out her hand, trying with the very last of her strength to help me from the water.

"See, I promised you would get out," I said.

But I had spoken too soon. From behind me, there came a crash and I turned in time to see the far wall of the basin, weakened from the explosions, cave in. A giant wave of water roared toward us, too big and powerful to stop. The force slammed me against the wall and took us both under, swallowing us into darkness.

26

I stepped onto the banks of the Wisła before dawn.

As I had climbed from the sewer, I reached back for the hand that should have been in mine, but was not. Now I stood beneath a vast, dark canopy of stars, alone. I had hoped to see someone, Kara or Saul maybe, waiting for me. But the riverbank was deserted, the others having left us for dead.

We're going to make it. A promise broken.

After the raging floodwaters had crashed through the basin wall, I had floundered, submerged in the dark, feeling for her beneath the surface for several minutes without success. At last I managed to find her and somehow pull us both onto the ledge. But it was too late. The water had filled her lungs for too long and she was barely breathing. There was a massive gash on her head, too, where the raging current had slammed her into the concrete basin wall. Blood gushed from it, impossible to stop.

"We can make it," I urged, trying in vain to pull her to her feet. "We'll go to Paris to paint and to study medicine." I dan-

gled our dreams in front of her, willing her to reach for them
and live.

But she was unable to walk and she used her last bit of strength
to push me away. "You have to go on for both of us," she said.
Then, with effort, she reached into her pocket and I was surprised when she handed me not one thing, but two.

"Take it," she breathed. "Tell him…" And I leaned close,
waiting to receive the message that she wanted me to deliver.
But she closed her eyes then, and the words never came.

I put my hand on her shoulder and shook her gently as if to
revive her, but she did not respond. "No!" I cried as the reality sank in. She was dying. My friend, the one who had given
everything for me, would not survive. I lowered my head close
to hers, my tears spilling over onto her cheeks. Her breathing
slowed.

When her chest rose and fell no more, I held her for several
seconds. I wanted to take her with me. I knew that I couldn't
carry her up the high ledge to get out of the chamber. The water
in the basin continued to rise. In another few seconds, it would
overtake the ledge and I would drown as well. Still I held her,
wiped the wet locks of hair from her beautiful face. My heart
screamed. We had sworn to leave the sewer together. How could
I abandon her now?

I kissed her cheek, the salt of my tears mixing with the dirty,
bitter water. She deserved a proper burial in a cemetery with
flowers. Of course, that was impossible. Still, I would not leave
her here for the Germans to find. Straining, I lifted her body
and pushed it from the ledge, returning her to the water. Her
face, peaceful and calm, lingered a second above the surface before it slipped below the waters and she disappeared as the sewer
claimed her for its own.

Then I began my final climb to freedom.

When I reached the riverbank, I stood motionless, trying to
catch my breath. A foghorn sounded long and low from a boat

unseen down the river. My wounds screamed with pain and I didn't know how I would go on from here at all, much less on my own.

Just then, I saw a familiar face appear over the horizon. My heart filled with joy. I had not imagined that he was still alive or would have waited. Seeing me, he sprinted forward, his face happy and relieved.

Then as he neared and realized I was alone, darkness clouded his eyes. "Where is she?"

"I'm sorry," I said, not wanting to deliver the news that would surely break him. "There was a flood. She saved me, but she didn't make it out alive." His eyes went hollow with grief. "I did everything I could," I added.

"I know." There was a note of resignation in his voice. He did not blame me. That any of us would have made it, much less all, was simply too much to hope. Still, the loss was a grievous one and I saw in his pained eyes how very much he had loved her.

"I'm sorry," I repeated. "She saved me. Only now I'm here and she isn't."

"It isn't your fault," he said, staring hard off into the distance and blinking back tears. "You did everything you could. She loved you, you know. She would be glad to know that you are alive."

"But she isn't!" I exclaimed, my sorrow bursting forth then. He drew me close and let me cry into the front of his shirt, heedless of the filthy water that soaked through.

"We should go," he said gently a moment later.

"No." I knew that he was right. But I was not ready to leave her behind. I turned back toward the entrance. We should be leaving together.

"We can't stay here," he said firmly. "She would want you to do whatever you had to in order to live. You know that, don't you?" I did not answer. "Don't let her death be for nothing." He pulled me up the riverbank. It was hard for me to walk, the thought of leaving her too much to bear. But she was gone. And staying here was not going to bring her back. Reluctantly, I let him draw me away from the exposed riverbank toward safety, but every step felt like a betrayal of the friend I left behind.

As we neared the street, I looked up at the tapestry of stars in the night sky. They seemed almost blue and it was as if there was one for each of the souls who had been set free. I saw *her* in the stars above and I knew that it was important that I go on for both of us. I could see it now, the constellations we had seen together that night, beckoning and leading me home.

When we reached the foot of the bridge, I looked back over my shoulder. Kraków, the only city I had ever known, sat shrouded in darkness, except for the sky, which burned pink along the horizon to the east. War still raged, my hometown under siege. And I was abandoning it. My guilt rose.

No, not abandoning, I corrected myself. I was leaving, but I would find a way to fight and honor her memory.

"Ready?" he asked.

"Yes," I said, putting my hand in his. Our fingers tightened around one another's and together we took our first step toward freedom.

Epilogue

═══════════════

Kraków, Poland
June 2016

The woman I see before me is not the one I expected at all.

As I near her table, I study the woman, who has not yet seen me. Though she must be over ninety, her smooth skin and perfect posture make her look much younger. She has not succumbed to the short hair of old age as I have, but wears her white curls in a high messy bun that accentuates her cheekbones and other strong features. She is, in a word, regal.

Still, close up there is something different about her than I expected. Something familiar. It must be the anticipation, I tell myself, the searching and waiting. The moment I have dreamed of for so long is finally here.

I take a deep breath, steel myself. "Ella Stepanek?"

She does not answer, but blinks once. The rain, which had gone as quickly as it came, had sent other patrons scurrying indoors. But the woman sits, undeterred. As her chocolate-brown eyes focus on me, they cloud with confusion. "Do I know you?"

"We've never met," I say gently. "But you knew my sister,

Sadie. I'm Lucy Gault." I use my family name, the one that had belonged to the parents and sister I'd never had the chance to know.

The older woman stares at me, as if seeing a ghost. "But how is that possible?" She tries to stand, but her knees wobble and she grips the edge of the table so hard that her tea sloshes over the edge of the cup, staining the tablecloth a darker blue. "That can't be. We were sure you had died."

I nod, a lump forming in my throat as it always does when I think of the improbability of my survival. By any measure, I should not have lived. I was born in a sewer, hidden from the Germans, who wanted to eliminate the next Jewish generation and killed them without mercy. I saw then the hundreds of thousands of children who had not lived. I should have been among them.

But somehow, at seventy-two, I am still here.

"How?" the older woman asks again.

I hesitate, searching for the right way to explain. Though I have imagined this moment a hundred times and tried to plan for it, words fail me and I struggle to figure out where to begin. "May I join you?" I ask.

"Please." She gestures to the chair beside her.

I sit down and turn over the coffee cup on the saucer before me. "It sounds strange to say, but I was born in the sewer. You know that part, don't you? And that my mother smuggled me out?"

Ella nods. "Your mother was trying to take you to a Catholic hospital that she thought was helping to hide Jewish children."

"Yes, but on her way there, a priest saw my mother on the street in poor condition and warned her that it was not safe to take the baby to the hospital. He hid the baby and then took my mother to the hospital for care. Only my mother was at the hospital when the Germans came for her. I was saved and later adopted by a Polish couple. My adopted parents, Jerzy and Anna, were wonderful people and I had a good life. They decided to emigrate to America when I was five and I had a happy childhood growing up in Chicago. When I was old enough, they shared what little they knew of my past. I learned the rest from Pawel."

"The sewer worker?" Ella looks stunned. "But he was arrested for helping the Jews. I assumed he died in prison."

"He was. But he talked his way out of jail and returned to his family."

"Pawel made it." Ella's eyes fill with tears. "I had no idea."

"Pawel returned to the sewer after he was released to check on Sadie and the others he had helped. But they weren't there. At first, he thought they had all been caught. Then he realized they fled the sewer or at least attempted to. He didn't know where they had gone or whether they had made it. But he knew one possibility, at least for my mother, was that she had given birth and left the sewer to hide the baby."

I pause as a waiter appears and pours coffee. When he has gone again, I continue. "Pawel was the one who had told my mother about the hospital in the first place. So he went there to look for her. He learned that she had come to the hospital, but not with the baby. He did some more digging and found the priest who had saved me and learned where I had been placed. When I was older, I corresponded with him for many years. He told me about my family. But there were so many questions he couldn't answer.

"So I came to find you to learn more about them, or at least about my sister. I would like to know her." This is what I wanted, to find the last link to the sister I had never known and to capture, now while I still can, the stories that would bring her back to life. This is why I had come all of this way. My entire family had been killed before I was old enough to know them. I have had a good life, filled with a husband who had loved me, two children and now grandchildren. But this piece has always been missing, a hole where my past should be. I want to know the people I had lost.

I put the bouquet of flowers down on the table. "These are for you."

Ella does not take the flowers, but stares at them for several seconds. "Mama was right," she whispers to herself.

"Excuse me?"

"She said that there would be flowers someday." Her words are confusing to me and I wonder whether the surprise of my coming has been too much. She presses her lips together, as if there is something else she wants to say but cannot. "So then how did you find out about me?" She still has more questions than answers.

"Saul," I reply.

"Saul?" Ella smiles as she repeats the familiar name, the lines about her mouth deepening. Her eyes dance. "He's still alive?"

"Yes, he's a widower living in California with many children and grandchildren. He never forgot about Sadie, though."

"He made it after all," she says with a quiver, sounding as if she is speaking more to herself than to me.

"Before Pawel died, he told me about the other family, the Rosenbergs, who had lived in the sewer," I explain. "Years later, I was able to find Saul. He gave me so many of the answers I was seeking about what had happened to my family. He had been separated from Sadie as they fled, and he was never able to learn what became of her. But he told me that she had a friend, a brave Polish girl, Ella Stepanek, who helped them escape. I began researching, trying to find this woman who had helped my sister. For years I hit a dead end, but then after Communism ended and I could get to the archives in Poland, I learned that there had been a young woman named Ella Stepanek who fought in the Warsaw Uprising. I thought it might be you." She blinks, not answering. "So I came to find you."

Yet as she sits before me now, something is still not right.

Taking in the familiar shape of her eyes, something inside me shifts. I know then that I have not found the woman I came looking for. "Only you aren't Ella, are you?" She does not answer. Her fine porcelain skin pales even more. "At least, you weren't always."

Her hand, resting on the edge of the table, begins to tremble once more. "No," she says, her voice scarcely a whisper. "I wasn't."

A realization rises up in me like a wave, threatening to sweep me under, the words so unreal that I hardly dare speak them. "Then I guess," I say slowly, "that makes you Sadie."

"Yes." She reaches out and touches my cheek with shaking fingers. "Oh, my baby sister..." Then, without warning, the woman whom I've met just minutes ago falls into my arms. As I embrace her, my mind reels. I came here looking for answers about my sister.

Instead, I found my sister herself.

A few seconds later, we break apart. I stare at her as the reality sinks in: Sadie, my sister, is alive. She clings to my arm like a life raft, not wanting to let go. "But how is it even possible?" I ask. "All of these years, I thought you had died in the sewer." I had searched, of course, every possible archive for a record of my sister, Sadie Gault. But after an entry in the ghetto records showing that she had been interned there, the trail went dark. I knew from Pawel and Saul that she had escaped to the sewer with our parents, and that our mother and father had both died. I assumed that Sadie had perished, too.

"When you were born, things became very difficult," Sadie begins. "We couldn't keep a baby from crying and giving us away in the sewer. So our mother took you to find a safe place to hide you. She left me with the Rosenbergs, Saul and his family." I feel then how awful it must have been for Sadie to have been left behind alone. She might have hated me for it. "Mama never returned. She died in the hospital." Her eyes fill with tears. Although I have grieved her my whole life, I am filled with newfound sadness as I think of the mother I never knew.

Sadie continues, "Several weeks after Mama left, Ella came to the sewer to rescue us. She said that our hiding place had been compromised and it wasn't safe for us to stay any longer. We would have to flee with her. But the Germans had laid mines in the sewer, and as we tried to escape, several detonated. The sewer walls collapsed, separating Ella and me from Saul and his father. We tried to escape another way, through a chamber, but it flooded. I couldn't swim. Ella saved me." As she relives the memory, her eyes fill with tears. "But the basin wall caved in and the waters swept us under. Ella was slammed against a wall and gravely injured. She died before we could get out."

"I'm so sorry," I say, seeing the pain in her eyes. I try to imagine the horror that they had been through, but find that I cannot.

"I made it out of the sewer, but I was alone and badly wounded. Saul and the others were too far gone for me to catch."

"So you were completely alone?"

"No, there was someone else. A young Polish man named Krys, who loved Ella. He was part of the Home Army. He was supposed to help Ella get us out of the sewer, but he was captured by the Germans. When the Germans were transferring him to a different prison, he escaped and made it back to the sewer. He was too late to help Ella, but he found me. He was going to Warsaw to fight as part of the uprising. I went with him to join the cause and do whatever I could."

"What became of him?" I ask eagerly. I am suddenly curious to know the fate of the man who had played a part in my family's survival.

"He was killed fighting the Germans, but I think part of his spirit was destroyed the moment I told him the awful truth about Ella's death. He was a good man." Her eyes cloud over. "I survived Warsaw somehow."

"You were so brave," I say.

"Me?" Sadie looks surprised. "I did nothing. Ella, Krys, Pawel, they were the brave ones."

I shake my head, smiling inwardly. Researching my family has made me into somewhat of an amateur historian and I have met several survivors of the war over the years. Each seemed to downplay his or her own role in the war, giving the "real" credit to someone else. "You were brave, too," I insist. "Saul told me so many stories about the courageous things you did."

"Saul…" Sadie smiles, seeming lost in her memories. "He was my first love. I tried to find him after the war, but I had no idea where he had gone. And later, when there were records, well, what was the point? I assumed that he moved on, had a life of his own."

"He never forgot you, though. I'm sure he would be glad to hear from you."

"Maybe." She falters, and in her hesitation to face the past, I recognize a piece of myself, the same reluctance that almost stopped me from crossing the market square and finding my sister. There are some pieces of the past too far gone to reach.

"But why have you used Ella's name all of these years?" I ask.

"Before Ella died, she gave me her identity card. I felt bad about taking it, but it was the one thing that would get me safely out of the city. At first, I used it to pass as a non-Jew. After the war, I decided to keep her name and live out my days honoring her. Sadie Gault was dead; she had no one. But Ella Stepanek could have a fresh start. I traveled to Paris, let Ella's brother, Maciej, know what had become of her. I settled there and realized my dream of studying medicine. I retired from my work as a pediatrician some time ago."

"You didn't come right back to Kraków after the war?"

She shakes her head. "But after Communism ended, Maciej was able to get back his and Ella's family home in Kraków. The government had taken it after the war when their stepmother was arrested as a collaborator. He left it to me when he died. It's a beautiful house not far from here. I didn't move into it, though. There were too many painful memories. I sold it. I have a small apartment now." She gazes out across the square. "I've lived all over the world. In the end, I came home. It was strange coming back to this part of the world after so many years abroad. But there was something that called to my soul. This is home now." I envy her peace, and her calm sense of belonging with her past.

"What happened to Ella's stepmother, the collaborator?" I ask. The woman means nothing to me, yet I am curious to fill in all of the missing pieces.

"She died in prison before she could stand trial. She was not a nice person and she caused Ella a great deal of pain. Still, it was a sorry end to a selfish life and I would not have wished it on her."

I try to process all that I have learned. My sister and I had lived all of these years, not knowing that the other still existed. We had lost so much time. "Tell me," I say, drawing my chair closer. "Tell me everything." I had found not just my sister, but a treasure trove of information about the family I never knew and a way to fill in the pages of blank history I thought were lost forever. "I want to know it all, about our parents, about our family before the war." I want to know more than how they died. I want to understand how they had lived.

But Sadie shakes her head. "I can't just tell you." I wonder if, as with so many survivors, the past is simply too painful to share. She stands, as if to go. Anxiety rises in me. We've lost so many years. Perhaps it is too late. "Let me show you instead." She holds her hand out to me.

I stand up. "I would like to see the places our family lived."

"I can show you where our apartment was before the war, and even the place we lived in the ghetto," she offers.

"But not the sewer?" Although it sounds macabre, some part of me is curious about the awful place where I was born, an indelible piece of our history.

"I'm afraid not. That was all closed up long ago. I considered going back down there. But it's for the best." I nod. Though I was born there, the sewer isn't who we are, just a tiny piece of our rich, full lives. "There are other places," she adds. "The places Papa and I used to walk and play, and a memorial in the ghetto." Tiny pieces, I mused, that would at last complete the puzzle of our family history.

"Did you ever have children?"

"No, I never married. I never had a family of my own—at least not until now." She squeezes my hand. "I'm all alone." She smiles brightly, but there is a catch in her voice that tells me she minds more than she would like to admit.

"Not anymore." Her fingers lock with mine, skin withered, but grasp firm and strong.

I notice then a necklace tucked within her collar. "What's that?"

Sadie pulls out the chain around her neck to reveal a small gold charm with the Hebrew letters making up the word *chai*. Sadie has chosen to live her days under Ella's name, yet she has not completely denied our family's Jewish faith. "This belonged to our father. Ella hid it for me during the war and I was able to get it back from her at the end." She reaches behind her neck and undoes the clasp, then passes it to me. "You should have this now."

"That isn't necessary," I protest. "It's yours." But it is the only memento of my family I have and I am secretly glad when she closes my fingers around it.

"Ours," she corrects. "Come. There's so much to see. We'll start now, even though it's late."

For a second, I am overwhelmed. "I'm supposed to be leaving tomorrow." Even as I say this, I know I won't be going so soon after I found my sister. Rebuilding our family history together is not the project of a single day, but a road we will build over time, stone by stone, now while we still can. "I'll have to see about extending my hotel."

"Stay with me," Sadie urges. "We'll have more time to catch up that way. I have a lovely apartment in the Jewish Quarter."

"Can you see the stars from there?" I ask. Astronomy has always for some reason been a passion of mine.

"All of them." She smiles. "Come, let me show you."

★ ★ ★ ★ ★

Author's Note

This book was inspired in part by the true story of a small group of Jews who survived World War II in the sewers of Lviv, Poland. The account that I have written and set in Kraków is wholly fictitious. I have nevertheless endeavored to remain true to the heroism of these brave people and those who helped them and to accurately depict the ways in which it was possible for them to survive. If you would like to read more about the true story, I recommend the nonfiction book *In the Sewers of Lvov* by Robert Marshall.

Acknowledgments

Like the year 2020, this book seemed, in many ways, doomed from the start.

The saga began in December 2019 when (keeping it real here) I turned in a book to my editor that was not at all right. We agreed that I needed to essentially start over, something that I had never done before. After a five-minute moan, I reminded myself of that quote from *The Godfather Part II*, "This is the business we've chosen," and set about the task before me. I scrapped 90 percent of the book and began to rewrite at breakneck speed with the unfathomable goal of finishing in about five months. To get this done, my Five A.M. Writers' Club suddenly became Four A.M.

In the course of the revision, I decided to move the book's setting to Kraków, Poland, and I planned a research trip there. (When I was younger, I had lived in Kraków for several years. However, due to family constraints, I had not been there in nearly twenty years.) I booked that trip to depart on March 11, 2020—the very week the COVID-19 pandemic erupted and international travel was largely suspended. The cancellation turned out to be a good thing, because the day I was supposed to fly to Poland, I instead found myself hospitalized for an emergency appendectomy! I returned home from the hospital to find the world shut down and the COVID quarantine in full effect. Like so many of you, I had to adapt to a new normal: homeschooling three kids and teaching remotely, all the while finishing this book.

Despite all of this, *The Woman with the Blue Star* came to life. I did not set out to write a book that was relevant to the pandemic. (How could I have possibly known?) Yet I found in the process of writing this book that themes emerged of coping with isolation and an uncertain future, which were more relevant to our current world situation than I ever could have imagined.

As I sit here writing this to you in late August 2020, we are still under lockdown, with so many of the things we took for granted still gone. Though writing is solitary, I am a person who thrives on community. I miss our elementary school and the moms on the playground, my colleagues and students at Rutgers Law, the synagogue and the Jewish Community Center and the five libraries I patronize each week. I want to walk into my local independent bookstore and hug readers again.

Yet even with all of the hardships we've all experienced, so many bright lights endure like the stars in the night sky Sadie dreamed of seeing from her confinement in the sewer. Our community of readers and writers still flourishes. Despite the months apart from readers and book friends, I still feel you out there and I am grateful for the ways in which books have been a lifeline and how the writing community continues to support one another, the librarians and independent bookstores and booksellers who keep finding ways to get books into our hands, the bloggers and book influencers and sites who have recognized that writers and readers need to connect now more than ever, the tribe of writers who lift each other, the readers who never stop believing.

This book would not be possible without so many people. I am forever grateful to my "dream team"—my beloved agent, Susan Ginsburg, and my epic editor-who-is-more-like-a-coauthor, Erika Imranyi, for their passion and commitment to making this book the very best it could be. My deepest thanks also goes to my wonderful publicist, Emer Flounders, and the many talented people at Writers House and Park Row and Harlequin and HarperCollins. (Looking at you, Craig, Loriana, Heather, Amy, Randy, Natalie, Catherine and so many others!) My gratitude for their time and talent is always immense, and even more so as they persevere in these challenging and unprecedented times.

I'm so thankful for the many people in Kraków who provided their assistance and expertise. First, my dear friends Barbara Kotarba and Ela Konarska at the US Consulate in Kraków, who helped me with trip planning when I thought I was going to Kraków and with long-distance resources when I discovered that I could not. I'm grateful to Anna Maria Baryla for her expertise on Kraków and the Polish language, and to Jonathan Ornstein of JCC Kraków for putting us in touch, and to Bartosz Heksel for his expertise on the Kraków sewers. I am indebted to amazing fact-checker Jennifer Young and copy editor Bonnie Lo. As ever, the mistakes are all mine.

I would like to thank all of the essential workers. I'm thinking of the doctors and nurses and health care workers, whose amazing work I witnessed firsthand when I was in the hospital. I am also extremely grateful for the grocery employees who have kept us fed, the delivery folks who have brought what we need, the teachers who show up every day, whether in person or online. None of what we do would be possible without you.

Being apart from the people we love has undoubtedly been the hardest part of this quarantine. I am sending all of my love and gratitude to my mom, Marsha, who is everything to us and helps with kids and puppy and much more so I can write; to my brother, Jay; to my in-laws Ann and Wayne; to dear friends Steph, Joanne, Andrea, Mindy, Sarah and Brya. May we all be together again soon.

Finally, and most of all, to those who have suffered me in quarantine, my beloved husband, Phillip, and the three small muses, I give all my thanks and love. I am grateful for the time together at home this quarantine has given us, the lazy mornings and long walks and countless hours in the backyard. I'm especially awed by the resilience of my kids and for the bond among them that has made all of this easier to bear. They give me hope that we will come out of all of this stronger and closer for the struggle.